ENGLISH LITERATURE ADVANCING THROUGH HISTORY - 6
The Victorian Age

ENGLISH LITERATURE ADVANCING THROUGH HISTORY - 6

The Victorian Age

WITH THEORETICAL INTRODUCTION AND PRELIMINARIES

Petru GOLBAN

TRANSNATIONAL PRESS LONDON

2025

Literature Series:

ENGLISH LITERATURE ADVANCING THROUGH HISTORY - 6

The Victorian Age

By Petru GOLBAN

Copyright © 2025 Transnational Press London

First Published in 2025 by TRANSNATIONAL PRESS LONDON in the United Kingdom, 21 Woodville Drive, Sale, M33 6NF, UK.

www.tplondon.com

Paperback

ISBN: 978-1-80135-174-4

Digital

ISBN: 978-1-80135-175-1

Transnational Press London Ltd. is a company registered in England and Wales No. 8771684

CONTENTS

PREFACE

The present book is the sixth in a series of works which aim to expose the complexity and essence, power and extent of the major periods, movements, trends, genres, authors, and literary texts in the history of English literature. Following this aim, the series will consist of monographs which cover the most important ages and experiences of English literary history, including Anglo-Saxon or Old English period, the Middle Ages, the Renaissance, the Restoration, neoclassicism, romanticism, Victorian Age, and the twentieth-century and contemporary literary backgrounds. The reader of these volumes will acquire the knowledge of literary terminology along with the theoretical and critical perspectives on certain texts and textual typology belonging to different periods, movements, trends, and genres. The reader will also learn about the characteristics and conventions of these literary periods and movements, trends and genres, main writers and major works, and the literary interaction and continuity of the given periods. Apart from an important amount of reference to literary practice, some chapters on these periods include information on their philosophy, criticism, worldview, values, or episteme, in the Foucauldian sense, which means that even though the condition of the creative writing remains as the main concern, it is balanced by a focus on the condition of thought as well as theoretical and critical writing during a particular period.

Articulating the literary phenomenon are literary voices and mediating its comprehension in the consciousness of the public are critical voices. Diachronically, they have different statuses. Homer, Euripides, Cervantes, Dante, Shakespeare, Donne, Austen, Dickens, Dostoyevsky, Proust, Joyce are among those literary voices whom the public has continuously perceived with an unchanged high intensity of interest and admiration. It is only natural that the "voice of an authentic author passes easier through time and possesses more longevity and resonance than that of the critics" (Munteanu, *Metamorfozele* 9). Indeed, Sarasin, Bayle, Lessing, Johnson, Herder, Taine, Sainte-Beuve, Gautier, Stephen, Lubbock are among those critical voices that can hardly be considered to be our contemporaries, and, in spite of the value of their critical discourse, time has eroded their ideas to such an extent that they do not constitute a viable presence in the contemporary literary theory and criticism any longer. Apart from these two groups, there is a third one represented by those poets, novelists and playwrights who manifested both as writers and critics. Here as well, with a few exceptions like T. S. Eliot, who is, to the present day, acclaimed as both writer and critic, or Pater, who is nowadays remembered mainly as critic not writer, the literary history has proven the assumption that in the case of the writer-critics, their literary voice attracts a wider audience and is more persistent in time than their critical one.

It also appears that literary work possesses eternal temporal validity due to its autonomous aesthetic value, whereas criticism provides points of view having temporary and transitory significance; in other words, criticism represents historical version of a particular type of approach to literature. Despite such claims, the vector of methodology in our series of books, dealing with the history of English literature, relies on Viktor Shklovsky, T. S. Eliot, Mikhail Bakhtin, and especially Yuri Tynyanov. In this issue of diachronicity, criticism, similar to literature, attempts to acquire longevity, but, contrary to literary work, whose system remains relatively stable in time, and because literary work necessitates a continuous actualization, critical endeavour requires a permanent renewal of its material. Hence literary criticism is in a continuous developmental process which, being influenced by different factors, involves constant and rapid transformation of its typology, methodology, concerns, and, especially, its attitudes and viewpoints.

What is the developmental process of English literary practice; and how it has come to constitute a particular system comprising various other systems representing different periods, genres, individual literary activities, and so on; along with its interrelatedness with the critical thinking having embarked on its own process of development, represent the main concerns of our books in the series.

As critical writing emerges with the appearance of creative writing, our emphasis on this interrelationship between literature and criticism sparks from the awareness that, particularly before the twentieth century, it is quite impossible to render literary history apart from literary criticism and theory, to separate the text from the context, as if trying to forget that literary criticism has roots in literary practice and vice-versa, and that most of the critics are actually practitioners of literature, rightly called "writer-critics" and situated between critical theory and imaginative writing as authors of two related discourses; only in English literature: Philip Sidney, Ben Jonson, John Dryden, Alexander Pope, Henry Fielding, Samuel Johnson, William Wordsworth, Samuel Taylor Coleridge, Percy Bysshe Shelley, Matthew Arnold, Walter Pater, Oscar Wilde, John Ruskin, Henry James, Virginia Woolf, T. S. Eliot, David Lodge, and many others. This awareness represents the starting point of the present books. Our main concern is to ensure that literary production is viewed in relation to literary criticism and the works of imaginative writing are examined in the light of the critical theory which inspires their creation and shapes their thematic and structural context, and vice-versa, the literary works shaping the critical thinking.

One of the most important writer-critics of all times and the exponent of English modernism, T. S. Eliot gave, towards the end of his life, his own definition of the type of criticism he had practiced, which is a highly revelatory statement, including for our own line of reasoning: "the best of my literary criticism", Eliot claims, is "a by-product of my private poetry-workshop; or a prolongation of the thinking that went into the formation of my own verse".

Other writers would use, or rather materialise, their own artistic credo and literary theory in their literary texts, such as Wordsworth reifying his theory of the origin of poetry from the Preface to *Lyrical Ballads* in his poems *The Prelude* and *Tintern Abbey*, or Pater exemplifying the principles of aestheticism in his novel *Marius the Epicurean*. For some, like for Sidney and Shelley, criticism was a means of defending the aesthetic value of literature; for others, criticism represented the instrument to be used in an attempt to found a new genre, as it did for Fielding and his "comic novel", or even to introduce into the contemporary culture and to validate a whole new literary movement, as it was for Wordsworth and Coleridge.

The interrelationship between literature and critical theory can be seen all the way through the periods, including the twentieth century, where the field of literary theory and criticism reveals a threefold perspective of development. First, one may argue that the development of literary criticism is dependent on literary genres and movements which are dominant in different periods. This is the case of literary criticism especially for the periods until the twentieth century. Douwe Fokkema and Elrud Ibsch (1-2)

4

exemplify this aspect by the theory of classicism which "should be understood as a generalization of the drama and epic of the time"; similarly, the biographical method in criticism is viewed as "one of the effects of Romanticism, which drew largely on autobiographical material"; another example would be the psychological novel which "is responsible for the psychological approach in literary criticism"; also, "the view has been defended that Russian Formalism is indebted to the ideals and slogans of futurism". Second, which is mainly the case of literary scholarship in the nineteenth and twentieth centuries, trends and schools in literary criticism are related to or rather determined by the new developments in science, philosophy, and society. Fokkema and Ibsch again claim: "[t]here is an unmistakable influence of Freudian psychology in psychologically-oriented literary criticism" and "Marxist literary criticism has been intertwined with particular political and sociological views"; also, the "search for a literary system or structure has certainly been inspired by *Gestalt* psychology. Russian Formalism is not only indebted to futurism, but also to new developments in linguistics". Third, these critics argue, where some trends in literary criticism "are closer to new trends in creative literature, [and] others are directly related to current developments in scholarship and society", there are also trends which "are somewhere in between" or they rather emerge, in particular some of the twentieth-century trends in criticism, from within the interpretative perspectives of the discipline of literary theory and criticism itself (for instance, narratology developed by structuralism).

In most general terms, with focus on art and, in this respect, on literature as one of the arts, it is art criticism that provides the analysis, study, and evaluation of individual works of art, as well as the formulation of general principles for the examination of such works. Literary theory and literary criticism are particular manifestations of art criticism developed and applied for the understanding and evaluation of literature; they constitute two distinct but interrelated disciplines which co-exist and are interrelated with a third one, the discipline of literary history, all three representing actually our instruments of approach to English literature which is conceived and constructed by us in its historical movement following the formalist, or rather neo-formalist, assumption that literature is a system of various central and peripheral elements – just as periods, movements, trends, genres, subgenres, and so on, are – and the advancement of literature through history is the substitution of systems.

Focusing on literary practice, applying critical theory and emerging from within our own teaching experience, the books in the present series, dealing with the history of English literature, are theoretical and surveyistic, like a monograph, whereas their more practical and text-oriented aspect should appeal as a student handbook for didactic purposes, in which certain literary texts or fragments from texts belonging to various writers from different periods are analysed and compared with regard to their source, form, thematic arrangements, message, ideas, motifs, character representation strategies, intertextual perspectives, structural or narrative techniques, and other aspects. Theoretical component apart, it is equally important to focus on particular literary works dealing with various concerns and building up different thematic perspectives, such as the process of growing up of the protagonist, because a particular theoretical contribution has no validity and efficiency unless it is well-rooted in the reality of the literary discourse which would eventually provide its practical argumentation. Thematic consideration of the text is indispensable from its structural analysis, be it a lyrical poem stimulating discussions on the use of figurative language for musical and pictorial effects, or a narrative text involving elements of formal organization such as narrator, narrative, narration, point of view, voice, or the principle of chronotope.

Chronos and *topos*, time and place, play a significant role as counterparts of one single mechanism of literary approach to the development of literature, in general, and of the image of its persona rendered in the work, in particular, and specifically in fiction. For Bakhtin, the chronotope is of several types, and, concerning literature, in the "literary artistic chronotope, spatial and temporal indicators are fused into one carefully thought-out, concrete whole. Time, as it were, thickens, takes on flesh, becomes artistically visible; likewise, space becomes charged and responsive to the movements of time, plot and history. This intersection of axes and fusion of indicators characterizes the artistic chronotope" (Bakhtin, "Forms of Time" 84). In Bakhtin dealing with the novel, the "chronotope" – the name (literally, "time space") being given to "the intrinsic connectedness of temporal and spatial relationships that are artistically expressed in literature" – is a key-element in his theoretical framework on genre (an important organ of memory and no less important vehicle of historicity) and, in particular, in his theory of the novel.

We still consider that an attempt to provide the learners of literature with a comprehensive and analytically structured insight into the movement of the literature of a nation or that of the world, in general, through history can be better achieved by drawing on theories of genre, system, and literary development. And we still believe that some of the most congenial theorizations, still valid and viable nowadays – emerging in the most recent books of literary scholarship, such as in those by Linda Hutcheon with her "system" and "constant", and Bran Nicol with the "dominant" – belong to Yuri Tynyanov, whose main reasoning would be that literature is a system of dominant, central and peripheral, marginalized elements – to us, "tradition" (centre) versus "innovation" (margin) engaged in a "battle" for supremacy, demarginalization, and the right to form a new literary system – and the development or historical advancement of literature is the substitution of systems.

The rise and development of genres represent an important aspect of our discussion, but our main concern is the diachronic movement of English literature through its main periods, movements, and trends which succeed each other, and each has its origin in certain precursors by rejecting some previous literary manifestations and continuing others – where innovation would reject what was before tradition and continue what was before innovation, and vice-versa – as well as being influenced by various contemporary developments and socio-cultural conditions. For this, we rely primarily on more traditional but established and recognized approaches to national literature, particularly on Tynyanov elaborating on system and formalism, on the whole, chiefly its emphasis on internal factors in literary historical movement and change, which, given their applicability nowadays through some changed perspectives of theoretical and critical consideration, may be viewed and labelled as "neo-formalism".

In viewing the literature produced in Britain as a literary system, we follow Tynyanov; in adding the historical dimension to the rise and development of an English – and not only – literature, we follow Tynyanov and Bakhtin again, among others, but more importantly is that our approach to the movement of English literature through history is conceived to go cyclically from theory (the existing theoretical categories of literary analysis) to practice (the direct approach to a number of literary works following the appropriate conceptions and points of concern according to specific features of the chosen texts), and then again to theory, or rather new theoretical arrangements which we hope would emerge in order to be used again in one's endeavours at practical, text-oriented criticism. In both theoretical and practical cases, the main purpose is to disclose and investigate the development and advancement of literary practice in relation to literary theory and criticism, and in this respect, the books focus diachronically on English literature from its beginnings in the Anglo-Saxon period to the present. By their interdisciplinary perspectives involving literary history, literary theory, and literary criticism, the present volumes should be useful to experts in literary studies, professional scholars of literary history and criticism, or to a more general readership, or anyone concerned with theoretical and practical consideration and understanding of literature, in general, and of English literary phenomenon, in particular, and whose knowledge on certain aspects of literature and literary thought in Britain might be enriched by reading these books.

The works represent an attempt of academic research in the field of literature but also meet the requirements of a teaching aid. The main target is student audience and the intention of the books regards the needs of students in their literature classes, aiming at introducing them to the domain of literary history. To students new in the field, at least, the books would supply insight into the historical study of literature; for them, these works would become an accompaniment to a course on literary history; and, we believe, by reading these books, they would secure a reliable grounding in major authors, texts, genres, subgenres, literary movements, trends, and periods. From the incompleteness and disembodiment of bibliographical assistance with regard to certain matters of concern, we believe to have progressed to certain interpretative modalities of our own, which consider the wholeness and complexity of the British literary history. These interpretative arrangements receive ultimate practical argumentation through direct approach to certain authors and their major texts, and they have been also validated by our teaching experience at universities in Turkey, Romania, and Moldova.

Our books are basically a survey tracing the development of British literature and literature related critical and theoretical thinking both as a unique experience and within the larger context of British and Western cultural and literary tradition. The first book in the series focuses diachronically on English literary phenomenon from its Anglo-Saxon beginnings to the end of the Middle Ages and covers the first two periods and experiences of English literary history, which are the Old English (Anglo-Saxon) and medieval ones. The second book considers the movement of English literature from the 1480s to the 1620s and covers the next periods and experiences of English literary history, namely the Renaissance, in general, and, in particular, Humanism, Reformation, and the Elizabethan Age. The third book is about the seventeenth century and offers insight into its main literary manifestations, including metaphysical poetry, Puritanism, and the Restoration. The fourth book considers the eighteenth century and covers some of the most important periods and experiences of the history of English literature in this long, complex and creatively potent age, namely neoclassicism, the rise of the English novel, and pre-romanticism. The fifth book in the series focuses on the period from the 1780s to the 1830s and covers one of the most important periods and experiences of English literary history, which is that of romanticism. This sixth book discloses the essence of the literary development in Britain from the 1830s to 1900 and focuses on other important periods and manifestations of English literary history, which are assigned together as the literature of the Victorian Age, in general, and, in particular, are known as post- and neo-romantic literature, realism, naturalism, and the avant-garde encompassing aestheticism, symbolism, and Pre-Raphaelite Brotherhood. The seventh book in the series is about the development of English literature in the twentieth century and focuses on the first half of the century with its Edwardian literature, the rise of modernism and experimental fiction, its poetry and drama, as well as the traditional literature of the period. The eighth book covers the second half of the twentieth century and offers an insight also into the contemporary literary background; its direct reference is to the post-war new realism of the Angry Young Men and other manifestations of the traditional novel versus a more visionary and philosophical continuation of the modernist and experimental trends, but the emphasis is on the postmodern theory along with postmodernism in its literary expression in fiction, poetry and drama, as well as on more recent alternatives to the postmodern thought and literary practice.

Before actually entering into the period or century in order to discuss its authors, works, movements, trends, culture, philosophy, critical thinking, and so on, our books contain an introductory part aimed to assist the reader to form an opinion on what is literature, what are the approaches to literature, and what are the major periods, movements, trends, authors and texts in the history of British and European literature. Coming after Introduction, the Preliminaries, relying on Yuri Tynyanov and others, would strengthen the understanding of literature as a system and the diachronic movement of literature as the substitution of systems whose central and marginal elements, tradition and innovation are in perpetual interaction and fight, rejection and continuation in order to build up – also as influenced by contemporary socio-cultural stimuli – new systems which we see as periods, movements, trends, genres, subgenres, and so on. Also, in three books in the series dealing with those periods in which a particular genre emerged to dominate the literary scene, there are chapters dedicated to the theoretical, methodological, terminological, and practical consideration of the narrative, lyrical, and dramatic genres. Namely, the theory of drama is explicated in the book on the Renaissance; lyrical genre is theoretically introduced and explained in the book on the seventeenth-century English literature; and, given the rise of the English novel in the eighteenth century, the book on this period contains a theoretical part on the narrative genre, including fiction, narrative poetry, categories and elements of narrative organization, and so on.

Apart from this, in every book of the series, the special emphasis is on those authors who manifested as important writers in the history of British literature, those who developed a national literary discourse making it a part of international cultural heritage. Their names need to be known, their main literary texts understood, and the historical order of events properly grasped in order to comprehend systemically and coherently the rise and development of English literature as a process, a diachronic advancement which encompasses periods, literary movements and trends, genres and subgenres, major authors and texts. Whether or not and to what extent this desideratum is likely to be accomplished by our endeavours, we shall see in the following.

INTRODUCTION
APPROACHING LITERARY PRACTICE AND STUDYING BRITISH LITERATURE IN HISTORY

Keywords: literacy, popularity, consumerism, literature, literary system, communication, aesthetic value, approach to literature, literary history, literary criticism, literary theory, diachronic versus synchronic, objective versus subjective, substitution of systems, innovation versus tradition, centre versus margin, to follow, to continue, to reject, contemporary stimuli, period, movement, trend, genre, author, literary work, text, ancient period, medieval period, modern period, postmodern period, post-postmodern period

In terms of a media-culture perspective, the decline of literacy and the indefinite future of the imaginative writing are nowadays matters of general lament, as it is the fact that literature might have lost its primary role to satisfy the aesthetic and intellectual needs of the post-postmodern man. Facing a complexity of new cultural alternatives, our contemporaries display exaggerated confidence in television, cinema, computers, and Internet; they often watch television or surf the net web-pages instead of reading books, use compact discs for learning languages or getting acquainted with Dickens's novels. The books, then, would apparently survive a limited time in the human cultural store, and many of them are in danger of being forgotten in a remote corner of an old library.

The concept of literacy is an essential principle for the survival of the books, yet, besides literature, literacy refers to many other types of mass communications and theories of mass culture, and literature is not the only reliable vehicle for cultural communication, or improvement of modern thought, or acquisition of information. In some of these respects, one may argue, television and computer are much more reliable, practical, and resourceful tools than the whole of imaginative writing.

On the other hand, the invention of television and the computer has not decreased the printing of books; moreover, the computer screen, Internet, and communication through e-mail display more alphabetic letters than images. Also, as every human being has a novel inside, critics metaphorically claim, "web-fiction" and other forms of online writing have allowed imaginative flight of the people to increase and their creativity to flourish.

The problem is not to oppose visual and written types of cultural communication. It is that, though the whole of image-oriented culture and media attempts to reify a new form of literacy, the problem consists in a general illiteracy caused by the open exposure to a form of visual illiteracy of the media and the insufficient exposure to important and mind-appealing books. In vindicating the role of imaginative literature, "do not fight against false enemies", argues Umberto Eco, because, first of all,

> we know that books are not ways of making somebody else think in our place; on the contrary they are machines which provoke further thoughts. Secondly, if once upon a time people needed to train their memory in order to remember things, after the invention of writing they had also to train their memory in order to remember books. Books challenge and improve memory. They do not narcotize it. This old debate is worth reflecting on every time one meets a new

communicational tool which pretends or appears to replace books. (Eco, *Apocalypse Postponed* 89-90)

Drama, poetry, and fiction have a long developmental history starting in ancient period; they have continuously developed types, forms, concerns, and for this, they are free from the danger of not surviving for years and centuries in the human cultural depository, or of becoming a handful of dust in a remote corner of an old forgotten library. They focus on those issues and tackle those thematic perspectives which reflect the period, its culture, answer to the aesthetic needs of the reader as a form of entertainment or didactic principles, and are imaginatively disclosed and theoretically and critically scrutinized.

Another criterion of their and literature, in general, survival is popularity which is provided and determined by consumerist, public and market demand, and another one is their literacy, or aesthetic validity, which is assessed and supported by academic and critical evaluation.

Today both concepts – popularity and literacy as essential principles of their survival – comprise many types of mass communication and theories of mass culture. According to this media-culture perspective, during the last decades a number of worrying reports have been produced in Western countries on the decline of literary value and the future of imaginative literature. One reason, perhaps, would be the overconfidence in and reliance on technology, internet, cinema, and other forms of communication, of which some have become alternative forms of art and which, apart from traditional arts, including literature, are simultaneously our contemporary forms of art and our contemporary sources of *utile et dulce*.

In order to keep literature at least on the same level with the newly emerged forms of art, strengthen its status, show and defend its aesthetic validity, a repeated insight into the historical advancement of the literary phenomenon is still a valid matter of scholarly concern, and, to us, also a matter of didactic interest aimed to assist the students in their literature classes. In this respect, the following issues are to be answered in this introductory part of the book:

---

1. What is Literature?
2. Approaches to Literature
3. The History of British and European Literature: Periods, Movements, Trends, Authors, and Texts

---

In relation to our attempts to provide a concise surveyistic perspective of **3. The History of British and European Literature** in order to assist students better comprehend its major periods, movements, trends, authors, and texts, prior to this, questions such as

---

What is a literary period?
What is a literary movement?
What is a literary trend?
Are there any differences between movement and trend?

---

would help our endeavour.

Another issue – **4. Literary Genres** – is equally important in literary studies; in our series of books, for didactic purposes, this theoretical aspect is the concern not in this introductory part but in certain chapters in books on specific literary periods and movements: theory of drama in the book on the Renaissance, poetry in the book on the seventeenth century, and fiction in the book on the eighteenth-century English literature.

---

1. What is Literature?

As for the definition, literature, a cultural phenomenon, one of the arts, the verbal art, is in the simplest way defined as imaginative writing. Apart from the long established opinion that literature is "imaginative writing", literature is also "creative writing" since it "employs a special form of language, more evocative and "conative" than that used in other forms of writing" (Castle 6).

Based on a strong critical tradition, having its roots in Saussurean declaration of language to be a system of signs as well as in the formal, including formalist and structuralist, critical theory, literature is understood as a system of elements framed within the boundaries of a communicative situation. The term "literature" is therefore used to designate "a certain body of repeatable or recoverable acts of communication" (Scholes 18).

It should be agreed, however, that in literature, like in art in general, the purpose is not only the communication of fact but also a kind of aesthetic communication involving "the telling of a story (either wholly invented or given new life through invention) or the giving of pleasure through some use of the inventive imagination in the employment of words" (Daiches 4-5).

Being a kind of "writing", literature uses language in "peculiar ways", "offending" language and deviating from its ordinary use; literature "transforms and intensifies ordinary language, deviates systematically from everyday speech" (Eagleton 2). It seems that this peculiarity of every artistic endeavour – be it literary or musical – to "deviate", "offend", "destroy" in order to create – was long ago acknowledged by the artist himself or herself, as to remember just *A Musical Instrument* by Elizabeth Barrett Browning.

Because its material is language, made of words expressed in relation to creative imagination, and besides its aspect of communication, the second important function of literature is the aesthetic one. Both functions are interrelated and of equal importance. The object of literature is the subjective and objective universe, the inner and outer world, and the verbal matter which materialises this object forms the beauty, which is established under the sign of joy and integrity and is in this condition communicated to the public.

In linguistic terms, the six elements in communication, in general, as identified by Roman Jakobson in *Linguistics and Poetics* (1963), drawing on Tynyanov's and formalist basic term "system" of elements, are the following (Jakobson 34):

| Addresser | Context

Message

Contact

Code | Addressee | - the addresser (usually but not necessarily the same as the sender)
- the addressee (usually but not necessarily the same as the receiver)
- the message (the particular linguistic form)
- the context (the referent or information, or more precisely, the contextual information on the world in which the message takes place; the social and historical framework in which the utterance is made; also, it refers to the circumstances or conditions relevant to a fact – a setting in which events occur; more recently, as prompted by Bakhtin, it is part of a text which determines its meaning, since the meaning cannot be understood outside the context)
- the contact (the medium or channel; the physical channel and psychological connection between addresser and addressee)
- the code (the language common to both addresser and addressee, which permits communication to occur) |

In the same study, Jakobson shows that corresponding to each element in this taxonomy is a particular function of language:

| Emotive | Referential

Poetic

Phatic

Metalingual | Conative | - the emotive (to communicate inner feelings and states)
- the conative (to attempt to determine/affect the behavior of the receiver)
- the referential (to carry information in order to describe a situation, object, state)
- the poetic (to focus on linguistic form)
- the phatic (to open the channel for practical or social reasons)
- the metalingual (to focus on language or dialect in order to clarify it or change it) |

Literature as a system, the literary system, constitutes a literary discourse to be communicated to the reader; in other words, it is involved in a literary communicative situation. The structure, simple but relevant to any learner of literature, is provided by Guy Cook. He shows that the six elements in communication, as identified by Jacobson in *Linguistics and Poetics*, each having a corresponding function of language, receive in literary communication their equivalent counterparts: "addresser" or "sender" is the "author" or "writer", "message" is the "text", "addressee" or "receiver" is the "reader", and so on. They constitute the elements of the literary system. Guy Cook identifies and places these elements in a simple but comprehensive structure of the literary communicative situation (128):

		Society	
Author	Text	(Performer)	Reader
	Texts	Language	

Every literary work represents a text, written or oral; it is a particular individual verbal expression, the product of an author, known to us or anonymous. The literary work addresses a reader. Even if no one has yet read a given text, the author is its reader. The material and means of expression of the text is language. It is produced in relation to a certain social background; it is the result of the literary production of an epoch, country, region; it is the expression of the social relations which occur at a certain historical moment. The literary work always exists in relation to other texts, which represent previous literary traditions or the period which is contemporary to the given literary work, by which disclosing intertextual relations on the structural and, above all, thematic level.

2. Approaches to Literature

The consumption of literature and the apprehension of its aesthetic values and effects go hand in hand with the approach to literature. The approach to literature has shown itself as a modality capable enough to reassure and strengthen the role of imaginative writing as an agent able to satisfy the intellectual needs of the humans by its permanent re-evaluation of the past national and international literary heritage as well as by its study and evaluation of the contemporary literary practice, in the context of what Matthew Arnold, during Victorian times, defined and described literary criticism as a disinterested effort or endeavour to learn and propagate the best which is known and thought in the world.

This endeavour, the nineteenth-century scholar believes, is the "real estimate", the real approach to literature leading to its true understanding and to "a sense for the best, the really excellent, and of the strength and joy". These ideas seem nowadays superfluous and obsolete, being long ago rejected and replaced by the more scientific and methodological critical perspectives of formalism, structuralism, psychoanalysis, deconstruction, and other approaches developed by the twentieth-century literary theory and criticism.

In the most general terms, the previous and subsequent to Matthew Arnold periods have developed in the field of literary studies three major perspectives of approach to literature, three directions offering theoretical and practical possibilities to study and understand literature, and which are commonly referred to as critical, theoretical and historical.

The three approaches to literature – **literary theory (the theory of literature), literary criticism, and literary history (the history of literature)** – despite the huge debates over their functions and even necessity, represent three distinct scientific disciplines with their own definitions, characteristics, terminology, objects of study, and methodologies. They are interconnected, having obvious points of identification and separation.

Prior to the discussion of these disciplines either from a historical perspective or as looking at their contemporary status, it is necessary to clarify their definitions, concerns, aims, relation to diachronic and synchronic elements, and to subjectivity and objectivity, as well as their interrelationship, interdependence and usefulness in the understanding of the literary phenomenon.

The standard dictionary definition regards **history of literature** or **literary history** as the **diachronic approach to literature which focuses on literary periods, movements, trends, doctrines, and writing practice (authors and works)**, all that represents the "objective facts of literary history" (Jauss, *Toward an Aesthetic of Reception* 51). Although in the contemporary state of terminology, "literary history" and "history of literature" are considered synonymous, it is also claimed that "history of literature gathers and classifies literary works, whereas literary history places and tries to explain these works by relating them to a series of historic, social, political, ideological, and cultural determinants" (Gengembre 4).

The modern "literary history was created in the Romantic age" (Perkins 338), with Herder in Germany as its founder, Madame de Staël and Chateaubriand in France, and in England with Robert Lowth, Thomas Percy, and especially Thomas Warton's *History of English Poetry* (1774-1781), which came to replace the older history of learning (*historia litterarum*) as promoted by Francis Bacon.

Literary criticism is the study, analysis, investigation, or approach to particular literary texts on both thematic and structural levels. Criticism interprets the text, discloses its meaning, and mediates between the text and the reader. If there are debates whether the average reader needs or not any help from criticism, concerning professional readers, academics and students, criticism has definitely acquired a solid position in the field of literary education, in which "criticism is both an end and a means, the natural culmination of study of an author and the instrument of literary training" (Culler, *Structuralist Poetics* vii).

In the process of critical interpretation, the complete meaning emerges out of the investigation of both content and form, thematic and structural dimensions of the text which are organically fused, since it is impossible to separate "what" is said in a literary work, or "what" is the text about, from "how" it is said, or the "way" in which the text is written.

The task of criticism as interpretation has a long history, from the medieval Biblical interpretation to "self-consciousness about the problem of textual meaning introduced by the Biblical hermeneutics associated with Schleiermacher at the beginning of the nineteenth century" (Collini 3-4) and then throughout the entire text and texts oriented theories of formalism, New Criticism, structuralism, and poststructuralism.

The theory and practice of interpretation range from the attempt to establish the exact meaning to Saussure's insistence on the arbitrariness of the signifier, Derrida's claim about the instability of all meaning in writing, and a more recent method by Umberto Eco of "interpreting the world and texts based on the individuation of the relationships of sympathy that link microcosm and macrocosm to one another" (Eco, "Overinterpreting texts" 45).

Literary theory looks at the nature of literature itself; it develops and offers terms, concepts, rules, criteria, categories, general strategies, methodologies and principles of research of the literary phenomena, including the text and other elements of the literary system. Theory "may connote a poetics or aesthetics concerned not with interpretation of texts but with theorising discourse in general" (Selden, "Introduction" 2).

Furthermore, theorizing within the field of literary studies "may have various objectives", but "the main aim has been to answer the question "What is literature?" Discourses addressing this question have traditionally been called "poetics", more recently "theory of literature"" (Fowler 3). In short, literary theory is "the systemic account of the nature of literature and of the methods for analysing it" (Culler, *Literary*

Theory 1).

Concerning the concepts of "diachronic" versus "synchronic", if the first, historical approach or history of literature embarks on a diachronic perspective in literary studies and investigates the development of national and world literature, the second, literary criticism, is considered synchronic, and the third one, literary theory, is referred to as general and universal.

In matters of subjectivism and objectivism, literary history and, especially, literary theory are designated as sciences, requiring normative and methodological objectivism. Literary criticism is also required to be objective and to concentrate solely on text, not context: as seen by Stanley Fish in *Yet Once More*, the literary critic "is a specialist, defined and limited by the traditions of his craft, and it is a condition of his labours (...) that he remain distanced from any effort to work changes in the structure of society" (Machor and Goldstein 29). Literary criticism, however, "cannot avoid being partial and selective" (Lodge 63).

Literary criticism, indeed, allows subjectivism to intermingle with objective reasoning, art with science, fusing in one discourse the personal responses to literature and the scientific research, but what the critical discourse requires most is the accurate balance between the subjective and objective components.

The predominance of subjective element makes a certain type of criticism to be more "practical", "personal", or, as it is often called, "impressionistic criticism" in which, usually in the form of essay, "you wrote about your feelings, perhaps saying how moving you found a poem or how it reminded you of something in your own experience" (Peck and Coyle 177). The essay form is particularly popular among the Anglo-American critics and writer-critics, being the most "creative" critical writing. It is then only normal that the great writer-critics of the twentieth century T. S. Eliot and Virginia Woolf embraced this form, the latter, in particular, taking "full advantage of the liberties of the essay form, drawing her readers into playful digressions, allegorical fancies, unanswerable queries, and inconclusive reveries, inviting us through a collaborative "we" to join in an unchaperoned dance of impressions and ideas" (Baldick 257).

On the contrary, the reliance on theory rather than on personal impressions makes the critical text objective, neutral, at the same time "theoretical" or belonging to "academic criticism", which is "more analytic (...) commenting on the subject matter and method of the text" (Peck and Coyle 177). According to their methods and principles, in addition to practical, impressionistic, and theoretical, the critics are also categorized as formal, historical, moral, analytical, descriptive, affective, psychological, and so on.

The principle of separation within critical practice works on the more general level amid the three disciplines as well. There are many and influential voices that isolate literature and literary criticism from historical context and literary history, to mention just I. A. Richards and F. R. Leavis. There are even voices that separate criticism from theory, arguing that the theoretical account of literature "isn't useful in criticism, and will simplify, if attempted, encumber critics with "preconceived ideas" which will get between them and the text" (Barry 20).

Where does the scientific/objective component in literary criticism come from? The answer is to be found in a more detailed presentation of the specificity of each of the three approaches to literature and in the explanation of the relationship of the three approaches to literature.

We have seen that literary history, or the history of literature, like literary theory and criticism, studies literature on the whole and the particular elements of the literary system.

However, if the contemporary field of literary theory and criticism discusses the literary work as a synchronic phenomenon, removing the text from its temporal and spatial context, the history of literature performs a historical (diachronic) investigation of literature and studies the national and world literary development in relation to its periods, movements, trends, writers and works.

It is a critical, or rather metacritical, cliché in the Anglo-American academic world to start a book on literary theory and criticism by bringing into discussion Rene Wellek and his view (in *Concepts of Criticism*, 1963) of literary criticism as dealing with concrete works of art and that of literary theory as "the study of the principles of literature, its categories, criteria, and the like".

It is also a cliché to mention the name of Matthew Arnold and his definition of criticism as "a disinterested endeavour to learn and propagate the best that is known and thought in the world".

This definition is for many people a reason enough to claim that both literary theory and literary criticism should rely on science, objectivity, reason, method, and terminology, and reject creativity and imaginative flight. This opinion would contradict the claims by Raman Selden and Geoffrey Hartman that "critical and theoretical writing could assume a status equal to the literature it had once been thought to serve" (Stevenson 88-89). Likewise, in the twentieth century, Northrop Frye said that the "subject-matter of literary criticism is an art, and criticism is evidently something of an art too" (3).

Against Frye are those who consider literary criticism to be a science, among whom T. S. Eliot, who claims criticism to be scientific by focusing on technical analysis; also, Wellek and Warren, in the celebrated *Theory of Literature* (1949), call criticism "a species of knowledge or of learning"; and Roman Jakobson, who in *Linguistics and Poetics*, uses instead of "criticism" the term "poetics" or "literary study" and demands poetics to be an integral part of linguistics, since linguistics is the "global science of verbal structure".

Siding with Frye are those who view criticism as art, among whom Friedrich Schlegel and his famous statement on literary criticism: "Poetry can only be criticized by way of poetry. A critical judgement of an artistic production has no civil rights in the realm of art if it isn't itself a work of art". D. H. Lawrence, in *John Galsworthy*, calls criticism an art because it is too personal and based on emotion, not reason; Wilde, in *The Critic as Artist*, views criticism as full art emerging from the same imagination and creativity which are required by the literary work it criticises; whereas others see criticism "an art, although only a minor one" (Gardner 6). Theories are employed and methodologies and concepts are used, but most critics "have seen their profession not as a science but essentially an art, i.e., the art of commenting illuminatingly on literary works, of explaining and assessing them so as to increase our understanding and appreciation of literature" (Shusterman 213).

And it is the condition of the writer-critics to stand apart from other types of critics and be the first to promote criticism to the high sphere of creativity and imaginative flight, even against all threats of becoming subjective, defensive, combative, prescriptive, reflexive and slaves of literary practice.

The current critical theory, be it art or a scientific method of literary analysis, displays immense vitality and productivity, representing a complex phenomenon of theoretical diversity and intellectual collision, and being a true exponent of globalization and internationalization. This aspect is remarkably captured by the writer-critic David Lodge in his trilogy of campus novels; in his non-fictional works, Lodge also conceives highly of literary criticism, which is for him a "highly developed intellectual discipline" and "since its subject is human eloquence it has a responsibility to maintain as much continuity as possible with human discourse" (Lodge 41).

Leaving aside the debates on scientific/objective versus creative/subjective binary opposition in literary studies, it is more important to assume that literary theory, literary criticism, and literary history (history of literature) are interrelated and interdependent, and co-exist in the field of literary studies as bound by their major and common object of study, which is literary work.

Their interrelationship and interdependence form a permanent circular movement from the historically placed literary practice to literary criticism, from literary criticism to literary theory and from literary theory back to criticism.

The text – either produced recently or representing an earlier period in literary history – is subject to literary criticism whose concluding reflections (the necessary outcome of literary criticism), if generally accepted and proved valid in connection to other thematically and structurally similar literary texts, emerge into the domain of literary theory, become its general principles of approach to literature, and are applicable to the study of other particular texts and to the understanding of literature, in general.

This activity of the critic makes him or her expect to acquire a kind of eternal position in the critical discourse moving on "perpetually from one text to another": "the critic, having had a say about a particular text, hopes that later interpretations will assimilate that "say", incorporating it into an interpretative tradition" (Scholes 3).

Literary theory is fed and supported by the outcome of the practical action of criticism, but it often also "develops out of the application of a more general theory (of art, culture, language and linguistics, aesthetics, politics, history, psychology, economics, gender, and so on) to literary works in the interests of a specific critical aim", meaning that theory "grows out of this experimentation with concepts, terms, and paradigms taken from other spheres of intellectual activity" (Castle 9).

Literary criticism uses theory in practical matters of research whenever the study of particular literary works is required, adding to the objective theory the critic's individual response to the text. The expected result is, on one hand, the development of new or alternative theoretical perspectives, and, on the other hand, the change, promotion, discouragement, revival or, in some other ways, the influence upon the literary practice of its own historical period, and the influence upon the literary attitude of the reading audience concerning the contemporary and past literary tradition.

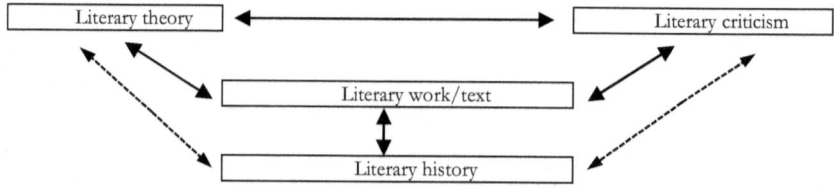

Literary criticism is thus not to be regarded as just the analysis or evaluation of particular literary works, but also as the formulation of general principles of approach to such works.

Co-existing in the field of literary studies with literary history and literary theory, literary criticism combines the theoretical/scientific and practical levels of literary analysis. Criticism as science follows and applies the general principles and methods of research from literary theory, but it also reveals an artistic/creative aspect when the critic personalizes the discourse by his or her own opinions.

The true literary critic uses literary theory to evaluate the literary text and out of the synthesis of the borrowed theory with his or her personal views, the critic develops other theoretical perspectives while keeping the proper balance between the objective and subjective component, between the use of theory and personal contribution. Otherwise, the criticism would be meaningless, "talking about literature in a way that cannot help to build up a systematic structure of knowledge" (Frye 18).

Since the balance is hardly possible, there is this often-made distinction between "theoretical criticism" (with its heavy reliance on existing theories and the attempt to develop new ones) and "practical criticism" (also known as "impressionistic", "interpretive", or "applied criticism", which applies theories but its main concern is individual text which is studied through observation, close reading, analysis, determination of thematic and formal qualities, intertextuality, and so on).

In the circular movement from criticism to theory and vice-versa, primarily the "theoretical criticism" both uses literary theory and proposes to develop "an explicit theory of literature, in the sense of general principles, together with a set of term, distinctions, and categories, to be applied to identifying and analysing works of literature, as well as the criteria (the standards, or norms) by which these works and their writers are to be evaluated" (Abrams and Harpham 61).

The "practical criticism" focuses on individual texts and expresses personal responses which the texts evoke. As such, this type of criticism is less concerned with developing theory or applying theory, and "the theoretical principles controlling the analysis, interpretation, and evaluation are often left implicit, or brought in only as the occasion demands" (Abrams and Harpham 62).

Whatever its typology, literary criticism focuses on individual texts and is connected to theory and history, but apart from these two fields, in the study of literature, the critical discussion cannot be separated from the domain of language in which a certain literature is produced. Literary criticism relies here on other domains, namely linguistics and stylistics. Literature and language are interrelated and interdependent, in that "the literature cannot be examined in any depth apart from the language, any more than the language can be studied apart from the literature", and the study of language can become "a complement and aid to the study of literature" (G. N. Leech 1). Furthermore, concerning the critical practice, Geoffrey N. Leech argues that

> The type of critical activity known as "practical criticism" or "explication de texte" relies more heavily on linguistic evidence than others. In addition, much of the basic vocabulary of literary criticism ("metaphor", "figurative", "antithesis", "irony", rhythm", etc.) cannot be explained without recourse to linguistic notions. As a meeting-ground of linguistic and literary studies, stylistics is the field within which these basic questions lie. (1-2)

Likewise, David Lodge considers that all good criticism

> is a response to language – that it is good insofar as it is a sensitive response – whether or not there is any explicit reference to language in the way of quotation and analysis. This applies not only to the "structural" approach, but to the moral, mythical, historical, psycho-analytical and thematic approaches too; and it explains, I believe, why we can profit from criticism using radically different approaches from our own. (63)

Umberto Eco, combining semiotics, cultural philosophy and literary criticism in one scholarly personality, extends the implication of language in critical interpretation of the literary works to the more general context of culture and literary history:

> a text is produced not for a single addressee but for a community of readers – the author knows that he or she will be interpreted not according to his or her intentions but according to a complex strategy of interactions which also involves the readers, along with their competence in language as a social treasury. I mean by social treasury not only a given language as a set of grammatical rules, but also the whole encyclopaedia that the performances of that language have implemented, namely, the cultural conventions that that language has produced and the very history of the previous interpretations of many texts, comprehending the text that the reader is in the course of reading. ("Between author and text" 67-68)

The relationship of the three approaches to literature – criticism, theory, and history – suggests that literary history is more of a distinct discipline, standing apart, whereas literary theory and literary criticism are stronger connected, which is also based on the assumption that there is no non-theoretical literary criticism. Theoretical principles and implications "lurk behind even the most "practical" forms of criticism, even the most text-oriented interpretations and evaluations" (Harland xi), and even the most personal opinions on literature.

Hence theory and criticism are being considered by certain scholars as one discipline under the generic name of "**literary theory and criticism**" or "critical theory".

Others provide a clear delimitation between literary theory and literary criticism, naming them "theoretical criticism" and "practical criticism" (also labelled "applied criticism"), respectively. But the former is just another label given to literary theory, since it "formulates the theories, principles, and tenets of the nature and value of art"; the latter, only sharing the same name with I. A. Richards's and F. R. Leavis's method, corresponds to literary criticism and "applies the theories and tenets of theoretical criticism [i.e. literary theory] to a particular work" (Bressler 7).

The names may differ, it is clear, but the essence concerning the object of study and aims does not change. The actual problem affecting the disciplines considers their outcome and utility.

There are strong voices recurrently providing apocalyptic declarations about the death of historicity, including the history of literature or literary history, as well as about the uselessness of any theory or critical study since there are doubts about the possibility to achieve originality, to construct and impose a meaning, and to employ language to represent or reflect whatever is the creative interest.

There have always been numerous and repeated efforts to revive and provide a scientific substratum to the historical study of literature. Yuri Tynyanov and the formalist school, on the whole, attempt to renovate literary history through the view of literature as a system, the theorization of literary evolution, and the discussions on genres. Hans Robert Jauss warns that history of literature is being reduced to a mere gallery of biographies and becomes an obsolete object of study, whose existence would be determined only by a didactic purpose and the necessity of being traditionally included as a part of cultural information. If literary history is to be rejuvenated, argues Jauss, "the prejudices of historical objectivism must be removed and the traditional approach to literature must be replaced by an aesthetics of reception and impact" ("Literary History as a Challenge" 13).

Earlier, Rene Wellek and Austin Warren (in *Theory of Literature*) claimed that "a history of a national literature as a whole, is harder to envisage (...) histories of groups of literatures are even more distant ideals (...) Finally, a general history of the art of literature is still a far-distant ideal". Strongly bound to their Russian formalist origins, namely Tynyanov's theory of literary system, Wellek and Warren claim that literary history must be the study of the systems of "literary norms, standards, and conventions", and must be "the tracing of the changing from one system of norms to another" (264-268).

Wellek and Warren believe that the separation of criticism from the diachronic dimension of the literary history and its subsequent consolidation as a distinct domain were caused by the distinction between the consideration of literature as a simultaneous order and the view on literature as a line of works arranged chronologically and regarded as constituent parts of the historical process. But the practice of historical approach to literature replied to Wellek and other challengers of literary history by such masterworks as Erich Auerbach's *Mimesis: The Representation of Reality in Western Literature* (1946) or Ernst Robert Curtius's *European Literature and the Latin Middle Ages* (1948).

Neither the research of the text as a synchronic phenomenon nor the historicism of the literary experience are to be neglected, but in order to achieve the adequate comprehension of the literary works of different writers and periods, it is necessary to overcome the gap between literary criticism and literary history by fusing the synchronic and diachronic dimensions in literary analysis, and by strengthening the relationship between text and context.

> It is the task of literary criticism – apart from the thematic perspectives of approach – to involve the diachronic perspective in the study of the text.

Otherwise, without understanding literature with what literary history provides, which is essentially a scrutiny of the literary phenomenon in its growth, the relationship between tradition and innovation, the origins of literary work, the author as artist possessing distinct psychology and sensibility, and the social and cultural circumstances which make the production of the work possible and which are reflected in the work, the critic would scarcely offer competent judgement on the value of the text. The "method of historical reception is indispensable for the understanding of literature from the distant past", claims Jauss, and how then the text can be properly understood if "the author of a work is unknown, his intent undeclared, and his relationship to sources and models only indirectly accessible"? (*Toward an Aesthetic of Reception* 29)

> The perspective is reciprocal: it is also the task of literary history to remain a scientific discipline by involving in the study on the rise and development of literature the synchronic dimension of the literary criticism and the scientific principles of research offered by literary theory. The history of literature, in order to claim the status of a science, must be a rigorous system equipped with scientific methodology.

Moreover, the

gap between literature and history, between aesthetic and historical knowledge, can be bridged if literary history does not simply describe the process of general history in the reflection of its works one more time, but rather when it discovers in the course of "literary evolution" that properly socially formative function that belongs to literature as it competes with other arts and social forces in the emancipation of mankind from its natural, religious, and social bonds. (Jauss, *Toward an Aesthetic of Reception* 45)

The literary work is undoubtedly a phenomenon dated in time, and represents, as Romul Munteanu clearly states it in *Metamorphoses of the Modern European Criticism* (1988), the product of a historical time in which a human community develops a particular view on existence, a view which comes to be expressed by exceptional individuals, the producers of literary works, themselves exponents of a particular historical background.

In this respect, as stated above, the discipline of the history of literature performs a historical investigation of literature, and studies the national and world literary development in relation to its periods, movements, trends, genres, types of text, writers, and works, which are inscribed in a process of becoming to reveal the victory of historicism in modernity – weakened but still alive nowadays – and strengthen George Calinescu's claim that literary history resembles an epic scenario on a vast cultural scene.

Like philosophy and history, criticism was conceived as part of a process, a becoming, a diachronic phenomenon, and even as part of history and philosophy, although the aesthetic legitimacy of the work to be judged by critical criteria would not be among the primary aims of the literary history.

Since the Renaissance through the nineteenth century, with empiricist, rationalist and positivist thinking at power, the literary work came to be conceived as a constituent part of a nation's spiritual existence more than it would be viewed as an act of artistic creation whose value emerges from its aesthetic indicators. Literary history would provide evidence about the life and specificity of a nation and become a means of understanding the national psychology as well as advance the literary work as the product and reflection of the milieu and history (Taine); earlier, the romantics already promoted the historical and national along with the individual significance in literary practice and literary studies through an anteriority and posteriority dualism, which later becomes the cause and effect dichotomy.

Literary history having embarked on diachronic research, the dominant opinion was that this discipline is nothing than history (Gervinus) and necessitates no insight into the specificity of the literary phenomenon. Earlier, Friedrich Schlegel negates both literary history and literary criticism by reasoning that if art should be science and the scientific research ought to acquire an artistic nature – since philosophy and poetry constitute a unitary phenomenon – than poetry can be criticised only through poetry, the aesthetic judgement having value only in so far as it is legitimized as an work of art (Munteanu, *Introducere in literatura europeana* 9).

Prior to the twentieth century, this separation of literary history from aesthetic judgement, including literary criticism, conferred low esteem to the historical approach to literature and discredited its status; Tynyanov, among the first, at the beginning of the last century, and later Jauss and others pointed at the systemic and methodological discrepancy in the field of literary history and attempted to provide it with scientific rigour and relate it to literary theory and criticism.

Apart from the debates on the status and usefulness of the historical approach to literature, there are still voices that argue for the uselessness of literary criticism too, which is summarised by Umberto Eco as follows: "Some contemporary theories of criticism assert that the only reliable reading of a text is a misreading, that the only existence of a text is given by the chain of responses it elicits, and that, as maliciously suggested by Todorov (...), a text is only a picnic where the author brings the words and the readers bring the sense" ("Interpretation and History" 24).

Critical text is a metatext, a second degree text, they say, a valueless imitation of the original literary text emerging in the process of reading. Northrop Frye speaks about the conception, popular among artists, of the critic as a parasite and consequently literary criticism as a

> parasite form of literary expression, an art based on pre-existing art, a second hand imitation of creative power. On this theory critics are intellectuals who have a taste for art but lack both the power to produce it and the money to patronize it, and thus form a class of cultural middlemen, distributing culture to society at a profit to themselves while exploiting the artist and increasing the strain on his public. (3)

Even the critics themselves may suddenly decide "that the true subject of criticism is ineffable, and criticism, as a consequence, unnecessary", whereas others may confess "that one is too stupid, too unenlightened to understand a book reputedly philosophical" (Barthes 34). Even if this were true, literary criticism has proved to be an important and necessary domain for centuries, providing, among other things, the establishment of literary traditions, advancement of literary practice, expression of literary value, and mediation between art and its audience. The question is not about the necessity of criticism but about the professional validity of such critics. Barthes again:

> But if one fears or despises so much the philosophical foundations of a book, and if one demands so insistently the right to understand nothing about them and to say nothing on the subject, why become a critic? To understand, to enlighten, that is your profession, isn't it? You can of course judge philosophy according to common sense; the trouble is that while "common sense" and "feeling" understand nothing about philosophy, philosophy, on the other hand, understands them perfectly. (35)

If literary history and literary criticism may be considered, unjustly, of course, by some as useless and helpless, then the sole surviving and necessary domain for literary comprehension is literary theory, still valued, developed and conceived as the only real science of literature. When not considered useless in defining literature, the role of literary criticism is minimized and perceived in the context of a mere reading experience. According to this first assumption, literary criticism is an alternative way of reading the literary text.

Criticism is a common practice helping readers to avoid discrepancies and misunderstandings, or it remains just a practical approach in universities explaining the text and improving the students' competence. In this respect, the critics "tend to minimize textual problems as reading problems. Their concern is usually with evaluating a poet's work or with arguing for a particular reading, rather than overtly demonstrating interpretive goals and reading strategies" (Fairley 311).

Contrary to this first convention, which regards criticism as being secondary to literature, there is another which argues that literary criticism "can be seen as a means of constructing the body of writing and knowledge which it appears to take as its object of study; in other words, literature can be seen as a product of and dependent on criticism rather than the other way round" (Webster 7).

Be theory of literature the most important discipline, yet the relationship of co-existence and interdependence of the three approaches to literature emphasises that literary theory, literary criticism, and literary history are parts of a single written discourse about literature. They are parts of a single science, the science of literature, having as its object of study an art, namely the art of literature, or, in other words, the work of literary art, which is the text, and all the elements which construct and condition the work of literature, where the literary work, or text, from a formalist perspective, would constitute the centre of the system of literature surrounded by and interrelated with all the other elements of the literary system.

The notion of "system" and its theoretical premises are congenial and applicable for the three approaches to literature – history, criticism, and theory, which build up the science of literature – as well: like every science, the science of literature "has as its final aim the truth, which is revealed through notions, and as such it is created as a system that is generally applicable. Being a science that focuses its system on an art, the literary science constitutes a meta-art and follows the disclosure, from a unique perspective, of the infinite individual patterns" (Bomher 11).

In addition, the relationship of the three approaches to literature points out that literary theory, literary criticism, and literary history are parts of a single cognitive system, a single discourse that assists the pragmatic function by its aim to form or facilitate a particular type of communication which involves the producer of literature and its receiver.

Interesting, comprehensive, systemic, and, above all, didactically useful for the learners of literature are the identification and explanation of the critical theories as provided by M. H. Abrams in his celebrated *The Mirror and the Lamp: Romantic Theory and the Critical Tradition* (1953).

According to him, in art, in general, four critical theories emerge and are dominant in different periods: "mimetic theory", "rhetorical" or "pragmatic theory", "expressive theory", and "objective theory". Abrams points out that all critical theories, as different as they could be, concentrate around four constituents, or major elements, which represent "the total situation of a work of art": (1) the "work", meaning the artistic product, the thing made by the maker; (2) the "artist", or the creator of the work; (3) the "universe", which is the world or nature which is imitated, where, when art is viewed as imitation, the materials of the real world and of the world of ideas become the substance of the work, out of which the work may be thought to take its subjects; and (4) the "audience", which is the receiver or addressee, to whom the work is addressed.

According to Abrams, the concern with one of these four elements results in a special critical theory on art. The critic that focuses exclusively on the "work" of art and views it as a self-contained entity, approaching art basically in its own terms, follows the so-called "objective theory". If art is discussed in relation to the "artist", the work being understood as the expression of the maker's own psychological and emotional states, the approach is called the "expressive theory". To view art in terms of "universe", which is in terms of what is imitated in the work of art, is to follow the "mimetic theory". Finally, to regard art in relation to the "audience", studying the effects of the work of art on the receiver, is to follow the "rhetorical" or "pragmatic theory".

Elements of art as a system	Corresponding critical theory
work	objective theory
artist	expressive theory
universe	mimetic theory
audience	pragmatic theory

Furthermore, Abrams believes, when viewed diachronically, the development of art and art criticism in the Western world reveals these theories to be dominant in different historical periods. In ancient classical age, the most characteristic theory was the mimetic theory, with Plato and Aristotle as its promoters. However, with Aristotle's *catharsis* as the effect of drama on audience and Horace's idea of art as *utile et dulce*, instruction and pleasure, the pragmatic theory emerged in ancient period as another dominant perspective to view art in critical terms. From Antiquity through the most of the eighteenth century, these two theories remain dominant, in particular the pragmatic theory with its focus on art's usefulness and its effects on audience, although in the Renaissance and, especially, in neoclassicism, the principle of imitation was also central to the evaluation of art.

The linearity of the aesthetic attitude of the Western world governed by the view of art as a major source of instruction mingled with delight and pleasure – and thus subject to normative prescriptions – and by the confidence in the imitative nature of art was broken by the romantic rejection of tradition and rules, by its claim of the freedom of artistic expression, the revival of innovative principle in art, and, especially, the emphasis on the artist's own emotional and psychological states.

Aristotle developed a kind of "reader-oriented" approach to literature, but with romanticism, the artist became the centre of attention, his or her power of imagination, creative flight, sensibility, subjective and psychological experience expressed in the work of art.

Thus the expressive theory – also known as the "expressive theory of authorship" – emerges as the most characteristic of the romantic attitudes towards art. Also, dominant in the nineteenth century and later in the twentieth century was the objective theory on art, based on the idea of art for its own sake, art *per se*, the work being viewed as a separate entity, complex enough in its thematic spectrum, range of symbols and imagery, along with its patterns of structure and form, to be a matter of critical concern in itself, as for the late nineteenth-century avant-garde (symbolism, aestheticism, decadence, and so on) and the twentieth-century formal approach to literature (Russian formalism, Anglo-American New Criticism, and French structuralism). However, the present diversity of approaches to art keeps the contemporary critic aware of all the four major theories in his or her endeavour to evaluate art, in general, and literature, in particular.

A closer look at the rise of the critical tradition in Britain reveals a process of development during certain periods or stages generally corresponding to periods and movements in English art and literature. British literary criticism, in particular, reveals some concerns with literature in the medieval period, but its actual beginnings are found in the Renaissance, and its development and consolidation occurred during the subsequent periods of the Restoration, neoclassicism, romanticism, and the Victorian Age, as to establish itself in the twentieth century as a scientific discipline, an objective, methodological and terminological domain developing and consisting of its own schools and trends of literary theory and criticism.

In order to understand better the whole range and complexity of the contemporary trends and schools in the theoretical and critical approach to literature, we may rely again on Tynyanov, Jakobson, and Cook with their grounding of the idea of system consisting of various interrelated elements.

Like with Abrams's distinction between four elements of the system of art and their corresponding critical theories, the literary work in itself and the different relations between the text and other elements of the literary system gave birth to different theories, trends and schools in modern literary theory and criticism. As a result, the contemporary literary critic faces a multitude of schools and theories which correspond to the categories from the structure of the literary system.

The methods of these critical trends compete with each other or conflict over the evaluation and interpretation of particular works, but they also complement each other, being united by the aim to provide an as much as possible comprehensive account of the literary work and to expose the total range of its meanings. But "there is no satisfactory total account of a work of literature except the work itself. It is only the work itself that presents all its meanings in the most significant and assimilable form" (Lodge 63). A writer cannot be asked to reveal the whole truth about life and likewise a critic cannot be expected to disclose the whole truth about a particular literary work.

Criticism cannot offer all the meanings of the work, since it does not and cannot reproduce the work of literature it discusses. Instead, criticism "sets beside this work another work – the critical essay – which is a kind of hybrid formed by the collaboration of the critic with the artist, and which, in this juxtaposition, makes the original yield up some of its secrets" (Lodge 63). Facing a large amount of contemporary critical theories, the question which naturally arises is whether an approach is better than any other. Instead of asking this question, one should "admit that any given method is justified by the use made of it by a particular critic" (Lodge 63). Also, instead of heavily borrowing ideas and providing quotations from the existing critical and theoretical studies, the critic may relate and apply them to his or her particular matters of concern. A more skilled critic considers the essence of different theories, modifying it according to the specificity of the research, and, by providing personal points of view and ideas, the critic progresses to certain interpretative modalities of his or her own.

Concerning the most important critical theories, trends and schools, and according to Guy Cook's literary communicative situation, corresponding to each category in his scheme are various types of critical theory. Thus, in the field of literary theory and criticism, the "author" is the matter of concern of literary scholarship and biography; "text" is studied by formalism, linguistics, linguistic criticism, and stylistics; "performer" by acting theory; "reader" by phenomenology, hermeneutics, reception theory, reader-oriented and reader-response theory, as well as by psychoanalysis, feminism, and poststructuralism; "society" by Marxist theories, cultural materialism, new historicism, and feminism; "texts" by structuralism, poststructuralism, and deconstruction; and corresponding to "language" are the theories of linguistics and stylistics.

author	literary scholarship and biography
text	formalism, linguistics, linguistic criticism, and stylistics
performer	acting theory
reader	phenomenology, hermeneutics, reception theory, reader-oriented theory, reader-response theory, psychoanalysis, feminism, and poststructuralism
society	Marxist theories, cultural materialism, new historicism, and feminism
texts	structuralism, poststructuralism, and deconstruction
language	linguistics and stylistics

Concerning intertextualism, themes, motives, influence, reception, and, in general, the different relations between the literary works, the initiative is that of comparative literature. The particular elements of the literary system and literature, on the whole, are also the matters of critical and theoretical concern of other theories and principles of research, such as those prompted by rhetoric, semiotics, Bakhtinian criticism, archetypal and myth criticism, folklore studies, ethnic literary studies, racial studies, colonial, postcolonial and transnational studies, cultural studies, environmentalism and ecocriticism, posthumanism, transhumanism, and other contemporary trends and schools in humanities and in literary theory and criticism.

These theories, trends and schools represent the twentieth century and the contemporary objective, scientific, and methodological literary theory and criticism. They also offer the picture of the science of literature as a large and chaotic domain concerning both the methods and aims of these types of literary criticism. In the celebrated *Nouveau dictionnaire encyclopedique des sciences du langage*, Oswald Ducrot and Jean-Marie Schaeffer reduce this diversity to five main directions: a) the evaluative criticism of the works; b) the historical and institutional analysis of literature; c) the interpretative disciplines; d) the theories of reading and reception; and e) all types of formal analysis (62-63).

Roman Jakobson's article *Linguistics and Poetics* has become a founding text of contemporary poetics and a point of reference for those critics who follow the formalist school and consider the applicability of linguistic methods in literary studies. Similar to literature, which represents a process of communication, literary criticism is a process of aesthetic reception, production and communication which involves the critic, author, and reader.

Jakobson's structure can, therefore, be applied to individualize both literary communication and critical communicative situation. Robert Scholes, for instance, adjusts Jakobson's diagram to describe the "reading of a literary text" and to arrange the active schools of critical theory "by their emphasis of particular features of this diagram" (8):

	Contexts Text	
Author		Reader
	Medium Codes	

In his book on literary criticism, Raman Selden gives another interesting interpretation to Jakobson's view of communication, in general, as a system of elements and changes the structure according to the purpose of criticism (*A Reader's Guide* 3-4). Considering that "contact" can be omitted in discussing literature, "since contact is usually through the printed word (except in drama)", Selden rewrites the diagram as

	Context	
Writer	Writing Code	Reader

and then places a number of critical theories according to their focus on a particular element in the diagram:

	Marxist	
Romantic	Formalistic	Reader-oriented
	Structuralist	

The long way of development of world literary theory and criticism has its origins in ancient period with its Greek and Latin critical theories, whereas concerning the rise and development of the theoretical and critical discourse on literature in Britain, one should consider the Renaissance and its subsequent periods until the rise of the formal approach to literature at the dawn of the last century.

In short, in the Western world, literary criticism starts its long developmental process in ancient Greece and Rome; it continues in the Middle Ages having a rather diminished status; the first modern methodological and analytical attempts at criticism based on the revived ancient tradition occurred at the beginning of the modern period in the Renaissance both in Britain and in Europe, in general.

Throughout the centuries, criticism developed within the context of the literary practice but gradually came to diversify its provenance, form, and category as to separate from the realm of literature in the nineteenth century and finally to flourish as an independent and scientific domain in the twentieth century and at the present time, which represent undoubtedly an age of criticism.

Throughout its history, criticism existed in a variety of forms, including dialogues, verse, essays, letters, prefaces, treaties, and books. Throughout its history, criticism belonged mainly to the domains of literature and philosophy.

Criticism has been continuously influenced by the literary process and has influenced in its turn this process. Criticism has been also continuously influenced by the new developments in thought as well as in natural and social sciences, art, culture, ideology, psychology, linguistics. As such, criticism has developed an impressive typology to which twentieth century and the present days have added a huge diversity of critical trends and schools.

Throughout its history, criticism has concerned first philosophers and later, to a much greater extent, artist-critics and writer-critics, especially poet-critics, as well as scholars from different fields (rhetoric, logic, mathematics, physics, sociology, psychology, linguistics, and so on), and finally reviewers, university academics, and just professional critics and theoreticians of literature, all those who are considered exponents of various contemporary schools and trends in literary theory and criticism representing a distinct scientific field of scholarly investigation into literature as a system with all its constituent elements.

3. The History of British and European Literature: Periods, Movements, Trends, Authors, and Texts

Before embarking on a surveyistic presentation of the historical advancement of literature, we should say a few words about a kind of rule of the development of literature, in general.

The place of literature in history is reified by the rise, development and consolidation of various literary periods, movements, trends, genres, writers, and literary works, which follow each other. Each of these is a particular literary system encompassing in its framework dominant (centre) and peripheral (margin) elements; the movement of these systems through history is their continuous development, change, or more precisely, substitution of systems.

Each of these is rooted in the previous ones, represents a continuation of the previous ones, and, at the same time, rejects the previous ones, attempting at suppressing them and taking their place in literary history. Also, each period, movement, trend, genre, etc., that is, every literary system, is determined by the contemporary developments in society, culture, philosophy, science, and so on.

Origins of the literary periods, movements, trends, genres, subgenres, and so on, each representing a literary system		
Relation to the past	1. continuation of the previous periods, trends, etc., where innovation follows innovation, and tradition relies on tradition	
	2. rejection of the previous periods, trends, etc., where innovation reacts against tradition, and tradition marginalises innovation	
Relation to the present	3. contemporary socio-cultural stimuli	

Each period, movement, trend, genre, subgenre, writer, and text is followed by another; each has its own rise, development, consolidation and decline, but not complete disappearance, as each one influences the next, gives its origins or is rejected by the next one, or the elements of its system are acknowledged in the systems of the subsequent periods, movements, trends, and literary works under different forms and functions. Each period, movement, trend, writer, and text represents one to another tradition and innovation, is placed one against the other, where a continuous "battle" takes place between their elements which are either central or peripheral within the structure of the literary system.

The place of literature in history is actually determined by the interrelationship, the "fight" between "**centre**" and "**margin**", "**tradition**" and "**innovation**", "**classical**" and "**modern**", "**conservative**" and "**experimental**", **dependence on rules** and the **freedom of artistic expression**. It is a correlation of two contrary factors whose interaction is the motor of change and development of literature, disclosing the **substitution of systems**.

In the history of literature, the concept of "tradition" is used to denote the ancient classical period, the revival of ancient classical tradition in the Renaissance, the eighteenth-century Age of Enlightenment (also referred to as classicism or neoclassicism), the nineteenth-century realism, and the twentieth-century and contemporary socially-concerned literature.

The term "innovation" denotes some literary experiences of the Renaissance period, metaphysical poetry, pre-romanticism, romanticism, the late nineteenth-century symbolism, aestheticism and other avant-garde trends, and the twentieth-century modernism in the first half of the century and postmodernism of the postmodern period, as well as other more recent experimental trends in literature.

The scholars and students of literature are familiar with the fight between **tradition and innovation** as the opposition and juxtaposition of **center and margin**; they also know this conflict between tradition and innovation under the name of "**the battle of the books**" or "**la querelle des anciens et des modernes**". Whatever the terms, it points again to the war between **innovation and tradition**, between **originality and authority**, between **classicism and modernism**.

The war started in Antiquity, was reinforced in the Renaissance, peaked in France and then throughout Europe at the turn of the seventeenth century and is still going on. In English culture, this conflict was remarkably captured by the neoclassical man of letters Jonathan Swift (1667-1745) in his satire on the battle between ancients and moderns known as *The Battle of the Books* (1704).

> In English literature advancing through history, just like in literature in general, innovation rejects tradition and innovation continues innovation or, better saying, **innovation continues as well as innovates the previous innovation.**

An example of the continuation of innovation, paralleled by the innovation of innovation occurring as an indispensable part of the literary development, would be romanticism, as innovation, assuming and changing, in order to advance further on the path of originality and experimentation, the innovation of pre-romanticism; in its turn, romanticism would be innovated by the nineteenth-century avant-garde which assumes some and change or totally reject other aspects of romanticism; likewise, Joyce and Woolf would adopt and innovate Pater's "impressions" placing them within the larger context of the abstract manifestations of the mind thematized in their modernist novels which focus on the psychological experience of the individual rendered by the stream of consciousness technique in the form of interior monologue.

The literary history studies the rise and development of a national literature and the world literary phenomena from its beginnings to the present day, and divides the historical process into literary periods, which may or may not correspond to the social or political ones.

Literary periods consist of literary movements and trends, which are represented by authors and their literary works and/or literary doctrine. The distinction made between movement and trend relies actually on the fact that a movement groups those writers who produce both literary works (which share similar thematic and structural features) and literary doctrine (texts of literary theory and criticism which share common ideas about their own type of literature) – romanticism, for example; whereas a trend is formed of the producers of only literary texts having common characteristics – the nineteenth-century realism, for example.

Literary periods are considered to refer to different sequences of time conceived in the temporal boundaries of an age, century, centuries, or years, but such an understating of the period may thwart any attempts at tracing clear demarcation lines between literary periods, movements and trends, or at clearly asserting them terminologically. The Renaissance, for instance, is certainly neither a movement nor a trend but a distinct period in the literary history. Metaphysical poetry, however, is first of all a trend which manifested itself only on the level of literary practice, but it is also a part of the larger period of the English Renaissance.

Romanticism represents a period: "Romantic Period", or the "Age of Romanticism", dated between the years of 1798 and 1824, or, in more general terms, between the last decades of the eighteenth century and the first decades of the nineteenth century. At the same time, romanticism is a literary movement: "Romantic Movement", consisting of both imaginative writing and the doctrine, literary texts (such as *Tintern Abbey* by Wordsworth, or *Kubla Khan* by Coleridge) and the critical ideas (from Wordsworth's *Preface to Lyrical Ballads*, for example, or Coleridge's *Biographia Literaria*) about these texts.

In British literature, neoclassicism is a period in literary history covering the last part of the seventeenth century throughout the eighteenth century; neoclassicism is a movement in literature with its poetic works and a strongly normative and prescriptive doctrine; and also neoclassicism is the creator of a particular trend in poetry, philosophical and satirical. Likewise, in both English and world literature, modernism is a period in the first half of the twentieth century, a complex artistic manifestation consisting of a number of distinct movements (futurism, for example) and developing a number of trends in the production of literary texts (for instance, the "stream-of-consciousness novel" of Marcel Proust and James Joyce).

In general, concerning both world and English literature, a diachronic perspective on literature in Britain reveals a historical process which follows the general European pattern, yet in some moments having its particular manifestations. A special problem here is the consideration of some more or less exact periods in the development of both British and world literature.

In most general terms, literature is regarded as passing through three major periods: ancient, medieval and modern, whereas since the middle of the twentieth century, humanity is in the postmodern period, a period claimed to represent the transition to globalization. The first period in European literature is the classical period of the ancient Greece and Rome, rejected and replaced by the Middle Ages.

Concerning British literature in the Middle Ages, historians have noticed the discrepancy between English and general world/European conditions: first, English literature does not have an ancient period to be claimed in relation to a particular civilization and culture, like Greece, Rome, Egypt, China, or India, and, second, its actual medieval period starts much later than the European one, which is the eleventh/twelfth century, for the simple reason that there was no English nation at all until that period.

It is hypothesized that until the sixth century BC, the British islands were inhabited by Iberians and from sixth/seventh century BC by Celts. The year of 55 BC is that of the Roman invasion, and the years between 410 AD and 441 AD date the period of the Roman retreat.

It was the fifth century AD which saw the invasion of the British islands by the Anglo-Saxon tribes coming from the Continent, which lasted for more than a century (449-600), and then the formation, the "becoming" of these people as English for more than four centuries, which marked a period called in the history of English nation, language and literature as "Anglo-Saxon" or "Old English" (449/600-1100/1200). Conquered in their turn by the Normans in the eleventh century (the starting point being the Hastings Battle of 1066), the newly formed English nation enters now "officially" into the Middle Ages which lasted for centuries until around 1500.

The medieval period is in its turn rejected and replaced by the age of Renaissance, which is considered either as the first part of the modern period – a view based on artistic line – which lasted until the middle of the twentieth century, or as a period of transition from the Middle Ages to modern period, now conceived as lasting from the seventeenth-century Enlightenment – a view linked to philosophical line – to the middle of the twentieth century.

The art and literature of the Renaissance already reveal two contradictory but co-existing aspects of "innovation" (for instance, sonnet in poetry) and "tradition" (the revival of ancient models, as, for example, in Renaissance tragedy), and a more detailed consideration agrees that henceforth the growth of literature displays a rather complex picture.

The emergence of the innovative spirit in literature continues after the Renaissance as the Baroque period (metaphysical poetry in English literature, also considered by some critics as the last manifestation of the British Renaissance), but this cultural extravaganza is rejected and suppressed by the much stronger and dominant traditional element which, based on the revival of ancient classical artistic doctrine and practice, becomes itself a period and dominates as Enlightenment (or neoclassicism, in England) the entire social as well as cultural and literary background of Europe for more than one hundred years starting with the middle of the seventeenth century.

By the middle of the eighteenth century, the doctrine of Enlightenment or neoclassicism is put into practice by the more pragmatic British mind, giving rise to Industrialisation and thus determining the decline and end of neoclassicism as a distinct period. It is also the eighteenth century that saw the rise of the novel in English literature, and by the middle of the period, the rise of the pre-romantic poetry. As a rejection of neoclassicism and the continuation of pre-romanticism, the romantic movement emerges at the end of the eighteenth century as reviving the innovative spirit in literature and breaking the linearity of literary development dominated for a long period after the Renaissance by the traditional and normative principles of the revived ancient classical doctrine. Romanticism ends as a regular trend by the middle of the nineteenth century, and henceforth in literature, "tradition" and "innovation" co-exist again under different names and in the framework of different movements and trends.

In the simplest consideration of the facts, romanticism gave, in the second half of the nineteenth century, symbolism, aestheticism, impressionism, expressionism, and other manifestations of the artistic avant-garde, which, in the first half of the twentieth century, continue into a more complex range of experimental and innovative trends and movements (surrealism, dadaism, cubism, "stream-of-consciousness" novel, etc.) assembled and assigned together as modernism, which in its turn continues in the second half of the twentieth century as the innovation and experimentation of postmodernism – this is the component of "innovation" in literary history, a line of development having its origins in the Renaissance, which continued in the Baroque, was suppressed by classical tradition but revived by romanticism, was developed by the late nineteenth century avant-garde trends and diversified by the twentieth-century modernism and postmodernism.

Some elements of the main "enemy" of romanticism, which is neoclassicism, re-appear in the second half of the nineteenth century in the system of the likewise conventional, normative and socially concerned realism, which emerges almost unchanged in its thematic and structural perspectives in the twentieth century, opposing with its traditional realistic concern the innovatory and experimental art – this is the component of "tradition" in literary history, a line of development having its origins in ancient period, which revived in the Renaissance, changed, developed and was institutionalised in the seventeenth and eighteenth century neoclassicism, was rejected and replaced by romanticism, but became present again on the literary scene as nineteenth-century realism, and continued and was diversified by the twentieth-century writers of social concern and realist interest.

To summarise, every new literary period, movement, trend results in and rejects the previous ones on the basis of the opposition between normative tradition and experimental innovation. Tradition and innovation are parts of a single process of literary change and development, contrary but interrelated, emerging in different periods under different names and in the system of different movements, trends and literary works, rejecting and succeeding each other, but from the second half of the nineteenth century to the present day co-existing as two distinct dimensions of literature. Apart from rejection and continuation, every new literary period, movement, and trend is determined by the contemporary developments in thought, science, and other domains.

Concerning the major periods in the history of British literature, the standard opinion, originated in the nineteenth century in relation to the development of English language, regards four periods: the period between 449/700 and 1100/1200 is called "Old English (Anglo-Saxon) Literature"; "Middle Literature" between 1100/1200 and 1500; and the period from around 1500 till the second half of the twentieth century is "Modern British Literature", followed by the "Postmodern Period". A more suitable consideration divides British literature into (a) "Old English (Anglo-Saxon) Literature", (b) "The Middle Ages", (c) "The Renaissance", (d) "The Seventeenth Century", (e) "The Eighteenth Century", (f) "The Romantic Movement", (g) "The Victorian Age", (h) "The First Half of the Twentieth Century", and (i) "The Second Half of the Twentieth Century". A more recent consideration of the major periods in the history of British literature is provided by Andrew Sanders in *A Short Oxford History of English Literature* (2004), who divides English literary history into "Old English Literature" (447-1066), "Medieval Literature" (1066-1510), "Renaissance and Reformation" (1510-1620), "Revolution and Restoration" (1620-1690), "Eighteenth-Century Literature" (1690-1780), "The Literature of the Romantic Period" (1780-1830), "High Victorian Literature" (1830-1880), "Late Victorian and Edwardian Literature" (1880-1920), "Modernism and Its Alternatives" (1920-1945), and "Post-War and Post-Modern Literature" (1945-present).

Each of these periods – except, perhaps, the Old English period and romanticism – has its own particular stages which correspond to specific sub-periods, or movements, or trends, or just some major authors. Thus, the medieval period of British literature, preceded by the Anglo-Saxon age, covers Anglo-Norman literature, Geoffrey Chaucer and his epoch, and the fifteenth century. The Renaissance is divided into the period of humanism and that of the Elizabethan Age. The seventeenth century includes metaphysical trend in poetry, the Puritan period, and the Restoration period. The eighteenth century consists of neoclassicism, the rise of the English novel, and pre-romanticism. Neoclassicism, actually, lasting from 1660 to 1780s, is divided into three periods: its rise during the Restoration period (1660-1700), its climax and dominance during the Augustan Age (1700-1750), and its decline during the Age of Johnson (1750-1780s). Following the period of the Romantic Movement, the Victorian Age covers the literature of realism, post-and neo-romantic writing, the Pre-Raphaelite Movement or Brotherhood, and aestheticism ("art for art's sake" doctrine). The twentieth century includes, in the first half of the century, Edwardian period, modernism, and the new realist writing, and, in the second half of the century, the Angry Generation and other manifestations of the traditional realistic writing, and the postmodern and postmodernist literature.

---

1. Old English (Anglo-Saxon) Period
- dated 447-1066, or between 449/600 (invasion of Britain by Angles, Saxons, and Jutes) and 1100/1200 (establishment of the Norman rule)
- no trends or movements, but some major authors (Caedmon, Cynewulf, the Venerable Bede) and texts (chronicles, the anonymous epic *Beowulf*, and a number of poems such as *The Seafarer* and *The Wanderer*)

---

2. Medieval English Literature
- dated 1100/1200-1500, or, more precisely, between 1066 (Battle of Hastings and the beginning of the Norman Conquest) and 1509 (death of Henry VII and accession of Henry VIII)
- the actual medieval period of British literature with no particular trends or movements
- covers three periods:
    - the Anglo-Norman literature (1100/1200-1350s): includes chronicles, poetry, but the most important literary manifestation is the medieval romance (also referred to as chivalrous romance, Arthurian legend, metrical romance, or prose romance); for example, *Sir Gawain and the Green Knight*)
    - Geoffrey Chaucer and his epoch (1340-1400): includes the poem entitled *The Land of Cockaygne*, the famous alliterative poem *The Vision of William Concerning Piers the Plowman* ascribed to William Langland, *Voyages and Travels of Sir John Mandeville* by Sir John Mandeville, the works of John Gower, but the period is entirely governed by Geoffrey Chaucer (1340-1400) and his writings, in particular *The Canterbury Tales*
    - the fifteenth century: includes Sir Thomas Malory's prose romance *Morte d'Arthur*, the poetry of John Lydgate and Thomas Hoccleve, the popular ballads, but the most important literary manifestation is the rise of drama (with many forms, both religious and secular, of which the most important ones are "mystery play", "morality", and "interlude")

---

3. Renaissance Literature, or the period of "Renaissance and Reformation" in British literature
- very difficult to date precisely:
    - the sixteenth century in general
    - between 1510 and 1620
    - between 1500 and the Commonwealth Interregnum (1649-1660)
    - begins in 1485 (the accession of Henry VII and the establishment of the Tudor dynasty) or in 1509 (the accession of Henry VIII)
    - ends in the early seventeenth century in Europe, in general, and the year of 1616 (the death of Shakespeare) in England, or by the middle of the seventeenth century in Europe, in general, and the year of 1649 (the execution of Charles I) or the year of 1660 (the restoration of monarchy) in England
- historically, it consists of "Early Tudor Age" (c.1500-1557) and "Elizabethan Age" (1558-1603); it may also include "Jacobean Age" (1603-1625) and "Caroline Age" (1625-1649), if one would consider that the Renaissance lasted until the middle of the seventeenth century
- concerning literature, Renaissance is divided into the periods of
    - humanism (first half of the sixteenth century)
    - Elizabethan Age (second half of the sixteenth century)
    - baroque (metaphysical poetry) in the first part and middle of the seventeenth century, if one would consider that the Renaissance lasted until the 1650s
- no clearly defined literary trends or movements, except humanism and metaphysical poetry
- the former is considered within the fields of philosophy and politics, and the latter in the context of the baroque, which is said to have followed the Renaissance period as part of the seventeenth-century mannerism and cultural extravaganza
- major genres: sonnet and drama
- important writings: *Utopia* by Sir Thomas More; sonnets by Thomas Wyatt and Henry Howard; Edmund Spenser with *The Shepherd's Calendar*, *Amoretti* (88 sonnets), and *The Fairie Queene*; Sir Philip Sidney with 108 sonnets printed as *Astrophel and Stella*, a pastoral novel *Arcadia*, and *Apologie for Poetrie*; prose by Francis Bacon, John Lyly, Robert Greene, and Thomas Nashe
- the most important literary manifestation: the Elizabethan Drama
    - Pre-Shakespearian drama: anonymous plays and various authors such as Thomas Kyd, John

Lyly, Robert Greene, and Christopher Marlowe (famous for *The Tragical Historie of Doctor Faustus* and *Tamburlaine the Great*)
- William Shakespeare: poetry (sonnets) and drama (historical plays, comedies, and tragedies)

---

4. The Seventeenth Century, or the period of "Revolution and Restoration" in British Literature
- dated between 1620 and 1690, or between 1603 (the death of Elizabeth and the accession of James I) and 1714 (the inauguration of the Hanoverian Dynasty by George I)
- major historical events: the rise of Puritanism, the abolition of monarchy (the execution of Charles I) in 1649, the Commonwealth Interregnum led by Oliver Cromwell between 1649 and 1660, the restoration of monarchy (Charles II restored to throne) in 1660
- concerning literature, the period consists of
       - metaphysical poetry (or Baroque, 1620s to 1670s)
       - the Puritan period (1649-1660)
       - the Restoration period (1660-1700)
- includes already clearly defined literary trends, such as metaphysical trend in poetry and the "comedy of manners" in the Restoration drama
- major literary voices: metaphysical poets John Donne and Andrew Marvell, the great playwright Ben Jonson, the Puritan writer John Milton, and John Dryden as the most important representative of the Restoration literature

---

5. The Eighteenth-Century Literature (1700-1780s)
- the period of French Revolution, Agricultural Revolution, and Industrial Revolution
- in literature, the eighteenth century consists of
- neoclassicism (1660-1780s)
       - the rise of the English novel (throughout the century)
       - pre-romanticism (1750s-1780s)
- the neoclassical period is divided into three parts:
       - the "Restoration Age" (1660-1700), or the "Age of Dryden"
       - the "Augustan Age" (1700-1750s), or the "Age of Pope"
       - the "Age of Johnson" (1750s-1780s), or the decline of Neoclassicism
- major trends and movements include:
       - neoclassicism as a movement in literature with its poetic works (namely philosophical and satirical) and a strongly normative and prescriptive doctrine
       - pre-romantic trend in poetry
       - different trends in the genre of the novel, or rather types of the novel: picaresque novel, sentimental novel, epistolary novel, comic novel, moral novel, and others
- major literary voices representing:
       - neoclassicism: Alexander Pope and Dr Samuel Johnson
       - the rise of the English novel: Jonathan Swift, Daniel Defoe, Samuel Richardson, Henry Fielding, Laurence Sterne, Jane Austen
       - pre-romanticism: James Macpherson and Thomas Gray

---

6. Romantic Literature
     - dated between 1780s-1830s, or between 1798 (the publication of *Lyrical Ballads*) and 1824 (the death of Byron)
     - romanticism represents a period: "Romantic Period", or the "Age of Romanticism"
     - romanticism is a literary movement: "Romantic Movement", consisting of both imaginative writing and critical ideas
     - important for breaking the linearity of literary development dominated for centuries by the traditional classical spirit and for reviving the innovative spirit in arts and the proclamation of the freedom of artistic expression, individualism, nationalism, authorship, emotional experience, imagination, nature and rustic life, dualism of existence, and so on
     - important for its literary doctrine: major critical texts include Wordsworth's *Preface to Lyrical Ballads*, Coleridge's *Biographia Literaria*, and Shelley's *Defence of Poetry*
     - the genres and representatives of Romanticism:
          - poetry: the most important genre, represented by William Blake, William Wordsworth, Samuel Taylor Coleridge, Robert Southey, Robert Burns, Percy Bysshe Shelley, George Gordon, Lord Byron, and

John Keats
- prose: the historical novel of Sir Walter Scott and the gothic fiction by Horace Walpole, Clara Reeve, Ann Radcliffe, and others
- drama: Percy Bysshe Shelley and George Gordon, Lord Byron

7. The Victorian Literature
- dated 1830s-1900, or between 1837 (Victoria came to throne) and 1901 (the death of Queen Victoria)
- in ideology, politics, and society, the Victorian Age was a period of innovation, invention, progress, complexity, and change: democracy, feminism, unionization of workers, Newton's mechanics, Darwin's evolution, Comte's view of society, Marx's view of history, Taine's view of literature, Freud's view of human psyche, industrialization, steam power, railway, telephone, telegraph, photography, etc.
- in literature and other arts: the Victorians attempted to combine the romantic emphases upon self, emotion, and imagination with the neoclassical concern with the public role of art and responsibility of the artist
- hence the Victorian Age consisting of a great number of movements and trends co-existing during one period and as such revealing the co-existence of the traditional and innovative elements in literature
- "tradition" is represented by realism, a major literary trend which manifests in novel writing and which rejects romanticism and continues the neoclassical emphasis on rules and ethics, and the interest in the actual, immediate reality
- close to realism, but also different in many respects, is the trend called naturalism
- "innovation" is revived by the defiant spirit of the romantic writers, rejects tradition, rules and prescriptive doctrines, and manifests as a continuation of the romantic rebellious attitude in art
- the element of innovation represents the real source of literary complexity in Victorian period since it consists of a number of trends and movements
- the innovation in literature and arts growing out of romanticism has a twofold perspective:
    - first, innovation from romanticism, heavily influenced by the romantic attitude and comprising a great number of romantic characteristics
    - second, innovation out of romanticism, less influenced by the romantic attitude but still continuing a number of its features
- the first kind of innovation manifests as post- and neo-romantic trends, including most of the Victorian poetry as well as some of the fiction of the period, such as Emily Bronte's gothic novel and the later colonial prose of Kipling, Stevenson, Doyle, Wells, and Conrad
- the second type of innovation manifests as symbolism, aestheticism, impressionism, expressionism, Pre-Raphaelite Brotherhood, and other trends which represent the artistic avant-garde of the second half of the nineteenth century
- the dominant literary form is novel, then poetry, and to a lesser extent, drama
- the novel belongs mainly to realism and the realist novel is the main type of fiction
- there are some exceptions, like the gothic/post-romantic novel *Wuthering Heights* by Emily Bronte, or *The Picture of Dorian Gray* by Oscar Wilde which reflects aestheticism
- poetry in general continues the romantic tradition, but is also influenced by aestheticism and symbolism
- to summarise, the Victorian Age covers the literature of such literary trends and movements as realism, post-and neo-romantic writing, the Pre-Raphaelite Movement, aestheticism ("art for art's sake" doctrine), naturalism, and others
- main literary voices:
    - prose: Charles Dickens, William Makepeace Thackeray, Charlotte Bronte, Emily Bronte, George Eliot, Lewis Carroll, Oscar Wilde, Thomas Hardy
    - poetry: Alfred, Lord Tennyson, Robert Browning, Matthew Arnold, Gerald Manley Hopkins, Dante Gabriel Rossetti, William Morris, Charles Algernon Swinburne

8. English Literature in the First Half of the Twentieth Century, or the period of modernism and its alternatives (1900-1945)
- British literature in the first half of the twentieth-century consists of a wide range of movements and trends which can be grouped under two headings:
    - the first one includes the literary works which continue the nineteenth-century realistic texts, preserve unchanged the traditional and normative type of writing, and is referred to as realism, meaning realist, traditional, and conservative literature
    - the second one rejects the traditional and conservative type of literature and consists of

innovative, original, experimental and avant-garde trends which represent the literary dimensions of modernism
- the first half of the twentieth century includes
    - the Edwardian period (1900-1910)
    - modernism (1910s-1930s)
    - realistic writing (throughout the period, although dominant in the first decade   (the Edwardian period) and in the 1930s and 1940s)
- modernism is a period in the first half of the twentieth century, an artistic movement, or rather a complex artistic manifestation consisting of a number of distinct movements and trends
    - in other words, it is more appropriate to use "modernism" as a generic term to be applied retrospectively to the wide range of experimental, avant-garde artistic and intellectual trends and movements of the first half of the twentieth century
    - the trends and movements of Modernism manifested in art in general, including painting, music, architecture, and literature
    - examples of modernist trends and movements: futurism, surrealism, cubism, dadaism, imagism, the stream-of-consciousness novel, and so on
    - composers such as Stravinsky and Schoenberg represent Modernism in music
    - the movements *les fauves*, cubism, and surrealism, and artists such as Picasso, Matisse, and Mondrian represent modernism in visual arts
    - in architecture and design, modernism is represented by Le Corbusier, Walter Gropius, and Mies van der Rohe
    - in literature, the leading figures of modernism are Guillaume Apollinaire, Louis Aragon, Jean Cocteau, Hilda Doolittle, William Faulkner, Ezra Pound, William Carlos Williams, Max Jacob, Federico Garcia Lorca, Franz Kafka, Marcel Proust, Gertrude Stein, Tristan Tzara, Paul Valery, and many others
    - in Britain, the major literary voices of modernism are James Joyce and Virginia Woolf in fiction (including the "stream-of-consciousness novel"), and T. S. Eliot and W. B. Yeats in poetry
    - other voice of Modernism in English fiction: D. H. Lawrence and Aldous Huxley
    - the realist literature of the first half of the twentieth century is represented by John Galsworthy, William Somerset Maugham, Graham Greene, George Orwell, George Bernard Shaw, and others

---

9. English Literature in the Second Half of the Twentieth Century, or "Post-War and Postmodern Literature" (1945-present)
- the second half of the twentieth century includes
        - the post-war literature (1940s and 1950s)
        - the postmodern literature (1960s to the present)
- the post-war literature is traditional and realist rather than experimental; the main trend is the Angry Young Generation (or Angry Young Men), whose representatives are Alan Sillitoe, John Wain, Kingsley Amis, and John Braine; however, the period also includes the visionary and philosophical writing of the 1950s and 1960s, which made possible the transition from realism of the post-war period to later flourishing of postmodernism, and which was at best represented by William Golding and Iris Murdoch
- the postmodern literature consists of two main parts:
        - realism, or the traditional realist writing, at best represented by Graham Greene, Evelyn Waugh, Charles Percy Snow, Sir Angus Wilson, Muriel Spark, Margaret Drabble, and others
        - postmodernism, or experimentation in art and literature
- like with modernism, postmodernism is a generic term used to name the wide range of contemporary experimental, innovative and original artistic and intellectual trends and movements of the second half of the twentieth century and of the first decades of the new millennium
- postmodernism in British literature can be divided in several trends and movements, among which:
        - the campus novel/global campus novel, at best represented by David Lodge
        - magical realism, at best represented by Angela Carter
        - historiographic metafiction, at best represented by Murial Spark, John Fowles, Graham Swift, and Ian McEwan
        - postcolonial writing, at best represented by Salman Rushdie and Monica Ali
- other postmodern and postmodernist voices in British literature: Julian Barnes and Peter Ackroyd in fiction; Ted Hughes, Dylan Thomas, Seamus Heaney, and Philip Larkin in poetry; John Osborne, Samuel Beckett, Harold Pinter, Tom Stoppard, and Caryl Churchill in drama

To summarise, with regard to the major literary trends and movements in English and general European literature, the students may consider the following:

humanism (Renaissance)
metaphysical poetry (baroque, Renaissance, seventeenth century)
cavalier poets (seventeenth century)
comedy of manners (seventeenth century, Restoration period)
Enlightenment (seventeenth century, eighteenth century)
neoclassicism (seventeenth century, eighteenth century)
pre-romanticism (eighteenth century)
picaresque novel (eighteenth century)
sentimentalism/sentimental novel (eighteenth century)
epistolary novel (eighteenth century)
comic novel (eighteenth century)
moral novel (eighteenth century)
romanticism (eighteenth century, nineteenth century)
gothic novel (eighteenth century, nineteenth century)
historical novel (nineteenth century)
post-romantic literature (nineteenth century)
neo-romantic literature (nineteenth century)
Transcendentalism (nineteenth century)
colonial literature (nineteenth century)
impressionism (nineteenth century)
expressionism (nineteenth century)
symbolism (nineteenth century)
aestheticism / "art for art's sake" doctrine (nineteenth century)
Pre-Raphaelite Brotherhood (nineteenth century)
realism (nineteenth-century, twentieth century)
naturalism (nineteenth century)
modernism (twentieth century)
futurism (twentieth century)
surrealism (twentieth century)
cubism (twentieth century)
dadaism (twentieth century)
imagism (twentiethcentury)
Harlem Renaissance (twentieth century)
the Lost Generation (twentieth century)
stream-of-consciousness novel (twentieth century)
Angry Young Men (twentieth century)
postmodernism (twentieth century)
campus novel (twentieth century)
magical realism (twentieth century)
historiographic metafiction (twentieth century)
postcolonial literature (twentieth century)
minimalism (twentieth century)
Beat poets (twentieth century)
confessional literature (twentieth century)
spoken word (twentieth century)

Concerning the differences in the history of British and general European literary phenomena, it has been often brought into discussion the so-called "complex of insularity" of the British cultural background, its strong regional and conservative features in relation to the rest of Europe. Throughout its history, British culture seems reluctant to accept the Continental influences, new developments in literature and other arts, new movements, trends and styles, whose origins have been in France and Italy, and to a lesser extent in Spain and Germany.

Hence the fact that English literature is a late phenomenon, from the very beginning and throughout its entire literary history. It may take a century or more to speak about English Renaissance and about the rise and consolidation of a literary tradition in English fiction, or decades for romanticism or symbolism, as if British literary background must finally yield to the acceptance of what in contemporary Europe has been already established as a dominant literary tradition, movement, or trend.

Still, many English authors on the side of the freedom of artistic expression remained for centuries unknown or wrongly evaluated, such as Donne and Hopkins, or, like Byron, Lawrence and Joyce, had to escape from the conservatism and reluctance of the fellow-citizens and produce their works in some other countries. It is claimed, however, that English literary "complex of insularity" ends with the synchronization in the first half of the twentieth century of the British with European modernism, due to the contribution of, among others, Joyce and Eliot, though in the second half of the last century English literature turns again to realistic and social concerns rather than literary experimentation, being traditional rather than innovative.

It might be that British literature, in general, has been traditional rather than innovative, but it passes nowadays, as many national literatures do, through a process of decentralization due to globalization, the country's former membership in European Union, new developments in sociology, anthropology, women's studies, cultural studies, and postcolonial and transnational studies. Perhaps the most significant factor of decentralization of British literature is the advancement of English as a world language, spoken worldwide by millions who have no other connection with Britain.

English literature might have been traditional rather than innovative, but it is an aberration to assume that it represents weak literary phenomena, lacking aesthetic strength and significance, and that it is investigated and taught merely because of some political, economic, colonial, postcolonial or linguistic causes.

British literature is rich and complex, studied in almost every country of the world and acclaimed by Anglo-American as well as international scholarship, as to remember just Emile Legouis and Louis Cazamian who, almost a century ago, in their celebrated *A Short History of English Literature* (1929), already saw English literature possessing "a greater capacity than other literature for combining a love of concrete statement with a tendency to dream, a sense of reality with lyrical rapture", and English writers characterized by "loving observation of Nature, by a talent for depicting strongly-marked character, and by a humour that is the amused and sympathetic noting of the contradictions of human nature and the odd aspects of life".

British literature is an important part of the world literary heritage, answering and assuming during its history most of the innovation and development in arts and literature, and having its own contribution to world literary practice and literary doctrine, attributable to such major British literary voices as Chaucer and Gower in the Middle Ages, Shakespeare, Marlowe, Spenser and Sidney in the Renaissance, Donne, Marvell, Milton and Dryden in the seventeenth century, Pope, Swift, Defoe, Richardson, Fielding and Sterne in the eighteenth century, Blake, Wordsworth, Coleridge, Byron, Shelley and Keats in romanticism, Dickens, George Eliot, Emily

Bronte, Charlotte Bronte, Tennyson, Robert Browning, Swinburne, Arnold, Ruskin, Pater, Wilde and Carlyle in Victorian Age, and, in the twentieth century, Joyce, Woolf, Lawrence, T. S. Eliot, Shaw, Hughes, Beckett, Pinter, Golding, Murdoch, Fowles, Barnes, Mitchell, Spark, Lodge, Larkin, Ackroyd, McEwan, and many other writers of all these periods, whose works are landmarks in the history of English as well as European and world literature and thought.

Finally, a few terminological explanations may properly conclude our answering of the three questions, which we have focused upon in this Introduction, as well as strengthen the acquired knowledge.

With regard to literary criticism, the interconnected terms "criticism", "critic", "criticise", "critical", and "critique" entered English language at the beginning of the modern period, largely around 1600. The etymology of all these words starts in ancient Greek, namely from Greek *krites* ("judge, a person offering reasoned judgement or analysis") and its derivation *kritikos* ("skilled in making judgement"), as well as *krinein* ("to decide, to separate") and *krinō* ("I judge", or "to separate and distinguish in order to be able to judge"), which is also the root for the word "crisis". From Greek they passed into Latin, then French and finally English.

The term "critic", for instance, having in 1580s the meaning of "the one who passes judgement" and from c.1600 on that of "censurer, the one who judges quality of books", entered at that time English from medieval French *critique*, which comes from Latin *criticus* ("judge, critic of literature") which derives originally from Greek. "Criticism", from "critic" and "-ism", meant around 1600 "the act of criticising" and from 1670s on "art of estimating literary works". "Criticise", formed by "critic" and "-ise/-ize", meant in 1640s "to pass, usually unfavourable, judgement", then "to discuss critically" from 1660s and "to censure" from 1704. "Critical", from "critic" and suffix "-ial", meant "censorious" in 1580s, received its meaning of "pertaining to criticism" in 1740s, but also had a medical meanings from c.1600 and the meanings "of the nature of crisis" (1640s") and "crucial" (1840s). "Critique", around 1700, meaning "the art of criticism", is from French *critique* or *critick* and Latin *critica* as the feminine of *criticus*, but it also derives ultimately from the Greek *krites*, *krinō*, and *kritikē* ("the art of discerning").

Concerning imaginative writing, it is interesting and also necessary to point out that in place of the terms familiar nowadays "author" and "literature", the words "poet" and "poetry" were used for centuries until late into modern period to label all creative literature and the writer, in general. The etymology begins in ancient Greece and Rome, with the Greek word *poiëin*, meaning "to make, to do, to compose". It gave the Greek *poesis* ("a thing made, composition, poetry"), *poema* ("thing made or created, work of poetry"), and *poetes* ("maker, poet, author"); the Latin *poesis* ("poetry"), *poema* ("poetry, verse"), and *poeta* ("poet, author"); Vulgar Latin *poesia*; Old French *poesie*, *poetrie*, and *poete*; Old and Middle English (c.1300) "poesy"; Modern English (c.1500) "poetry", "poem", and "poet".

Thus, the terms "poetry" and "poet" signified literature and author, in general, and referred to all genres, which was mainly due to the fact that the greater part of imaginative literature produced until the rise of the novel was actually written in verse form. Philip Sidney in *The Defence of Poesie* insists that "it is not rhyming and versing that maketh poesy. One may be a poet without versing, and a versifier without poetry". Literature was, therefore, named as "poetry", a text of literature of whatever genre as "poem", and the author as "poet". Drama was labelled "poetry", as in Dryden, for whom plays are "dramatic poesie" and Shakespeare and Jonson are "poets". Even novel was included in poetry, as in Fielding, who calls his novel *Joseph Andrews* a "comic epic poem written in prose". Gradually, in the course of literary history, the words "poetry" and "poet" were limited to the meaning of literature written in verse form.

The term "literature" originates from the Latin *littera*, meaning letter of alphabet, and its form *litterarum*, referring to books, manuscripts, letters, acts, memories, and literary and scientific works. Terry Eagleton points to the fact that throughout the periods of literary development in England, and especially in the eighteenth century, "the concept of literature was not confined as it sometimes is today to "creative" or "imaginative" writing", that it "meant the whole body of valued writing in society: philosophy, history, essays and letters as well as poems", "conformed to certain standards of "polite letters"", and that it was only in the romantic period that the modern definition of "literature" began to develop, "the privilege accorded by the Romantics to the "creative imagination"" leading to "a narrowing of the category of literature to so-called "creative" or "imaginative" work" and literature became "virtually synonymous with the "imaginative"" (Eagleton 15-17).

Today, the term "literature" denotes the entire imaginative writing and all the works which belong to all literary genres and forms, including narrative, lyrical, dramatic, or fictional prose, poetry, drama, or, to be more specific, novel, short story, poem, play, epic, tragedy, ode, satire, dramatic monologue, etc. Also, the term "literature" has another meaning: "if we describe something as "literature", as opposed to anything else, the term carries with it qualitative connotations which imply that the work in question has superior qualities; that it is well above the ordinary run of written works" (Cuddon 505-506).

This is the reason why anyone concerned with the history of literature and that of literary criticism should pay attention to the ways in which certain terms derive etymologically from others and the ways in which they change their meanings, as one should bear in mind that the criticism of "poetry" and "poets" produced before the nineteenth century actually means criticism of imaginative literature, in general.

To conclude this rather long but necessary part of our book, the argument to be considered in the field of literary studies dealing with the history of English literature is that the literary texts produced by different writers in different periods of British history and civilization are not merely a category which needs to be included in an overall literary system of English or international cultural heritage for the sake of rendering its completeness and aesthetic validity.

It is rather that they are different in kind, unique and representative of a type of literary discourse which should be studied as a system in itself, and which, if properly comprehended, may perform the function of breaking down the existing views and theories about English literature, in general, or a particular literary manifestation in Britain, reorganizing them and suggesting new ones.

In our series of books, we attempt to argue that, following the principles announced by Yuri Tynyanov, the investigation of literary history is possible in relation to the view of literature as a system, interrelated with other systems and conditioned by them and by assuming that the movement of literature through history represents substitution of systems.

A more detailed and comprehensive presentation of Tynyanov's principles and opinions on historical investigation of the literary phenomenon may provide a vector methodology to those concerned with the diachronic movement of literature, as we shall see in the Preliminaries to this book.

PRELIMINARIES
LEARNING LITERARY HERITAGE THROUGH
CRITICAL TRADITION OR BACK TO TYNYANOV

The point is that most people don't want what you and your colleagues think of as history – the sort you get in books – because they don't know how to deal with it. Personally, I've every sympathy. With them, that is. I've tried to read a few history books myself, and while I may not be clever enough to enrol in your classes, it seems to me that the main problem with them is this: they all assume you've read most of the other history books already. It's a closed system. There's nowhere to start. (A character in *England, England* by Julian Barnes, London: Jonathan Cape, 1998, pp. 70-71)

Keywords: Tynyanov, Shklovsky, Eliot, Bakhtin, system, literary system, system of elements, substitution of systems, centre versus margin, innovation versus tradition, internal change, function, order, depersonalization, *ostranenie* (defamiliarization), literariness, intertextuality, dialogism, chronotope

---

It is a remarkable coincidence that the *fin de siècle* of all centuries before and during modernity represents an important breakthrough in the literary advancement: around 1370, *Sir Gawain and the Green Knight* is said to have emerged on the literary scene; around 1387, *The Canterbury Tales* came to claim the rise of Englishness in the literary art; 1470 saw the publication of *Morte d'Arthur*; the end of the sixteenth century saw Elizabethan drama and Shakespeare; the end of the seventeenth century proclaimed the age of reason and, particularly in English literature, neoclassicism; the eighteenth century ended in romanticism and the dominance of poetry (in English literature, with Blake, Wordsworth, and Coleridge), and, also in English literature, the novel is founded; the nineteenth century ended with the innovation of symbolism and aestheticism as origins and precursors of modernism; and the last decades of the twentieth century, as postmodern, also revealed the flourishing of literary innovation and experimentation under the auspices of postmodernism, which mainly manifest themselves in imaginative prose.

The movement of English literature (or any other national literature, or the world literature, in general) through history is the main concern of the history of literature (literary history), a distinct discipline of literary evaluation which is nowadays alive and applied – and still developed and attempted to be conferred with scientific and methodological apparatus – despite the postmodern laments over the death of history, originality, meaning, reality, and authorship, along with the mourning of the end of reflexiveness, reflexivity, reflection, and the impossibility of language to truthfully represent whatever an artist would endeavour to reflect.

In its diachronic perspective focused on literary periods, movements, trends, authors, and texts, the historical investigation of literature is interrelated with literary theory (offering terminology and general principles of research) and literary criticism (providing the way of approach to particular texts), which, in turn, are indispensable from literary history (history of literature), as we have seen in the Introduction to this book.

In the discussion of the rise and consolidation of an English literary tradition, one should focus on the elements of the literary system in order to conduct a general, surveyistic as well as coherent approach to the complexity of the literary phenomenon considered diachronically from its Anglo-Saxon beginnings to the present day.

Rewriting Jakobson's structure of communication, Guy Cook identifies author, reader, text, performer, society, texts and language to be the main elements of the literary communicative situation, or the elements of the literary system. Among these elements is language; the formal, particularly structuralist and post-structuralist, interpretative arrangements of Shklovsky (*O teorii prozy*, 1929) and Lotman ("Lektsii po strukturalinoi poetike", 1994) – concerning art as language and system of signs, and the written language of the novel, poem and other literary works as their instrument and material – argue that language influences diachronically the essence of every cultural system, including literature and fiction. In turn, written language is indispensable from the instability and dynamics of various historical and cultural circumstances.

In order to be closer to the objective theory of art, from a formalist perspective, the aestheticization of written language, as a central aspect or element in the literary act of communication, prompts literariness and becomes possible by means of a set of literary devices, figures of speech, verbal nuances, and so on. Shklovsky, over a century ago, already showed that these devices would eventually make things unique and complicate the form of a work of art in order to increase the difficulty and time of perception since this process in art is an end in itself and must be prolonged.

This principle working in art and literature, called *ostranenie* ("defamiliarization"), has become the fundamental credo of modernism and is still successfully applied nowadays in literary practice, such as in the works of magical realism.

Adding Bakhtin to Cook, Shklovsky, and Lotman, other canonical principles, underpinning the development of literature and representing elements of its consolidated pattern, include chronotope, *raznorechie* (heteroglossia), polyphony, carnivalesque, and, especially, dialogism.

Adding Tynyanov to Bakhtin, Cook, Shklovsky, and Lotman, literature is to be viewed as a system of elements with centre and margin, with dominant and peripheral elements which fight to move into centre, to resist what denies them.

These elements do not disappear; they always are; they just exist; they are "Lord's", as Shklovsky says about his "images", just as T. S. Eliot speaks about impressions and experiences which do not change but are continuously recombined and rearranged.

Based on Tynyanov, a "rule" of literary development would declare periods, movements, trends, genres, subgenres, even texts, and so on, to be literary systems placed in a diachronic relationship of substituting, following or succeeding each other by continuing and rejecting each other, as well as by being influenced by contemporary socio-cultural stimuli and developments in philosophy and science.

In the light of Tynyanov's ideas on literary work and literature conceived as systems, speaking solely about literary practice, its development in the context of literary history is based on the "fight" between the aspect of "innovation" and that of "tradition". These two aspects are represented diachronically by different periods, movements, trends, types of text, and so on, which either continue or reject and either follow or replace one another.

These aspects, therefore, constitute the central (tradition) and marginal (innovation) elements within a literary system, which are engaged in a battle for dominance and to be central, to achieve defamiliarization, by which allowing development, change, and advancement of literature through history.

The movement through history of a national literature can be better explained by drawing on theories of genre and literary development, of which one of the most congenial theorization, still valid and viable nowadays, belongs to Yuri Tynyanov, whose main reasoning would be that **literature is a system of central and peripheral elements** – in other words, tradition (centre) versus innovation (margin) in the fight over supremacy, which means for tradition to stay in the centre, whereas for innovation, it implies to proclaim demarginalization, to move into centre, and by this, to claim the right to build up a new system – **and the development or historical advancement of literature is the substitution of systems**, in other words, the substitution of various periods, movements, trends, genres, subgenres, styles, textual typologies, and so on.

Amid the huge amount of critical attention given to English literature, in general, and amid the multiplicity of theoretical perspectives to be applied to its analysis, Tynyanov's theories are appropriate and applicable also because they characterize national types of literature with their own characteristic features and peculiarities of historical development.

Drawing on the assumption that a literary work, like literature in general, is a system of interrelated and interdependent elements, the Russian formalist scholar discusses the genre in his essay entitled "Literaturnyi fakt" ("Literary Fact") and the development (history) of literature in "O literaturnoi evolutii" ("On Literary Evolution"), both written in 1927. Both works postulate the formalist theory of system and that of internal change in literary history.

In "Literary Fact", in matters of its principles, rise, development, sources, death and rebirth, these aspects of the genre, along with the migration and transformation of the genre, co-exist with and depend on the larger literary process, namely, the emergence of new literary trends, movements, forms, as well as views and conceptions in literary history.

The genre represents, in this respect, Tynyanov argues, not "a fall from the system", "not a planned evolution", not a "development", but "a jump or leap" and a shift, "a substitution of systems", and is therefore innovative and "unrecognizable"

("Literaturnyi fakt" 255-256). Like a literary work or movement, or literature in general, a genre is a system, but not a static, motionless system; it is a structure that may fluctuate, emerge from other systems, and weaken to become vestiges of subsequent systems.

A new genre replaces an old one, or becomes its successor, and the decline and rebirth of a genre are to be understood, as Tynyanov shows, in relation to the concentric model of literature, which is organized by the principles of "centre" and "margin": moving within this structure, a genre degenerates or dies out when it departs from the centre towards the periphery, but revives its literary potential when it approaches the centre, or "in its place from the trifles of literature, from the backyards and bottoms of literature, a new phenomenon emerges in the centre" (Tynyanov, "Literaturnyi fakt" 257-258).

Tynyanov emphasizes the diachronically inconstant feature of the literary periods, movements, and genres, which are viewed as literary systems, their dynamic, not static, essence, which is based on the perpetual clash between tradition and innovation, the permanent conflict over hierarchy, which involves various elements in their position within the system as centre and margin, in other words, as central or peripheral, dominant or marginal elements. An element or a form originally not considered literary is placed into a literary system, or it diverges from another element or form, and thereby it may give birth to a new trend or genre as a new system. Once established, a literary genre or trend never goes out of existence since its elements may emerge in either dominant or marginal positions in various other systems, namely newly emerging periods, movements, trends, genres, subgenres, and so on.

The medieval ballad, for instance, receives a new expression in romanticism by Coleridge. Also, in this period, the historical element becomes dominant in the system of what is established as the historical novel by Scott. In Wieland and especially Goethe, the element of ordeal from medieval romances re-emerges as an important element in the Bildungsroman literary system to determine the inner change of the character and prompt his or her identity formation.

Focusing primarily on literary genres, Tynyanov develops the formalist theory of internal change in literary development. After providing a concentric model of literature, he postulates the principle of the conflict between centre and margin, theorizes the obliteration and rebirth of genres, and insists on the migration and transformation of genres, according to which, moving within the literary system, a genre is forgotten or silenced if it moves away from the centre, and is renewed when it comes closer to the centre.

A particular genre becomes dominant in a certain period and develops its system of elements: it attracts writers, who become more imitative than creative, expands temporally and territorially, and, in this way, a literary tradition or convention is established. Confronted by innovation and originality, the genre may lose its dominant position and be replaced by a new one which becomes dominant.

The way in which Tynyanov discusses the genre is true for literary periods, movements, trends, species, and works, i.e., all literary phenomena which constitute, in the formalist view, literary systems with distinct characteristics.

We also follow in our study the **theory of internal change**, and start from the premise of literature to be a system of elements which denote either centre or margin prompting a battleground for innovation and tradition.

In order to explain this practically with direct reference to a literary tradition established as literary system, a good example would be the subgenre of the novel known as the Bildungsroman. Just like with various genres, in Tynyanov's opinion, the thematic and, to a lesser extent, structural elements of various literary systems – literary systems are represented diachronically from ancient times to the end of the eighteenth century by different periods, movements, trends, genres, subgenres and text categories – perform individual breakthroughs and survive, or are modified, receive new positions, and interrelate anew around the central element of identity formation as established by Goethe in his canonical novel of formation *Wilhelm Meisters Lehrjahre*. In doing so, these elements, primarily thematic, are placed into and become elements of the new Bildungsroman literary system; among them, pseudo-biographical material, childhood experience, education, ordeal, chronotope of road, epiphany, and others become central and peripheral elements of the literary system of the Bildungsroman, whose dominant and central element is formation.

The Bildungsroman, being currently perpetuated by various writers around the world, reveals that changes still occur within its literary system. These changes have occurred and occur for both internal and external reasons, such as the newly emerging trends (magical realism, for instance), the audience, the publisher, or various social, cultural and political developments.

Unlike the romance, or the picaresque novel, or the gothic narrative, the Bildungsroman stays to the present day one of the few "strong" genres, or rather subgenre of the novelistic genre, as to be more correct terminologically in accordance to the categorisation by literary theory and criticism. The Bildungsroman proves, historically, literary vitality and multifaceted creative consistency, since, in its depiction of the life of a particular individual, this fictional subgenre relies on and confirms the view that literature has always been and will always be, to a lesser or greater extent, a reflection of the personal experience of the author.

The formalist theory of internal change covers the domain of genres, and also those of literary periods, movements, trends, types of texts, including the Bildungsroman, and so on; nowadays it is also applied in feminist, minority and cultural studies and in postcolonial theory. In postulating intertextuality – new texts emerge as imitating, completing, competing, negating, or parodying other texts – the formalist theory of internal change alludes to Bakhtin's dialogism, Shklovsky's *ostranenie*, and Eliot's new combinations of elements.

"A new art emotion" is what T. S. Eliot declares, in "Tradition and the Individual Talent" (1919), to be novelty in literature, its significance and the real artistic and poetic achievement. Tradition is for him an "order", which is a term identical to that used by Tynyanov; for Eliot, likewise, order is not static or ideal but is continuously modified by new works which attempt to acquire their place in literary history, making order simultaneous, bringing it into the present of literary activity when intertextuality is at work.

The poet is not an individual separated from history, and the significance of his poetry stands in its relation to the past: "No poet, no artist of any art, has his complete meaning alone. His significance, his appreciation is the appreciation of his relation to the dead poets and artists" (Eliot 44).

The ideal order established by tradition becomes a simultaneous order when the past and present are united and expressed concomitantly: the simultaneous order is a kind of archive. Accordingly, the individual talent does not need to invent something or attempt to produce originality, since everything has been already written, but to recombine, rearrange the elements of order, keeping in mind – and here Eliot is not far removed from "dialogism" in Bakhtin and "intertextuality" in Kristeva – that "the past should be altered by the present as much as the present is directed by the past" (Eliot 45).

Another important aspect in the act of artistic creation is, for Eliot, the "process of depersonalization" based on the continuous surrender to tradition and "self-sacrifice": the poet does not express a personality, but "a particular medium"; poetry, in Eliot's famous anti-Wordsworthian declaration, "is not a turning loose of emotion, but an escape from emotion; it is not the expression of personality, but an escape from personality" (Eliot 52-53).

Actually, the process leading to novelty or "new art emotion", as articulated by Eliot, is not far removed from a formalist perspectives: it begins with (1) learning, acquiring the knowledge of canonical works as standards of greatness (as later Harold Bloom would insist), in other words, evolving an awareness of the past tradition, order and the world, the human condition; it continues with (2) self-sacrifice or surrender to past tradition; which leads to (3) poet losing personality and acquiring "depersonalization" or impersonality; so that (4) the poet becomes a medium for the expression of existing elements, "impressions and experiences"; (5) the poet thereby produces new, original combinations of impressions, experiences, images, feelings, phrases, etc.; which results in (6) the ideal order becoming simultaneous; which means, finally, that (7) a "new art emotion" emerges to take its place in the order or, in Tynyanov's terms, in the literary system.

The modernist author T. S. Eliot is viewed, as a critic, in relation to Anglo-American "New Criticism", whereas Yuri Tynyanov represents Russian "Formalism"; they are united in their pursuit of a formal approach to literature, hence certain similarities of their critical thinking.

Examples of a common pursuit and similar concepts and perspectives of literary investigation are to be found in the work of the formal and formalist Viktor Shklovsky, namely in his "Art as Technique" (1917), in which self-sacrifice and depersonalization become *ostranenie* ("defamiliarization") and the key concepts are again "rearrangement", "recombination" of elements and images so as to pursue the technique of art which is "to make objects "unfamiliar", to make forms difficult, to increase the difficulty and length of perception because the process of perception is an aesthetic end in itself and must be prolonged" (Shklovsky 778). "Art is thinking in images", and poetry is a special way of thinking, namely, thinking by means of images, where thinking in images allows for "economy of mental effort" (Shklovsky 775).

"Images", in Shklovsky (or "elements", in Tynyanov, and "impressions and experiences", in Eliot), change little diachronically, or, actually they are the same; they pass or are taken unchanged from poet to poet: "from century to century, from nation to nation, from poet to poet, they flow on without changing" (Shklovsky 776); they belong to no one but the Lord, and they are identical in the works of various poets.

Like Tynyanov and Eliot, Shklovsky draws attention to the fact that a certain poet would never invent or produce new images. Like Tynyanov, for whom elements are linked to co-exist in the system in correlation and interrelationship, and, like Eliot, for whom impressions and experiences are combined in new and original ways to produce a new art emotion, Shklovsky contends that the poets should remember images rather than create them – since images are given to poets – in order to rearrange and combine them in new and original ways.

As in Tynyanov and Eliot, elements, images, experiences, feelings, themes, concerns, motifs, ideas, etc. are static; what is continually changing is their relation, or combination, or arrangement. The motivation for such arrangements and combinations focuses on impression, in that poetic imagery "is a means of creating the strongest possible impression" (Shklovsky 776). Shklovsky's "impression", like that of Henry James and especially Walter Pater, concerns the process of artistic perception; as in Pater, personal impression is a means of fighting stereotype or unconscious existence, or, as Shklovsky calls it, fighting "habitualization", the process of "algebrization", "the over-automatization of an object" (Shklovsky 778).

Hence, the requirement for successful and accomplished artistic endeavour is "ostranenie" or "defamiliarization", by which the sensation of life is recovered, things are felt, the stone is made "stony", and the purpose of art is achieved, namely, "to impart the sensation of things as they are perceived and not as they are known", since "Art is a way of experiencing the artfulness of an object; the object is not important" (Shklovsky 778). One should remember here that the romantic critical theory already pointed at this feature of literature – Wordsworth and Shelley stipulating the ability of poetry to achieve unusual, unfamiliar expression – as later the nineteenth-century avant-garde did.

Shklovsky's view of the arrangement of images in various new ways – just like Tynyanov's view of elements and Eliot's of impressions which are arranged and combined in new, original ways – represents one way to understand the historical movement of literature through periods, movements, and trends.

Poets and their works are classified or grouped according to the arrangement of images, the "development of the resources of language", and "the new techniques that poets discover and share" (Shklovsky 776), where this "grouping" would allow the foundation of new trends and movements.

To us, such ideas represent a congenial way to understand the movement of literature as a system diachronically, including the rise, consolidation, fall, further development, and change of various periods, movements and trends.

In matters of literary genre, Viktor Shklovsky talks about "the canonization of minor genres", such as the romance, the picaresque novel, or the gothic narrative. The Bildungsroman is also such a historically emergent literary fact, first in German pre-romanticism with Goethe, to become aesthetically strengthened by the realists and modified and diversified by the modernist and postmodern writers.

To revert to Tynyanov, a literary system, as a particular period, movement, trend, literary species, category, type, genre, or subgenre, demonstrates in the system of literature, in general, that "the literary fact is multi-structured and in this respect literature is a continuously evolving order" ("Literaturnyi fakt" 270) consisting of a myriad of diverse forms within which occur a myriad of "merging episodes of the constructional principle with the material" ("Literaturnyi fakt" 269).

Tynyanov further applies his conception of literature as a system to the discussion of literary development, or, in his words, "literary evolution", whose principles are, also in his terms, "fight" and "substitution". In his study "O literaturnoi evolutii", Tynyanov compares the domain of the history of literature to a colonial state driven by an "individualistic psychologism" and "a schematically causal approach to the literary order" (270). The divergence between them leads to a methodological discrepancy in the field of the historical investigation of literature. The former type replaces the problem of literature with the question of the author's psychology and the issue of literary evolution with that of the genesis of literary phenomena. The latter leads to the disagreement between the literary order and the standpoint from which the observation of this literary order takes place.

This place of observation constitutes social orders, and the construction of a closed literary order and the approach to evolution inside it (that is, to literary variability) would frequently come up against neighbouring cultural, domestic and, in the broad sense, social orders, and as such are doomed to incompleteness. Moreover, the theory of value in literary science has brought about the danger of studying major but isolated works and has changed the history of literature into what Tynyanov calls "the history of generals", meaning "great works" or masterpieces of literature (the literary canon), to the detriment of the study of mass literature.

The very term "history of literature" is a problem as well, continues Tynyanov, as it seems to be extremely broad and pretentious, suggesting the study of the history of *belles lettres*, the history of verbal art, and the history of writing, in general. Meanwhile, the historical investigation of literature has forked into the investigation of the genesis of literary phenomena and the investigation of the "evolution" of the literary order, or literary mutability.

The problem plaguing the historical approach to literature is the lack of theoretical methodology and the lack of an awareness of the character of research. The solution for making the history of literature a science, conferring on it the necessary methodological rigour, must be its striving for "reliability" and veracity ("O literaturnoi evolutii" 271). The study of literary development must avoid the theory of "naïve evaluation" and the subjective response; it is also necessary to reconsider the notion of "tradition", which is the abstractization of one or more literary elements in a system.

The central concept in literary evolution, which is responsible for literary change and development, is the "substitution of systems" ("O literaturnoi evolutii" 272). In order to analyse this essential issue in the context of studies on literary history, Tynyanov starts from the fundamental assumption that a literary work is a system, as is literature itself. In his opinion, the foundation of a science of literature and the investigation of the historical progress of literature are possible only in the view of literature as a system interrelated with other systems and conditioned by them.

All the elements of a literary work are the elements of a system, in the sense of a literary system which is a system of functions of literary order which are in continual interrelationship with other orders. All the elements of the system of a literary work are interrelated, interdependent and interacting. Some elements of a work in prose, such as rhythm, are also elements of the system of a work in poetry, and their study shows that the role of such elements is different in different systems.

The interrelationship of each element with every other in a literary work as a system, and, therefore, with the whole, is what Tynyanov calls the "constructional function of the given element" ("O literaturnoi evolutii" 272). This function is a complex entity: it shows that a distinct element is, on the one hand, interrelated in the order with similar elements of other works-systems and even of other orders, and, on the other hand, interrelated with other elements within the same system. Tynyanov names the former "auto-function" and the latter "syn-function". Both operate simultaneously but are of different relevance. The lexis of a given literary work, for instance, is related at once to the literary lexis and the general verbal lexis, and to other elements of this work.

Tynyanov points to the mistake of extracting certain elements from a system and, without their constructional function, of correlating them outside the system with a similar order of other systems. It is also impossible to study synchronically a literary work as a system outside its relation to the general system of literature; otherwise, such a study is another abstractization. The isolated study of the literary works is applied, successfully enough, to the evaluation of contemporary works, since the interrelationship of a contemporary work to contemporary literature is involuntarily taken as an established fact.

However, Tynyanov argues, even in contemporary literature, isolated study is impossible because the very existence of a text as literary depends on its differential quality, which is on its interrelationship with either literary or extra-literary order. In other words, its existence depends on its function: what in one period would be a matter of casual social communication, in another would be a literary fact, or vice versa, depending on the whole of the literary system in which the given text appears.

Therefore, "studying the work in isolation, we cannot be sure that we speak in correct terms about its construction" ("O literaturnoi evolutii" 273). The auto-function (the interrelationship of an element to the order of similar elements in other systems and other orders) is a condition for the syn-function (the constructional function of the element).

To summarize, according to Tynyanov, the constructional function is the correlation of each element of the literary work with other elements of the system, and thus with the whole system. It is a mistake to separate the elements from the system and to correlate them outside the system, which is to neglect their constructional function. The existence of a literary fact depends on its differential quality, meaning its function.

Next, Tynyanov offers examples of poetry and prose, and focuses on the novel and its adjustment genres of story and novella to insist again that "the evaluation of literary phenomena does not occur outside their interrelationship" ("O literaturnoi evolutii" 276) and that, unfortunately, the evolutionary relation between the function and the formal element has not been studied. There are examples in literature of how the evolution of literary form determines the change of function; examples of how a form with indefinite function calls and builds up a new one; and examples of how function searches for its form.

The variability of functions of a formal element of the system, the appearance of a new function of the formal element, and its association with the function are important issues of literary evolution. Again, the whole research depends on the consideration of literature as an order, a system, where "the system of literary order is first of all the system of functions of literary order in continuous interrelationship with other orders" ("O literaturnoi evolutii" 277). Each literary work is correlated with a particular literary system depending on its deviation, its difference, as compared to the literary system with which it is confronted. Moreover, since a literary system is a system of the functions of the literary order which is in continual interrelationship with other orders, such as social and cultural, orders or systems change in their composition, but the differentiation of human activities remains.

Due to the specificity of its material, the growth of literature, like that of other cultural orders, coincides neither in rate nor in character with those systems or orders, such as social, with which it is interrelated. The evolution of the constructional function occurs rapidly; that of the literary function occurs over epochs, and the one concerning the functions of the whole literary system in relation to the neighbouring systems occurs over centuries.

> To follow Tynyanov's line of argumentation, to understand the development of literature as the "substitution of systems" is to perceive it as the change in the interrelationship of the elements of a system, which is the change of functions and formal elements.

A system does not represent an equal interrelationship of all elements, promoting instead the differential interaction of its elements, where through a group of dominant elements producing the deformation of other elements, a new literary work emerges in literature and acquires its literary function by means of these dominant elements.

Drawing especially on these theoretical assumptions by Tynyanov, as well as on those by Shklovsky and Bakhtin, the books of our project focusing on English literature aim to demonstrate the diachronicity of the literary phenomenon as an order or system of elements. We argue that English literature is a literary system which has passed through development and change of its thematic and formal elements and functions in order to establish itself as a continuous movement of periods, trends, genres, subgenres, authors, texts, and so on, each a literary tradition or system with preceding systems as cornerstones.

The substitutions of literary systems leading to new ones vary from epoch to epoch; they may occur rapidly or slowly; they do not necessarily require the complete renewal or replacement of the formal elements of the systems, but rather "a new function of these formal elements" (Tynyanov, "O literaturnoi evolutii" 281). A potential collation of certain literary phenomena must consider functions in addition to forms.

Tynyanov concludes his study by summarizing his ideas: the study of literary evolution is possible only by viewing literature as an order, a system which is interrelated with other orders, systems, and is conditioned by them. The study must move from the constructional function (the interrelationship of each element with other elements of the system, and thus with the whole system of the literary work) to the literary function (the interrelationship of a literary work with the literary order), and from the literary function to the verbal function (the interrelationship of a literary work with the social conventions), while clarifying the issue of developmental interaction of functions and forms. Also, the investigation of literature in its development "must go from the literary order to the nearest correlated systems, not some distant ones, although these could be important" ("O literaturnoi evolutii" 281), such as social conventions, cultural doctrines, historical background, the author's psychology, daily life and personal experience, and the tastes and interests of the reading audience.

Concerning the two components – social or historical, on the one hand, and biographical or psychological, on the other – that is, the author's times and life, from a formalist perspective, literature is above all interrelated with social conventions, and as such the correlation takes place first of all through its verbal aspect. In other words, the interrelation between literature and society is realized through language, and in relation to the social background the prime function of literature is its verbal function. Using the term "orientation" to denote the author's creative intention, Tynyanov and the formalists suggest that the intention is changed by the structural function (the interrelationship of elements within a work) into a catalyst, that "creative freedom" yields to "creative necessity", and that the literary function (the interrelationship of a work with the literary order) completes the process.

Simply stated, the "orientation" of a literary work proves to be its "verbal function", its interrelationship with social conventions. It would be futile to study the verbal function of literature in relation to some distant conditions, such as economic, as it is useless to study the author's psychology, environment, daily life, and class directly in order to establish the origins of the literary phenomena. Clearly, Tynyanov and the formalists believe, the problem here is not one of individual psychological conditions, but of objective, evolving functions of the literary order in relation to the adjacent social order.

Likewise, in discussing practical criticism, David Daiches states that the approach to the literary work should be different from going to biography or psychology to discover the author's intention, for "it is less personal intention than artistic tradition that is the real question" (265), where literary tradition is the object of study of the history of literature. Earlier, W. K. Wimsatt together with Monroe C. Beardsley condemned both "affective fallacy", which leads to a confusion between ends and means in judging the literary work in terms of its results in the mind of the audience, and "intentional fallacy", which is an error of evaluating a literary work by trying to assess what the author's intention was and whether it has or not been fulfilled.

In the historical studies of British literature, or any national literature, or the history of world literature, on the whole, it is clear that literary history, which provides a chronological vision on literature, is confronted with repeated methodological crises, as this discipline is unable to fully synchronise itself with the innovations which constantly take place in modern literary theory and criticism. As Tynyanov has already warned on this matter in his formalist attempts to renovate the history of literature through the theories of literature as a system, literary evolution, and the genre, the historical investigation of literature might still have no clear theoretical awareness of how to study a literary work or what the nature of its significance is. Rene Wellek and Austin Warren, in their celebrated *Theory of Literature*, also claim that the history of a national literature is hard to envisage and remains a distant ideal; strongly bound to their Russian formalist origins, they assume the theory of the literary system and claim that literary history must be the study of systems of "literary norms, standards, and conventions" and must be "the tracing of the changing from one system of norms to another" (264-268).

Wellek and Warren believe that the separation of criticism from the diachronic dimension of the literary history and its subsequent consolidation as a distinct domain were caused by the distinction between the consideration of literature as a simultaneous order and the view on literature as diachronic order, a line of works arranged chronologically and regarded as constituent parts of the historical process. Our study attempts to balance the levels on the assumption that neither the research of the text as a synchronic phenomenon nor the historicization of literary experience are to be neglected. To achieve an adequate comprehension of the literary works of different writers and periods, it is necessary to overcome the gap between literary criticism and literary history by fusing the synchronic and diachronic dimensions in literary analysis, and by strengthening the relationship between text and context.

To revert to Tynyanov, the two main types of the historical investigation of literature – the investigation of the genesis of literary phenomena and the investigation of the growth of a literary order or system – are both problematic, as problematic is to re-examine the problem of "influence", one of the most complex issues of literary history, in relation to the existence of specific literary conditions. Also, coming back to the concept of "tradition" in literature, it is to be remembered that what may be called "traditionalism" is, as to give an example from Tynyanov, the fact that each literary movement in a given period seeks its supporting point in the preceding systems, as each new genre, or form, or type of literary text does.

In the process of literary development, tradition continues tradition and rejects innovation, just as innovation continues innovation and rejects tradition, making literary systems – which we view as literary periods, movements, trends, genres, subgenres, texts, and so on – follow, replace, substitute each other. This process implies the struggle between tradition and innovation in terms of a binary opposition involving centre and margin, or central and peripheral elements, where the differential interaction of the elements of a system, the existence of some "dominant" elements which produce as such the "deformation" or marginalization of other elements, mean actually, in Tynyanov's opinion, literary evolution as substitution of systems.

Yuri Tynyanov's views on the literary work and literature conceived as systems and on the development of literature as substitution of systems are applicable in other domains of the humanities, such as linguistics (since language itself is a system), translation studies, and cultural studies, and in different literary disciplines, such as comparative literature, where, in particular, the issue of "reception" – the study of the process of reception of a literature (as a system) in another literature or another cultural background (also conceived as systems) – receives a strong theoretical and practical basis. Although highly important for the elucidation of the status and role of literary history as a scientific discipline, Tynyanov's theory of the literary system, due to its normative principles and methodological rigour, may not always be appropriate to the study of literature. This is especially the case when we face some national peculiarities of literary history, or when the individual creative imagination is both ready to assume an established tradition, model or pattern of writing and to pursue unexpected innovation, literary experimentation, and modernization of the literary discourse.

However, like many other concepts and principles of the formalists, and from the Russians' ranks also those of M. M. Bakhtin, Tynyanov's idea of literature as a system of dominant and peripheral elements turns out to be an important issue for postmodern theoretical and ideological debate regarding the "centre and margin" dichotomy. Bakhtin himself focuses on the concepts of "self and other"; he also coins the terms and discusses chronotope, polyphony, *raznorechie*, carnivalesque, dialogism, unfinalizability, *roman vospitaniya* ("the novel of education" or Bildungsroman), where these and other principles and ideas on literature are the most congenial to our approach to the rise and development of a national literature, English, and world literature, in general.

To return to the idea of system and the "centre and margin" dualism, this binary opposition is nowadays discussed in cultural, postcolonial, social, feminist, and literary studies. The postmodern attitude towards dominant elements, and, in particular discourses, is twofold: (1) to come within dominant discourses and try to modify them from within, and (2) to accept and proclaim marginalization and try to make fringe move into centre.

The relationship of centre and margin, or dominant and peripheral elements, can be applied to literature both diachronically and synchronically. From a diachronic perspective, we would link two explanations in the discussion of the development of literature, in general, one late modern by Tynyanov, based on his theory of system, and another postmodern, based on the concepts of margin and centre. In its shift from centre or a dominant position to margin or periphery, literature becomes ex-centric (outside the centre), and "ex-centric" means "eccentric", in the sense of being unconventional, original, new. Thus, innovation emerges by rejecting tradition as centre within tradition, and moves towards the margin to become a peripheral phenomenon; if strong enough, innovation may eventually become a centre and establish itself as tradition, as it happened with baroque, romanticism, symbolism, modernism, and, more recently, with magical realism.

Innovation and tradition in literature are reified by various following each other periods, movements, and trends as literary orders or systems; their rise is based doubly on rejection of some prior literary systems and continuation of other previous literary systems, and is influenced by contemporary developments in other more or less distant systems, such as cultural, linguistic, scientific, sociologic, and so on.

Although postmodernism rejects the notion of system, we should still pay attention to Tynyanov pointing to literature as a system containing dominant and peripheral elements when we speak about centre and margin from a postmodern standpoint to explain the development of literature by recourse to such concepts as innovation and tradition. We ought especially to recall Tynyanov's theorization of literature as a system, the evolution of literature as substitution of systems, and the elements of the literary system as interrelating and interacting both (1) among themselves and (2) with the elements of other literary and non-literary (social, cultural, political, ideological, artistic, etc.) systems.

From a synchronic perspective and within national boundaries, a literary system may be described in terms of three criteria of development with regard to the interrelationship of its elements: (1) concerning individual authors, for example Alexander Pope as centre and Thomas Gray as margin, or Shakespeare as centre and Ben Jonson as margin; (2) the substitution of periods and movements, for instance neoclassicism as centre and romanticism as margin at the end of the eighteenth century, where subsequently romanticism becomes itself a centre and replaces neoclassicism; and (3) the shift of periods and movements, for example realism as centre and modernism as margin changes to modernism as centre and realism as margin in the first half of the twentieth century.

The centre and margin dichotomy in feminism and in social studies is actualized as male/man as centre and female/woman as margin, heterosexual versus sexual minorities, dominant nationality or race versus national or racial minorities, and so on. In postcolonial studies: white versus non-white, colonizer/West/Europe as centre and the colonized/Non-West as margin. The opposition emerges also within each of the two elements taken separately. In Europe as centre, for example, Western Europe is centre and Eastern Europe is margin, which can be seen in literature as well: in anthologies of literature you would barely find Alexe Rudeanu in the company of Ian McEwan. The margin may move into the centre, along with the emerging issue of identity, when an author is translated but especially when he or she assumes the language of the centre, its values, mentality and attitudes, but, above all, enhances the centre, just as Eliade, Ionesco, Kundera, Kis, Safak, and others have done. Another example would be Latin America as margin which, in its relation to the West as centre, nevertheless produced a type of reversal of the binary opposition: after producing outstanding literature (Marquez and Coelho, among others), the erstwhile margin becomes centre when it is imitated by the already existing centre, as is the case, in English literature, of Angela Carter and her novels of magical realism.

The basic term "system" in Tynyanov and formalism receives a new life through Linda Hutcheon's "constant" and "system" as well as Bran Nicol's "dominant" in their explanation and evaluation of the postmodernist literature. Hutcheon, in *A Poetics of Postmodernism* (1988), speaks about a constant, meaning a central, dominant element, in postmodern fiction, namely that "the assertion of identity through difference and specificity is a constant in postmodern thought" (59). Furthermore, Hutcheon views modernism and postmodernism as two incompatible ideological "systems", where postmodern fiction rejects from the system of modernism such elements or features as the modernist ideology of artistic autonomy, individual expression, and the deliberate separation of art from mass culture and everyday life.

Nicol, likewise, considers "postmodern" as adjective to refer to "a particular period in literary and perhaps cultural history" and, at the same time, to a system or "set of aesthetic styles and principles", whereas, postmodernism, as an aesthetic phenomenon and the reflexive or reflecting mentality and artistic practice of postmodernity, refers to a system or "set of ideas developed from philosophy and theory and related to aesthetic production" (2). Furthermore, Bran Nicol introduces the notion "dominant" in his consideration of three main features or elements, which are mostly important, or dominants, in the postmodern novel (xvi), itself conceived as a literary system. They are identified by Nicol in his book as (1) a self-reflexive acknowledgement of a text's own status as constructed, aesthetic artefact; (2) an implicit (or sometimes explicit) critique of realist approaches both to narrative and to representing a fictional "world"; and (3) a tendency to draw the reader's attention to his or her own process of interpretation as s/he reads the text (6).

In conceiving the postmodern fiction as a system with certain dominant or central elements, Nicol relies on Jakobson's formalist concept of "dominant" which determines and rules the other components or elements of the system or structure, stays in the centre of the system and guarantees its integrity, and changes over literary history.

It is certain and there is no further need to argue that Jakobson with his theory of communication relies entirely on the formalist conception of the system containing various elements possessing specific functions and, to the present, his theory has remained highly influential in both linguistics and literary studies. It is also worth mentioning here another approach which, drawing on the assumption that a particular literary work is a literary system within the larger system of a genre within the general system of literature and interrelated with other socio-cultural systems, is based on Itamar Even-Zohar's theory of polysystem. Even-Zohar views literature as a polysystem, a system of systems, a complex and heterogeneous structure, coherent yet dynamic, in that its elements are in a constant agonistic relation among themselves. Applicable along with formalism to the study of literary history and genre, this view of literature as a kind of system widens the approach to literature, whose system is regarded in relation to other systems and domains such as culture and cultural studies, translation, anthropology, and so on.

Jakobson and French structuralism, on the whole, later Hutcheon and Nicol, to say nothing about Itamar Even-Zohar, to a certain extent Julia Kristeva, and even Homi Bhabha – as well as our humble contribution, we would like to believe – maintain Yuri Tynyanov's line of thinking and concepts alive, which have developed and emerged nowadays more like a kind of "neo-formalism".

Within this neo-formalist framework of reasoning, in order to strengthen the understanding by the students of the mechanisms working to make possible the movement of literature through history, it is to comprehend again that speaking solely about literary practice in the light of Tynyanov's ideas, its development in the context of literary history is based on the "clash" between "innovation" and "tradition". They stand to each other as centre and margin, the dominant element versus marginal element in the system of literature, each striving against marginalization and for the supremacy of its aesthetic validity, longevity and potency. They are represented diachronically by different periods, movements, and trends which follow and replace one another. Just like the literary genres, they are systems whose elements are correlated as depending again on their central and peripheral nature. Literature on the whole is a system with an on-going battle between central and marginal elements, where mutations happening on the level of any element generate and determine mutations on the general level of the system.

If we conceive of the **literary work and literature, on the whole, as systems**, the interrelationship between "tradition" and "innovation" in the historical advancement of literature acts upon a literary system, which, by placing a group of its elements in the "dominant" position, makes the marginalization and deformation of other elements possible. A new work, or writing style, or subgenre, or genre, or trend, or movement emerges in literature and takes on its own literary function through this "dominant": this is the factor which stipulates the **substitution of systems** and determines the change and development of literary phenomena in the course of succeeding periods.

This is true as much of genres as of periods and movements. For instance, the literary system of the medieval romance changes in the Renaissance into the system termed by the noun *roman* ("novel") when elements of extended narration, setting, character representation and others become "dominant", whereas others, like verse form and the supernatural element, are extinguished.

On the contrary, when other elements, such as love intrigue, subjective and psychological experience, the fantastic and the irrational involved in action, are placed in the "dominant" position, the literary system of the romance is substituted in the second half of the eighteenth century by the system of a particular type of poetry called by the adjective "romantic". Another example: the element of "the revival of ancient classical tradition" in the literary system of the Renaissance becomes "dominant" in relation to the social and cultural orders (systems) of the seventeenth and eighteenth centuries, making possible the substitution of the system of the Renaissance literature by that of Enlightenment and neoclassicism.

This is also true about any particular literary tradition, or type of literary text. The "dominance" of such elements as adventure, ordeal, trial, the road chronotope, moral issues of personal conduct, love experience, autobiography, change of condition with respect to the social background, representing the system of the picaresque novel, to which the "dominant" element of *Bildung* or character formation (emergence or becoming, as in Bakhtin), implying inner change, is added in Goethe's *Wilhelm Meisters Lehrjahre*, makes possible the rise of the fictional system of the Bildungsroman in the nineteenth century. This type of novel, now a literary tradition, seeks its support in the previous systems, especially in the ancient and picaresque narratives and the romantic tradition, but places, in turn, a group of its elements in the "dominant" position, which makes possible the deformation of other elements, and as a result the related fictional types of *Entwicklungsroman*, *Erziehungsroman*, and *Künstlerroman* emerge in world literature.

A literary system can, therefore, be a literary period, such as the Renaissance, whose main elements are humanism, individualism, observation, rationalism, deduction, revival of the ancient classical tradition, etc.; it can be a literary movement, such as romanticism, whose central elements are imagination, subjective experience, dualism of existence, escapism, rebelliousness, and so on. A literary system can be also a genre, such as the novel, or a subgenre, for instance, the Bildungsroman.

Concerning this novelistic tradition, as to further exemplify our line of reasoning, we regard the literary discourse of the Bildungsroman as a well-structured literary pattern and likewise as an ordered system of elements whose aesthetic values stand within the larger system of the novel. The novel, as a self-standing system, belongs, along with other literary genres and types of text, to the system of literature. Literature, in turn, is a system framed within the general system of culture and should be approached in relation to other cultural systems. Such an analysis takes into consideration the national peculiarities of a literary system (here English), its relation to world literature, as well as the interrelationship between national culture and the world cultural phenomenon in general.

The peculiarity of the Bildungsroman as a literary work centred on the process of character formation – as both self-formation and guided formation – implies certain interpretative considerations. A critic should examine such elements of its system as (1) the author, particularly in his or her relation to the character, and the degree of their identification and separation, as well as the character as an autodiegetic narrator, since the Bildungsroman is an autobiographical type of fiction; (2) the reader, since the Bildungsroman is intended to be representative of the human condition; but, especially, (3) the content, or the thematic level, and (4) the form, or the narrative level, with their distinct but interrelated arrangements within the text of the whole process of an individual's development and formation.

In matters of (3) the content, or the thematic perspectives, particular concerns represent the milieu or society, the family background, parental figures, education, professional career, sentimental experience, ordeal, the philosophy of living, epiphany, moral didacticism, and others. In matters of (4) the form, meaning the structural perspectives, the focus is on the type of narration, point of view, narrator, narratee, mode, voice, and especially chronotope and its typology, and language as a means of both textualization of the process of growth and maturation and expression of the authorial point of view on this process. These elements are at the same time the main thematic and narrative aspects of the Bildungsroman literary system.

The elements to be focused upon in the study of such a particular type of text as the Bildungsroman may recall the elements of Roman Jacobson's structure of communication in general (sender, receiver, message, context, contact, and code) and those of literary communication as stated by Guy Cook: author, reader, text, performer, society, texts, and language. Such elements emerge from the condition of the Bildungsroman as a literary phenomenon which represents a specific type of fictional discourse framed within a specific type of communicative situation, a literary discourse intended to be communicated to the reader; in other words, the text of the novel of formation is involved in a literary communicative situation, it is the central element of a particular type of literary communication involving its author and reader and being organized as a literary system.

The Bildungsroman is to be considered a particular novelistic subgenre structured as a literary system in the line of such established literary and non-literary traditions as picaresque fiction and biography. Romanticism is a literary system in the line of such movements and trends in literature as metaphysical poetry, neoclassicism, aestheticism, or realism. The Renaissance is a literary system similar to such periods in the history of literature as medieval period, Victorian Age, the period of modernism, or the postmodern one.

They are phases and aspects of the diachronic movement of English literature and, as such, they are matters of concern of literary history, theory, and criticism. However, one should avoid making his or her study of English literature a compilation of unverified critical and theoretical categories simply due to their wide dissemination. In our case as well, instead of heavily borrowing ideas and providing quotations from historical, critical and theoretical studies in an attempt to relate and apply them to the analysis of English literature, it is necessary to consider the essence of different opinions and ideas, to adapt them according to the vector of research, and, especially, to follow the interpretative perspectives emerging from the direct, textual, contextual and comparative approach to English literature.

> We suggest to our students that a particular subgenre, such as the Bildungsroman, as well as the novel or fiction, generally, together with a poetic or dramatic text, or poetry and drama, or a particular literary period, movement, and trend, along with literature, in general, can be studied as systems of elements which would become concerns and objects of study of various trends and schools of the large domain of literary theory and criticism.

Literature, on the whole, and the particular elements of the literary system represent the main concern of the history of literature as well, especially in the light of Paul Ricoeur's hermeneutic perspectives of the textual arrangement and text analysis with regard to the human experience considered diachronically: (1) the implication of language as discourse, (2) the implication of discourse as a structured literary work, (3) the relation between verbal and written forms in the discourse and the structured literary work, (4) the structured literary work/discourse as the projection of another world, (5) the structured literary work as the projection of the authorial life which is transfigured through the discourse, and (6) the structured literary work as the self-comprehension of the reader (94).

In our books, the "world" of the literary system of English literature receives evaluative attention from three perspectives, which are the long-established domains of literary theory, literary criticism, and the history of literature. An accurate approach to English literary phenomenon would require the symbiosis of the three directions of research; unfortunately, much of the modern literary theory and criticism addresses the literary work as a synchronic phenomenon, removing the text from its temporal and spatial context.

The study of literature may avoid references to some distant systems, such as science and economy, but it should not ignore the importance of the private, social and/or historical factors, and especially cultural, philosophical and theoretical ones, since it is within these contexts that the literary significance of the work can be better clarified.

We agree with those who, like Brian Vickers, attempt to balance the impact of the internal and external factors acting upon the historical movement of literature in that a particular period, movement, trend, or genre is punctuated by social events, such as changes of governments or industrialisation, but it also necessarily obeys its own internal logic and is subjected to the organization and interrelationship among the elements of its system.

In his presentation of the seventeenth century, Vickers states that "[p]olitical events do impinge on literature, nowhere more dramatically than in the closing of the theatres in 1642, but the introduction, development, and ultimate decline of literary modes or genres follow their own laws, depending on the innate vitality of a form of the inventiveness of the writers using it" (160).

The emphasis on cultural, theoretical, philosophical, scientific, and historical dimensions and the consideration of various social and biographical influences on literary work must not, of course, exclude the synchronic dimension, methodological principles and the scientific rigour of literary theory and criticism to which literary history has access. Especially in the case of the diachronic advancement of English imaginative writing – which has a long developmental history – without understanding literature in its movement through history, the dualism of tradition and innovation, the origins of the literary work, the author's artistic sensibility and especially his or her theoretical and philosophical views, and the social and cultural circumstances and context of the act of literary creation, the critic would scarcely offer competent judgement on the value of the text, its author, period, movement, trend, or genre.

Despite the apocalyptic death verdict announced by so many concerning the future of literary history, the fact that any literary work is not historically determined, or that no literary text is an expression of an epoch, or that its production has no connection with the individual experience of the author, would never be proved. It is counterintuitive to think that a literary work can be properly understood by some criteria lacking temporal significance.

Therefore, it is crucial to shoulder the effort of joining the synchronic and diachronic research, and to examine the literary work as projected on a diachronic scale, in relation to both its past and its contemporary perspective. In this case, the history of literature should endeavour to find ways to innovate its discourse by getting support from other disciplines of the humanities, such as cultural anthropology, social history, sociology, linguistics, and cultural studies, but especially from the most recent and world-wide acknowledged theoretical and critical modalities advanced by literary theory and literary criticism.

Possessing scientific consistency, the history of literature is expected to form together with literary theory and criticism a distinct unified discourse of aesthetic evaluation of the literary phenomena. If continuously and adequately modernized, this discourse would be efficient enough to sustain the proper study of national and international literary heritage, and even eliminate the general illiteracy caused by the deformed vision of the literary truths from the past.

The books of imaginative writing might then remain an important stimulus for the aesthetic and intellectual needs of the human race, despite the complexity of new cultural alternatives and the changing rhythm of human existence at the beginning of a new millennium.

Likewise, the books of literary history or history of literature might remain important guides into the cultural heritage, which needs to survive and stay known, despite the claims, which are still heard nowadays, in the aftermath the postmodernity, that history and historicism are dead or writing history is an equivalent to writing stories which encompass, like fiction, events and characters specific to the narrative. A character, in Julian Barnes's *England, England*, states that concerning the reception by readers of the historical books, it occurs in view of history as a system which is closed and the reader is expected to have already read other books of history. The statement is given at the start of these Preliminaries.

To justify our own series of books on the movement through history of English literature, and contrary to what is stated in Barnes's novel, we do not expect readers to have read books about English literature since we aim our work to be their starting point in learning or strengthening the knowledge about a remarkable share of the international cultural depository, a part of which – focused on particular periods, or movements, or trends, certainly on genres and unavoidably on various authors and their works – our readers will discover in the following.

1.
THE PERIOD AND ITS LITERARY PRACTICE

The period in English literature called "Victorian Age" – literally describing things and events during the reign of Queen Victoria – covers roughly some seven decades starting with the end of romanticism as a regular movement in early 1830s until the dawn of the twentieth century. In literature, thematically embracing the romantic concern with individual existence and adding to it the concern with social background, realism emerges among the dominant literary trends in the nineteenth-century literature. Like on the Continent, in Britain realism develops as a reaction against romanticism and as a continuation of some (neo)classical principles, but it is mostly influenced by the rising in the period social theories, positivist philosophy, and especially sociology and historicism. Also, like in other countries, English realism co-exists with a number of other trends and movements that represent alternatives to realism by continuing certain romantic attitudes, pursuing experimentation and innovation, and developing new principles in art by which rejecting their contemporary realist ones.

English literature, in general traditional, accepts late the literary innovation that in mainland Europe is already a dominant period, movement, or trend. The innovation once accepted in Britain, it becomes a strong normative practice, as with romanticism, which is a strong tradition in itself rejecting changes and innovations. Hence is in Britain a strong nineteenth-century romantic presence in literature, and like on the Continent, especially in France, due to the continuous attempt to innovate the literary discourse, and due to a mobile innovation, there is "innovation *of* romanticism" (post-romanticism as a minor innovation and neo-romanticism as a major innovation) but most important is "innovation *from* romanticism", which is frequently called "avant-garde" and encompasses symbolism, aestheticism, impressionism, decadence, Parnassianism.

1.1 The Social and Cultural Context

The Victorian social and cultural scene is a complex, even paradoxical phenomenon, thwarting any attempts at describing or labelling it precisely. In literature, we ought to avoid calling it generically the period of realism or realist fiction, as in Marxist criticism, given the persistence of the romantic mode of writing throughout the entire nineteenth century, alongside the emergence of avant-garde trends, though in point of literary genre, the Victorian novel parallels Elizabethan drama in terms of both popularity and literary achievement.

Queen Victoria (1819 – 1901) reigned from 1837 until January 1901: she was probably the greatest queen after Elizabeth and gave her name to an epoch of expansion of wealth, power, and culture; a period which appeared to mark the apogee of national and imperial glory, improve standards of distance and morality, an age of stability, peace, imperial expansion and increasing prosperity. However, the Victorian standards, beliefs, and values of the social and the personal – such as hard work, moral strength, religious orthodoxy, sexual reserve, family virtues, confidence in personal and historical development – were often challenged by criticism for the epoch's unquestioned acceptance of authority and orthodoxy, its great amount of hypocrisy, conscious rectitude, deficient sense of humour, and a self-satisfaction engendered by the increase of wealth.

The Victorian Age was not unified, as one may think given Victoria's reign which lasted so long that it comprised several periods. Above all, it was an age of paradox and power: the Catholicism of the Oxford Movement, the Evangelical movement, the spread of the Broad Church, and the rise of Utilitarianism, socialism, Darwinism, Freudism, and scientific Agnosticism were all in their own ways characteristically Victorian; as were the prophetic writings of Carlyle and Ruskin, the criticism of Arnold, and the empirical prose of Darwin and Huxley; as were the fantasy of George MacDonald and the realism of William Thackeray and George Eliot. More than anything else what makes this age Victorian is its immense sense of social responsibility (remarkably expressed in the novels of George Eliot, for instance), a basic attitude that obviously differentiates it from romanticism, its immediate predecessor.

Victorian Age is, nevertheless, one of dynamic change and assiduous activity, fermentation of ideas and recurrent social unrest, great inventiveness and expansion. In this period, England was caught in a whirl of social, economic, and religious changes. Like all major periods of transition, this one did not come easily: the first part of the Victorian Age (1832 – 1848) was one of tumult, where the rapid industrial expansion and the laissez-faire economic system allowed for the justification of horrible working conditions, especially for children, together with high tariffs on grain, which caused food shortages. It also caused the early 1840s' depression, but, by the middle of the Victorian period, the situation changed to some extent: tariff and labour reforms helped to bring back general economic prosperity and contentment. The second half of the nineteenth century is also to be regarded in relation to the revolutions of 1848 on the Continent; the Chartism and its failure; the development of science applied to practical purposes: telephone, telegraph, photography, steam engine, electricity; the great discoveries in the natural sciences, and so on.

This aspect of great development comprising astonishing innovation, rapid change and remarkable diversity of the Victorian age is characteristic to all domains of social existence. The most common terms used to describe the period are stability, positivism, optimism, progress, and consolidation, an "immense consolidation in terms of peace and prosperity, in terms of wealth and power, and in terms of artistic productivity" (Blamires 259). At the same time, the Victorian period was an age of paradox, "an age of conflicting explanations and theories, of scientific and economic confidence and of social and spiritual pessimism, of a sharpened awareness of the inevitability of progress and of deep disquiet as to the nature of the present" (Sanders 398). In science and technology, there was the advance of invention, and "England became highly industrialized and a modern economy was developed. The force of steam power was used for railways, printing presses and a merchant fleet which had no equal in the world. England invested in all countries and was the world's banker" (Galea 10).

In science and technology, the Victorians invented the modern idea of invention, the notion that one can create solutions to problems, that human beings can create new means of bettering themselves and their environment. In ideology and philosophy, the Victorians identified many of the modern problems and attempted solutions, again from a diversity of perspectives including those developed and prompted by Darwin, Comte, Marx, Taine, Freud, as well as Utilitarianism, the Oxford Movement, Chartism, and others. In religion: Evangelicalism, the Broad Church, and Tractarianism. The Victorians would experience a great age of doubt, being the first to call into question institutional Christianity on such a large scale. Indeed, controversy would often shift from social and economic issues to religion: for instance, the Utilitarians, reflecting on what they considered to be the basic human needs, decided that a society that listened to the voice of reason had no need for religion. The Utilitarian views distressed the religious conservatives, who argued that the Victorian Age, with its excesses and social problems, was in dire need of the stability and comfort offered by traditional Christianity.

In literature and other arts, Victorianism sought to combine the romantic emphases upon self, emotion, and imagination with neoclassical ones upon reason, the public role of art and the social responsibility of the artist. Except that part of literary practice and criticism which regards art *per se*, much literature in the Victorian England "necessarily extends itself on every front, into every area of discourse and concern: social, economic, political, epistemological, moral, religious, and cosmological" (Davis 9). As a cultural phenomenon, Victorianism "might be defined by the complementary action of opposite tendencies: individualism and self-denial, material pursuits and idealization of existence, the influences of science and the force of religion" (Galea 13), determining here as well remarkable progress and diversity. Indeed, in Europe in general, the nineteenth century saw an extended public interest in art paralleling a remarkable increase in the number of artists from different fields – writers, musicians, painters – to whom new fields were added as a result of the period's inventions and advances in science and technology:

Only in Germany, the number of painters and sculptors increased from 8890 to 14000 between 1895 and 1907. In 1891, in Great Britain the number of musicians was twice than the number of bank clerks. The enormous flux of the artists was only partly absorbed by the new organizations on the art market and by the expansion of new fields in art: photography, graphic illustration of the publications, reproduction industry. (Frevert and Haupt 265)

In philosophy, politics, society, and studies on art and literature, the nineteenth century brought in astonishing innovation and change: the principles of democracy, feminism, unionization of workers, socialism, aestheticism, Darwin's evolution, Comte's view of society, Marx's view of history, Taine's view of literature, Ruskin's and Pater's views of art, and Freud's view of human psyche. All these theoreticians and many others elaborated hypotheses in their own fields of expertise, which are seemingly beyond the domain of literature, but which influenced both the literary practice and literary criticism in the nineteenth and twentieth centuries.

Subject to controversy and debate since its publication in 1859, *On the Origin of Species* by the naturalist Charles Robert Darwin (1809 – 1882) exposed the scientific theory of evolution and natural selection. According to Darwin, life has "its own laws of reproduction and variation, leading to an endless prospect of dynamic change" (Parrinder 12). The theory received enough evidence from the author to be accepted during his lifetime and to be applied to the discussion of man, socio-economic milieu, culture, art, and literature. The human being, social institutions, religion and myth, art and literature came to be considered within processes of evolution similar to that of nature. The evolutionist method and the comparative studies in anatomy and biology sustained the nineteenth century conflict between science and religion, but they also prompted the rise of new disciplines, such as anthropology, or the development of new trends in literature, such as naturalism. According to Radu Surdulescu, "the socio-cultural anthropology adopts in its incipient stage the comparative-evolutionist method, as it may be noticed in *Primitive Culture*, published by E. B. Tylor in 1871, and *The Golden Bough* by Sir James Frazer", published in 1890; also, "the acceptance of anthropology as a science, which was much insisted on by Tylor, was conditioned and supported by the social studies adopting the theory of evolution from the natural sciences" (Surdulescu 22).

Among the most influential thinkers was the theoretician and doctor Sigmund Freud (1856 – 1939) who developed a structural model of the psyche and the theory of the *id* (unconscious) in an attempt to provide the explanation of the psychological phenomenon with a scientific method. The main element is unconscious, "responsible equally for our daytime bungling and the terrors of the dreamer, the neurotic or psychotic: all are the subject to the "same laws"" (Stonebridge 271). Freud's revolutionary change in the science of the mind had its impact not as much as on the nineteenth century as on the twentieth century, given that in 1900 he published *Interpretation of Dreams*, and, in 1901, *The Psychopathology of Everyday Life*. As the founder of the psychoanalytic school of psychiatry, Freud had a number of predecessors earlier in the nineteenth century, among whom Thomas Laycock, W. B. Carpenter (who spoke of an "unconscious cerebration"), and especially the mid-century physicians Henry Holland and A. L. Wigan who pointed to a "double brain" and a "duality of mind". On the more general level of psychology, instances of such an approach could be found in Antiquity, with Aristotle, in his definition of tragedy, speaking about emotions of terror and pity in the production of *catharsis*; later Philip Sidney and Samuel Johnson commented on the moral effects of poetry; but especially romantic poet-critics psychologised literature by their expressive theory of authorship and their theories of the imagination. Coleridge emphasises "unconsciousness" in his theory of poetic imagination and reveals it as a theme in his *Kubla Khan* and *The Rime of the Ancient Mariner*. Wordsworth speaks in *The Prelude* of an "unconscious intercourse" with nature that may heal the wound of the self, where "Wordsworth evokes a type of consciousness more integrated than ordinary consciousness, though deeply dependent on its early – and continuing – life in rural surroundings" (Hartman 51).

The psychoanalytic theories of Freud and his followers were highly original by their insistence on the unconscious, as was psychoanalysis as a modern psychological approach to literature. Freud's theories emerged from his experience as a neurologist, but many ideas were also suggested by literary works, as Freud himself declared: "poets and philosophers discovered the unconscious long before what I discovered by scientific method which permits to study the unconscious". Just like Carl Jung would employ folklore, fairy tales, and religion to develop his theories, Freud "employs Greek myths (most prominently Oedipus and Narcissus) for his crucial concepts" (Emig 175). Rainer Emig finds the psychoanalytic position in literary criticism to be similar to what modern literary theory calls "intertextuality":

> Text-based in its methods, psychoanalysis shares with literature the poiesis of images and expressions, the poetics of their arrangement, the grammar of narratives, but also a theory of interpretation. The latter frequently abandons the idea of an origin of symptoms (...) and instead refers to other texts, previous traumas or archetypal images and stories that are closely related to myths. (175)

Indeed, it is easy to find in Freud's work references to literature, which had an important role in the rise of psychoanalysis, namely to Sophocles and Shakespeare and with regards to "Oedipus complex". According to Ileana Malancioiu, both Oedipus and Hamlet represented one of Freud's main and continuous concerns from 1897 to 1938. In an 1897 letter to Wilhelm Fliess, Freud speaks about a possible analogy between *Oedipus Rex* by Sophocles and his own feelings of love towards mother and hatred towards father. *Oedipus Rex*, "explains Freud, makes the child's dream become real", whereas in *Hamlet*, the infantile wish "is repressed and manifests as neurosis" (Malancioiu 11-12). According to Freud, Hamlet is a human personality possessing passions, thoughts, conscious and unconscious, whereas Oedipus has no unconscious since he represents the human unconscious itself. The legend of Oedipus is the symbolic representation of a complex, that is to say, of a desire which is a memory of a real incident from primitive times. Oedipus is thus also a myth, and myths, according to Freud, are related to "dreams, works of art, and neurotic manifestations" and represent "precipitates of the unconscious processes which are projected over the external world" (Surdulescu 53). Freud's theories stipulated new interpretations of man's gestures and his peculiar responses to external reality. Freud's ideas put in a totally new light the issue of determinism, and oppose the classical ones, as well as Romantic views, and the sociological and Marxist ones concerning social determinism. In this respect, Freud's theories gave rise to tragic and pessimistic views concerning the human being's possibilities, proving that the individual is no longer a master of his destiny but subject to obscure, unknown, uncontrolled and illogical passions and instincts (such as *libido*) coming from the *id*. Freud's ideas are included in the domain of philosophical speculation, the main reason being that Freud's theoretical hypotheses regard a number of consequences that open questions which philosophy cannot ignore. Among these issues, the "main problem is to know whether the hypothesis of an unconscious determinism of our behaviour and thinking is in contradiction with the classical definition of freedom as self-determinism and autonomy" (Graf 29).

Later, Carl Jung (1875 – 1961) develops new ideas on memory, personal unconscious, collective unconscious and archetypes, which diverge from those of Freud but which are also of great importance and influence. Like Freud establishing and influencing the psychoanalytic criticism, Jung is a major influence on mythological and archetypal criticism, and his primary contribution to these approaches is the theory of archetypes and racial memory. A student of Freud, Jung breaks and disagrees with his master, primarily in terms of unconscious and the principles governing the personal unconscious, which are, for Freud, libido, Oedipus complex, and others. Unlike Freud who "assessed the evolution of the individual in a particular cultural setting, Jung extended his theories to the history of humanity", but both "aspire towards universal validity" (Emig 180).

A similar fascination with the unconscious as depository of ideas and the unconscious history of ideas was shared earlier in the nineteenth century by John Stuart Mill and Auguste Comte. To Mill, the ideas that survived as "intuitively natural and foundational", "such as the so-called "laws of nature", disguised the working of material self-interest in history; they created an anachronistic language that prevented thought just when it seemed to be expressing it" (Davis 171). To Comte, according to Mill in *Auguste Comte and Positivism* (1865), the shared ideas have social implications regarding a single system of thought: "To combat both the individualistic muddle and the specialized division of labour in the nineteenth century, Comte believed that the more the thoughts fitted into one whole rationally agreed framework, the more the individuals who held them might fit into a genuinely uniform society" (Davis 171).

Concerning literary practice and literary criticism, Freud's theories have proved to be more potent and influential than those of Jung. It was Freud's psychoanalysis that showed the fact that the use, or rather the materialization, of a theory or doctrine, literary or philosophical, in the literary text, has been a common practice among those writers who manifested also as thinkers, or among those authors who embraced different doctrines as developed by others. Among the writers of the latter type, D. H. Lawrence revealed in his novel *Sons and Lovers* a number of principles, theories, and concepts, such as Oedipus complex, as put forward by Freud. Actually, the principles of psychoanalysis influenced the literary practice of the twentieth century perhaps more than other contemporary trends in thought, especially in the first half of the century and in particular the literary activity of those writers who are acclaimed as exponents of modernism. Among them, and apart from Lawrence, are Virginia Woolf, James Joyce, Eugene O'Neill, and many others. In the field of literary theory and criticism, the principles of psychoanalysis as developed by Freud gave rise in the twentieth century to a whole new trend in critical thinking, called "psychoanalytic criticism", best represented by Jacques Lacan, Harold Bloom, Geoffrey Hartman, Juliet Mitchell, Luce Irigaray, and others.

To revert to nineteenth century, another influential philosopher of the period is Friedrich Nietzsche (1844 – 1900), whose work, highly methodological though not systematic, covers a great number of concerns ranging from the function of language to theories on myth. Nietzsche's most important ideas are on subjectivism in human perception and search for truth, the cognitive role of language, art as human most effective means of dealing with existence which is essentially tragic, the rejection of conformity and dogmas, and the support for the one who has the capacity to create, to be "free spirit" or "new philosopher", and whom Nietzsche calls *Übermensch* ("superman" or "overman"). His anti-dogmatic and anti-Christian views challenged the Victorian confidence in progress and influenced the literary activity of many twentieth century and contemporary writers. His ideas became important points of reference in later philosophy and literary criticism, as in Freud, existentialism, and the poststructuralist writings of Jacques Derrida and Paul de Man. For instance, "deconstructionist criticism, as in Derrida, Roland Barthes, Paul de Man, Jean-Francois Lyotard, Gilles Deleuze, and J. Hillis Miller, has found his theothanatology especially virtuous for the propagation of autogeneal, autotelic, "grammarless" reflection" (La Bossiere 435).

Apart from *Übermensch*, in *Thus Spoke Zarathustra* and other writings, some of Nietzsche's best-known and influential concepts include *der Wille zur Macht* ("will to power"), "eternal return", as well as his principles of nihilism, rejection of morality and the anti-Christian claim that "God is dead". Likewise, Dostoevsky argued that in a universe in which God is dead everything is permitted, the only rule being to break rules. In existentialism, since in the world God is dead, one solution is to rebel, as for Camus, or choose and act in order to become, as for Sartre. In testing the solitude of man, existentialism "follows through the nihilism of Nietzsche, denies all essences, all a prioris in the human condition, and achieves a transvaluation of values despite itself" (Hassan 143). Also comes to the mind the famous remark of Georg Lukacs that the novel is "the epic of a world abandoned by God".

Concerning Nietzsche's relation to literature and literary studies, "his thought, as much as his style, reveals him as a son of the Romantic movement" (Durant 439), as Nietzsche values the individualistic and egoistic impulses and fails to recognize the value of the social factors. He rejects the opinions and interpretations which are made according to the values imposed by culture and religion, and assigns to criticism the task to unmask all the pre-determined values governing the human estimation and understanding of the text. His belief is that

> as there is not a single mode of life, good for all people, so it is not clear that there can ever be a single, overarching interpretation of a particular text that everyone will have to accept. "The" world and "the" text are equally indeterminate. The problem with this approach, in morality as well as in literature, is that every unmasking must itself proceed from a particular point of view, which it must take for granted while it is depending upon it. Thus, every revelation of the partiality of a previous point of view will contain within it an unquestioned commitment to some further point of view. The genealogical enterprise therefore cannot ever be fully completed. Even the claim that there is no truth, that the world and the text are equally indeterminate, in being claimed, is claimed to be true. (Nehamas 547)

Related to literary field is Nietzsche's famous *The Birth of Tragedy* (1872), which asserts that the genre originates in the Dionysian celebrations, and, "for some exegetes Dionysus becomes the path to understanding and interpreting Greek culture, while for Nietzsche, who opposes Dionysus to Apollo, he becomes the path to interpreting tragedy" (Golban 25). As conceived by Nietzsche, the Dionysian element provides a paradoxical experience to humans: "the horror felt by the individual faced with a primal lack of differentiation and the violence unleashed in the sacred celebration; and the "delicious ecstasy" provoked by the breakdown of the principle of individual existence and the feeling of melting into the primitive One" (Dumoulie 872). In short, "in Nietzsche's view, tragedy is born out of nostalgia for the Primitive in a world of Will, and out of the reconciliation of these two "artistic drives of nature", which are opposing, but also complementary, since "the eternal suffering and contradiction" needs "a lovely appearance" in order to find comfort" (Golban 25). According to Nietzsche's theory about the beginnings of Greek tragedy, by the sacrifice of a he-goat, a sacred animal for Dionysus, where the sacrifice exists before dramatic representation, the passion of Dionysus might have been the first subject rendered in tragic drama, followed by the elements of violence, madness and crime which are characteristic to ancient Greek tragedy. Rising the critical discussion to the philosophical level, Nietzsche points at the failure of modern people to sustain the confidence in the eternal truths offered by the tragic myth and Greek tragedy. By its range of ideas on ancient tragedy, Nietzsche's *The Birth of Tragedy* "contributed to the modernists' increased interest in myth (Eliot, Pound, Joyce), the consideration of a new aesthetics (Eliot, Pound, Woolf, Joyce), and an analysis of human relations based on will (Conrad, Lawrence)" (Ciugureanu 21). In his turn, even if viewed as being rooted in romanticism, it is said that Nietzsche developed his philosophy as a reaction to Kant, Mill and Schopenhauer (by Santayana, among others), and that the real roots of his thinking should be found in the pre-platonic philosophers and later seventeenth century French moralists, as well as in Alfred Espinas, Paul Bourget, Stendhal, Baudelaire and Dostoyevsky.

In the literary field, reacting against romantic paradigm, realism, one of the most important nineteenth century literary trends, was shaped by the ideas of Comte, Taine, Feuerbach, Darwin, Hegel, and Marx. Realism manifested itself predominantly in fiction, requiring faithfulness to actuality in its representation, the concentration of the novelist on everyday events, the milieu, the social and political realities, and ordinary people. These ideas were largely suggested by Champfleury in *Le realisme* and developed by the great writer-critics of the period Balzac, Stendhal and Zola.

On the general European level, the realist critical view of literature and the realist novel of the nineteenth century owe much to the positivist philosophy of the period, in particular to the ideas of Hippolyte Taine (1828 – 1893), who considers literature to be the product of *la race, le milieu et le moment*, and Auguste Comte (1789 – 1857), whose studies on society and science influenced the realistic writings of the period and, together with Marx's theories of society and Taine's opinions on literature, shaped a new model of literary studies combining historical with sociological approach to literary production.

Where for Matthew Arnold criticism would consider the effects of literature on society, for Taine, Marx and the entire sociological criticism of the period the main interest is in society as the cause of literature and literature as the product of society. In the nineteenth century, after the end of romanticism as a regular movement, literature came to be viewed in relation to social issues, among which the most important is the sense of historical and scientific determinism which found its utmost expression in the works of, among others, Darwin and Marx. Also, in Taine, and in no lesser degree, "science's methodology, philosophical assumptions, and practical applications found an admiring adherent and a strong voice" (Bressler 39). The key word in Taine is "determinism", and according to him, the study of literary works should consider race, milieu, and moment, which he explains as "forces arising from racial inheritance", "social and political environment", and "the moment of time in which the literature or the historical figure emerged", respectively. Taine's famous phrase "race, milieu, and moment", elaborated in his *History of English Literature* (1864), points to hereditary and environmental types of determinism.

Concerning the estimation of a literary work, Taine asserts these three important factors to be the main sources for the elementary moral state of the human being.

They are to be taken into consideration in the study of past literature: "race" discloses that the writers of the same nation share similar emotions and ideas expressed in the work; "milieu", meaning environment or surroundings, helps the critic to understand the intellectual and cultural issues expressed in the work; and "moment" or epoch offers through the information on the period's values, customs, outlooks, culture, and science the true understanding of the meaning expressed in the work. When their influence is revealed, the three factors of race, milieu, and moment provide the understanding of any literary period, and, when the focus is on individual literary works, these factors are also to be taken into consideration, since the work is determined by the author's psychology and the psychology is determined by race, environment, and moment of time. In his *History of English Literature*, Taine speaks about the role of the climate as an important circumstance acting upon race and its psychological traits, where, in the case of the British, "rain, wind, and surge leave room for naught but gloomy and melancholy thoughts".

By subordinating literature to sociology, Taine is the founder of the sociology of literature, recommending the study of literature in the direction of disclosing its representation of individual as a social being and of constructing from literary texts, which are also literary documents, the moral and social history of mankind. In this, literature is superior to history, because "a great poem, a fine novel, the confession of a superior man, are more instructive than a heap of historians with their histories", and they are instructive because "they are beautiful; their utility grows with their perfection, and if they furnish documents it is because they are monuments". But the study of literary authors and texts, as Taine explains in the Introduction to *History of English Literature*, requires a scientific approach, it is better done in a scientific manner, in particular by applying the methods of biology, as to penetrate the "mass of faculties and feelings" that make the inner man, to "get inside" the life and works of an author in order to better disclose the social and moral rather than individual features of the human being. Literary criticism is thus a kind of add-on to social and moral history, because, Taine argues, a literary text "is not a mere individual play of imagination, the isolated caprice of an excited brain, but a transcript of contemporary manners, a manifestation of a certain kind of mind" from which "we might discover (…) a knowledge of the manner in which men thought and felt centuries ago".

The critical reflection on literature through the lens of "historicism" is already present in the Enlightenment, emphasised in the romantic period, and flourishes in the nineteenth century. The historical approach provides "new views on literature and art which are understood both as an anteriority-posteriority relationship and as bound to some national events that are meaningful for the existence of certain peoples" (Munteanu 8-9). The positivism of the nineteenth century added to the anteriority-posteriority relationship that of cause-effect, and the act of literary creation came to be explained more and more by factors that are beyond the text. In Victorian Britain, the view of history as a congenial factor and that the contemporary society represented an improvement over the preceding historical periods came from Thomas Babington Macaulay (1800-1859). His optimistic views are quite opposite to those of Arnold, Carlyle, and Ruskin who pointed to the sense of completion, material acquisition and possessiveness of Victorianism and "deplored the disappearance of the idyllic, patriarchal mode of life" (Galea 48).

The new reflections on history emerging in the eighteenth and nineteenth centuries gave rise to a new discipline in literary studies, called "literary history". Although nowadays discredited as ineffective and obsolete, the literary history established the diachronic research of the literary phenomenon. It also provided "evidence on national peculiarities", represented "a means of understanding the psychology of a nation (Taine), and, after escaping the classical models, a proof of the existence of a nation, not as an act of creation evaluated by its aesthetic principles (Taine)" (Munteanu 9). It is claimed that the discipline of literary history was founded at the end of the nineteenth century by Gustave Lanson (1857 – 1934), who follows two directions. First, the French scholar expands Taine's concept of *la race, le milieu et le moment* and adheres to the idea that literature is the expression of society. Second, Lanson promotes also the idea of the author as the producer of the text and "claims that the best act of criticism is that which reveals the truth about the text according to what the author wanted to express" (Gengembre 6). Prior to this, in 1800, Madame de Staël (1766 – 1817) contributed to literary history in *De la litterature consideree dans ses rapports avec les institutions sociales* by promoting the idea that the consolidation of different types of literature is determined by the period, national spirit, climate and religion, and criticism must examine in detail "the moral and political causes that change the spirit of literature". Madame de Staël was a cosmopolitan spirit, like her contemporary Claude Charles Fauriel (1772 – 1844) who wrote on her work and on the history of philosophy, but he is mainly acclaimed as the Professor of foreign literature at Sorbonne. Fauriel, his successor Frederic Ozanam (1813 – 1853), and Edgar Quinet (1803 – 1875) of University of Lyon are considered the forefathers of a new discipline, which is comparative literature. However, Francis Claudon and Karen Haddad-Wolting consider their way of treating foreign values, customs and literature to be populist and journalistic, and as lacking a method. Instead, these two critics claim that the method in comparative literary studies was borrowed from the French naturalist and zoologist Georges Cuvier's (1769-1832) *Leçons d'anatomie comparée* and that Jean-Jacques Ampere (1800-1864) is the real founder of comparative literature (Claudon and Haddad-Wolting 9-10). One ought to remember also M. Noël's and M. de La Place's *Cours de litterature comparee* (1816) or Stendhal's *Racine et Shakespeare* (1823), and the first mentions of the term "comparative literature" by Abel-Francois Villemain in 1827 and Matthew Arnold in 1848. In English, accredited for the foundation of comparative literary studies is the Irish-New Zeeland H. M. Posnett in *Comparative Literature* (1886). The term "comparative" appeared in the eighteenth century, and this century, "with its cosmopolite and internationalist tendencies, represented the best soil for the growth of the comparative ferment which was being prepared" (Cioranescu 14). For Daniel-Henri Pageaux, the discipline of comparative literature emerged in the nineteenth century, first in France, by "conquering the universities", among which its introduction by Ferdinand Brunetiere at Ecole Normale Superieure with the purpose "to confront the development of French literature with that of other Western literatures, to follow the evolution of genres (similar to the evolution of species), and to understand the ways in which French literature assimilated foreign influences. One may see here the two notions that will give rise to a particular type of comparative literature: evolution and influence" (Pageaux 15). The flourishing of comparative literature took place in the twentieth century, in particular with the first issue of the *Journal of Comparative Literature* in 1903 and with the publication in 1931 of the *Comparative Literature* by Paul Van Tieghem. But it was the nineteenth century literary theory and criticism that revealed the first, though rudimentary, methodological attempts at comparative literature with its emphases in the critical act on literature *per se*, on one hand, and on the other hand, on the relationship between literary practice and society, science, morality and history.

Emphasising the importance of history was also Georg Wilhelm Friedrich Hegel, although the German philosopher is primarily considered in relation to the late eighteenth- and early nineteenth-centuries German philosophical movement called "Idealism", which is closely linked to both the Enlightenment and romanticism. Influenced by Aristotle, Descartes, Goethe, and Kant, Hegel's view of history, idealism, freedom and nature, immanence and transcendence, Master versus Slave dialectic, and "dialectic of existence" (described in *Science of Logic* (1811, 1812, and 1816) as involving *Sein* ("pure Being") and Nichts ("pure Nothing") united as "Becoming") influenced many writers and philosophers of the nineteenth century, among whom Schopenhauer, Nietzsche, Heidegger, Russell, and Marx. Karl Heinrich Marx (1818 – 1883) produced his own, Marxist, or materialistic, dialectics, rejecting, together with Friedrich Engels, the philosophical idealism of Hegel and claiming that:

My dialectic method is not only different from the Hegelian, but is its direct opposite. To Hegel, the life-process of the human brain, i.e., the process of thinking, which, under the name of "the Idea", he even transforms into an independent subject, is the demiurgos of the real world, and the real world is only the external, phenomenal form of "the Idea". With me, on the contrary, the ideal is nothing else than the material world reflected by the human mind, and translated into forms of thought.

In other words, "the idealist method, which starts from what humans imagine or represent to themselves as to reach the real and actual man, will be replaced by Marx with the method which starts from the processes of real life as to reach the thinking that results from it" (Graf 4). Marx's ideas mark the end of philosophy in the traditional sense, replacing some of its schemes by scientific, sociological and economic concepts. Marx developed social and economic theories, in particular on consciousness being determined by life, on means and forces of production, on infrastructure and superstructure, on ideology, money, market, labour, capital, and many others.

Literature was not one of his main concerns; yet Marx's theories contain references to art and literature; art "is included in the superstructure, and indeed subsumed under ideology; cultural production must be seen as subordinate to the rhythms of material production" (Callinicos 89). Douwe Fokkema and Elrud Ibsch identify Marx's literary assessment to be based on three criteria: first, "the criterion of economic determinism, which is concerned with the question whether a literary work represents advanced or regressive developments in the economic basis"; second, "the criterion of verisimilitude, which is in full accordance with the literary code of his days"; third, "the criterion of personal preferences, such as for the writings of Aeschylus, Shakespeare and Goethe, which belong to the literary canon of his time" (Fokkema and Ibsch 83).

In general, Marx's theories force discussions on the ways in which literature is a product of the society and the ways in which literature reflects the social and economic development of the society from which it emerges. Marx's views of society were highly influential upon literary practice and especially critical thought, resulting in Marxist criticism, which, in the twentieth century, gave some first-rate critics, such as Georg Lukacs, Terry Eagleton, Walter Benjamin, and others.

Apart from Marx, Taine, Comte, Nietzsche, Pater, Ruskin, and Arnold, a special impact on the nineteenth century, as well as twentieth century, literary practice and critical scholarship came from the rising feminism. In rejecting the patriarchal model of their contemporary society and the gender discrimination, a great number of the late eighteenth- century and nineteenth-century women writers and thinkers protested against the supposed physical and intellectual inferiority of women, on this matter producing theoretical analyses of women's position in society in relation to education, profession, family, art, and other social aspects.

Among them, Mary Wollstonecraft (1759 – 1797), who, with her best known *A Vindication of the Rights of Women* (1792), was among the first thinkers to argue "that the normative definition of femininity reflects the wish to perpetuate women's dependent position and that the education of girls is abused as a means of teaching them to internalise a sense of their intrinsic inferiority" (Knellwolf 194). Reflected in the novels of Charlotte Brontë, George Eliot, and later Virginia Woolf, the feminist conceptions gave in twentieth century the feminist school of literary criticism, which consists in a number of feminist theories, methodologies, and approaches to literature. Whatever the approach or method, the feminist criticism analyses and challenges the established literary canon – that a male-dominated society stereotypes women into images of physical and moral inferiority – and develops approaches to literary works from a female point of view, developing a model of literary criticism based on a female consciousness ("gynocriticism"). It focuses on culture and society, in particular the cultural forces in the society that shape women' identities, and on female psyche, body, and language as reflected in literary texts or the ways in which these are related to the writing process.

With respects to the realist literary practice, of greater influence was Comte's six-volume *Cours de philosophie positive* (1830 – 1842), which made possible the appearance of the science of sociology, the term which he also invented. The work expresses "Positivism" as a philosophy and its scientific attitude towards social behaviour, the cause-and-effect relationship in economics, religion, culture, and other areas of human existence, and which explains the human conduct. Indeed, Comte is "credited as the author, not only of sociology, but also of "positivism", that is, the doctrine that society and the human condition can be studied by means roughly analogous to the methods of the natural sciences" (Milner 18). In his work, Comte traces the famous "law of three stages", stating that knowledge begins in theological form, passes to the metaphysical form, and finally becomes positive. In Comte's own words, "The law is this: – that each of our leading conceptions, – each branch of our knowledge, – passes successively through three different theoretical conditions: the Theological, or fictitious; the metaphysical, or abstract; and the Scientific, or positive".

Developing one of the first theories of the "social evolutionism", Comte saw three phases in the development of human society – theological, metaphysical, and positivist – claiming that Europe was in the last of the three stages, which he calls "scientific" and "positive", and which is to embark on scientific research and scientific explanation of phenomena based on observation, experiment, and comparison. The scientific method is a means of positive affirmation of different theories which would offer the only authentic knowledge, which is the scientific one. The positive spirit would achieve universality "only if it generalises its way of thinking, that is to say, only if it extends over the study of moral and social phenomena which have been so far conceived solely according to the theological-metaphysical mode" (Graf 62). The positivist aim being a universal scientific knowledge, the universality of the positive method would replace theology and metaphysics and would make possible the transition from positive science to positive philosophy.

Comte's views influenced the realistic and naturalistic writings of Stendhal, Balzac, Flaubert, Zola, Maupassant, Dickens, Thackeray, George Eliot, Hardy, and many other writers, of which some turned literary critics. In Britain, for instance, such novelists entering the critical arena were Dickens and Thackeray, but their status as critics ranks lower than that as writers. A more interesting critic is the author of *The Egoist*, George Meredith (1828 – 1909), remembered for *An Essay on Comedy* (1897), "a stimulating exercise, remarkable for the sheer concentration of the exposition and the energy of thinking behind it" (Blamires 287).

Of a higher significance in the history of criticism is George Eliot (1819 – 1980), another writer influenced by Comte and positivism. In the January 1851 number of *Westminster Review*, she praised positivist science for offering "the only hope of extending Man's knowledge and happiness" (Larkin 57). A major representative of realism, George Eliot speculated on art and life in terms of social observation, wishing someone to

> devote himself to studying the natural history of our social classes, (...) the degree in which they are influenced by local conditions, their maxims and habits, the points of view (...) and the degree in which they are influenced by religious doctrines, the interactions of various classes on each other, and what are the tendencies in their position towards disintegration and towards development.

Such a person who would devote to such a task was Eliot herself, in particular in her masterpiece *Middlemarch*. As revealed in her novels and expressed in her critical writing, George Eliot preached reason and scientific coherence in the literary treatment of various topics. She rejects idealism, the melodramatic and the sensational, including the public's demand for a happy ending, as expressed in her 1856 article *Silly Novels by Lady Novelists*, even at the cost of popularity. Her novels prove it, having no satisfaction given to readers, which is also the reason for their being considered "English novels written for grown-up people", as Virginia Woolf puts it. George Eliot provided critical speculation on literature insisting on the necessity to combine in one literary discourse the faithfulness to fact and reality with the detailed rendering of individual psychological states. The failure to do so means the lack of artistic truthfulness or artistic incompleteness, which she discusses in relation to Dickens's failure, in her opinion, to link character delineation to social concern: Dickens is "one great novelist who is gifted with the utmost power of rendering the external traits of our town population; and if he could give us their psychological character (...) with the same truth as their idiom and manners, his books would be the greatest contribution Art has ever made to the awakening of social sympathies."

In France, influenced by Comte, Honore de Balzac (1799 – 1850), in the famous Preface to the *La Comedie humaine* (1842), claims that the reform of the society is useless if the spirit of its citizens is not formed and if they do not acquire new understandings that correspond to the scientific progress. Hence the special requirements for the novelist as put forward by Balzac: "the writer must not be only an artist, but also a scientist and a philosopher"; "art is not a neutral reflection of reality" but necessitates "a philosophical attitude on the part of the writer, an attitude which is able to organize the isolated fragments (...) into a coherent system" (Grigorescu and Alexandrescu 15). Balzac believed in the existence of social mysteries, and the writer, omniscient and doctor in social sciences, has the task to detect and explain them by his literary work. The literary practice is impossible outside history, and the novelist is, as Balzac himself claims to be, a "secretary" of the most important historian which is society itself. As a secretary, the novelist, with his intelligence and power of observation, writes the history of the society. Revelatory in this respect is Balzac's claim from the Preface:

By drawing up an inventory of vices and virtues, by collecting the chief facts of the passions, by depicting characters, by choosing the principal incidents of social life, by composing types out of a combination of homogeneous characteristics, I might perhaps succeed in writing the history which so many historians have neglected: that of Manners.

The novelist is an artist, philosopher, historian, moralist, and in all these hypostases the writer should grasp the reason of social "movement", the relation between cause and effect, and the many particular circumstances of real life. Balzac, however, is conscious of the differences between reality and imaginative writing, and therefore asks for the circumstances of real life to be transfigured into an ideal sphere, and for characters to acquire features that resemble those of real people, but to be, at the same time, original.

Concerning the relationship between morality and literature, Gustave Flaubert (1821 – 1880) seems to have a different opinion from Balzac. Like Balzac, Flaubert did not produce any dogmatic treaties on the realistic direction of novel, but made the ideas from his large correspondence into a veritable *ars poetica* on the nature of fictional work. Unlike Balzac, the author of *Madame Bovary* (1857) opposed the doctrinarian beliefs and "the tendency of the period to transform literature into a means of affirmation and dissemination of moral values", but "accepts the ethical essence of literature" (Grigorescu and Alexandrescu 23). Flaubert considers that the "moral ideal" in art, like in nature, is reached by its elevation and becomes useful by its sublime; also, the moral ideal "should be transmitted through a particular intermediary factor: the literary style" (Grigorescu and Alexandrescu 24). Like Balzac, Flaubert considers art to be close to science and accepts the scientific principle in rendering the truth in literature, but, unlike Balzac, Flaubert equalizes this principle to "the objective precision of observation and to the departure from involvement in social life, whereas Balzac thought that the writer is obliged to involve in it" (Grigorescu and Alexandrescu 25). Flaubert disregards the prefigured structure of a novel and insists on the arbitrariness of the plot and on the flexibility of the chain of events provided by the imaginative flight:

> The story, the plot of the novel is of no interest to me. When I write a novel I am at rendering a colour, a shade (...) In *Madame Bovary*, all I wanted to do was to render a grey colour, the mouldy colour of a wood-louse's existence. The story of the novel mattered so little to me that a few days before starting on it I still had in mind a very different Madame Bovary from the one I created: the setting and the overall tone were the same, but she was to have been a chaste and devout old maid. And then I realised that she would have been an impossible character.

Concerning the relationship between reality and literature, Stendhal (Marie-Henri Beyle, 1783 – 1842) also seems to have a different opinion from Balzac. The place of Stendhal in literary history between romanticism and realism is still a matter of critical debate, but one can hardly go against such critical voices as that of Erich Auerbach who, in his celebrated *Mimesis*, claims that Stendhal enters into his "contemporary reality" much more than many of his contemporaries and considers him to be the first in the line of realism: "Insofar as the serious realism of modern times cannot represent man otherwise than as embedded in a total reality, political, social, and economic, which is concrete and constantly evolving – as is the case today of any novel or film – Stendhal is its founder" (Auerbach 408).

Stendhal is acclaimed as a practitioner of realism and *Le Rouge et le Noir* (1830) as the first realist novel, but critics find elements related to other trends, such as romantic, sentimental, psychological, historical, and others. The first paragraph of the novel is a romantic passage on idealised and nostalgically viewed nature and countryside. Julien Sorel is a "romantic character", and, indeed, "his plebeian pride and hatred of those in power, his ardent temperament and calculating intelligence, his ambition, and his hypocrisy forced upon him by circumstances" (Ginzburg 230) are among the features of a romantic hero. Yet this romantic hero is included in a strictly normative historical, social, and moral system, since Stendhal displays verisimilitude by showing realistic and convincing development of his character who is grounded in actual reality and who reveals himself as a typical representative of his time.

Stendhal is considered to mark the transition from romanticism to realism, or as representing an early stage of realism. The term "subjective realism" used to name Stendhal's fictional style, along with those of "mirror-novel" and the novel of social concern. On the theoretical level, as a writer-critic, Stendhal reveals his alliance to realism at least in two ways. First, he is praised for his theory of writing developed in *Le Rouge et le Noir* by the very famous description of a mirror and which is considered to be a moment of reflection of realism itself:

> a novel is a mirror, taking a walk down a big road. Sometimes you'll see nothing but blue skies; sometimes you'll see the muck in the mud piles along the road.

And you'll accuse the man carrying the mirror in his basket of being immoral! His mirror reflects muck, so you'll accuse the mirror, too! Why not also accuse the highway where the mud is piled, or, more strongly still, the street inspector who leaves water wallowing in the roads, so the mud piles can come into being.

This theory fits Stendhal's view of the world as theatre and implies "the necessary presence of the author and the presumed one of the reader, attempting to reconcile the principles of lyrical objectivity and subjectivity" (Sirbu 147). Second is Stendhal's "moment of crystallization", or the law of passionate love, from *De L'amour* ("On Love", 1822), which shows how science plays an important role in the rise of realism. During the experience of falling in love, the love object is "crystallized" in the mind in a process similar to a trip from Bologna to Rome. The trip is a transformative process that involves four steps of admiration, acknowledgement, hope, and delight. At the end of it, the hero is supposed to work out his destiny. Allen Thiher describes it as a "metaphorical manoeuvre" which represents "a unique attempt on Stendhal's part to create explicitly a science of the psyche, though he did incorporate the "laws" he discovered into the construction of fictions like *Le Rouge et le noir* ("The Red and the Black") or Lucien Leuwen" (Thiher 32). Stendhal's "moment of crystallization" is demonstrated in his novel, in which the romantic and ambitious Julien Sorel is involved in relationships with Mathilde de la Mole and Madame de Rênal, but the conflict in him between ambition and love makes the awareness of true values emerge late in his consciousness, and he understands eventually that Madame de Rênal is his true love. In other words, she is the real love object being in the process of crystallization in his mind, as Stendhal describes it in *De L'amour*.

Likewise, the famous essay *Experimental Novel* (1879), written by Emile Zola (1840 – 1902), shows the influence on literature exerted by the contemporary naturalistic philosophy and science. In this work, Zola explains the literary categories that he has come to develop as naturalism. Charles Darwin's theory of evolution, in particular, prompts the idea that man is a substance of chemical action and reaction and thus subject to biological heritage, and the product of the socio-economic milieu, whose institutions are in a process of evolution similar to nature itself. Zola and naturalism consider the human being to be influenced by heredity, social background, and history. Apart from the social determinism, naturalism includes in its aesthetics the determinism of the French physiologist Claude Bernard (1813 – 1878), another follower of Darwin, according to which every effect has a cause, and the determinism of Taine, according to which the writer is determined by the three factors of race, milieu, and the particular circumstances of the epoch. Naturalism refuses "the transfiguration and organization of the material according to some formal criteria" (Ceuca 21). To be an experimental novelist is then for Zola, to adopt and adapt to the newly developed scientific methods in the literary creative process as to achieve "the study of separate facts, the anatomy of special cases, the collecting, classifying, and ticketing, of human data". Zola himself claimed to have applied to his novels the experimental scientific method from the experimental medicine developed by Claude Bernard who explains the differences which exist between the sciences of observation and the sciences of experiment. He [Bernard] concludes, finally, that experiment is but provoked observation. All experimental reasoning is based on doubt, for the experimentalist should have no preconceived idea, in the face of nature, and should always retain his liberty of thought. He simply accepts the phenomena which are produced, when they are produced.

Like a doctor studying the organism, the novelist is a scientist not only observing but also objectively experimenting to better understand the human intellectual and emotional life and the social background which together with the biological heritage shape the character. The novelist then, writes in a realist manner – developing his plot as a chain of events linked by the cause and effect relationship – to reveal the destiny, or rather the struggle, of a human being presented with a certain biological heritage against specific socio-economic conditions. Apart from Darwin and Bernard, Anca Sirbu enumerates the theory of Geoffroy Saint-Hilaire and those of Prosper Lucas and Charles Letourneau as representing an intellectual attitude for those writers who asked science for a method and saw themselves as scientists (Sirbu 192-193). Along with the relationship being established in the nineteenth century between literature and science, there was also the growing awareness of literary criticism, especially in the twentieth century, about creative writing and science, "once thought to be two separate and oppositional activities", being in fact two "fruitfully interrelated cultural practices" (O'Gorman 230). In English criticism, one should mention at least Lionel Stevenson's *Darwin Among the Poets* (1932) and Leo Henkin's *Darwinism in the English Novel, 1860-1910* (1940).

Zola, Stendhal, and Balzac are the great theoreticians of realism, its most important writer-critics, but the first theoretician of realism is an obscure writer: Champfleury (Jules-Francois-Felix Husson, 1820 – 1889). His *Le realisme* (1857) became actually the manifesto of the new literary doctrine, though the author himself disapproved of the term "realism", and in many respects regarded the newly emerging movement as undesirable, and the term as equivocal, open to multiple connotations.

Opposite to naturalism and realism, and continuing romantic paradigm, were the principles of aestheticism, Parnassians, symbolism, decadence, impressionism, and the entire spectrum of the late nineteenth-century artistic avant-garde trends. The major emphasis is on the idea that art must be autonomous, which has its starting point in the 1830s with the French writer, painter, and critic Théophile Gautier (1811 – 1872) proclaiming the doctrine of *l'art pour l'art* ("art for art's sake"). Rejecting romantic worship of nature, Gautier, Baudelaire and other French symbolists assert the artistic to be superior to the natural: "Nature is stupid, without consciousness of itself, without thought or passion", declares Gautier, "art is more beautiful, more true, more powerful than nature". Also, according to Gautier, the formal, aesthetic beauty is the very purpose of a work of art, and, as he claims in the Preface to his novel *Mademoiselle de Maupin* (1835), art has no utility: "Nothing is really beautiful unless it is useless, everything useful is ugly, for it expresses a need, and the needs of man are ignoble and disgusting, like his poor nature. The most useful place in a house is lavatory". The view of beauty as an independent value and the doctrine of "art for art's sake" infiltrated into France and the rest of Europe from Kant and his philosophical successors who developed the idea that there is an aesthetic sense by which we appreciate the beautiful – a sense quite independent of our moral judgement, independent of our intellect. If that is true, it follows that the artist works through this special sense, and that it is quite irrelevant to introduce moral or intellectual standards into the appreciation of a work of art. Kant said works of art had "purposefulness without propose", by which he meant that they seemed to have been created to serve some special end; yet they had no clearly defined function like a chair or a machine: rather, they were like a flower. (Highet 444)

With Gautier claiming that art has no utility and Poe theorizing the "poem *per se*" and rejecting "heresy and other critics", the history of criticism encounters the objective theory of art, by whose standards art is autonomous, self-sufficient and serves no other purpose (moral, didactic, political, or propagandist) than the pursuit of beauty, and should accordingly be judged only by aesthetic criteria. These are actually the main principles of Aestheticism, or the "art for art's sake" doctrine, an important movement in the second half of the nineteenth century, dominated in Britain by Walter Pater and Oscar Wilde. The main theoretician of aestheticism in England, Pater actually introduced the ideas of French aestheticism into Victorian England and coined the phrase "art for art's sake" in English. Unlike Matthew Arnold who believed that art had the power to transform the cultural milieu, Pater and Wilde argued that art is self-sufficient and quite useless. Wilde also insisted on the separation between art and morality, holding in *The Critic as Artist* that art and ethics are "absolutely distinct and separate" and rejecting any "ethical sympathy" in the artist. Following Gautier, Wilde proclaims in *The Decay of Lying* nature to be inferior to art: "what Art really reveals to us is Nature's lack of design, her curious crudities, her extraordinary monotony, her absolutely unfinished condition".

Aestheticism developed a theory reflecting the French influence of Symbolism – not of Mallarme and Valery as much as of Gautier and Baudelaire – combined with native ideas, but its roots go back to the romantic doctrine of Kant, Schiller, Coleridge and others. Arthur Symons (1865-1945) is claimed to have encouraged the recognition in Britain of the French symbolist poetry (in *The Symbolist Movement in Literature*, 1899) and to have influenced W. B. Yeats in writing poetry and criticism (namely, the essay *The Symbolism of Poetry*, 1900).

Associated and even confused with symbolism, and having its roots in Poe's poetry and Gothic fiction, is the "decadence" of the *fin de siècle*. Unlike aestheticism being "characterised by the tension between art and life", the decadent artists (Joris-Karl Huysmans, Arthur Rimbaud, Arthur Symons, and others) are characterised "by socio-psychological tensions between the one and the many" (Gagnier 41). Urban and elevated, they are first of all introspective, emphasising the psyche, detaching the individual from society, and thus representing together with symbolism, impressionism, and aestheticism a part of the transition from romanticism to modernism.

It is said that the first ideas of aestheticism date from Gautier's assertion that art is useless, but as a movement it was developed by Charles Baudelaire (1821 – 1867), who was greatly influenced by the critical doctrine of E. A. Poe and influencing in his turn Mallarme, Verlaine, Flaubert, Pater, Wilde, Swinburne, Yeats, Eliot, and many others. Baudelaire is acclaimed to be "the first to portray the modern and decadent artist as someone with an overdeveloped nervous system" and for him "the nerves are motors of creative energy, of gigantism, stridency, multiplication, as well as hyper-sensitive registers of sensation" (Scott 214). Also important is that Baudelaire and symbolism, on the whole, changed the traditional view of poetic language: "language was no longer treated as a natural outcrop of the person but as a material with its own laws and its own peculiar forms of life" (Scott 212).

Acquiring the consciousness of language is also Edgar Allan Poe (1809 – 1849), the most important American writer-critic of the nineteenth century, who, after practicing criticism as a reviewer of books, turned to a more serious critical endeavour in *The Philosophy of Composition* (1846) and other essays. The main source of his criticism is British and European romanticism, namely Coleridge, as to mention just Poe's definition of poetry from the Preface to his 1831 volume – "a poem, in my opinion, is opposed to a work of science by having, for its immediate object, pleasure, not truth" – which is almost a quotation from Coleridge. Like Pater and aestheticism in England, Poe in *The Poetic Principle* (1850) establishes the autonomy of art, speaking about "poem *per se* – this poem which is a poem and nothing more – this poem written solely for the poem's sake". Poe's opinion is "perhaps the first instance on artistic or poetic autonomy by an American writer" and his insistence on artistic autonomy "may have been a call to consider the beauty of a poem regardless of its political, as well as its moral content; given that his notion of beauty was somewhat Platonic; it may also have been an attempt to lift art out of and above the sphere of everyday life and its entanglement in bitter political and social struggles" (Habib 464).

Prefiguring aestheticism, Poe rejects any personal source for the poem, focuses on text in itself, the poem *per se*, and develops critical theories on form and techniques of composition of poetry, the genre which he defines as "The Rhythmical Creation of Beauty", and which is also his main method used, among others, in the creation of *The Raven*, his most celebrated poem. A representative of Romanticism and a follower of Coleridge and the Continental poetic theories, Poe nevertheless would neither adhere to the expressive theory of poetic creation nor believe in Wordsworth's "spontaneous overflow of powerful feelings", since *The Philosophy of Composition* argues for a design and the proceeding "step by step to its [*The Raven*'s] completion with the precision and rigid consequence of a mathematical problem". *The Raven*, claims Poe, is not the product of "accident or intuition", but the result of his intention to write a poem "that should suit at once the popular and the critical taste". The poet aimed at the effect of beauty mingled with melancholy, and the topic that would better combine both and achieve the expected effect is the mourning of the death of a beautiful and beloved woman. Melancholy is "the most legitimate of all the poetical tones" and suggestive of this emotional experience is also a particular word used as a refrain and possessing the sonority of the sound "r" in relation to "o", hence the word "Nevermore". Furthermore, there should be a non-human creature that would repeat this word, making it an element of structural cohesion, and, after thinking of a parrot, the chosen one was raven, indeed a powerful symbol in the poem. In presenting in *The Philosophy of Composition* the ways in which he composed *The Raven*, Poe "not only denies the operation of chance in literary composition – he also severely restricts the element of choice. He claims to have begun with an abstract, impersonal aim which was attained by a series of exclusive artistic decisions, each of which logically and inexorably dictated the next" (Lodge 70).

In his critical work, and in the determent of prose, in particular the realist one, which he considers to be produced by "that evil genius of mere matter-of-fact", Poe places poetry in his hierarchy of literature at the top, as the most important species of composition. Anticipating aestheticism, for Poe, the real meaning of the text is beneath the vivid surface of the work, and since the aim of poetry is "beauty" (whose highest manifestation relies on the tone of "sadness" or "melancholy") and its effect only "pleasure", the text transcends any didactic and moral doctrine. Indeed, as argued by Poe, the most dangerous of the heresies regarding poetry is the "Heresy of the Didactic" since "poetry has nothing to do with either morality or truth, not because these are unimportant but because it is not in the poem that they are best treated" (Regan 23).

It is worth mentioning that Poe developed interesting and influential approaches to prose fiction, considering the structural level of the text. The novel's plot, its narrative construction, everything should be, like in poetry, under authorial control as subject to a pre-established plan of composition. Poe draws both on novel and short fiction; in his essay on Nathaniel Hawthorne, he "sees the novel as a genre devoid of a true unity of impression, while the short story is for him the most artistic prose genre, because the unity of effect on the reader can be calculated and preserved" (Onega and Landa 18).

Also in America and in the nineteenth century emerged a literary and philosophical group that, based on the ideas of Plato, Kant, and Coleridge, developed a doctrine of idealism against the social and religious premises of the contemporary culture. Called "Transcendentalism", this movement found its spokesman in Ralph Waldo Emerson (1803 – 1882) who, in his lecture "The Transcendentalist", the famous essay *Nature* (1836), and other writings, provides original views on American natural environment, but what is more important is that he develops a kind of "philosophy of intuitionism", a type of "Transcendental idealism", by putting forward the idea of the individual spiritual existence "transcending" the physical through personal intuition. As transcendental philosophy "can be seen as a systemic reflection on the interrelation between experience and the self", in his approach Emerson "radically individualizes the problem of experience in that he pulls emotions, moods, and changing personal states of consciousness into the centre of his analysis, and then pursues their inherent problematic" (Putz 50).

In Europe rather than in America, aestheticism established itself as a movement containing both critical theories and artistic practice. The view of aestheticism that art is superior, self-sufficient, and has no use or moral effect, emerged in opposition to the dominance in the second half of the nineteenth century of realism, positivism, the historical and scientific thinking, and "in defiance of the widespread indifference or hostility of the middle-class society of their time to any art that was not useful or did not teach moral values" (Abrams and Harpham 4).

In the literature of Victorian Britain, the views of aestheticism are primarily theoretically developed by Walter Pater and practically thematised in literary work by his disciple Oscar Wilde. The principles of aestheticism help define the reverence for beauty of the Pre-Raphaelites (Dante Gabriel Rossetti, William Morris, Charles

Algernon Swinburne) and their return to medievalism and escapism into art away from the contemporary actual reality, as it is revealed in their poetry, painting and critical thinking, for instance in *The Art of the People* by William Morris, which is influenced by Carlyle. Aestheticism also helps define the concern with the form of the Parnassians (Lionel Johnson, Andrew Lang, Ernest Dowson, Edmund Gosse) and, in the first half of the twentieth century, some thematic and structural aspects of the experimental writings of modernism. Aestheticism asserts that art is self-sufficient, that there is no connection between art and morality, and that art should provide refined sensuous pleasure rather than convey moral or sentimental messages, have a didactic purpose, or be in some other ways useful – these and other principles on art are first of all directed to challenge and undermine the dominance of realism and realist fiction in the epoch.

1.2 The Condition of Fiction: Realism, Realist Novel and Its Alternatives

Victorian Age is a great art and literature producing and consuming period and in this age of print, the novel stands as the dominant literary form. It was created by the new profession of novelists, a group that now included women as well as men; it was printed quickly and inexpensively on the new steam-powered printing presses and distributed efficiently over the kingdom on the new railway system; it was welcomed as a source of moral and social instruction as well as of delight and entertainment by the newly expanded reading public.

For the Victorians, the modern distinction between the literary novel and the popular best-seller had not yet come into existence. The novels of Charlotte Brontë, Charles Dickens, George Eliot, Anthony Trollope, and Thomas Hardy were read not merely by a literary elite, but widely throughout the expanding middle class and, particularly in the case of Dickens, by the working class as well. This wide readership was aided by new methods of presentation and distribution. Early in the century, Dickens pioneered publication in inexpensive separate numbers with *Pickwick Papers*, and the practice was followed throughout the century with, for example, William Makepeace Thackeray's *Vanity Fair* and George Eliot's *Middlemarch*. Then, the novel usually appeared in a three-volume edition, a "three-decker", that readers borrowed from private lending libraries, of which the most famous was Mudie's. Eventually, the three-deckers were made available in less expensive form, cheap editions and railway editions, the equivalent of modern paperbacks, distributed through national chains of booksellers, as well as in more expensive collected editions.

Despite its consumerist aspect, the Victorian novel is undoubtedly a complex, aesthetically valuable literary phenomenon. Like the age itself, the novel expresses its own paradoxical status: there is the same worshipping of independence and of individual self-assertion, the same overwhelming self-confidence, along with the same contradiction between morality and the system, the same belief in institutions, democracy, organized religion, philanthropy, sexual morality, the family and progress.

In terms of literary movement or trend, the contrary to romantic movement is the literary trend called "realism", and most of Victorian fiction is realist, but there is no violent contestation between them, as, for instance, the deep gap between romanticism and neoclassicism. Still, where romanticism champions subjectivity of the individual, the realistic fiction "frequently appears to deal rather in social relationships, the interaction between the individual and society, to the increasing exclusion of the subjectivity of the author" (Belsey 68). Better say, in dealing with the relation between society and self as its main subject, realism takes "the emphasis on self and individualism that characterizes the Romantic period and shows it to be pressured by increasingly powerful ideologies of capitalism" (Shires 61). It is a long-established critical opinion that "realism is not conditioned only by aesthetic circumstances, namely by the anti-romantic reaction; most of literary historians who dealt with this problem agree that realism represents an attitude towards the social world within which it developed" (Grigorescu and Alexandrescu 9). Realism coincided with the expanding industrial capitalism, changing exterior world, invention, experiment, advances in science and technology, and developments in thought. On the cultural level, realism co-existed with the flourishing from within the romantic tradition aestheticism, symbolism, and other avant-garde trends of the second half of the nineteenth century. One may also argue that realism, though a continuation of neoclassical model, is less rational and normative, and that its concerns with psychological issues continue the individualised and personalised character as defined by the romantics. Another example would be the historical concern in literature. In romanticism, the historical romance deals with medieval and other earlier settings, whereas in realistic novels, both history and psychology receive a true-to-life perspective under the representation of the contemporary society.

The "rule" of literary development claims that the emergence of every new trend is conditioned by contemporary factors and that it also simultaneously rejects and continues some previous literary traditions. In this respect, realism is a reaction against romanticism but also has its origins in some of the neoclassical principles. In England, realism is also a direct continuation of the eighteenth-century verisimilar novels of Defoe, Richardson, and Fielding through Jane Austen and Sir Walter Scott. But what in earlier fiction was just an element, though a dominant one, in Victorian prose it became the reason for the existence of a whole new type of novel – the "realist novel" – and gave its name to a whole new trend – "realism" – which to the present has remained highly popular and productive. Like with other terms having general human connotations, the notion of the difference between "realism in life" and "realism in literature" should be present in mind. The former "connotes a way of estimating, evaluating, or assessing a situation; having "an eye for the main chance", making a fair or comprehensive and adequate judgement; but "realistic" is also synonymous with clever, sharp, expedient, all the way to cynical and unscrupulous"; the latter, as an element in literary work but especially as the emerging in the nineteenth century literary trend called "realism", "connotes a way of depicting, describing a situation in a faithful, accurate, "life-like" manner; or richly, abundantly, colourfully; or again mechanically, photographically, imitatively" (Stern 40). Realism is thus, as Frye puts it, the art of verisimilitude, an art of implicit simile, when what is written is like what is known.

The shift from romanticism to realism is the shift from the individual to general human, from subjective to the social, from the human beings as masters of their destiny to a multitude of character types as social units, from the narrow circle of personal existence to the wide social panorama containing many social sectors and character types presented in social interaction. Realism tends to present its characters as being defined by social and economic factors. The key-terms are "determinism", "environment", "heredity". Unlike the realism of the eighteenth-century fiction, the nineteenth-century realism has a greater concern "for material reality as a shaper of Man: a concern which invested the detail of daily existence with an active creative role in the lives of the novelist's main characters, instead of being largely a back-cloth to their activities" (Larkin 2).

But there are also individuals in the realistic novels that escape being so defined because "they are essentially free" and, in this case, "realism suggests that the characters that it presents find the reasons for their actions and decisions inside themselves" (Bertens 6-7). Hans Bertens refers to this view of the subject in the nineteenth century and modern culture as "liberal humanism", meaning a philosophical and/or political set of ideas, in which "the ultimate autonomy and self-sufficiency of the subject are taken for granted" and which states that the humans are free and create themselves on the basis of their individual experiences (Bertens 6).

Responsible for realism, like for many other movements and trends, were the French writers. Realism emerged in the 1830s and, starting with the 1850s, it was already a definite literary trend in European and American literature. The term *le realisme* was firstly used in *Mercure francais du XIXe siècle* (1826), in which it refers to "a point of view or doctrine which states that realism is a copy of nature and reveals to us the literature of truth" (Cuddon 774). The term was first defined negatively and often rejected as undesirable, as by Courbet, Champfleury, and Baudelaire, but it received the deserving esteem with the works of Flaubert, Balzac, Zola, and Maupassant, and with its spreading to other countries of Europe and to America. In Britain and Europe alike, after the death of the romantics, a shift in the cultural background was produced and which manifested itself on the level of artistic concern, techniques, and genre. If the English Romantic Movement was a great period of poetry, in which writers presented a cultural and aesthetic vision of human existence and the world in verse form, the Victorian period was a great age of fiction in English literature. Indeed, the imaginative prose was the dominant literary form and actually the majority of the population was a prose-reader. The English novel in the nineteenth century originated as a literary discourse of the growing middle-class audience and became the logical reading-matter for this social level. The Victorian readership sought and found in contemporary novels instructions for living amid the complexity and change of the actual social background. These guidelines are closely linked to a number of topics of special interest to them, such as family relationships and virtues, religion and morality, social change and reform, and so on. In turn, novelists made sense of their enormous variety of experiences and choices, appealing to their audience with the semblance of real world. The novel, unburdened by tradition, was flexible and adaptable to the portrayal of the multitude of changing situations in Victorian life.

To an era of existential uncertainties and frustrations, commercialism and chaotic industrialism, escapism, especially in poetry, has become a psychological necessity, and realism – especially in prose and as a kind of justification for the conscious reader as escapism – was the actual satisfier of his unconscious needs. Furthermore, realism, as the product of the middle-class art, finds its chief subjects and protagonists in the middle-class life and manners, values and actions, avoiding situations with tragic or mysterious implications, and applying a tone of humour, irony, often satire. Another essential characteristic of the Victorian novel is its concern with character, where most characters are middle-class and most settings, preoccupations, and values are also middle-class, and the general tendency is an acceptance of middle-class ethics and mores. It is for the middle-class character to achieve emotional perfection, and, when praiseworthy acts are performed by lower-class representatives, it is either accidental or curiously and strongly implied to be the result of middle-class conformity. Also, the patronizing notes reserved for lower-class personages made possible exotic grotesque postures, which probably increased the sense of security of the Victorian middle-class audience, while the upper-class protagonists were viewed with a mixture of envy and scorn.

In the Victorian novel, the emphasis is placed on social aspects, and the shift from rendering the inner experience and exploring the psychological issues of the character makes new and interesting thematic perspectives possible. The character's personality is important for the Victorian author, but the character functions within a highly organized and structured society.

Realism emerges in the Victorian cultural background as a means of rendering fidelity to actuality in its representation. It defines a particular literary trend, a literary method and a range of subject matter, and is loosely synonymous with verisimilitude, meaning the concentrated expression of the relation between the literary text and the social, cultural and literary context. More precisely, Tzvetan Todorov's *vraisembable*, or verisimilitude, as the concentrated expression of the relation between the literary text and the social, cultural and literary intertext; also, to remember Paul Valery's affirmation, every work is the work of many things besides the author, and the novel becomes a process of integration, usually unconscious, of some alien discourses.

In this respect, every work is the work of many things besides the author, and the novel becomes a process of integration, usually unconscious, of some alien discourses. Realism also implies a synchronic representation of the contemporary to its practitioners' everyday life, whereas verisimilitude may focus on other spatial and temporal realities, as in Walter Scott's historical novel. Realism has its origins in the major contemporary developments in thought and changes on social level (technological inventions, scientific discoveries, social and philosophical trends) as effects of Industrialization. In strict literary terms, realism rejects romanticism and is a continuation of certain neoclassical principles.

The most commonly referred to characteristics of the realist novel include the following:

(1) in a realist novel, the major concern is the contemporary to the writer realities of social background (social concern) and human existence (individual experience), both aspects attentively observed, faithfully represented in the text, as well as in a simple and direct mode of narration with the highest possible degree of impartiality on the part of the writer;

(2) the human condition is always reflected in relation to the social background in a low-mimetic perspective (Thackeray, Dickens) or high-mimetic (George Eliot);

(3) the relationship between individual experience and social background is presented and analysed in relation to the principle of determinism (or cause and effect), meaning the effects and influences of the society on the individual subject;

(4) the representation of the relationship between individual condition and social background excludes supernatural, fantastic, idealistic, and non-real elements, that is, social background and human existence should be true to life and should reflect semblance to reality;

(5) the realist novel is reader-oriented, and the language is plain but emphatic, in order to make the message accessible to the reader;

(6) as reader-oriented, the realist novel often contains a moral lesson, and the reader finds instructions for living, learns ethical values, such as virtue, as well as the proper aspects of social behaviour, family relations, and so on;

(7) the narrative organization of a realist novel reveals its linear narration, omniscient pointy of view, a complex sequence of events, a great range of characters (flat, round, static, or dynamic) most of whom, usually except the protagonist, represents social and moral typologies.

These characteristics are common to realist works, in general, but they receive different thematic perspectives, as in the following novels:

David Copperfield	*Great Expectations*	*Jane Eyre*
The concern is with the individual rather than milieu, as the title suggests, although society receives a panoramic representation, a complex picture.	The social background is a concern stronger than individual existence, and is clearer and more concisely rendered.	The balance between the social concern and the concern with individual experience; for instance, Jane leaves Rochester as being determined by both social (according to Victorian ethics, it is immoral to be a mistress) and individual (the refusal to be inferior in a father-daughter-like relationship) standards; also, the female personality struggles to accomplish in a male-dominated world.
A romantic perspective in which human personality is highly emphasised and the character is a master of his destiny, independent, and able to fulfil personally in spite of all social interaction and determinism.	The character is highly individualised but reveals strong bonds with the background; the character is dependent on his milieu; he is subject to social determinism and as such subject to inner and outer change.	The character is highly individualised and reveals strong bonds with the milieu; the female character is dependent on society and subject to determinism. As such, the character is subject to inner and outer change, but also rebellious and self-confident.
The determinism of the milieu is strong but not successful; there is no real social influence or effect on the development of personality. Hence is the success of the	Social determinism is strong and successful; society influences and affects in a negative way the development of personality, and hence is the failure of the character	Social determinism is strong and in most cases successful, but the character manages to accomplish and impose successfully her personality in a male-dominated society.

character formation.	formation.	
Exclusion of the supernatural and fantastic elements, but exaggeration with the melodramatic, sentimental and idealistic tones, as well as the individual traits of the characters.	Exclusion of the supernatural and fantastic elements, as well as of the melodramatic, sentimental and idealistic tones.	The intrusion of romantic elements in the narrative, in particular gothic, and the exaggeration of the individual traits of characters (such as the cruelty of Jane's aunt, or teacher Temple as the feminist ideal of a fully independent female personality).
The moral lesson regards the importance of character to follow moral values and inner drives which, if properly assumed and kept unchanged, represent the source of accomplishment.	The moral lesson refers to the necessity to follow ethical principles which, if changed or eradicated by the effects of social determinism, lead to the failure of formation.	The moral lesson regards the importance of the adherence to moral values and inner stimuli which, if fought for and imposed on others, represent the source of personal accomplishment and acquirement of a social status.
The language is with sentimental and emotional overtones; words are chosen and sentences are developed to impress, stimulate pity, and express a high degree of subjectivism.	Plain and emphatic language with words and sentences linked to realistic reasoning.	Plain and emphatic language with words and sentences that hide the expression of emotions by an analytical reasoning.
Autodiegetic narrator, omniscient point of view, melodramatic tone, linear narration but disorganized due to a great number of events and characters, almost all of them being flat, except David (round), and all of them static, including David.	Autodiegetic narrator, omniscient point of view, rational tone, linear narration, concise and well structured, fewer events and fewer characters, all of them round, including Pip, and static, except Pip (dynamic).	Autodiegetic narrator, omniscient point of view, rational tone, linear narration, concise and well organized in distinct narrative units, fewer events and fewer characters, all of them round, including Jane, and static, except Jane (dynamic).

These three novels are also united by the common theme of character formation. The formation of personality is the main thematic perspective in a Bildungsroman, and to achieve character formation means to work out one's destiny, to fulfil expectations, and to accomplish as an individual. Produced in the age of realism yet also discussing the issue of the spiritual and moral progress, the novel of formation focuses mainly on the growth and development of the protagonist within the context of a clearly defined milieu. Thus, the final formation and initiation imply a search for a meaningful existence in society, including social integration and professional and financial success.

In England, in particular, the Bildungsroman became one of the most favourite literary models for Victorian realists, because its fictional pattern, consisting of the literary treatment of the process of development and formation of a character in relation to society, offers the necessary extension and complexity to the literary concern with individual experience and social background. In the context of realism, as Bildungsromane, these three novels differ in the treatment of the theme of character formation and the emerging ideas in relation to this theme:

David Copperfield	*Great Expectations*	*Jane Eyre*
The development of personality in relation to milieu, where the formation of personality is a success on personal, professional, and social level in spite of social determinism.	The development of personality in relation to milieu, where the formation of personality is a failure on personal, professional, and social level as the result of obstructing social determinism.	The development of a female personality in relation to the social background, where the formation of personality is a success on personal and social level in spite of social determinism.

Apart from these three novels, *Pendennis, The Ordeal of Richard Feverel, Wuthering Heights, The Mill on the Floss* are other important Victorian Bildungsromane. But the main concern of realism – the relationship between individual subject and social background – was treated through other modalities as well, such as the sociological perspective in George Eliot's *Middlemarch*. Moreover, unlike the realist novels of Thackeray, Dickens or Charlotte Brontë, in this novel the characters are no longer social or moral types, but complex individuals, the author revealing important psychological and emotional insights into character, whereas the background (provincial town of Middlemarch), although receives a complex, panoramic, and detailed presentation, is static and conventional, allowing no change or challenge of its established conventions. In the novel, the relationship between the character and milieu is a complex experience which is studied in all its diversity and according to the three narrative directions corresponding to the experiences of the main characters:

Character	Background	Relationship	Outcome
Dorothy (and Ladislaw)	Middlemarch	Social rebelliousness	Escapism (to London)
Lydgate	Middlemarch	Social determinism	Compromise (becomes a fashionable doctor in London)
Fred (with Mary)	Middlemarch	Social conformism	Integration (in Middlemarch)

Apart from rejecting romanticism, its most important "enemy", where romantic writers transcend the immediate to find the ideal, realism opposes idealism and nominalism, but asserting that only ideas are "real", it seems idealistic; when the ideas are only names, as in the case of nominalism, they confusingly may be regarded as realistic. Realism also opposes naturalism and, where naturalists take the actual or superficial to find the scientific laws that control human actions, realists "centre their attention to a remarkable degree on the immediate, the here and now, the specific action, and the verifiable consequence" (Holman and Harmon 392). Realists move toward a pragmatic theory of art, because, on the one hand, they seek to find a relativistic truth associated with consequences and verifiable by experience, and, on the other hand, they are interested in the effect of their work on the audience (this aspect is revealed, for instance, by the narrator's omniscient point of view). Realist writers also tend toward a mimetic theory of art, for the materials they select to describe (common, everyday, usual) are imitated and concentrate mainly on rendering the closest correspondence between the representation and the subject.

Victorian fiction, as the embodiment of various aspects of realism, follows the traditional patterns of novel writing, concerning itself mostly with ethical issues (French realism is more scientific and speculative, while Russian is religious and mysterious), the necessity of selecting and presenting these issues being accurately implied. In this respect, realism requires, besides the aspects of the milieu and the characters easily recognizable in real life, the fidelity on the level of technique of the narrative discourse.

The human existence and the existence of the environment, as perceived by realism, lack symmetry and the coherence required by a narrative discourse; fiction, truthfully reflecting existence or life as it is, must avoid symmetry and coherence. Then, in Dickens's case, for instance, the failure to provide any unity or symmetry to his literary discourse comes from his truthful representation of reality, rather than from his intellectual weakness, making him more realistic than the Brontë sisters, whose fiction reveals a strong romantic impulse in the nineteenth-century literary background.

Realist writers have a common point in praising the individual and valuing the characterization as the centre of the novel, but, while Thackeray and Eliot render in their fiction socially representative types, others, like the Brontë sisters, stress on the inner existence of the protagonists and their spiritual universe, often concerning themselves with psychological issues and expressing special insights into personal consciousness. In other words, Dickens, Thackeray and especially George Eliot are linked to the concept of correspondence, which implies the fact that the external world can be understood by scientific research, documentation and definition, requiring a referential language and an objective point of view, and these writers are considered more realist than others. Charlotte and Emily Brontë link their narratives to the principle of coherence, which suggests that the external world is knowable by insight and intuitive perception, requiring a subjective language and point of view, which means that their realist worldview is mingled with romanticism. However, given the mixture of realistic and romantic elements in the fiction of all these writers, as well as the inter-penetration of languages and viewpoints, it is difficult to draw absolute divisions. One can just suggest that some novels are more realist than others in the writers' attempt to picture life with fidelity, without the idealization of things, neither rendering them the way they are not nor presenting them as transcendental, fantastic, unreal, fanciful, improbable, or as imaginative flights, invented dream worlds, and other antitheses of realism.

In Victorian England, the dominant genre was prose fiction and its dominant type was the realist novel. True followers of Richardson and Fielding are Thackeray, Dickens, Eliot, and other exponents of realism, and, "although often extremely able story-tellers", "it is evident that it is not to the story that they attach most importance, but to the social, the economic, the political lesson which is to be delivered from it" (Beach 55). Generally, the Victorian narrator expresses a complex or mixed system of possible points of view and represents a narrative voice talking not to himself/herself or nobody, but addressing an audience, ready to control it as he/she often controls the character, and to impose his/her own system of values. It seems that Dostoyevsky is the first nineteenth-century writer who attempted to withdraw from the narrative discourse, introducing in novels dialogue and the polyphonic construction, and perhaps George Eliot does this in *Middlemarch*.

In general, since "Victorian literary discourse intersects with many other important cultural discourses of the period, most prominently religion, science, and political economy", there are these and other discourses that divide the Victorian novel into sub-genres, which come close to or depart from realism, "such as the historical novel, the domestic novel, the silver fork novel, the detective novel, the industrial novel, and the science fiction novel" (Shires 68). To these sub-genres, one should add the novel of formation, or the Bildungsroman, a very important type of Victorian novel.

Like on the Continent, in British literature there are, however, stronger and more important alternatives to realism and realistic fiction, which react against the social concern, moral outlook, and consideration of characters as determined by the milieu and as social or moral types. Among them, the emphasis on art in itself in aestheticism (Walter Pater, Oscar Wilde, Pre-Raphaelite Brotherhood) and symbolism (influence on Pre-Raphaelite poetry and later on Yeats) in literature, impressionism in painting, as well as in Britain rather strong post-romantic (emotional determinism replacing the social one in Emily Brontë's Gothic *Wuthering Heights* and the individualism and escapism of Victorian poetry in general) and colonial, also called neo-romantic (Stevenson, Kipling and later Conrad) trends. Harold Bloom and other critics consider Victorian poets to be representatives of the romantic movement in their fourth and fifth generations. Indeed, a Victorian poem such as *Ulysses* by Tennyson displays in its form as dramatic monologue some strong romantic elements, such as the theme of escapism and the concern with individual experience of a romantic persona who is solitary, alienated, superior, egocentric, and rebellious. Another example can be *Wuthering Heights* which, by its uncommon concentric narrative organization, also expresses a number of romantic elements, such as the concern with individual emotional experience rather than with the social, characters are emotional rather than social or moral types, and inter-human determinism rather than that of the milieu, alongside Gothic elements which make it one of the most famous Gothic novels in English literature.

From the aftermath of romanticism to the present, there has been a continuous return to the themes and values of romanticism, including "subjectivity, personal vision, myth – and the pursuit of remote of exotic subjects in mythology, history, literature, and art", as during the Second World War and the post-war period in which the "New Romanticism" was a state of mind that "aspired to escape from drab or grim reality into a world of the imagination, as opposed to the complementary impulse to render that reality truthfully in writing" (Bergonzi 63), and which manifested mainly in poetry and painting.

The major attack on realism would come in the first half of the twentieth century by the modernist experimental fiction of Proust, Mann, Joyce, Woolf, and others. Their novels are called by Roland Barthes in *S/Z* (1970) as "writerly" (*scriptible*), in which "the reader [is] no longer a consumer, but a producer of the text" (Barthes 4), in opposition to the "readerly" (*lisible*) text, which is classic or realistic work, "an art of Replete Literature: literature that is replete" (Barthes 5). The main antecedent of the "writerly texts" in English literature is Laurence Sterne's anti-novel *The Life and Opinions of Tristram Shandy, Gentleman* (1760). Like Sterne, amid the rising realist tradition, and Joyce and Woolf, surrounded by realists, the Victorian Oscar Wilde, Emily Brontë, and to a certain extent Thomas Hardy "threatened to break up the stable synthesis of the realistic novel" (Lodge 7). The history of the novel shows that its development relies on the attempts to break the laws, to evade the tradition, to change and innovate the fictional discourse, and to search for new thematic concerns and means of literary expression. Hence is the claim that if the realist work is actually the "novel", and the novel is less a genre than an anti-genre, then the history of the novel is the history of anti-novels. The novel in its development attempting to break the conventions of fiction and to renew its discourse has nowadays acquired a cultural self-consciousness by which novelists explore a theory of fiction through the practice of writing fiction. The fiction has thus become "metafiction", which is a kind of fictional writing that "self-consciously and systematically draws attention to its status as an artefact in order to pose questions about the relationship between fiction and reality", and in offering a "critique of their own methods of construction, such writings not only examine the fundamental structures of narrative fiction, they also explore the possible fictionality of the world outside the literary fictional text" (Waugh 2). Against the traditional realist view that language only passively reflects a meaningful universe, the "metafictional" writers see it as an independent system generating its own meanings. Hence the complexity of literary expression reflected in the theoretical diversity of the "metafictional" approach.

Even within the nineteenth-century realist tradition, seemingly highly normative and conventional, realism is not regarded as a wholly unified trend, especially concerning the issue of the relation of individual to society. Realism is often divided into a low-mimetic perspective (Thackeray, Dickens) and a high-mimetic one (George Eliot, Mrs Gaskell, Trollope). Also, "High Realism" and the novel of "pure realism" co-exist with realist novels having romantic elements, or novels as romances, novels of domestic realism, and even the sensation novels. There is a distinction made between two realist Bildungsromane, *David Copperfield* and *Pendennis*, already noticed at the moment of their publication by David Mason who asks, "Why is Mr. Dickens, on the whole, genial, kindly, and Romantic, and Mr. Thackeray, on the whole, caustic, shrewd, and satirical in his fictions?" (as cited in Davis 301-302). There is also a clear contrast between the realist works of one writer: *David Copperfield* shows a maximalist young writer who romantically believes in the power of the individual to shape the future in spite of all determinism, whereas *Great Expectations* reveals a mature, realist author understanding the impossibility of escaping the influences of the milieu. On the more general level, one may speak about "the less realistic generation of Dickens, Gogol and Balzac leading on to the more realistic generation of Eliot, Tolstoy and Flaubert, in turn leading on to the hyper-realistic generation of the naturalists" (Harland 81).

1.3 The Condition of Poetry and Drama: Romanticism and Aftermath

In Victorian period, the dominant literary form was novel, then poetry, and to a lesser extent drama. The dramatic work finds its prominence in the works of playwrights such as Edward Bulwer-Lytton, Catherine Gore, Robert Reece, and especially Oscar Wilde and George Bernard Shaw. Victorian drama also made Shakespeare a best-seller, but in matters of its own creativity, it was melodrama, as its most important characteristic and dominant type, though overshadowed by the more prominent literary doctrines of romanticism and later realism, that actually came to dominate the Victorian stage. Moreover, the theatrical melodrama with its tactics and modes emerged into the novel as a means of rendering a highly charged emotion (in the thematisation of criminal conduct, family conflict, bodily torture, and so on) in its social context, as well as a literary, often polemical response to the invasive effects of market culture. Both the melodramatic tactics and romantic attitudes emerged in the fictional discourses of the Victorian Age (as in the novels by Dickens and the Brontë sisters, for example), but, Elaine Hadley reasons in *Melodramatic Tactics: Theatricalized Dissent in England's Marketplace, 1800 – 1885*, although both modes launched critiques of the period's unique style of governance, in which theatricalised displays of state power disguised the economic restructuring of hierarchical England into what is now called a class society, the procedures of these modes were different. Much of the romantic viewpoint facilitated the ongoing fragmentation of the public sphere and its model of social exchange. By contrast, the melodramatic mode resisted the classification of English society and romantic internalisation of the human by insisting on the vitality of traditionally public, social formations, which represented identity in terms of familial and communal relationships. The writers who adopted the melodramatic tactics in their fictional writing also attempted to detect and resist the modern principle of classification. Caroline Norton, for example, in her writings of the 1840s and 1850s, applied the melodramatic mode to the discussion of family relationships, familial sentiment, the principle of classification being now intricately encoded by gender. Another example of the relationship between the melodramatic mode, typical of all instances of social melodrama, and the aesthetic values of the fictional discourse, is provided by Dickens in *Oliver Twist*, where the melodramatic tactics are employed to resist the alienating and classifying effects of The Poor Law Amendment Act of 1843, finally seeking radical change based on reactionary values. But such nostalgic idealism never quite succeeded in abolishing the modern principle of social class and control in the nineteenth century

The condition of Victorian poetry renders its general marginalisation and inadaptability within the new cultural realities of the nineteenth century. Matthew Arnold embarked on an assiduous campaign as a poet and critic "for the nobility of poetry – "the grand style" – in what nonetheless Arnold recognised as the unpoetic age of the democratic realist novel" (Davis 225). The "premature death of the second generation of great Romantic poets – Keats in 1821, Shelley in 1822, Byron in 1824 – only helped to produce such a situation", as it was also helped by the changed literary taste of the Victorians facing "the changed social, industrial, and urban conditions of the later nineteenth century" (Davis 223).The Victorian poetic production, though complex and diverse in its literary implications, was viewed as a marginal literary discourse, an unimportant genre that did not suit the needs of the Victorian audience for realism, as a continuation of the romantic poetry into the third and fourth generations (this opinion belongs to Harold Bloom), and even as a betrayal of the romantic writers' imaginative honesty and autonomy. Indeed, it seems that the poetry of Victorian age began in a vacuum after the death of the romantics, and that the Victorian poets were unable or unwilling to sustain the confidence in the freedom and priority of imagination and in aesthetic autonomy cherished by romantic authors.

Victorian poets were influenced imaginatively and stylistically especially by Keats (Tennyson, Arnold, Hopkins, Morris, Rossetti) and Shelley (Browning, Swinburne, Hardy), and demanded sincere expression in the poetic practice, accompanied by simplicity of utterance and emotional truth. They would prefer indirectness in the expression of the inner self, poets assuming multiple identities within the poetic technique of dramatic monologue (a conscious innovation of the Victorian poets), replacing the concern with subjectivity by a new concern with imaginary situations, the development of a purely imaginative writing as invention or re-creation of situations not real or true, and the concern with other temporal and spatial realities (such as Greek Antiquity, European Middle Age, or Renaissance), which would provide possible alternatives to Victorianism and fundamentally render the major theme of escapism in Victorian poetry, as in Tennyson's *Ulysses* and *The Lotos-Eaters*. As a means of expression linked to escapism, the latter poem displays the psychological state of ataraxy as intermediary between life, awakening, day and death, sleep, night, which is rendered in the poem in close relation to natural objects and phenomena, where life and death are not desirable but a transitory status between them. Sometimes, the Victorian lyrical persona would vividly tend towards death, as in Swinburne. The refuge may also be found in the creative act and in art itself, as in Robert Browning's *Andrea del Sarto*, as well as in the aesthetic and hedonist poetic production of the Pre-Raphaelite Brotherhood.

This perception of the Victorian poetry as marginalised and escapist comes from the social and cultural circumstances and the peculiar condition of the poet during the Victorian age. As Walter Pater made clear in 1889, the "imaginative prose" is "the special art of modern world" because of the chaotic variety and complexity and "the all-pervading naturalism" unpropitious for the restraint proper to verse form. Convinced of their eminence in society and the world, in an age of commercialism and social inequalities and uncertainties unsuitable to poetry, poets saw the essence of their role as one of a disseminator of moral and humanistic values, of truth and wisdom, the bringer of freedom (Tennyson in *The Poet*), with a social and spiritual responsibility (Matthew Arnold stating that "poetry is at bottom a criticism of life"). Many important critical voices, among whom T. S. Eliot, established the critical misfortunes of the Victorian poetry, denouncing it as offering a hypocritical picture of the age, as being moralistic in a dishonest way, and, unwilling to be conscious of the realities which might have challenged the image of a well-ordered, solidly established society, revealing a facile optimism or duplicity, a multiplicity of attitudes, hence a multiplicity of styles, which made the period seem directionless and lacking unity. The latter aspect, for many a regrettable fact, was clearly emphasized by Matthew Arnold in his *Preface* to *Poems* (1853): "The confusion of the present times is great, the multitude of voices counseling different things bewildering, the number of existing works capable of attracting a young writer's attention and of becoming his models, immense".

Victorian poetry is, nevertheless, a major imaginative achievement of the nineteenth-century English literature, extraordinary varied and intense, and, above all, an important predecessor of modernism. Indeed, another distinct feature of Victorian poetry is its being the poetry of transition between classical, romantic poetry and the twentieth-century, modernist poetry with all their literary implications, similarities and differences. The former is generally characterised, on the level of verse technique, by a complex use of figurative language, stylised diction, metaphorisation and ornamentation of the poetic discourse, whereas on the thematic level, meaning apparently requires little effort of comprehension: the "harmonious madness", in the case of Shelley, stands for "poetry", and many other examples can be added. In twentieth-century poetry, the fragmentation of message and the simple, often colloquial use of language usually complicate rather than render the poetic message and meaning explicitly: "And I am dumb to tell the lover's tomb / How at my sheet goes the same crooked worm", as in Dylan Thomas, for example. Victorian poetry constitutes both a continuation of the former mode of writing, as in Tennyson or Arnold, and an opening for the modernist perspectives in the verse making endeavours, as in Elizabeth Barrett's poetry or Robert Browning's experiments with dramatic monologue, language and syntax, and culminating with the strikingly modernist Hopkins's "I caught this morning morning's minion, kingdom of daylight's / dauphin, dapple-dawn-drawn Falcon".

A remarkable, conscious innovation of the Victorian poets is "dramatic monologue"', a lyrical poem in which a single speaker, who is not the poet, utters the entire poem at a dramatic or critical moment in his or her life. The speaker has a listener within the poem, often unidentifiable and silent, but the readers, too, are listeners, and they learn about the speaker's character from what the speaker says. The speakers may reveal unintentionally certain aspects of their personalities, as in Tennyson's *Ulysses* and Browning's *Andrea del Sarto* and *My Last Duchess*, for instance, which reveal a "soul in action" through the speech of a character in a dramatic situation.

The dramatic monologue is actually a new form given to the old tradition of soliloquy, but it must be distinguished from this dramatic practice by its inclusiveness, as it is also to be distinguished from the epistle, the monodrama, the solo, and other kinds of the monologue, all of which involving a single sustained utterance, typically by a character about whom the reader knows something beforehand. The Victorian dramatic monologue and its circumstances surrounding the conversation are made clear by implication; the reader has to grasp the reality of the character and of the situation he or she is involved in from between the lines, thus making possible an insight into the character of the speaker. Most of the successful poems of this category are uttered not by the newly created persons, but especially by historical personages, the favourite historical background for the poems being Renaissance as the age of humanistic individualism, as well as characters from myth, legend, or literature, the poetry becoming a psychological study and a mental analysis as a result of the poet's interest in the spiritual freedom of the human personality, in individual self-assertion. The poets of Victorian age seem to have been fascinated by the possibilities of the duplicitous discourses of the dramatic monologue, as introspective drama, or drama into character, where the speaker is no longer a subject controlling and guiding language at will, but is subjected to language as it speaks over against the speaker. The interest of the Victorian poets in the individual character is motivated by the extremely complex and active external life and thought of the epoch, and the element of lyrical persona helps them to achieve escapism and express emotions and themes not necessarily admitted by the social standards, such as eroticism, irreligious attitudes, and so on.

Robert Browning perfected the form of the dramatic monologue in English poetry, and he is also credited with its creation, though the name was not used by the nineteenth-century masters of the form. Tennyson used the form on occasion, and the twentieth-century poets found it congenial, too, as in the works by Robert Frost and T. S. Eliot; the latter's *The Love Song of J. Alfred Prufrock* is a remarkable example of modernist dramatic monologue fusing meditative poetry and interior monologue.

Among the Victorian poets, there is a particular group that represents a unique movement called the "Pre-Raphaelite Brotherhood", which was founded in 1849 by William Holman Hunt, D. G. Rossetti, John Everett Millais, William Michael Rossetti, James Collinson, Thomas Woolner, F. G. Stephens, William Morris, Charles Swinburne, and Edward Burne, who first met as a group in 1848.

The term "Pre-Raphaelite", which refers to both visual art and literature, is confusing because there were essentially two different and almost opposed movements, the second of which grew out of the first. The term is now widely used to denote a distinctive aspect of decor, design, and style. The term itself originated in relation to the Pre-Raphaelite Brotherhood, an influential group of the mid-nineteenth century *avant-garde* painters associated with John Ruskin, whose praise of the artist as prophet had great effect upon British, American, and European art. Those poets who had some connection with these artists and whose work presumably shared the characteristics of their art include Dante Gabriel Rossetti, Christina Rossetti, George Meredith, William Morris, and Algernon Charles Swinburne. In addition to the formal members of the movement, other artists and writers formed part of a larger Pre-Raphaelite circle, including the painters Ford Madox Brown and Charles Collins, the poet Christina Rossetti, the artist and social critic John Ruskin, the painter-poet William Bell Scott, and the sculptor-poet John Lucas Tupper. Later additions to the Pre-Raphaelite circle are J. W. Inchnold, Edward Burne-Jones, William Morris, and even J. M. Whistler. The second form of Pre-Raphaelitism, which grew out of the first under the direction of D. G. Rossetti, was Aesthetic Pre-Raphaelitism, and it in turn produced the Arts and Crafts Movement, modern functional design, and the Aesthetes and Decadents. Rossetti and his follower Edward Burne-Jones emphasized themes of eroticized medievalism (or medievalized eroticism) and pictorial techniques that produced a moody atmosphere. This form of Pre-Raphaelitism has most relevance to poetry; for although the earlier combination of a realist style with elaborate symbolism appears in a few poems, particularly those of Rossetti, this second stage finally had the most influence upon literature. All the poets associated with Pre-Raphaelitism draw upon the poetic continuum that descends from Spenser through Keats and Tennyson – one that emphasizes lush vowel sounds, sensuous description, and subjective psychological states. Pre-Raphaelitism in poetry had a major influence upon the writers of the Decadence as well as upon Gerard Manley Hopkins and W. B. Yeats, both of whom were also influenced by Ruskin and visual Pre-Raphaelitism.

At the beginning an entirely painters' movement, the Pre-Raphaelitism attempted at revitalizing the arts, or they rather hoped to create an art suitable for the modern age by testing and defying all conventions of art. The Pre-Raphaelites displayed a keen connection to aestheticism and the doctrine of "art for art's sake", as they revealed a reverence for beauty and its independent values, striving, in poetry, to create beautiful musical effects rather than a clear sense, and reviving an extensive use of Classical mythology as a framework for expressing ideas (medievalism, interest in chivalry and romance being themselves an important part of the aesthetic cult). The Pre-

Raphaelites also attempted to withdraw from the materialism and complacency of the later Victorian period. As a painters' movement, they were against the conventionalism of the nineteenth-century academic painting. If the Royal Academy schools taught art students to compose paintings with pyramidal groupings of figures, one major source of light at one side matched by a lesser one on the opposite, and an emphasis on rich shadow and tone at the expense of colour, the Pre-Raphaelites painted with brilliant perversity bright-coloured, evenly lit pictures that appeared almost flat. They saw themselves as rebels against the Victorian life, in general, and their return to the past coloured the rebellious aims of their artistic products with a definite sense of nostalgia.

The members of the Brotherhood rejected and ignored Turner and Constable; they turned to the Italian *quattrocento*, and, rejecting Raphael, intended to continue the tradition of the painters of the early fifteenth century who proceeded him. Though they aimed at fidelity to nature (or "back to nature" expressed in clarity and detailed observation of natural objects) and moral strength (expressed in the rendering of some religious themes or symbolic mystical iconography), they ended in the medieval concept of reality as a symbolic one rather than in nature. Turning medievalists, they insisted on the symbolic meanings of objects, which is an approach proper to medieval art. The subject, in turn, is involved in a process which emphasizes precise, almost photographic representation of even humble objects, particularly those in the immediate foreground, which were traditionally left blurred or in shade, thus violating conventional views of both proper style and subject. In other words, their realism is actually a kind of naturalism, because they cultivated the detail/object in a very artificial way, investing it with significance. Following Ruskin, they attempted to transform the resultant hard-core realism by combining it with typological symbolism, and the Brotherhood produced a magic or symbolic realism, often using devices found in the poetry of Tennyson and Browning.

Believing that the arts were closely allied, the movement encouraged artists and writers to practice each other's art. The movement itself was highly literary, as its periodical *The Gern* (1850) suggests, and, looking for new subjects, which turned to be medieval as well as literary, its most striking paintings were inspired by Shakespeare, Dante, Keats, and Tennyson, but its members would also often turn into colour and line their own poems. The Brotherhood's most important poets are Dante Gabriel Rossetti, William Morris, and Charles Swinburne.

1.4 The Condition of Literary Criticism: The Idea of Literature as a Critical Concern

In the course of development of English literary criticism, the Victorian critical thinking is a criticism of transition, a criticism becoming independent from literary practice, forming its own typology and turning into a scientific, rigorous approach. Harland argues that it was not until "the advent of Naturalism that the claims of Realism were articulated in a theoretically confrontational manner" (Harland 81). In this respect, paralleling the shift of the literary concern from subjectivity to society, and conditioned by the growing influence of history and science over the thinking and practical activities, literary theory moved from the expressive theory of authorship to social and scientific theories of literature. However, the critical scene was much more complex than that: in the field of literary theory and criticism, apart from romantic theory, which remained influential after Romanticism seized to exist as a regular movement from about 1830 onwards, the nineteenth century saw realistic, naturalistic, impressionistic, aesthetic, historical, biographical, sociological, and humanistic criticism, offering an impressive typology that became more diversified in the twentieth century.

Also, a major change took place about the status of the critic that was on the way of becoming professional, since literary criticism started to be produced less by writers than by academics (usually from university chairs for study of literature, like editing of texts and providing scholarly, historical and biographical research) and journalist-critics (of different periodicals, producing informative essays and reviews). At its beginning, the literary article occupied few pages in any number of *Edinburgh Review* (founded 1802) and its rival *Quarterly Review* (1809) which focused primarily on intellectual issues regarding science, politics, economics, exploration, and travel. Gradually literature became a serious topic, and literary criticism an important domain, which was also due to being published in various magazines – *Blackwood's Magazine* (founded 1817), *London Magazine* (1820), *Fraser's Magazine* (1830), *All the Year Round* (1859), and many others – in the form of essay and review and alongside the works of literature. Linked to industrialization, printing technology, circulation and commercial coverage, not only imaginative writing but also criticism was extensively published and by the early 1830s, British periodicals were viewed as a powerful literary engine. The review became an important critical tool next to the more traditional essay, but its value was disputable, for it contained primarily some personal responses to writers and works treated through the lenses of subjectivity. For example, Thomas Babington Macaulay's review of Thomas Moore's biography of Byron, known as *Moore's Life of Lord Byron*, clearly discloses the author-aristocrat's angry retort at Byron's anti-aristocratic, rebellious attitude. "It is always difficult to separate the literary character of a man who lives in our own time from his personal character", says Macaulay, and continues:

> It is peculiarly difficult to make this separation in the case of Lord Byron. For it is scarcely too much to say, that Lord Byron never wrote without some reference, direct or indirect, to himself. The interest excited by the events of his life mingles itself in our minds, and probably in the minds of almost all our readers, with the interest which properly belongs to his works. A generation must pass away before it will be possible to form a fair judgment of his books, considered merely as books.

Macaulay is anxious first of all about Byron's egocentrism, which is critically true, in that all the hypostases of the Byronic hero are textual reflections of the Byron himself: "He [Byron] was himself the beginning, the middle, and the end, of all his own poetry, the hero of every tale, the chief object in every landscape. Harold, Lara, Manfred, and a crowd of other characters, were universally considered merely as loose incognitos of Byron; and there is every reason to believe that he meant them to be so considered."

Expressing subjective criticism were the Victorian writers themselves, which also diminished their status as literary critics. Charles Dickens, the most popular and influential Victorian novelist but a rather weak literary critic, in the Preface to the third edition of *Oliver Twist*, gave a rather pathetic critical account of his aims and topics in writing the novel, partly only justified by that the preface was written as an answer to the accusations of immorality and vulgarity. Defending his position as a writer is another major Victorian novelist, William Thackeray, in the Preface to *The History of Pendennis*, who, like Dickens, is also disconsidered as a critic.

Apart from the reviews and essays in periodicals, the Victorian literary criticism strengthened its status also as a result of the expansion of education and of literature becoming a university discipline. It is interesting that the establishment of English literature as a university course in England was a late phenomenon: it occurred happened at University College London in 1828, whereas at Oxford only in 1893 and at Cambridge in 1911. The reason was, on the one hand, the monopoly of the Church of England over the two universities, Oxford and Cambridge, with their subjects in classics, divinity and mathematics, and, on the other hand, the conservative forces that since the Middle Ages allowed no change in subjects, religion, and gender. The events can be summarised as follows:

The breakthrough came in 1826 when a University College was founded in London with a charter to award degrees to men and women of all religions or none. From 1828 English was offered as a subject for study, and they appointed the first English Professor of English in 1829. However, it was not really as we know it. It was mainly the study of English language, merely using literature as a source of linguistic examples. English literature as such was first taught at King's College, London (another college of what later became London University) beginning in 1831. (Barry 12)

Gradually, literature came to be considered the last standpoint of civilisation and, in particular in Britain, with Matthew Arnold and others, the study of English literature was seen as a means of emancipation, learning, culturalization, social progress, political stability, and even as a kind of substitute for religion. The implementation of English studies in universities culminated with the foundation of the Cambridge English in 1911, which led in its turn to the great 1920s when the academics I. A. Richards, William Empson and F. R. Leavis produced new and truly scientific critical theories and methods, probably the most influential ones in the twentieth-century Anglo-American criticism.

Meanwhile, in the nineteenth century, criticism became a general European practice of literary evaluation. Different critics from all over the Continent representing different literary groups or philosophical theories contributed to the development of literary criticism which became more scientific and theoretical, receiving its methodical and methodological input from the rise in that period of different scientific, philosophical, social and literary movements. Particularly, in

English literary world, the literary movement called "aestheticism" became extremely popular among young avant-garde artists with its pursuing art for art's sake, declaring the uselessness of art, and viewing art as the source of aesthetic hedonism.

These are some of the principal ideas of the main theoretician of aestheticism in England, Walter Horatio Pater (1839 – 1894). Pater was born at Shadwell, in East London, the second son of Dr Richard Globe Pater and Maria Hill Pater. All his life, Pater was a reclusive Oxford scholar, but insubordinate to Victorian standards and assumptions, at the same time a historical relativist, sceptical about all fixed and dogmatic doctrines or theories. He coined the phrase "art for art's sake" in English, introduced the impressionistic methods in criticism and wrote on art, style, beauty, reception, and hedonism. Walter Pater's first essay, on Coleridge's philosophy, was published in 1866, and, a year after, an essay on Winckelmann, both in the *Westminster Review*. Pater's other critical studies include a number of essays, in *The Guardian*, the *Athenaeum*, *Pall Mall Gazette*, and other periodicals, on Leonardo, Botticelli, Michelangelo, and other artists, as well as on Wordsworth, Lamb, and romanticism, in general. His lectures were posthumously published as *Greek Studies*.

Pater's most famous and influential book is *Studies in the History of the Renaissance* (1873). His contribution to English thought and literature also includes a volume of philosophic descriptions of characters carefully set in their environment, entitled *Imaginary Portraits* (1887); *Appreciations, with an Essay on Style* (1889), a collection of writings and an essay on his own theory of composition; a volume of highly stylized college lectures published as *Plato and Platonism* (1893), and designed to introduce the ancient philosopher and clarify his historical position; and *Marius the Epicurean* (1885), his most valuable legacy to imaginative literature, a novel written in the tradition of the Bildungsroman to illustrate through complex and sophisticated sentences the perfection of prose style and the ideal of the aesthetic life.

In his novel, Pater also elaborates on ancient philosophy and religious beliefs and attempts to clarify his own philosophical and aesthetic position. The ancient principles of Platonism and Stoicism and especially of Epicureanism and hedonism are juxtaposed to those of the newly emerging Christianity to form a complex framework for the discussion of aesthetic issues and for identification of a congenial religion and philosophy of existence in an age of uncertainty, change and transition, which Pater regards as resembling his own period. In showing his protagonist's pursuit of a satisfying philosophy, Pater is careful to distinguish between hedonism, which might pass as amoral among the Victorians who read his Conclusion to *Studies in the History of the Renaissance*, and Epicureanism, which advocates pleasure attained through modesty, austerity, serenity, ataraxia and aponia. Epicureanism and hedonism, as well as Platonism and Stoicism, are contrasted to Christianity. Christian faith promises eternal life and offers hope for resurrection. Art and beauty are superior, because they promise nothing that they do not provide; they preserve integrity, because they do not pretend to provide anything else then themselves. Pater's position violates the Victorian religious and moral doctrines, and is even more aggravated by such ideas that, as humans have only "one chance", "without hope of a life after death we can only strive to make our lives on earth as rich in experience as possible". Conceiving that such ideas from the Conclusion might possibly mislead some young men, in particular his Oxford students of aestheticism, Pater omitted the Conclusion from the second edition of *Renaissance*, but reprinted it in later editions with some changes to clarify the original meaning; also, he claims, "I have dealt more fully in *Marius the Epicurean* with the thoughts suggested by it".

Pater's *Studies in the History of the Renaissance* sets the impressionistic criticism as a new trend in art criticism and focuses on the effects of a work of art on the viewer. Here Pater displays at full length his aesthetic hedonism, advocating "a refinement of sensation in pursuit of an ultimate truth in Art and Life and in order that an ecstasy of passionate response might be maintained. In the face of the transience of life, he suggests, the cultivation of the momentary appreciation of the beautiful, and therefore of the "truthful", could serve to fire the spirit" (Sanders 461). Pater's ideal is an aesthetic life based on the pursuit of insight, perception and impression. In the Preface to *Renaissance*, Pater introduces the term "impression" to argue that the key to aesthetic criticism is to "know one's impression as it really is". Impression means "not non-literary sensation, but the very instance of aesthetic representation" (Matz 13). Impression represents the highest form of truth, which "makes it a species of metaphor – a style of figuration that would reproduce the inchoate feelings that Impressionism locates between sensing and thinking", where "impressions bring to consciousness the same kind of truth that metaphor brings to language" (Matz 65).

In this respect, Walter Pater argues that the best impression is that most strongly felt. In order to understand a work of art in all its complexity, the critic should discover the impressions it produces in the receiver and to discriminate between these impressions and the impressions produced by experiencing other works of art:

the function of the aesthetic critic is to distinguish, to analyse, and separate from its adjuncts, the virtue by which a picture, a landscape, a fair personality in life or in a book, produces this special impression of beauty or pleasure, to indicate what the source of that impression is, and under what conditions it is experienced. His end is reached when he has disengaged that virtue, and noted it, as a chemist notes some natural element, for himself and others; and the rule for those who would reach this end is stated with great exactness in the words of a recent critique of Saint-Beuve: De se borner à connaître de près les belles choses, et à s'en nourrir en exquis amateurs, en humanists accomplish.

Studies in the History of the Renaissance is also famous for many phrases and passages of poetic prose, as the one describing Leonardo's *Mona Lisa*, beginning with "she is older than the rocks on which she sits", but the most influential part of the book is the epilogue, Pater speaking here of "the desire of beauty, the love of art for art's sake". The phrase "art for art's sake" was coined by Pater in relation to the general European aesthetic doctrine that art is self-sufficient, could not or should not be in any way useful, and need serve no social, moral, or political purpose. *Studies in the History of the Renaissance* renders the author's conviction that it is in art where the finest sensations are to be found and where the human existence has the possibility of preserving the intense but fleeting moments of experience. The human life is indeed uncertain and fleeting, and, instead of pursuing inaccessible ultimate truths, man should strive to purify his sensations and passing impressions, so that, as Pater puts it in the Conclusion to *Renaissance*, "we may well grasp at any exquisite passion, or any contribution to knowledge that seems by a lifted horizon to set the spirit free for a moment, or any stirring of the senses, strange dyes, strange colours, and curious odours, or work of the artist's hands, or the face of one's friend." The artistic reception is possible when the spirit of the receiver is free from any constraints of tradition or theory, as art itself is autonomous and self-sufficient. Pater promotes what Abrams call the "objective theory" of art by asserting the freedom of artistic reception over normative and prescriptive nature of the "philosophical theories or ideas, as points of view, instruments of criticism", which determine neither the artistic production nor the receiver's understanding, but only "may help us to gather up what might otherwise pass unregarded by us".

The doctrine of "art for art's sake", which dominated the late nineteenth-century avant-garde culture in Europe and England alike, made Pater the leading mastermind of the English aesthetic movement of the 1880s and the most important influence on the works of the aesthetic writers of the closing years of the century. Among them, Oscar Wilde openly proclaimed himself a disciple of Pater and the cult of "art for art's sake", his novel *The Picture of Dorian Gray* explicitly materialising aesthetic doctrines and ideas. Especially close to Pater is Wilde reacting against the ethical artist and rejecting the idea of art to be a moral teacher, stating instead in *The Decay of Lying* (1890) that the "final revelation is that lying, the telling of beautiful untrue things, is the proper aim of Art".

Pater's influence also continued in the literary context of the early twentieth century, namely that of modernism, where his "impressions" and "moments" – "where every moment some form grows perfect in hand or face; some tone on the hills or the sea is choicer than the rest; some mood of passion or insight or intellectual excitement is irresistibly real and attractive to us" – were transformed into the "image" of Ezra Pound and the imagist poets, and into the "epiphany" of James Joyce. Pater and his followers advocated aestheticism, aesthetic hedonism, the aesthetic doctrine of "art for art's sake", and the refinement of sensation in pursuit of an ultimate truth in art and life, defying conventional opinion and the social, moral or political purpose in art. In *Legitimate Criticism of Poetry*, the writer-critic Robert Graves (1895 – 1985) calls the condition when the artist or writer responds by his/her work to some extra-literary demands as "careerism". Careerism was the plague of the nineteenth century, as it is of modern literature, claims Graves. To him a good poem is "one that makes complete sense; and says all it has to say memorably and economically; and has been written for no other than poetic reasons", and, continues Graves, "by "other than poetic reasons" I mean political, philosophical, or theological propaganda, and every sort of careerist writing" (Graves 277).

In Victorian age, Pater's work was revered by Wilde, Swinburne, Rossetti, and all decadent and art-centric writers of the late Victorian period, who developed the cult of beauty, which they considered the basic factor in art, believing that life should copy art. In art and literature, they prompted suggestion not statement, sensuality not morality, and the use of symbols and synaesthetic effects, meaning the correspondence between words, colours and music. Pater states that life needs to be lived intensely, following an ideal of beauty, his work showing a change in his thinking from the abstract idealism of Ruskin to more concrete reflections on beauty. In the Preface to *Renaissance*, Pater rejects the use of abstract terms in critical study, and argues that beauty is not an abstract concept but a concrete one and should be defined by concrete terms.

Walter Pater, the major British aesthete, is the founder of impressionistic criticism (which should be distinguished, as having little in common, from impressionist painting). According to him in *Renaissance*, the real understanding of literature is less a result of the objective judgement than of the critic's individual, based on personal impressions, responses to particular literary works and the critical act would be a beautifully expressed appreciation of the work.

Further developing this view, Wilde considers the objective evaluation of literature as irrelevant and develops in *The Critic as Artist* a type of "creative criticism", which he calls "aesthetic" and which, based on the critic's own personality being added to the original work while reading, would "treat the work of art simply as a starting-point for a new creation". Influenced by Pater, Wilde believes that the critic's personal views and impressions represent the substratum of criticism. Unlike Arnold for whom the critic has a secondary role, for Wilde the critic is an artist, a creator and he insists on this "creative" nature of criticism. Also, while Arnold claims that the critic's responsibility is to see an object as it really is, Wilde claims in *The Critic as Artist* that "the primary aim of the critic is to see the object as in itself it really is not". From the perspective of aestheticism, the literary work is independent and self-sufficient, and from the perspective of aesthetic or creative criticism, the literary work reveals its value if open to multiple interpretations. The true criticism, according to Wilde, must not confine itself to discover the real intention of the artist and accept that as final, because "when the work is finished it has, as it were, an independent life of its own, and may deliver a message for other than that which was put into its lips to say".

Another Victorian critic dealing with art and beauty, and rejecting the dogmatic principles of his period, was John Ruskin (1819 – 1900). Much of his education was given at home, then at Christ Church, Oxford, where he developed confidence in the Bible, stern political views, strong affection for romantic literature, attraction to contemporary landscape painting, and what he claimed to be his main interest: the study of the facts of nature. Ruskin produced a number of Byronesque poems and short stories written for Christmas annuals, but he is mainly known as an art and social critic, the only work of literary criticism being *Fiction, Fair and Soul* (1880). His many essays, lectures, and letters are written on a great number of subjects, revealing an astonishing diversity of concern, including painting, architecture, culture, natural history, travel, geology, war, trade, work, economy, and ethics. In short and "in a sense, everything that Ruskin wrote is an attempt to understand human beings in a complex natural and industrial environment" (Sanders 364). Many of these subjects are among his concerns in his most famous and important work represented by the five volumes of *Modern Painters* (the first appeared in 1834; the second, after seven months' work on its preparation in Italy, appeared in 1846; the third and fourth were published in 1856; and the final volume in 1860). The work expresses, first, Ruskin's conceptions on art, artist, natural beauty and its representation. It also discusses the medieval buildings of Europe before they should be destroyed by neglect and restoration (*Modern Painters II*), the greed as the deadly principle guiding English life (*Modern Painters V*), and challenges the self-centred and scientific spirit of his period, promoting instead the recovery of medieval, heroic and Christian values, and urging to see nature as a source of inspiration. To Ruskin, nature offers "a language of creative discovery – a deeper, more validated, more mysterious, unpredictable, and sacred language, he believed, than any offered by contemporary science, economics, or politics. But the law is that nature can rightly serve human beings only when it makes them feel that they are serving it" (Davis 83-84).

But Ruskin's view is not entirely romantic, not Byron's "The desert, forest, cavern, breaker's foam,/Were unto him companionship; they spake/A mutual language", or Wordsworth's "golden daffodils;/Beside the lake, beneath the tress,/Fluttering and dancing in the breeze,/(...) And then my heart with pleasure fills,/And dances with the daffodils". Ruskin rather rejects the romantic consideration of nature to be the proper place for human emotions, resulting in "illegitimate emotional projection operation falsely upon the objects of perception" – he calls it "pathetic fallacy" – meaning the "unwarranted linguistic tendency in the nineteenth century for the ascription of human feelings to non-human objects in the landscape" (Davis 80).

Ruskin's influence emerges from his critical spirit, often provocative and offensive, and highly demonstrative. Believing in the human potential in art and literature, Ruskin sets for himself the task to open the contemporary Victorian mind to beauty as perceived and represented in earlier times. He believed art should be elevating, and, unlike Pater or Arnold, "because the artist should be concerned with human experience, art for art's sake had no meaning for him. He was against the pursuit of beauty for its own sake since the role of art was to interpret and edify" (Galea 48). Ruskin attempted to awaken the Victorian spirit to both ethical and environmental principles, although by 1880 he became rather sceptical with regard to the success of any social changes.

Though exerting pervasive influence on many of their contemporary writers and, in the first half of the twentieth century, on writers of modernism, Ruskin, Pater, and Wilde were outshined in their own time by the critical voice of Matthew Arnold, a major Victorian poet and critic, and, as a critic, the founder of a new school of criticism called "new humanism", or humanistic, and also referred to as "moral criticism" or "moral humanism".

Arnold's first important critical study was the Preface to the volume of *Poems* of 1853. Here he introduced for the first time the principle that a major concern of criticism must be the work's effects on emotional and moral health of the receiver, in particular, and of the nation, in general. Arnold the critic assumed himself a distinctly prescriptive role, for the "confusion of the present time is great", and a young writer needed both "a hand to guide him through the confusion" and a voice "to prescribe to him the aim he should keep in view".

Arnold's most famous critical study is *The Function of Criticism at the Present Time*, in which he describes the mission of criticism and argues why his own age was unpropitious for the creation of some "master-works" of literature and why he himself turned from poetry to criticism. According to Arnold, poetry is a "criticism of life" and the task of criticism is "to try to know the best that is known and thought in the world and by in its turn making this known, to create a current of true and fresh ideas". In this work, as well as in his later criticism, especially in the essays which became *Culture and Anarchy*, Arnold argues for an idea of culture containing within it the combination of past achievement with fostered progressive improvement. In his work, he also argues for an ideal civilized mind, referring to it as "sweetness and light", which suggests at once openness and insight: the habit of perfection would direct a divided society towards a true and satisfying ideal, a culture of intellectual sweetness and moral light. Against the threat of popular anarchy, he prompts the concept of culture that should contain the sum of both poetry and religion, and should act as a catalyst to the rigid advances of modern social, philosophical, and scientific changes. In *The Study of Poetry*, Arnold extends the discussion on poetry and its social function:

> mankind will discover that we have to turn to poetry to interpret life for us, to console us, to sustain us. Without poetry, our science will appear incomplete; and most of what now passes with us for religion and philosophy will be replaced by poetry. Science, I say, will appear incomplete without it.

Relying on Wordsworth's and Shelley's ideas on poetry and combining them with those of the classics, Arnold, in *The Study of Poetry*, might have exaggerated the role of poetry in his period when conferring to it the place of philosophy, or seeing it as a replacement for religion, or considering it an important part of scientific research, the best source of knowledge for humankind. But it is his view of criticism as one of the most useful activities of mind, which sustains the expansion and appreciation of criticism in the Victorian period. Similar words with great resonance in Victorian England, although spoken at the beginning of the twentieth century, belong to George Stuart Gordon (1881 – 1942), a famous Professor of English Literature at Oxford, who argued in his inaugural lecture for professorship that "England is sick, and (...) English literature must save it. The Churches (as I understand) having failed, and social remedies being slow, English literature has now a triple function: still, I suppose, to delight and instruct us, but also, and above all, to save our souls and heal the State". Likewise, Arnold gives to poetry an "almost sacred function", building his reflections on

> ideas that earlier in the nineteenth century had been formulated by Romantic poets like Percy Bysshe Shelley (1792-1822), who had attributed a special, visionary status to poetry, and on a long tradition, going back to the classics, that likewise gives literature, and especially poetry, special powers. It was only natural, then, for Arnold to put forward poetry as the major embodiment of "culture". (Bertens 2)

Arnold's view of criticism (in *The Function of Criticism at the Present Time*) is both humanistic and moral, according to which criticism is "a disinterested endeavour" whose function is "to learn and propagate the best that is known and thought in the world". He introduced this concept of "disinterestedness" of the critic to reject the subjective and individual response while insisting on objectivity and neutrality of the critic who should "see the object as in itself it really is". Surprisingly, one could see certain affinities here between Arnold and Wilde, although the former is a moralist believing that art or poetry has "profound culture-transforming powers", whereas for Wilde art is quite useless and he insists (in *The Critic as Artist*) that art and ethics are "absolutely distinct and separate":

Like Arnold, Wilde believed that the aesthetic experience took place outside "the practical view of things" (...) both Arnold and Wilde subscribed to the notion of a distinct and separate art-object that stood in a luminous extra-social aesthetic space, a space that guaranteed the work's purity for Arnold and its triviality for Wilde. (Harpham 374-375)

In *The Study of Poetry*, Arnold expands his discussion on criticism, and speaks about "real estimate", the only true type of literary criticism, and "historic estimate" and "personal estimate", both of which are fallacious. The basis for the real criticism is the method called "Touchstone", which is one of Arnold's key critical devices. "If we have tact and can use them [touchstones]" we become critics, and the critics, claims Arnold, must have "always in mind lines and expressions of the great masters, and apply them as a Touchstone to other poetry", meaning that the notion of Touchstone "avoids any definitions of desirable literary qualities, and merely suggests using aspects of the literature of the past as a means of measuring and assessing the literature of today" (Barry 26).

The literary critic, therefore, is asked to be objective, concrete and illuminating in his endeavour to discover the truest values expressed not only in his native literature, but also the universal values expressed in other literatures, in order to introduce them to reader and to encourage creative genius. Here Arnold's *Culture and Anarchy* is revelatory, which shows Victorian critic's understanding of modern literature as essentially comparative rather than national in its range of critical concerns, an idea anticipated by Goethe earlier, who stated in 1828 that "our present active epoch with its increasing communication between nations might soon hope for a world literature".

A similar high estimation of poetry and its consideration as superior to prose and other forms of writing were provided by John Stuart Mill (1806 – 1873). At first under the influence of Jeremy Bentham and his father James Mill, both leaders of Utilitarianism, Mill focused on ethical discussions involving social and economic issues and having also literary implications. In his essay *Coleridge* and especially in *What Is Poetry?*, Mill rejected "the utilitarian idea that the effect of poetry was to form opinions through the subversion of rational judgement, using the art of persuasion", and, by exalting the significance of individual inner life and feelings and by extending "the meaning of poetry to music and the fine arts", Mill argued that "poetry acted upon the emotions and offered interesting objects of contemplation to the sensibilities" (Galea 31). For Wordsworth, poetry is the "spontaneous overflow of powerful feelings"; likewise, for Mill, poetry is the "expression of a feeling" of naturally gifted creator, which supports the view of *poeta nascitur, non fit* ("poets are born, not made"). Mill's most famous work is the essay *On Liberty* (1859), which shows his support for the Reform Bills, advocacy of democracy and individual freedom, and of liberty of citizens and mutual tolerance of the society members.

Another key figure in the development of British literary criticism was Thomas Carlyle (1795 – 1881), who influenced the literary activity of, among others, Charles Dickens, Elizabeth Gaskell, Alfred Tennyson, William Morris, and John Ruskin. Carlyle, sometimes called "the last product of the Scottish Enlightenment" and sometimes as representing the aftermath of romanticism, emerged from within the intellectual background of the *Edinburgh Review*. He is considered in the aftermath of romanticism as a follower of Goethe and Coleridge, demanding imagination and feeling amid Victorian pragmatism and materialism. He is also viewed as a humanist like Matthew Arnold, being concerned in his theories of culture with man as the creator of culture "in epochs of spiritual crisis and moral decline", in that both Carlyle and Arnold "demanded a more spiritual interpretation of life, an awakening to a fuller and richer insight into reality" (Galea 37). But where Arnold attacks the ignorance and narrow-mindedness, Carlyle points to the mechanic, materialistic and possessive features of his age, and unlike Arnold, speaks on a more general level involving history and society besides culture, which he examines from various perspectives. Hence the modern consideration of Carlyle as a social thinker as well, obliging "his contemporaries to face the evident enough contradictions within their civilization and to attempt to make some sense of the disorder around them", and the conflict which "he identified was not simply that of faith and doubt, of tradition and innovation, or of conservatism and reform, but of a gulf between the rich and the poor" (Sanders 334). Carlyle sees the lack of spirituality to be one of the most important problems of the contemporary world; he conceives of literature as a means of recapturing the genuine values. Hence are the "heroic" nature of the art of writing and the "heroism" of the writer. In his *The Hero as Man of Letters*, Carlyle considers the "genuine" man of letters to be the "Hero", and

Hero as Man of Letters will be found discharging a function for us which is ever honourable, ever the highest; and was once well known to be the highest. He is uttering forth, in such way as he has, the inspired soul of him; all that a man, in any case, can do. I say *inspired*; for what we call "originality", "sincerity", "genius", the heroic quality we have no good name for, signifies that. The Hero is he who lives in the inward sphere of things, in the True, Divine and Eternal, which exists always, unseen to most, under the Temporary, Trivial: his being is in that; he declares that abroad, by act or speech as it may be in declaring himself abroad. His life, as we said before, is a piece of the everlasting heart of Nature herself: all men's life is, - but the weak many know not the fact, and are untrue to it, in most times; the strong few are strong, heroic, perennial, because it cannot be hidden from them. The Man of Letters, like every Hero, is there to proclaim this in such sort as he can. Intrinsically it is the same function which the old generations named a man Prophet, Priest, Divinity for doing; which all manner of Heroes, by speech or by act, are sent into the world to do.

All six lectures *On Heroes, Hero-Worship and the Heroic in History* (1841) are also of particular significance, in which Carlyle stresses "that heroism manifested itself in a wide range of human activity and that the "hero", whether king or prophet, poet or philosopher, was a challenger of convention and of sham and a reformer of the defunct and the empty" (Sanders 403).

In Victorian age, Arnold speculates on culture, criticism, and poetry; Pater and Ruskin develop critical theories on art, in general, and, in particular matters, refer rather to painting than literature. Since William Hazlitt, there were no significant theoretical or critical comments on drama, as it was viewed, like poetry, as a marginal literary discourse, a minor genre that did not suit the Victorian audience's need for realism. A remarkable exception in this respect was the great Irish playwright George Bernard Shaw (1856 – 1950), who produced – apart from a great number of plays and five novels serialised in magazines – many critical articles and essays on art. Based on his admiration for Wagner, Ibsen, Bergson, and Nietzsche, the most famous are *The Perfect Wagnerite* (1898) and *The Quintessence of Ibsenism* (1912). The literary criticism by Shaw points to the opposition between Shaw-orator from his prefaces and essays, wishing to persuade and to explain everything endlessly and in detail, including himself, and Shaw-playwright, delighted by his own creation, gifted with a huge creative imagination, a remarkable capacity of living, and a provoking laughter.

The plays were published with long prefaces of dramatic criticism in which Shaw clearly expresses his views as a non-romantic champion of reason. The dramatic conflict is the conflict of thought and belief, not that of neurosis or physical passion. The discussion is the basis of his plays, and his intelligence provides the reader with the idea that mental and moral passion could produce remarkable dramatic material. He believes that war, illness, and frustration diminish the "Life Force", which is a flux of creativity having its roots in the power of human will and which is essential to any progress and the survival of the human race. The concept of the "Life Force" is detectable in many of his plays, such as *Man and Superman*, which is a paradoxical version of the Don Juan story. The concept is somehow similar to Bergson's *élan vital*, but the echo in his works is rather Nietzsche's revision of all values, rejection of Christian morality as morality of the slave, doctrine of power, and affirmation of Superman.

In Victorian period, the dominant literary form was novel, then poetry, and to a lesser extent drama. Matthew Arnold embarked on an assiduous campaign as a poet and critic "for the nobility of poetry – "the grand style" – in what nonetheless Arnold recognized as the unpoetic age of the democratic realist novel" (Davis 225). The "premature death of the second generation of great Romantic poets – Keats in 1821, Shelley in 1822, Byron in 1824 – only helped to produce such a situation", as it was also helped by the changed literary taste of the Victorians facing "the changed social, industrial, and urban conditions of the later nineteenth century" (Davis 223).

Therefore, apart from Arnold, only a small amount of criticism was dedicated to poetry and even in his case the critical discussion takes place in general terms regarding its nature, status, and purpose. An exception is the poet Gerald Manley Hopkins who, paralleling James in the discussion of fiction, examines poetry in its own terms. To be more exact, his own experimental poetry which requires explanations of its technique. Hopkins's innovations of metre and other aspects of the structural level led him to develop in various notes and letters an original terminology of criticism, such as "inscape", "instress", or the "sprung rhythm" in opposition to the traditional "running rhythm". Other critical opinions on poetry belong to Algernon Charles Swinburne, an admirer of Pater and aestheticism, which are expressed in his prefaces, essays, and other studies.

Also, the literary criticism of the period included women writer-critics as well, who juxtaposed the critical concern with literary value or ideological positions to the emerging gender issues:

Of the many women who wrote literary criticism, chiefly for periodicals, the best-known names earned their fame as poets or novelists. Elizabeth Barrett contributed critical essays to R. H. Horne's *A New Spirit of the Age*, an important volume of 1844; Mary Ann Evans (George Eliot) wrote extensively for the *Westminster Review*, Margaret Oliphant was a loyal *Blackwood's* writer, and Mary (Mrs Humphry) Ward reviewed for *The Times*. (Latane 399)

In Europe, in general, the nineteenth century saw an impressive amount of literary theory and criticism dedicated to novel. The main theoreticians "were novelists who reflected on their art and attempted to justify it from either an ideological perspective or from that of literary technique" (Valette 30). Only in France, mention should be made of Chateaubriand's prefaces to *Atala* (1801), Madame de Staël's to *Delphine* (1802), Hugo's to *Notre-Dame de Paris* (1831), Gautier's to *Mademoiselle de Maupin* (1834), Balzac's foreword to *La Comedie humaine* (1842), Zola's *Le Roman experimentale* (1880), and Maupassant's *Etude sur le roman* (1887). It is not a coincidence that Balzac published his Preface to *La Comedie humaine* in 1842, the year in which Comte's *Cours de philosophie positive* appeared. The theoretical ideas of Balzac and other writer-critics, alongside their literary practice, most of which being related to the tradition of realism, were influenced by the principles of positivism and by the new developments in natural sciences and their determinist conceptions:

the precision of analysis, the respect for objective facts, and the practice of observation of phenomena would provide literature with characteristics that Romanticism did not possess. But especially positivism, with its vigour and relationships established between phenomena, would influence deeply the novel [and criticism] of the period. (Grigorescu and Alexandrescu 11)

In England, George Eliot and George Henry Lewes (1817 – 1878) in their essays proved to be among the critics who defended realism as a moral responsibility of the novelist. These critics focused on the thematic level of the novel, emphasising not the work's "plot but its mimetic aim in the depiction and characters and setting", favouring the "novel of character" over adventure novel or romance, privileging the moral intention over the simple copying of nature, and demanding the novel to be "a psycho-social study, one that reveals new truths about human feelings and relationships" (Onega and Landa 17). Hence Lewes's admiration for Jane Austen, expressed in his *The Novels of Jane Austen*, in which Lewes develops the idea of the study of the author's life and lays emphasis on the so-called "domestic realism". Jane Austin may be "not capable of producing a profound agitation in the mind", says Lewes, but her achievement lies in the "economy of art", by which he understands "the easy adaptation of means to ends, with no aid from extraneous or superfluous elements", and that "the only names we can place above Miss Austen, in respect of this economy of art, are Sophocles and Moliere". Likewise, George Eliot advocates the study of the author's life revealing an interest in the psyche and inner impulses that are responsible for human behaviour. In *Leaves from a Note-book*, Eliot develops a theory of authorship and the benefits of writing as a social activity. "The author's capital is his brain-power – power of invention, power of writing", claims Eliot, but his/her excellence relies on being involved in a social activity. To write "prose or verse as a private exercise and satisfaction is not social activity" and, in making critical judgements on authors, that is, in "endeavouring to estimate a remarkable writer who aimed at more than temporary influence, we have first to consider what was his individual contribution to the spiritual wealth of mankind?" and "Did he animate long-known but neglected truths with new vigour, and cast fresh light on their relation to other admitted truths?"

In an age of novel in England, unlike in France (where Zola, Gautier, Balzac and Flaubert were the main writer-critics), the critics focused primarily on author and the humanistic and moral nature of literature, and that there were few methodical attempts at either theory or textual criticism of the novel.

Henry Fielding gave a good start in the eighteenth century, followed by Walter Scott and William Hazlitt in the romantic period, but in the Victorian period, fiction was theoretically neglected, except some reviews of novels in periodicals made by novelists (Scott, George Eliot) or by different reviewers (Lewes, Bagehot, Hutton, Stephen) who wrote on contemporary fiction, especially on Dickens's, Thackeray's, and Eliot's novels. These reviewers, together with some biographers (Morley, Trollope, Gosse), maintained a minimal theoretical interest in the novel. Following the eighteenth-century novel-criticism with its concern with social and especially moral function of art, the nineteenth-century critics focus mainly on the thematic level. They are interested in the ways in which the fictional content makes use of realism to teach right values and conduct and to achieve moral improvement, as, for instance, David Masson in *British Novelists and Their Styles* (1859) and George Henry Lewes in *Principles of Success in Literature* (1865). Earlier, in his Preface to the 1839 edition of *Oliver Twist*, Dickens "wrote that vice and virtue are inextricably mixed in contemporary fiction and one can hardly tell them apart: they sound like reality. But he felt he had to introduce some moral principles in his novels to separate good from evil and even to give some hope to the moral reader" (Mindra 69).

A more important critical voice belongs to George Saintsbury (1845 – 1933), a leading figure of academic criticism, Professor of Rhetoric and English Literature at the University of Edinburgh, whose historical approach from *A History of Nineteenth Century Literature, 1780-1895* (1896), *A Short History of English Literature* (1898), and *The English Novel* (1913) includes accounts of the concepts of "tradition" and "canon", and loose evaluations of the characteristics of some Victorian novelists. His "approach to Victorian novel was to defuse its political or social force", and he neither "considered that Victorian novels intervened in contemporary debates in and about society" nor dwelt on "specific novels, and barely quoted from them (the New Criticism with its emphasis on close textual reading eclipsed Saintsbury's method in the mid-century)" (O'Gorman 22). "The Book of History is the Bible of Irony" is one of his most famous quotes. Together with Shakespeare critic Andrew Cecil Bradley (1851 – 1935), Saintsbury revealed interest in the history of literature and began the modern critical history. They produced monographs on canonical writers, contemporary or from earlier British and Continental literature, tracing their lives and literary activity, and thus combining the historical commentary with biography, and the biographical commentary with descriptive criticism. In their efforts, unlike other critics, "Bradley and Saintsbury did not write across a range of non-literary subjects; they confined their efforts instead to what Leslie Stephen dubbed in 1876 'aesthetic criticism'" (Latane 392). Other critics would often involve social and scientific issues in the discussion of literature, or some "complex philosophical approaches spread into literary criticism proper, as for instance in the writings of Walter Pater" (Latane 392). Those who advanced the study of literary history focused on Coleridge, Shelley, Swift, Fielding, the Elizabethan period, Shakespeare (the first Shakespeare Society being founded in 1840), and going back to Bible and the Greek and Roman classics. Among those who favoured literary history and biography were Symons on Sidney, Trollope on Thackeray, Stephen on Pope and Johnson, Hutton on Scott, Pattison on Milton, Morley edited Macmillan's *English Men of Letters* series, Dowden on Shakespeare, Southey, and Eliot, Gosse on Donne, Gray, and Swinburne, Saintsbury on Dryden. George Saintsbury is also the author of the once celebrated *A History of Criticism and Literary Taste in Europe* (1900-1904) and *Loci Critici* (1903). The former, covering the period from ancient Greece to the 1900, is regarded as the first university history of criticism.

Besides the interest in the history of literature and advancement of literary history as a modern discipline, there was the interest in the history of books. The Bibliographical Society was founded in 1892 and one of its most prominent members, Walter Wilson Greg (1875 – 1959), provided an important qualitative advancement in the history of Renaissance theatre and Shakespeare, namely in *Principles of Emendation in Shakespeare*.

Historical or synchronic, biographical or textual, sophisticated or emphatic, aesthetic or moralistic, and in general hardly disinterested, Victorian critical discourse unveil the values of the past literary tradition and reflect by contrasting with them the contemporary achievements in poetry, especially of Tennyson and Browning, and in prose fiction, especially of Thackeray and Dickens, and with regard to realism and social concern. Outside Britain, an interesting account in social terms of Victorian novel belongs to the French scholar and academic Louis Cazamian (1877 – 1965) who in *Le Roman Social en Angleterre, 1830-1850: Dickens, Disraeli, Mrs Gaskell, Kingsley* (1903) speaks about the struggle between "individualism" and "idealism", the former belonging to economists and the latter's "best weapon" against individualism being the Victorian "literary realism".

Unlike in England, in France criticism fuses the concern with subject matter with that with the form of the novel, as Flaubert, in *Madame Bovary* is aware of the inseparableness between the content and form, the expression of the ideas and the technique of writing: "You tell me that I pay too much attention to form. Alas! It is like the body and the soul; form and the idea, for me, are one and the same thing, and I don't know what the one is without the other". Flaubert diminishes the role of realism as the subject of the novel in favour of the novel's internal beauty and internal value which are achieved through a universal style and a musical language, declaring his preference for a book without any subject, or at least with an "invisible subject". A mild attempt in England to discuss novel in its narrative construction by contrasting it with drama belongs to Edward Bulwer Lytton in his essay *On Art in Fiction* (1838).

It was not until the end of the nineteenth century that serious critical theories of novel, in general, and in particular, of the narrative specificity appeared in England, which was primarily due to Henry James, another writer-critic of the century. Henry

James is firstly acclaimed as a novelist, whose literary works (*The Portrait of a Lady*, *The Ambassadors*, *The Golden Bowl*, and others) "subscribe to the tradition of the European prose, in particular English", first of all concerning the writing technique and namely "the point of view of the character through whose consciousness the action is filtered" (Cartianu and Preda 196). James's novels are placed in the framework of modernism in the line of those authors who deal with the artistic dilemma of the relationship between art and reality and who attempt to catch the atmosphere of the mind in rendering the psychology of the characters. The major voices of modernism in British fiction are those of the stream of consciousness novelists – Dorothy Richardson in *Pilgrimage*, James Joyce in *Ulysses*, Virginia Woolf in *Mrs Dalloway* – but apart from the stream of consciousness novels, the English experimental fiction includes other innovative manifestations, such as the expression of the psychoanalytic principles by D. H. Lawrence, or the dystopian novels of Aldous Huxley and George Orwell, or the psychological realism of Henry James. These writers, however, unlike the stream of consciousness novelists Joyce and Woolf, are no longer regarded as exponents of modernism but considered experimental only in the context of the fictional innovation of the first half of the twentieth century.

Henry James (1843 – 1916) was born in New York, the son of Henry James, an eccentric philosopher and religious visionary, and brother of William James, an influential American psychologist and philosopher. He spent his early childhood in Albany, New York, before the family left for Europe when he was twelve. In 1882, after the death of his parents, James settled definitely in England, and in 1898 moved to Rye, Sussex, where he spent the rest of his life. By the time he reached maturity, Henry James had already published reviews and short stories in some of the leading American journals, such as *Atlantic Monthly*, *Galaxy*, and *Nation*. His mature career is usually divided into three periods. In his first part, which culminates with *The Portrait of a Lady* (1881), he touches the so-called international theme, which is the drama of Americans in Europe and of Europeans in America. In the second part he turns to experimenting with various themes and forms, with novels dealing with social and political currents of the 1870s and the 1880s, then with writing drama and short fictions aimed at revealing the relationships of artists to society and reality, and the psychology of people placed in difficult situations. In his last period, called "major phase", James returns to cosmopolitan and international subjects, to the confrontation between the European and American culture, to the theme of freedom, and, especially, to "the very atmosphere of the mind", the rendering of the complex inner life of his characters' psychology. Now recognised as one of Britain's and America's major novelists and critics, as a psychological realist in fiction and a formal critic of the work of fiction, Henry James produced during his lifetime twenty novels, more than one hundred shorter fictions and ten volumes of travel books, essays and literary criticism. Among his novels, the best are *The Portrait of a Lady*, *The Bostonians* (1886), *The Tragic Muse* (1889), *The Wings of the Dove* (1902), *The Ambassadors* (1903), and *The Golden Bowl* (1904). His most popular shorter works include *Daisy Miller: A Study* (1878), *The Real Thing* (1892, 1909), *The Turn of the Screw* (1898), *The Beast in the Jungle* (1903), and others.

As a literary critic, James is first praised for his theoretical discussions of the technical problems of novel in *The Art of Fiction* (1884), especially concerning the point of view, which "are among the first and the best available" theories (Martin 20). Many of them prefigure later advances, such as his theory of the point of view anticipating structuralism, or his distinction between the "subject" and the "wrought material" of the novel prefiguring the Formalist opposition between *fabula* and *siuzhet*. Together with his contemporary writer-critic Vernon Lee (Violet Paget, 1856 – 1935), who was influenced by the aestheticism of Walter Pater, James provided the shift of the critical concern from the thematic to structural level, from content to form and narrative technique. Unlike the socially and morally concerned writers and critics of his period – such as Saintsbury who does not focus on particular novels, or H. G. Wells who follows the tradition of Johnson and Dickens – James values the work of literature in itself, to a certain degree coming closer to aestheticism, and conceives technical issues as the main critical preoccupation.

In matters of narrative technique, James rejects the author's involvement, the direct statement, and the omniscient point of view, by which the narrator is the controlling voice in the narrative, allowing his/her characters no freedom to act and speak on their own behalf, and hurrying up with assumptions and interpretations so the reader concludes and understands the narrative message from the authorial point of view. James rejects hereby a very popular mode of narration in Victorian fiction, known as "moral retrospect", found especially in the Bildungsromane, in which the character is the narrator situated at the end of the narrative process, more mature, able to remember and interpret his own activities in the light of his later, greater wisdom.

James's theoretical criticism of the novel may appear to have no intrinsic value, or his ideas might be viewed as obsolete and redundant, yet his merit is prompting the interest in the critical and theoretical potential of the novel, and, indeed, in the twentieth century and nowadays the novel has been critically the most discussed literary form.

In Victorian age, the novel was a form of entertainment, and the majority of the Victorian population was actually prose-readers. Also, for the Victorians, the modern distinction between the literary novel and the popular best-seller had not yet come into existence. The novels of Brontë sisters, Dickens, George Eliot, Trollope, and Hardy were read not merely by literary elite, but widely throughout the expanding middle class and, particularly in the case of Dickens, by the working class as well. The establishment of the novel as a dominant literary form resulted in the need for its critical evaluation and theorization. In James's famous *The Art of Fiction* the aim is clear: as English novel "had no air of having a theory, a conviction, a consciousness of itself behind it – of being the expression of an artistic faith, the result of choice and comparison", then in this study and in the prefaces to his own novels, James assumes the task to provide such a theory of writing for the novel. In doing so, he insists on the aesthetic value of fiction, on the fact that the novel should be viewed as art and as the expression of the author's personal impressions of life and not merely as a form of entertainment subject to the principle of realism that requires fidelity to actuality in its representation as well as the moral effect of art. For James, the novel is not a depository of "realistic data from real-life experiences", but is "organic" and "has a life of its own that grows according to its own principles or themes" (Bressler 43).

Apart from realism, James reacts against the biographical method in critical assessment and promotes a method which focuses on psychology of the writer and which would demonstrate the art of writers' texts by outlining "their unique individuality of style, tone and vision, their artistic, but not biographical, personalities" (Dutton 65). James exposes his own methods of writing fiction and insists on the "artistic personality" of the author which he describes impressionistically. In terms reminiscent of Pater, James, in *The Art of Fiction*, asserts impression to be an essential condition of fiction: "A novel is in its broadest definition a personal, a direct impression of life; that, to begin with, constitutes its value, which is greater or less according to the intensity of the impression". Henry James insists also on the unique "personality" of the work of fiction and describes the novel, in terms reminiscent of Coleridge's theories of growth and of the interrelationship between the whole and the parts in literature, as a living organism, "a living thing, all one and continuous, like any other organism, and in proportion as it lives will it be found, I think, that in each of the parts there is something of each of the other parts." Like Coleridge with poetry, James insists on the need of the work of fiction to achieve "organic form", since "form alone takes, and holds and preserves, substance – saves it from the welter of helpless verbiage that we swim in as in a sea of tasteless tepid pudding". James's approach shows resemblance to a formalist one, as he implies the interdependence of various fictional elements such as theme, idea, narrative, setting, image, and so on.

James was sympathetic to and agreed with his brother's pragmatism, although their theoretical paths had limited connection. While Henry excelled in the field of literary practice and criticism, William James (1842 – 1910), after producing in 1890 one of the most famous and influential works of psychology, *Principles of Psychology*, turned to philosophy and, with his *Pragmatism* (1907), became "the central literary figure in the pragmatic movement"; his pragmatism, largely a philosophy of religion, was "anticipated by Pierce", the pragmatic philosopher of science, and "revised by John Dewey", the pragmatic philosopher of morals (White 155).

In the first half of the twentieth century, Henry James the novelist influenced many contemporary writers, among whom Joseph Conrad (1857 – 1924) who in *Henry James: An Appreciation* speaks highly of his "master", in front of whose "magnitude" the "critical faculty hesitates" and whose "books stand on my shelves in a place whose accessibility proclaims the habit of frequent communion", but laments the fact that James's work is not fully appreciated. Here and in the prefaces, for instance in the Preface to *The Nigger of the "Narcissus"*, Conrad develops his own critical views of novel and, like James, insists on fiction being an art. "A work that aspires, however humbly, to the condition of art should carry its justification in every line", claims Conrad, and defines art as "a single-minded attempt to render the highest kind of justice to the visible universe, by bringing to light the truth, manifold and one, underlying its every aspect." The prose fiction, if it aspires to be art, "appeals to temperament" and must be, "like painting, like music, like all art, the appeal of one temperament to all the other innumerable temperaments whose subtle and resistless power endows passing events with their true meaning, and creates the moral, the emotional atmosphere of the place and time". To be effective, reasons Conrad, such an appeal "must be an impression conveyed through the senses; and, in fact, it cannot be made in any other way, because temperament, whether individual or collective, is not amenable to persuasion". Therefore, concludes Conrad, all art "appeals primarily to the senses, and the artistic aim when expressing itself in written words must also make its appeal through the senses, if its high desire is to reach the secret spring of responsive emotions".

Indeed, as a critic and theoretician of novel, Henry James stimulated important though conflicting discussions on fiction. On the one hand, he was acclaimed as a

"Master" by those critics who favoured formal perfectionism and technique, among whom Percy Lubbock. On the other hand, James was condemned for considering the point of view as central to the art of novel in the determent of character, as by E. M. Forster, and, as by H. G. Wells, for thwarting "the freedom of the novelist to exhibit his own personality and opinions, to comment openly upon his fiction, to indulge in parody and burlesque, and to discuss contemporary ideas" (Baldick 159).

Henry James's own novels and his ideas on novel writing "were representative of the transition between the classical realist novel, with its emphasis on story, setting and character, and the modernist novel with its stress on writing and composition" (Onega and Landa 21). In *The Art of Fiction* and in his prefaces, James proves a precursor of Percy Lubbock in *The Craft of Fiction* (1921), Joseph Warren Beach in *The Twentieth Century Novel: Studies in Technique* (1932), as well as of Norman Friedman, Wayne C. Booth, Tzvetan Todorov, Gerard Genette, Roland Barthes, David Lodge and others who discuss and emphasize the narrative elements and narrative strategies in the novel.

In the nineteenth century, among the precursors of the contemporary approach to narrative, Henry James provides the first systemic and methodological instances of technical assessment of the novel. James does so by bringing into discussion issues concerning the structural or narrative level of the fictional text, narrative techniques in novel, author's perspective and multiple perspectives in the novel, reception of the fictional material by the reader, principles of discrimination and selection, relation – or rather non-relationship – of morality to the form and theme of the novel, and others.

Contrary to this critical tradition that focuses on the narrative level is the consideration of the novel's thematic perspectives as containing the representation of human and social life in all its diversity. This empirical and pragmatic view, emphasizing the historical, social, realistic, scientific, philosophical, psychological, moral, pedagogical and whatever other aspect of the external component of fiction, is expressed in the theories of Georg Lukacs, Walter Allen, Ian Watt, Robert Scholes, Robert Kellogg, René Girard, Marthe Robert, Northrop Frye, Lucien Goldman, Walter Reed, Lennard Davis, and others.

The incipient stages of these two novel-related critical directions appeared in the nineteenth century and they corresponded to the general tendencies in the critical theory of art and literature of the period, which developed and diversified, moving criticism away from the constraints of literary practice to the relative independence as methodological and scientific approaches. Like in mainland Europe and in later periods, the Victorian England saw a greater variety of critical outlooks on literature: realist, naturalistic, impressionistic, aesthetic, historical, humanistic, moral, and other types of criticism. Romantic aesthetic doctrine remains influential throughout the nineteenth century and many of Victorian critics would follow romantic views of literature, as Matthew Arnold in *Essays in Criticism* (1865, 1888). Others would be more original, like Henry James's examination of the novel, or John Ruskin's and Walter Pater's critical texts on art and culture.

Victorian criticism marks the transition from the previous literary criticism – dependent on literary practice and literary movements, as well as subjective, defensive, normative and prescriptive – to the twentieth-century independent and scientific approach to literature. The primary cause of the "separation" between criticism and literature is the literary diversity in the Victorian age, and the diversity of literary trends is a result of romanticism breaking the linearity of literary development dominated by classical views, reviving the innovative spirit in art, rejecting tradition and rules, and proclaiming the freedom of artistic expression. Like on the Continent, Victorian literature includes a number of movements and trends that co-exist during one period and as such reify the co-existence of traditional and innovative elements in literature.

Marked by these developments and facing a literary diversity, the nineteenth-century literary criticism developed its own diversity, its own typology which may or may not correspond to the literary or artistic one. As diverse as they were – historical criticism, humanistic criticism, moral criticism, biographical criticism, realistic criticism, naturalistic criticism, impressionistic criticism, aesthetic criticism, and others – it was a common practice at the time to attach a general discussion to a particular criticism. Overall, Victorian critics dealt with the nature of culture, art and literature, mainly poetry and novel. They brought into discussion such topics as the social function of art and literature, hedonism and its relation to art and literature, morality and immorality in art, imaginative faculty of the artist, the style of the literary work, the theory of the comic genre and the presence of the comic spirit in the novel, and many others. Also, the subjective component in criticism and the critical dependence on literary practice, together with the prescriptive nature of criticism, are rejected and become extinct, as one may see in the great works of Victorian criticism by the leading critics of the second half of the nineteenth century Matthew Arnold, Thomas Carlyle, John Stuart Mill, John Ruskin, and Walter Pater. Amid the ravages of "the fierce intellectual life of our century", as Arnold puts it, the rise of different literary movements and trends (realism, naturalism, impressionism, symbolism, aestheticism and the doctrine of "art for art's sake") co-exists in the second half of the nineteenth century with the major discoveries in science and developments in philosophy. Most of them helped the rise of different types of literary criticism in that period, many of which already revealing the separation of literary criticism from the constraints of artistic trends and movements, while relying on the new developments in philosophy, psychology, science, and social studies.

Indeed, where the previous periods show that literary criticism is dependent on literary trends and movements which are dominant in different periods, the nineteenth century shows that literary criticism is rather dependent on new developments in science and philosophy, of which those of Comte, Taine, Darwin, Marx, Freud, Nietzsche, and Wollstonecraft are mostly influential on both literary practice and literary criticism.

However, it was the twentieth century to witness the actual expansion and diversification of independent from art and literature critical approaches and their typology organized in schools and trends representing the modern scientific and methodological literary theory and criticism. The twentieth-century criticism neither belongs nor responds to particular artistic or literary trends, but develops its own trends and schools aiming at approaching theoretically and critically the literary practice from a multitude of perspectives.

Still, some of these critical trends, like the literary criticism of the previous periods, are dependent on trends and movements of creative literature (like formalism on futurism); others are dependent on different developments in science, philosophy, and society (hermeneutics, psychoanalysis, Marxist or feminist approach); and others are somewhere in between or emerging from within the interpretative perspectives of literary scholarship itself (like narratology as a by-product of structuralism starting with Todorov's *Grammaire du Decameron*, 1969).

Some of the twentieth-century trends in literary scholarship continue the nineteenth-century artistic and philosophical input, and many established types of criticism (biographical, social, historical, Marxist, psychological, impressionistic, aesthetic) continue to flourish at the beginning of the century. At the same time, new branches of literary criticism emerge, which reject the nineteenth century literary studies and which are "anti-Romantic, anti-humanistic, and anti-empiricist", and which reject "the privilege of emotion, the belief in the unity and identity of human subjectivity, and the blind faith in observation and experience as the only sources of knowledge" (Selden 4). On the other hand, the human and social sciences from the first half of the twentieth century, unlike physics or biology, were concerned, according to Lawrence Cahoone, "not merely with facts but with the *meaning* of facts for human subjects", and a number of theories – which also gave particular trends in literary theory and criticism – emerged with the task "to diagnose contemporary alienation". These theories, continues Cahoone, embarked on a historical analysis

> of how human society and the human self develop over time, in order to see how and why modern civilization had gone wrong. What was needed, it seemed, was a return to the true, or authentic, or free, or integrated human self as the centre of lived experience. This meant not an abandonment of modern industry, technology and secularism, but some reconstruction of society (for Marx), or of moral culture (for Freud), or of our openness to the vicissitudes of our own authentic experience (for phenomenology and existentialism). (Cahoone 3)

In fact, in the first half of the twentieth century "literary criticism underwent a revolution" (Baldick 258) and the century begins with a reaction against the nineteenth-century traditional, historical, humanistic and moral criticism, a reaction coming from a number of critics focusing on literary text in itself, its form and structural organization. This first modern critical perspective represents the formal approach to literature and includes three major schools of literary criticism: Formalism, New Criticism, and structuralism. The formal approach rejects and supersedes the humanist and moral literary criticism, replacing its subjective and prescriptive nature with a scientific one. Also, due to the fact that the humanist literary criticism has been "progressively superseded by much less prescriptive versions of literary studies which have sought to analyse and explain how writing is written, read, distributed and exchanged", the "literary studies threatens to become part of a much wider intellectual enterprise", nowadays designated as "cultural studies" (Milner 14).

2.
MAJOR LITERARY VOICES

Prose fiction was the dominant genre and the realist novel was its main type. The main literary voices of the period – Charles Dickens, William Makepeace Thackeray, Charlotte Brontë, George Eliot, Thomas Hardy, and others – were prose-writers and exponents of realism. There were some exceptions, like the Gothic/post-romantic novel *Wuthering Heights* by Emily Brontë, or *The Picture of Dorian Gray* by Oscar Wilde, which reflects aestheticism. In this age of print, the novel opens to mass audience and becomes "consumerist", as to remember just the forty thousand copies of the first issues of *The Pickwick Papers*. In Victorian age, the novel was welcomed as a source of moral and social instruction as well as of delight and entertainment by the newly expanded reading public. It was created by the new profession of "novelists", a group that now included women as well as men. It was printed quickly and inexpensively in three-decker form on the new steam-powered printing presses and distributed efficiently over the kingdom on the new railway system. Poetry, despite its Victorian marginalisation by the (realist) prose fiction, is a heterogeneous phenomenon owing its aesthetic significance to such outstanding literary voices as those of Alfred Tennyson, Robert Browning, Elizabeth Barrett Browning, Matthew Arnold, Gerald Manley Hopkins, and the Pre-Raphaelites.

2.1 Charles Dickens

Charles John Huffham Dickens (1812 – 1870), the son of a clerk in the Navy pay office, was born in Portsmouth and spent the happiest period of his boyhood in Chatham. This was followed by a period of intense misery and suffering which deeply affected him, during which his father was imprisoned for debt in the Marshalsea and he himself, aged 12, worked in a blacking warehouse. This period of pain inspired much of his fiction, especially the early chapters of his autobiographical *David Copperfield*. He then worked as an office boy, studied shorthand, and became a reporter of debates in the Commons for the *Morning Chronicle*. His collaboration with the periodicals of the time continued and proved to be extremely productive. Dickens contributed to the *Monthly Magazine* (1833 – 5), to the *Evening Chronicle* (1835), and to others the articles subsequently republished as *Sketches by 'Boz'. Illustrative of Every-Day Life and Every-Day People* (1836 – 7). They attracted much attention and led to an approach from Chapman and Hall, which resulted in the creation of Mr. Pickwick and the publication in twenty monthly numbers, beginning April 1836, of *The Posthumous Papers of the Pickwick Club*. The work was published in volume form in 1837 when Dickens was only 25 years old. The series soon achieved immense popularity and promised a prominent future and career.

In 1837, *Oliver Twist* began to appear in monthly numbers in *Bentley's Miscellany*, a new periodical of which Dickens was the first editor. It was followed, also in monthly numbers, by *Nicholas Nickleby*. In 1840, a new weekly was founded, written wholly by Dickens, called *Master Humphrey's Clock*: it was intended to include short sketches and instalments of the full-length novels *The Old Curiosity Shop* (1840 – 1) and *Barnaby Rudge* (1841). Later, however, as the novels proved popular, the linking by Master Humphrey was dropped. In 1842, with his young wife Catherine Hogarth, Dickens visited America, where he was well received, and where he advocated international copyright and the abolition of slavery. His first favourable impressions of the American life soon caused disillusion; this was expressed in his *American Notes* (1842) and through the portrayal of American stereotypes in *Martin Chuzzlewit* (1844, the sales of which were disappointing), both books causing much offense in America.

This period was followed by the success of *A Christmas Carol* (1843), the first in the series of Christmas books, including *The Chimes*, *The Cricket on the Hearth*, *The Battle of Life*, *The Haunted Man*. Dickens himself described these works as "a whimsical sort of masque intended to awaken loving and forbearing thoughts". In 1846, he founded a new paper, radical by the standards of the time, called *Daily News*, briefly edited by him. Dickens contributed to it the *Pictures from Italy*, produced as a result of his long visit to Italy in 1844. In 1846, during a visit to Switzerland, he began *Dombey and Son*, published in 1848. Two years later, he started the weekly periodical *Household Words*, incorporated in 1859 into *All the Year Round*, which he was to edit until his death.

The periodical saw the publication of much of his later writings, such as the Christmas stories, which replaced the Christmas books. *David Copperfield* appeared in monthly numbers in 1849 – 50; *Bleak House* in 1852 – 3; *A Child's History of England*, irregularly, in 1851 – 3; *Hard Times* in 1854; *Little Dorrit* in 1855 – 7; *A Tale of Two Cities* in 1859; *Great Expectations* in 1860 – 1; *Our Mutual Friend* in 1864 – 5. During these years of intense productivity Dickens produced public readings of his own books; in 1867 – 8 he revisited America and delivered a series of readings there, and on his return to England continued to tour the provinces. Charles Dickens died suddenly in 1870, leaving unpublished his last important novel, *The Mystery of Edwin Drood*.

The first thing that anyone would normally think about Dickens, when it comes to discuss his personality and literary activity, is his immense popularity, Dickens capturing the popular imagination as no other novelist has done before, but which may diminish the objectivity of any critical approach. The writings being familiar with the wider public, many receivers of one's critical attempt to discuss Dickens know what is talked about, and this can be considered the main advantage of his popularity. Yet to criticize Dickens, to talk about the existence, besides merits, of any defeats in his novels, is often "regarded by some of his more devout English readers as almost on a par with criticizing the Royal Family" (Churchill 119). Indeed, in some respects, Dickens is the greatest genius in British literature, but, the same critic believes, "no writer of any distinction at all has ever produced so much rubbish" and "unfortunately the genius and the rubbish exist side by side in the same novels" (Churchill 119).

This aspect makes him unique among the Victorian novelists, the most unequalled of all, but, at the same time, certain characteristics place him within the literary conventions of his time, making him a typical Victorian writer. This paradoxical status of Dickens is given again by the coexistence of both merits and defeats in his literary production. It has been noticed that his defeats come from the immaturity of the novel form and the uneducated taste of the middle-class that formed the main corpus of his reading audience. Dickens, himself a middle-class, was not an intellectual and educated, not a conscious artist, compared to Thackeray or George Eliot, and not able to understand his faults and to analyse and coordinate his observations; he did not have the power to structure and systematize the narrative material raised by his strong creative imagination, talent and inspiration. He was also accused of sensationalism and sentimentality, and of his inability to portray female characters other than innocent, idealized or grotesque. Dickens remarkably tells the story, capturing and holding the readers' attention, but an objective critic cannot help pointing out that intellectual weakness is the main cause of his failure to discover and work with patterns and laws governing fiction, in general, and his own genius, in particular. Dickens cannot impose order on his imagination and inspiration; he cannot construct and he is lacking the sense of form, for, indeed, many of his novels have no organic unity required by a narrative discourse, are full of detached episodes, sometimes too much plot and a complicated intrigue which is hard to follow. It seems that Dickens is still bound by the formal conventions of the picaresque novel and that imposed by Richardson and Fielding in the eighteenth century. One may argue that Dickens's weakness is also the cause of his uncertain grasp of character, for, writing outside his range, he brings in all sorts of types outside his own background, aristocrats or lower-class representatives, to whom he fails to render any strong personalities, and, failing over his characters, he cannot draw complex, serious protagonists able to act according to their own personalities because of the incoherent changes in their situations, which thwart their personality. Many of Dickens's characters, of course with a few brilliant exceptions like David Copperfield or Pip, seem to serve no purpose in the running of the plot, making it more agglomerate than complex or coherent, and, in many cases, one cannot help noticing their alliance to the conventional melodrama types. The melodrama, as a distinct genre, flourished in nineteenth century and produced a kind of naively sensational entertainment, but the melodrama in Dickens's novels disturbs the unity of tone, Dickens over-using the pathos and overstating the tragic condition of some of his characters, colouring them with strong sensationalism and extravagant emotional appeal.

However, creating on a larger scale and covering a huge range of characters and incidents is also a merit, and Dickens's merits are given by the same strong creative imagination, almost unprecedented in the history of English literature. It has been called a "fantastic imagination" – for his range consists mainly of those aspects of life that permit the fantastic treatment and perhaps because of the author's willingness to exaggerate – fascinated by the grotesque, which modifies the narrative material accentuating its characteristic features to a fantastic degree, and horror, which creates remarkable characters and impressive atmosphere and setting. The setting of his novels reveals the power of both creating the atmosphere and describing the actual appearance of humans. Yet both his characters and the situations they are involved in are melodramatic and conventional, but the combination of realism and the macabre still produces special, sometimes shocking, effects on Dickens's readers. Besides the power to create setting and atmosphere, but linked to these two, other distinctions and merits of Dickens are his poetry and humour. It is the poetry that gives vitality to his descriptions; "poetic fantasies", comic and macabre, for Dickens's poetic imagination is stimulated mostly by the gloomy and the sinister. Claimed by many to be the greatest humourist that English literature ever produced, Dickens combines both satire and pure humour, both fantastic in their exaggeration, but also effective because of reference to reality. The characters of his novels are humorous rather than realistic portraits, and the humour in Dickens is often a repetition of a set phrase, a tag, like Mrs. Micawber's in *David Copperfield*, or it is linked to a certain obsession, to someone bound to an invariable ritual habit, our sense of superiority towards an obsessed person being another source of laughter.

The structure of Dickens's fiction, as Northrop Frye points out in "Dickens and the Comedy of Humours" (1978), is that of the New Comedy, which originated in Greece in the third and fourth centuries BC, with emphasis on amorous intrigues with a happy ending, the best known playwrights being Philemon and Diphilus. It came down to Dickens from the Roman imitators Plautus and Terence, who, in turn, influenced Ben Jonson (whom Dickens admired) and later Moliere. The main action, Frye believes, is a "collision" of two social types or societies: "the obstructing and the congenial society". Dickens continued its tradition by creating a number of stereotyped plots and characters, and he was very conventional in applying the New Comedy plot structure to his own novels. The congenial society is centred on the love between hero and heroine – Dickens, more than anyone, being the slave of the formal convention of his time, which taught him that these types were essential to a novel – the obstructing on the characters who often can be regarded as parental figures related to the main characters and who try to smother this love and the self-accomplishment of the protagonists. As in a New Comedy plot structure, the characters of the obstructing society dominate most of the action and range of incidents, but towards the end a change in the plot reverses the situation and the congenial society dominates the happy-ending. In building his characters, Dickens proves again typically Victorian and bound to the New Comedy structure: he does not look at them from the intellectual point of view, he has no special insight into the qualities which are characteristic of man as man, and he does not tell much of the inner life of the character. It is in contact with other humans that the individual characteristics reveal themselves most vividly, Dickens rendering remarkably well those qualities which separate an individual subject from the others, by which disclosing one of the most important aspects of human nature – its individuality.

In his novels, Dickens seems to have introduced the satire, almost non-existent in a typical New Comedy artistic pattern, but he continues the creation of some humorous characters, belonging to both the congenial and the obstructing side. The differences between these characters create the condition of the action and opposition between the two social types: the humour of the congenial society is merely dramatic, good and consisting of some harmless eccentricities; that of the obstructing one helps rendering society with all its false standards and values, for comedy in Dickens's novels was not merely comic relief. Hence is the appearance of satire, which makes the characters of the latter social type appear ridiculous, cruel, and even dehumanized. The humour (comedy) is naturally connected to the morality (play), and the comic allusions to social levels, which define the English comic tradition that shifted from the eighteenth-century concern with man and human nature to the nineteenth-century "social comic genre". Even the parental figures attached to the central character belong to these societies: there are, besides actual parents who are often dead before the story begins (or who mysteriously emerge at the end bearing names unrelated to the story), the parental figures of the obstructing society, who are generally cruel and often similar to the step-parents of folklore, and the parental figures of the congenial society, who assume a protective role and relation to the main character. The family was actually the only social unit that Dickens regarded as genuine; it was the key to social identity, and the comic action often moved toward recognition scenes, the discovery of unknown parents, and the articulation of correct family relationships.

N. Frye's opinion is just one possible way of understanding the narrative structure of Dickens's novels, given the complexity and polyvalence of his literary discourse. One may talk about the picaresque form of his novels, or the characteristic features of his narrator who renders the universe of childhood and reveals the author's own concern with the experience of childhood. It seems that Dickens writes best when he does so from a child's point of view, for he is instinctive, possesses a strong imagination and vivid sensations, and the first parts of both *David Copperfield* and *Great Expectations* can be regarded among the best pictures of childhood in English literature.

Dickens renders the major Victorian concern with social phenomena and the status of personality as integrated or not in the social structure. For Dickens, the structure of society reveals chiefly the sinister and the absurd aspects of it, aspects which are often invaded by comic action. But Dickens seriously tended to suspect all institutions and social structures; the natural human kindness and basic human values are set against the cruelty of the impersonal, soulless institution, church, charitable society, government office, laws, inhuman theory, or simply individual selfishness, for he felt that they were attempting to destroy the good which could only arise from the spontaneous action of the individual. Like the writers of old moralities, Dickens presents a strong moral outlook, which determines the emotional content of his novels, peopling his books with a wide range of virtues and vices, believing in the universal value of the primary, benevolent, natural impulses and affections of man, and thus being more than an artist – a prophet expressing a viewpoint of life and drawing a scale of values that has universal application.

Among his novels that reveal this concern, but also among his best writings, are *David Copperfield* and *Great Expectations*. They have much in common: both are picaresque tales of adventure, in both the story is told as a first person narration, and the hero is shown as developing from childhood to maturity in the tradition of the Bildungsroman.

"Of all my books I like this best", wrote Dickens about *David Copperfield*, and it has always been a favourite with the reading public. The novel, in spite of the hero's early miseries, is a high-spirited and optimistic book, David finally becoming a famous author and making a happy marriage, which is in the spirit of Victorianism. In the novel, as in other Victorian Bildungsromane, the author tells the story of his own life interpreted through fiction. Highly autobiographical, for the emotional identification of the author with the character is very strong, the novel follows the hero's development and presents his experiences and events he is involved in at the same time with influences of the milieu. The narration slowly moves from childhood through youth and early adult life to a more stable adult maturity; it consists mainly of memories about the formation of a personality through suffering and tragic life experiences. The happy sensory universe of childhood is shadowed by the appearance of Murdstone, a typical parental figure of the obstructing society, although any emotional link between beautiful and kind Clara Copperfield and cruel Murdstone seems quite improbable. Such characters are used by Dickens to increase the depth of the hero's suffering; Murdstone inspires fear to the little boy and treats him as wild nature that needs to be tamed. With his childhood under terror, imposed by other characters and the milieu, the hero will eventually preserve his innocence and resist the cruel destiny. After the death of his mother, David is sent to school and then to menial employment in London, where he lives a life of poverty and misery. Finally, after a multitude of events involving many characters and incredible situations, rendering the development of his artistic side in parallel with his affections, the plot ends with the marriage between David and Dora Spenlow, a "pretty empty-headed doll", reminiscent of his mother, mainly because of the workings of his "undisciplined heart" rather than conducted by mature reasoning, but who dies after a few years and David marries the much idealized and right for him Agnes Wickfield. Perhaps it will not be much to say that David's final accomplishment and entrance upon maturity is to rise to the level of Agnes. Along with these protagonists, there is a number of other characters that people Dickens's novel, some of them raised at the level of high importance for the narrative and thematic structure of the novel, and others being merely shadow figures with no evident purpose in the running of the plot. Yet they are also highly individualized according to Dickens's own interest and concern in expressing his point of view to the reader: in the case of Uriah Heep, for example, Dickens uses the ideolects and sociolects in order to reveal both the psychological features of the character and the ideological and sociological issues.

Great Expectations, in which life is not a laughing matter, renders the tragic condition of the hero, who has cruelly discovered for himself the disreputable social basis on which his well-being is founded. Dickens's radicalism was almost burnt out when he came to write this novel, for he no longer nursed much hope of changing the world for the better and he had lost much of his feelings that the simple, rustic existence (a romantic element) is better than the sophisticated, urban civilization. Like *David Copperfield*, *Great Expectations* focuses on the formative process from childhood until manhood, but, while David remains static in his idealized perfectibility in spite of the trials and ordeals provided by the milieu, Pip changes at the moment of coming into contact with the larger society, represented in the novel by the city, its institutions, other characters, and especially money. Perhaps the curse of money, for it changes the character for the worse and is unacceptable because of its source, the convict Magwitch and not fairy-good for him Miss Havisham. Actually, Pip's relationship with Magwitch is at the heart of the narrative, and one of the climatic points of the plot is Pip's discovery in Chapter 39 that his social position, that of a gentleman, to which his "great expectations" are linked, is based on money coming from a fallen man, even if it represents the product of hard work, not crime. This is a moment that represents the end or loss of his illusions. "Crime and punishment" renders the character's psychological transformation from a complex, sensitive, and imaginative type into a snob cutting off his roots, revealing a strong social embarrassment set against his previous condition, which is again due to the money and his anxiety to become a gentleman. The end of the narrative suggests, however, the hero's return to the basic human values known to him from childhood and taught to him by Joe.

Through the character of Pip, the author is able to express the anguish and passions of his own nature. But, at the same time, the character is nothing more than a pathetic victim of the external world. At the beginning an innocent and pure child, together with Estella, symbolically representing the primordial couple in the garden of Miss Havisham, Pip goes to the city, the agent of corruption, which leads to his loss of personality, acquisition of experience and end of innocence. Similarly, Estella loses her personality when becomes an instrument of revenge against men in Miss Havisham's hands, who also influences the formation of Pip (he naively believes in her good intentions, only much later to understand her true intentions). Joe is the first parental figure for the orphan Pip, who provides formative attributes to his personality (provincial existence, uncorrupted by civilization, some basic human drives, kindness, honesty, links to nature, at the same time ignorance, even mediocrity). Next comes Mrs. Joe, his cruel sister, who teaches him the sense of property, and Miss Havisham, who creates in Pip the world of great expectations and the impulse to change his condition, which he started hating even after their first meeting. A strange character in a strange setting, creating an expressionist-like film set, Miss Havisham in bridal clothing and her room are unforgettable, frozen forever in their static existence. The most important parental figure is Magwitch, the destroyer of the great expectations, an ambivalent figure whose later decent and honourable behaviour wins the readers' approval, but not Pip's, who expresses repugnance on his appearance. The author himself intended to make him a pathetic figure, an inferior being, dog-like in his yearning for approval and appreciation. It seems that Dickens expresses the Victorian fear of the criminal element in society, but, making him escape from the soldiers, the author will eventually attribute to his personality a rebellious aspect against social structures (unlike Orlick, another criminally inclined character, who does not reveal any repentance for his evil doings). But Magwitch also makes Pip look at life realistically, understand that one must not only receive, but also give, even if, as in Estella's case, he destroys Pip's personality by creating of him an instrument to fulfil his own never-produced social accomplishment.

2.2 William Makepeace Thackeray

William Makepeace Thackeray (1811 – 1863), whose parents were of Anglo-Indian descent, was born in Calcutta, the son of Richmond Thackeray, a Collector of a district near Calcutta. His father died of fever in 1815, and his son was sent home to England at the age of five to be educated, and later was joined by his mother, who married again in 1820. Though Thackeray's recollections of his early years in India were scanty, the culture of Anglo-Indians figures prominently in a number of his works, including *The Tremendous Adventures of Major Goliah Gahagan*, *Vanity Fair*, and *The Newcomes*. Thackeray was given the education of a gentleman at private boarding schools (so-called public schools), including six years at Charterhouse, where he was not happy, and the abuses he suffered in these institutions became the basis for remembrances in essays, such as *The Roundabout Papers*, as well as episodes in novels (*Vanity Fair* and *The Newcomes*). He then was educated at Cambridge, where he entered Trinity College. His tutor was William Whewell (philosopher of natural science, nowadays of interest for his theory of discovery), but Thackeray saw little of the inaccessible don, preferring to spend his time at wine parties. Adding to these his own inability to excel at mathematics, the poor preparation he had received at Charterhouse, and a penchant for gambling and trips to the Continent, Thackeray left the university without a degree in June 1830. He visited Paris and spent the winter of 1830 – 1 in Weimar, where he met Goethe. Thackeray took away from Weimar a command of the language, a knowledge of German romantic literature, and an increasing scepticism about religious doctrine.

On his return from Germany, Thackeray lived the life of a propertied young gentleman, including more gambling, drinking in taverns, and sexual encounters with women. Thackeray's next attempt at finding an occupation led him to the Inns of Court, where he briefly tried to study law and gathered instead more of the atmosphere of "gentlemanly idleness", for he had little enthusiasm for law and never practiced as a barrister. He began his career in journalism, and in 1833 he invested part of his patrimony in a weekly paper, *The National Standard*, which he took over as editor and proprietor. Though the paper went under quickly, it gave Thackeray his first taste of the world of London journalism and an entree to the London literary world. He also pursued his enthusiasm for art, studying in a London art school and a Paris atelier. His father had left him an estate of approximately 17,000 pounds, but by the end of 1833 virtually all his fortune was lost, mostly through the failure of an Indian bank: this financial disaster forced Thackeray out of idleness and into serious work as a journalist. He lived in Paris from 1834 until 1837, making a meagre living from journalism, and for a while he had a regular income as Paris correspondent of the *Constitutional*, a newspaper bought by his step-father, but which soon failed, and Thackeray returned to London. Meanwhile, in Paris, he met his wife, Isabella Shawe, and the two settled briefly here (in 1836) before returning to London. Their first child, Anne, was born in 1837. Thackeray began to contribute regularly to *Fraser's Magazine*, the *Morning Chronicle*, *The Times*, and, most successfully, to *Punch*.

A second daughter was born in 1839, but she did not live long, and after the birth of their third child, Harriet Marian, in 1840, Isabella Thackeray suffered a mental breakdown which proved permanent. He was forced to place her in the care of a French doctor, and later in a private home in England, and to send his children to live with his mother in Paris.

Before the success of *Vanity Fair*, Thackeray worked as a free-lance journalist for about ten years, publishing literary criticism, art criticism, topical articles, and fiction either anonymously or under a number of comic pseudonyms. During the 1840s, he began to make his name as a writer. Earlier, in 1836, he published *Flore et Zephyr* in volume form. But he first came to the attention of the public with *The Yellowplush Papers* (1837 – 38), followed by *Catherine* (1839 – 40), *A Shabby Genteel Story* (1840), *Samuel Titmarsh* and the *Great Hoggarty Diamond* (1841), and *Barry Lyndon* (1844), all appearing in *Fraser's*, while *The Book of Snobs* (1846 – 7) gave Thackeray his first notoriety when it appeared as *The Snobs of England* in *Punch*. During these years, Thackeray also produced his first books, collections of essays and observations published as travel books. *The Paris Sketch Book* (1840) sold well enough to cover its costs, provide to its author a decent payment, and, perhaps most importantly for Thackeray, interest publishers in seeing more of his work. He sold *The Irish Sketch Book* (1843, with a *Preface* signed, for the first time, by Thackeray in his own name) to Chapman and Hall, the publishers of Dickens and Carlyle, and also turned a comic series done for *Punch* about a trip to the East into another book, *Notes on a Journey from Cornhill to Grand Cairo* (1846).

His children returned to live with him in 1846. In 1847, his first major novel, *Vanity Fair*, began to appear in monthly numbers, with illustrations by the author. The novel had a slow start: the first chapters were rejected by several publishers, but eventually it sold in the neighbourhood of 7,000 numbers a month. Just as importantly, it was the talk of the town, and Thackeray finally had a name that gained notice and reviews in journals such as the *Edinburgh Review*. As further proof of Thackeray's more complex, more playful nature, one cannot omit his *Rebecca and Rowena* (1849), a mock-heroic story, a "pastiche" after Scott's *Ivanhoe*, with everything upside-down, as indeed it should be in a parody – even beginning with the title, which gives priority to the Jewish woman.

Pendennis followed in 1848 – 50, considered one of the greatest autobiographical novels of all times. In 1852, *The History of Henry Esmond* was published as a 3-volume novel without first being serialized and with special type meant to imitate the appearance of an eighteenth-century book. Thackeray's novel shows the signs of what he recognized as the "cutthroat melancholy" he felt at this time (perhaps because of his increasing love for Jane Brookfield, the wife of an old Cambridge friend, which led to a rupture in their friendship). This is his only non-satirical novel, and it is often considered the greatest historical novel in English. It was followed by *The Newcomes*, published in numbers in 1853 – 5, a dynasty novel of three generations, supposedly narrated by Pendennis.

Thackeray followed in Dickens's footsteps with a lecturing tour of America, and he twice visited the United States to deliver lectures, in 1851 – 3 and 1855 – 6. He also continued to produce lighter works: he wrote for *Punch* until 1854, and produced a series of *Christmas Books* which he illustrated himself. In 1851, he gave a series of lectures on *The English Humourists of the Eighteenth Century*, and in 1855 – 7 he lectured on *The Four Georges*. In 1857 – 59, he published *The Virginians*, a novel set before and during the American Revolution, which is a sequel to *Henry Esmond*, and which Thackeray intended as a fond tribute to the country where he made a number of friends. In 1860, he became the first editor of the *Cornhill Magazine*, for which he wrote his *The Roundabout Papers* (a series of conversational essays modelled after his own favourites, Montaigne and Howell), *The Adventures of Philip* (1861 – 62), and the unfinished *Denis Duval* (1864). Thackeray died suddenly on the Christmas Eve of 1863.

The realism of *Vanity Fair* – the book which established Thackeray as a novelist – constitutes the first thing that anyone would normally discusses when approaching this novel. The characteristics of realism may help one's attempt to understand the novel, or one may follow Anthony Burgess's claim that while Dickens wrote of low life and was a warm-blooded romantic, Thackeray wrote of the upper-class and was anti-romantic. Indeed, no other English novel so minutely depicts a whole social class, and no other English writer has excelled at portraying his own social level with such irony and often cynicism. The novel, undoubtedly, is also a satire on a hypocritical society, and that the author belongs to it would not stop him from revealing, through his hatred of rank and privilege, the deeds, traits of character, options, ideas and ideals of the Victorian upper-class. He attacks every single criminal abuse of unearned rank and privilege, the mediocrity of the mind, the extreme brutality, and other vices through the depiction of a number of socially representative types, such as Sir Pitt Crawley, Sir Francis Clavering, Lord Steyne, and others. Lifting his title from *The Pilgrim's Progress*, Thackeray attempted to depict and neutralize the hypocrisy of a "ready-money society", though sometimes his task of demonstrating the comprehensiveness of a rather limited aspect of human existence (embodied within a social class), which represents the main part of his outlook, is dominated by the moral reference which is hardly that of a great novelist. In this respect, it seems that Thackeray's characteristic literary voice comes out strongly when he describes the characters of Dobbin and Amelia, while Becky represents the means of exerting the author's moralizing tone over the narrative. Through her desire to rise upward the social ladder, and the relations she establishes with a number of characters, Thackeray manages to portray his own social level the way it really exists.

The character of Amelia Sedley is a parody of the romantic persona, for, as romantics themselves, she creates her own universe of existence, but, having no personality, she becomes a mere parody. Nevertheless, she stands for a number of standards which are genuine, valid and valuable, or how the upper-class social level ought to be. In the case of both female characters, the chief subject of the narrative is the contrast between human pretensions and human weaknesses. Also, in the case of both Amelia and Becky, the contrasting curves of their destinies would point to the same morality: in a stable society, as the embodiment of Victorian deities of home, family, marriage, children, which Thackeray obviously praises, the violator of these norms (Becky) may momentarily seem triumphant but will eventually be cast down, for the author severely charges at her incapacity to be moved by either. Amelia, respectively, the dutiful follower of accepted mores, though momentarily in decline, will eventually be rewarded. Modern readings of the novel have brought new interpretative nuances, and, perhaps because of the realization that literature cannot possibly teach or make things right, and the complexity of Becky's personality, her duplicity and femininity, it is no less important to assume that Becky, along with Amelia, was the author's beloved offspring.

It is also more sensible to assume that in this novel "without a hero", there are two heroines; or the hero is the author himself, given his omniscient point of view throughout the entire narrative, attempting to significantly intervene into the process of the reader's comprehension of the meaning and the message of his book; or, to follow the traditional approach, the novel is indeed without any heroes (although it displays a huge number of characters) because the social background, or the society – the main concern of the narrative – can hardly be regarded as a principal character in a work of literature, while Thackeray would eventually argue about the non-existence of any heroic characters in his novel. The narrative's concern with a definite social stratum, which results into a loose representation of any mental activity, is a conscious innovation which disregards the conventional intrigue plot of the contemporary novels. The world of the novel is the world of London's society, its extension into the rural community, and even to the Continent and India; the work thus gives an impression of a lucid and fluent style of prose, allowing the author to achieve a panoramic effect of social and historical movement which is impressive despite, as mentioned above, some heavy moralizing tone.

2.3 The Brontë Sisters

The Brontës, or the Brontë sisters, is a generic name for the family of the Victorian female authors Charlotte Brontë, Emily Brontë, and Anne Brontë.

Emily Jane Brontë (1818 – 1848), was sister of Charlotte and Anne Brontë and daughter of Patrick Brontë, an Irishman, perpetual curate of Haworth, Yorkshire, from 1820 until his death in 1861. Her mother died in 1821, leaving five daughters and a son to the care of Elizabeth Branwell, their aunt. Emily briefly attended the school at Cowan Bridge with Charlotte in 1824 – 5, but was then educated chiefly at home, where she was particularly close to Anne, with whom she created the imaginary world of Gondal, the setting for many of her finest poems. She was at Roe Head in 1835, but suffered from homesickness and returned after a few months to Haworth. In her nature, she was more intensely than her sisters attached to home, whose moorland scenery she often evokes in her works. Emily worked as a governess in 1837 at Law Hill, near Halifax. In 1842, she went to study languages at the Pensionnat Heger in Brussels with Charlotte, but returned at the end of the year on her aunt's death to Howarth, where she spent the rest of her brief life. Unlike Charlotte, she had few but strong loyalties, yet no close friends, and her enigmatic character, her vein of violence (exemplified in the story of her subduing a dog with her bare hands), and her mysticism combined have given birth to many legends but no vivid certitude. Now recognized as one of the most original poets of the century, the most considerable poet, and perhaps novelist, of the three sisters, Emily produced one of the Victorian masterpieces, the novel *Wuthering Heights*, though it was less understood at the moment of its publication, while Emily's own response to its apparent lack of success, like so much in her character, still remains enigmatic.

Emily's only novel, *Wuthering Heights*, even more powerful and valuable than *Jane Eyre*, was written between October 1845 and June 1846, and was published by T. C. Newby after some delay in December 1847. "Wuthering" may be a Yorkshire variant upon "weathering" (which is "stormy"), and, indeed, one may say that the storm is violent, as the lives and events of the characters, but at the end it stops, along with the happy ending of the narrative, and the nature is calm and brightened making people smile again, which is more of a romantic allusion about nature mirroring and being linked to human existence, and which creates actually the novel's poetic appeal, its poetic and moral structure, so representative of the author's own imaginative powers. Indeed, one may definitely notice that the novel is less concerned with rendering social and moral issues, and concentrates on the complexity of human insight, telling the story of the family living at Wuthering Heights and the family of Thrushcross Grange.

Emily Brontë's adds to the complexity of the narrative organisation of Victorian fiction, in general, and the Bildungsroman, in particular, by its "concentric" structure, in which a narrative within a narrative within a narrative, and so on, are arranged according to a certain principle of narrative concern. *Wuthering Heights* can be seen as a Bildungsroman in its presentation of the process of formation of a number of characters, centres on the theme of love and revenge, which is rendered by a narrator who gives an account of a tale told by someone else, and within this tale there are further narratives, and the "movement 'inwards' at the beginning is complemented by a movement outwards at the end, a return to the original narrative relationship" (Cook 144).

Though the construction of the novel is often regarded as its weakest point, and it has been called clumsy by more than one critic, for indeed the various parts contributed by the narrative voices of Mr. Lockwood and, through him, Ellen Dean, have a tendency to provide digressions and cut the story into segments, the narrative structure is nevertheless close-packed, every incident having its place in this extremely complex plot, contributing to the feeling or the impression left by the character. The first chapters represent an introduction aimed at creating the atmosphere, forming a logical beginning for the further account of the story, which soon turns back on itself, quickens up, takes in other narratives – for instance a diary is read, which goes back 30 years – and so on, a narrative within a narrative within a narrative on different temporal and spatial levels: the present day and then back, forward nearly 20 years and then back again, speech within speech, incident within incident, culminating with a movement into the future when Mr. Lockwood unexpectedly revisits Thrushcross Grange, still its tenant, just to return to a temporal reality which not long ago represented "the present day". The last chapters are actually an addendum to the main story, a concession to the popular taste, to provide the happy-ending demanded by the reading public.

Among the narrative voices of the novel, that of Nelly Dean is quintessential. Putting the telling of the story into the mouth of this extraordinary teller, the author seems to get over certain inconveniences: for instance there is no need to explain how Heathcliff made his money, for Nelly just does not happen to know. Nelly Dean provides the real beginning of the story, in Chapter IV, when Lockwood asks her, speaking of Heathcliff, "Do you know anything of his story?", and she omnisciently replies: "It's a cuckoo's, sir. I know all about it". She is involved in all the main events of the narrative, knows everything about everybody, even their inmost and intimate thoughts, but sometimes the reader cannot help noticing that her vocabulary and her remembrance of small details over a period of 30 years are improbable, which is very important for the critic's attempt to dissent from her viewpoint. However, she is the unifying factor of the narration, the reasoning principle of this almost fantastic tale, and, in this narrative of frequent pagan allusions, the Dean suggests a religious meaning, as she is almost the only one who reminds people of the existence of a supreme God. Similarly, Lockwood is no less important for the understanding of the novel, though he is less concerned, compared to Nelly Dean, with giving explanations on the events and being involved in the lives of characters. Even his name suggests closeness and obtuseness, as one may notice in his response to Nelly's suggestion of a possible affair between him and the young Cathy.

Among the characters of the novel, it seems that Heathcliff, compared to the others, embodies both love and revenge, two main themes implied in the narrative, thus being more complex as a personality than others who either love (Catherine, Edgar Linton) or are driven by and exist for revenge (Hindley). These categories provide the basis and purpose of their existence, and, when lost, they have no reason to live further, become insane and eventually die: Heathcliff is bereaved of love (Catherine's death) and revenge (Hindley dies and he becomes the owner of both Wuthering Heights and Thrushcross Grange, thus accomplishing his aim), and having no one to love or hate, which is having no purpose in life (never had another one), his end is no less tragic and meaningless than that of the others. Similarly, Hindley's sense of life consists of hate and revenge against Heathcliff, and when the latter leaves Wuthering Heights after hearing about Catherine's intention to marry Linton, Hindley loses the purpose of living, degrades and finally, "assisted" by Heathcliff on his return, dies in misery, changed from human to animal condition. Like romantics earlier, Emily Bronte describes childhood as the age of spiritual understanding from which further life is either developing or falling away. This experience as antecedents of childhood makes possible the psychological delineation of specific human characteristics (love and revenge) which eventually become characteristic to the entire personality. It is to notice that Heathcliff is less violent within the story, responding to others' attacks and violent actions towards him. If Catherine has been called the driving force of the story, he would become its structure, remaining passive as other characters act upon him.

The ties that bind Heathcliff and Catherine – two characters whose interrelationship constitutes the nucleus of the narrative, representing the struggle of universal forces as archetypes – are beyond sex, and from the stormy intercourse of their elders, resolved in the union of death, young Hareton and Cathy would eventually form a balance in life of the active and the passive. The love of Hareton and Cathy may be considered an anti-climax to the love of Heathcliff and Catherine, which dominates the narrative, though it seems that one could not find its consummate force without the other. At first regarded as excessively morbid and violent, met with more incomprehension than recognition, unlike *Jane Eyre*, it was not until Emily's death of consumption that *Wuthering Heights* became widely acknowledged as a masterpiece, gradually re-assessed, praised as a masterful fusion of romance and realism, though its author's personality and much of her character still remain enigmatic.

Charlotte Brontë (1816 – 1855), with three of her sisters, was sent to a Clergy Daughters' School at Cowan Bridge, portrayed as Lowood in *Jane Eyre*, an unfortunate step which Charlotte believed to have hastened the death in 1825 of her two elder sisters and to have permanently damaged her own health. The surviving children continued their education at home, reading widely and becoming involved in a rich fantasy life influenced by their admiration of Byron, Scott, and others. It resulted in the creation of microscopic magazines in imitation of their favorite *Blackwood's Magazine*. They began to write stories, and Charlotte and Branwell collaborated on the invention of the imaginary kingdom of Angria, while Emily and Anne on the invention of Gondal. In 1831 – 2, Charlotte was at Miss Wooler's school at Roe Head; she returned as a teacher in 1835 – 8. In 1839, she was a governess with the Sidgwick family, near Skipton, and in 1841 with the White family at Rawdon. The next year she went to study languages in Brussels, but they were recalled at the end of the year by their aunt's death. In 1843, Charlotte returned alone for a further year. She fell in love with M. Heger, who failed to respond to her letters from Haworth after her return. She intended to establish her own school, with her sisters, but the project soon failed. The period of misfortunes continued with the death in September 1848 of Branwell; Emily died in December of the same year, and Anne the following summer. The loneliness of her later years was alleviated by the friendship with Mrs. Gaskell, whom she met in 1850 and who was to write her biography in 1857, and, in 1854, after much persistence on his part and hesitation on hers, by the marriage with A. B. Nicholls, her father's curate. Charlotte died a few months later of an illness probably caused by her pregnancy.

Charlotte's literary activity materialized in 1845, when, convinced of the quality of Emily's poems, she projected a joint publication resulting in a volume of verse entitled *Poems by Currer, Ellis, and Acton Bell* (the pseudonyms of Charlotte, Emily, and

Anne) which appeared in 1846. By that time, each of them had finished a novel: *The Professor*, Charlotte's first, was never published in her life, but Emily's *Wuthering Heights* and Anne's *Agnes Grey* were accepted and published by Thomas Newby in 1847. Not much affected by the rejection, Charlotte immediately began *Jane Eyre*, which was published in the same year by Smith, Elder, and achieved immediate success. Because of much speculation about its authorship, and the suspicion that the Bell pseudonyms concealed but one author, Charlotte and Anne visited Smith, Elder, in July 1848 and made themselves known. Although her identity was known in the literary world, Charlotte continued to publish as "Currer Bell". Through the tragic period which followed, Charlotte wrote *Shirley* which appeared in 1849. *Villette*, based on her memories of Brussels, appeared in 1853. A fragment of *Emma* was published in 1860 in the *Cornhill Magazine* with an introduction by Thackeray, and many of her earlier works were published subsequently.

During her lifetime, Charlotte was the most admired of the Brontës, although criticized for her emotionalism, didacticism, and the need of being loved, which was considered unbecoming for a clergyman's daughter, but more widespread were praise for her special insight into the depths of feeling and human psychology, and high popular and critical esteem.

Emily Brontë tells the story of her novel through the narrative voices of Nelly Dean and Lockwood, two minor characters of her own creation. Her sister Charlotte renders it as a first person narration of the main character, but the narrative structure of *Jane Eyre* is no less complex that that of *Wuthering Heights*. *Jane Eyre*, focusing the reader's attention on the emphasis placed by the author on the female personality, reveals the existence of a general well-rounded plot consisting of a number of sections or units, each meeting the requirements of independent, rounded, in the traditional way, plots and corresponding to a typical Bildungsroman thematic pattern. The narrative structure of the novel consists of three main plot units and a minor plot developed within the structure of the third one: the Gateshead section (corresponding to childhood, generation gap, provinciality); the Lowood section (institutionalized education and early miseries); the Thornfield section, which actually allows for the development of another plot unit within its narrative structure – the Moor House section – or continues after this one justifying the happy-ending and the final accomplishment of the heroine – the Ferndean section (corresponding, respectively, to the larger society, alienation, two love affairs – one with Mr. Rochester, of a passionate, almost carnal attraction, suitable to her personality, and another on a spiritual level, with no perspectives of inner fulfilment, with St. John – at the same time the search for a vocation and a place in the world, development of the professional side, rediscovery of family relations, and final accomplishment while entering upon maturity).

The work abounds with romantic allusions and elements, though Charlotte herself, an admirer of Thackeray, dedicated her most unrealistic and un-Thackerayan novel to him. Jane acts as both character (protagonist) and narrator (autodiegetic), through whom the author attempts to express a point of view communicated to the reader. Never before had the English novel claimed that a woman possesses so much of a personality and a complex inner structure, or that a woman's passion can equal or exceed that of a man. The narrative movement of the novel encompasses events around the strong characters of Jane and Rochester. Like many of Dickens's characters, Jane gradually narrates as she is spiritually and biologically developing, in parallel with a more mature narrator who remembers everything that is narrated, and is governed by reason and with less subjectivity in telling the story. Throughout the narrative, she teaches herself not to indulge in romantic hopes, and when Rochester is gone away, for instance, the reader is determined to think that she is apparently indifferent. But she also has the freedom to choose incidents in order to emphasize her strong personality, this aspect being possible while rendering a number of oppositions between characters and throughout the entire story which is founded on a typical Bildungsroman narrative structure. Orphaned as a child, Jane is under constraints and experiences unhappiness in the household of her relatives, the Reed family. She is shown highly intelligent, strongly imaginative, with astonishingly powerful feelings and sensibility, fancying that the spirit of Mr. Reed may return into the Red Room, but she is also capable of rational debate in her account to her cousins and Mrs. Reed, displaying a strong sense of right and wrong. Later, at Lowood school, Jane continues her self-depiction as a life-fighter, while learning to be passive and endure without resistance, as with Shelley's idea of the non-violent resistance to evil. The opposition here is provided by the character of Helen Burns, who preaches the orthodox lessons of forgiveness and endurance, and who also becomes merely a narrative device used by the narrator to emphasize Jane's own personality, or the way a female personality should be, and, when no more needed after Jane leaves the school, Helen dies. Jane is now determined to face existence, to make her own way in life, needing no advice and guidance from another person. This happened after Miss Temple left the school, under whose personality Jane's lively spirit was successfully subdued. At Thornfield, as a governess, Jane renders her professional development and her attitude towards a student, which is far from being sentimental, and is drawn to her employer, Edward Rochester. The professional development goes hand in hand with her growing affection towards him ("the bonny wanderer", "the pilgrim", and so on). Rochester is shown from the very beginning as a masterful character whom Jane refuses to be afraid of; during their long conversations, she meets the challenge successfully, and one may notice her professional pride when she is really upset by his suggestion that she may have been helped in her paintings by an artist. Such aspects, along with her courage in facing the physical danger of the fire in the bedroom, or listening, as an innocent governess, to Rochester's story about his French mistress, were unfamiliar qualities in a Victorian heroine. Finally, the love-starved governess wins this most unlikely man, the substitution of her never-known father, the romantic libertine, himself totally unfit for the Victorian typology of character representation, and is about to marry him. She learns that he is married, and his lawful insane wife is imprisoned in the upper room of the mansion. She leaves him refusing to become his mistress, pleading conscious as a sufficient excuse for the Victorian reading public, for, the power and extent of her female personality being so strongly emphasized, her position as a mistress, not wife, will eventually diminish and disregard her individuality. Also, with such a strong personality, she is unwilling to accept the father-child relationship under his masculine dominance, and the inferior state as a mistress. The feminist critical narrative has made of Rochester's wife locked up in the attic a symbol of oppressed Victorian womanhood (particularly by Sandra Gilbert and Susan Gubar in their canonical *The Madwoman in the Attic: The Woman Writer and the Nineteenth-Century Literary Imagination*, 1979), mad and imprisoned, which might have been comprehended by Jane, as if in an epiphanic experience, to be her future alter-ego.

Departing from Rochester, Jane is befriended by the family of Riverses, especially by St. John Rivers whose marriage proposal she rejects. St. John is the right man in all respects except that of love; Rochester is the wrong man in all respects save that of love. When Rochester's insane wife (the symbol of his guilt and the compulsory punishment) burns down the mansion killing herself, Jane hurries to him and they marry. It seems that the marriage meets the terms of her own personality and inner nature, for Jane returns triumphantly to establish the mother-child dominance over him. The story reverses the earlier Gothic narratives in which pretty ladies are enslaved by the masculine will of the male protagonists. The conventional ending of the narrative links the characters' strength of elementary life forces and provides a sustainable continuity of their existence together, which is even more basic than sex. Though sometimes overusing pathos and sentimentality, the presence of some grotesque coincidences and the inability to portray the milieu as the spatial premise of the story, the author and her novel held and still do a high popular esteem and admiration.

The Bildungsroman in the case of the Brontë sisters is concerned with the character and plot more than with the portrayal of the social background (at least, in the case of Emily) and typologically representative protagonists, which are elements required by the realist fiction. In turn, their novels contain aspects reminiscent of the romantic literary tradition, alongside mysterious elements and the authors' methods of artistic individualization of characters while exploring their psychological depths and range of feelings. The novels of the Brontë sisters renders the development of the main characters as a gradual process from childhood to maturity; their structure consists of a biographical substratum which is fictionalised; the formation of the character corresponds to her own nature and its counterpart nurture, and consists of the ever-existing ideals and disappointments, true and false virtues, as necessary stages of maturation. Also, in the case of Charlotte and Emily Brontë, Bildungsroman takes on new perspectives in that it represents the result of women writing, the novels developing a specific language for female experience within a continuing tradition of women's literature. The female novel of development is central, and the major issue for the female protagonist is the search for autonomy and selfhood in opposition to the social constraints placed upon her, including the demand to marry. In the whole of the Victorian female authorship, this conflict, usually with autobiographical resonance and often framed in metaphors of imprisonment (social, cultural, and sexual), is best embodied in Charlotte Brontë's *Jane Eyre*, Emily Brontë's *Wuthering Heights*, and George Eliot's *The Mill on the Floss*.

2.4 George Eliot

George Eliot (1819 – 1880), by her real name Mary Ann, later Marian, Evans, was the youngest surviving child of Robert Evans, estate agent in Warwickshire. In her childhood, she was particularly close to her brother Isaac, but from whom she was later estranged. At school, she was deeply attached and became a convert to Evangelicalism. She was freed from this by the influence of Charles Bray, a free-thinking Coventry manufacturer, but remained strongly influenced by the religious concepts of duty, love and morality (expressed in her works which contain many affectionate portraits of clergymen). She read widely, pursuing rigorously her education; translated Strauss's *Life of Jesus* which appeared without her name in 1846. In 1850, she became a contributor to the *Westminster Review*, to which she became assistant editor in 1851. Also in 1850, she met J. Chapman, and moved to 142 Strand, London, in 1851, as a paying guest in his house, where her emotional attachment to him proved an embarrassment. In 1851, she met Spenser, for whom she also developed strong feelings which were not reciprocal, but they remained friends. Her second translation was Feuerbach's *Essence of Christianity*, published in 1854. At about that time she joined G. H. Lewes in a union without legal form, for he was already married, which lasted until his death. They traveled to the Continent and on their return they set up house together. Lewes proved to be a constant support throughout her life and literary activity, and their relationship was gradually accepted by their friends. Lewes died in 1878; in 1880, she married the 40-year-old John Walter Cross, whom she met in Rome in 1869 and who became her financial adviser. She died seven months later.

George Eliot's literary activity, apart from some earlier translations, begins with *The Sad Fortunes of the Rev. Amos Barton*, the first of the *Scenes of Clerical Life*, which appeared in *Blackwood's Magazine* in 1857. This, along with the others, attracted praise for their domestics and humor, as well as speculation about the identity of "George Eliot", supposedly a clergyman or a clergyman's wife. Her first important novel, *Adam Bede*, appeared in 1859. *The Mill on the Floss* appeared in 1860 and *Silas Marner* in 1861. *Romola* was published in the *Cornhill Magazine* in 1862 – 3. *Felix Holt, The Radical* appeared in 1866, and her dramatic poem *The Spanish Gypsy*, conceived on an earlier visit to Italy and inspired by Tintoretto, was published in 1868. *Middlemarch*, critically considered her masterpiece, was published in installments in 1871 – 2, and *Daniel Deronda*, her last great novel, in the same way in 1874 – 6. Alongside the novels for which she is remembered, Eliot also wrote various poems, short stories, letters, and journals.

Adam Bede is Eliot's first novel which was received with enthusiasm and which established her as a leading novelist. The major concern represents the rendering of moral and religious standards, or rather the author's interest in reciprocal influences of one human personality upon another, in moral and religious issues, and final moral regeneration: the deep change in Arthur, the mental drama of Hetty, the latter's moral misery changed by the persuasive influence of the Methodist woman Dinah Morris. Hetty's moral despair and her rebellion change to sorrow and a sense of guilt, and, by the moral influence of another human and through religious considerations, she is morally regenerated. The morally strong Adam and Dinah eventually marry founding a happy family. Adam, who by means of honest work comes to happiness, illustrates the author's appreciation of those contented with their lot and contributing to social harmony. Eliot reveals in her novel the ethical intention of demonstrating the workings of retribution and the weight of responsibility. In her view, people should be concerned with duties and not with their rights, and the moral perfection attained through suffering and helplessness of conscience matters to her more than the vindication of human rights. It seems that George Eliot endorses Feuerbach's view that religious belief is an imaginative necessity for the human being and a projection of his or her interest in his or her own species. The readers of her fiction only gradually become aware of this heterodoxy.

George Eliot's next book, *The Mill on the Floss*, is more complex and reveals a new stage in her literary maturation. The novel itself is a typical Bildungsroman so far as it presents the gradual formation of two characters, Maggie and Tom, from childhood until their maturation. The novel expresses the author's own emotional and spiritual struggles in childhood, and the first section is actually dominated by the brother-sister relationship between Maggie and Tom (Marian Evans and her brother Isaac). This is one of the finest "childhood idylls" in English fiction, for the infantile experience and its period lay the foundation for the positive emotions of adult life. But their childhood is idyllic as well as a time of intense suffering, sorrow and frustration: Maggie cutting off her hair, forgetting to feed Tom's rabbits, and pushing Lucy into mud are childhood episodes whose representation makes them common devices of stories for children, but in Eliot's novel they also constitute and determine the extension of fictional subject-matter. Childhood, as a time of emotional intensity, is opposed not only to mature, intellectual life, but also to convention. The period of childhood and education of proud Tom and his brilliant sister end with the foreclosure upon the Dorlcote Mill by the debt of Mr. Tulliver, its owner, to lawyer Wakem. Tulliver remains as manager, but vows his son to eternal hatred of the Wakems. Maggie becomes interested in Philip Wakem, the son of the new owner, against her family wishes. Stephen Guest, engaged to Lucy Deane, takes Maggie for a boat-ride, and, though she refuses, they are forced to spend the night in the drifting boat. Tom, who is now running the mill that he has been able to buy back, and her father cast off Maggie as a fallen woman, which is actually the climax of the novel. The "the drama of brotherhood love", this impossible moral conflict, is solved by an external agent, the autumnal flood of the river Floss, during which Maggie hurries to her brother and is drowned with him.

Like Charlotte Brontë, George Eliot attempts to emphasize the complexity of a female personality, creating a highly emotional and intelligent character, whose life is a perpetual conflict between aspiration and possibility, happiness and duty, natural rights of the human being and the restrictions of morality, religion, and convention. Maggie is more intelligent than her brother, whose existence is founded on a straightforward fight for getting and keeping, and who is unworthy of Maggie's devotion. However, it seems that even the highly intellectualized author sensed the feminine need to lean upon the masculine assurance and will. The two characters, Tom and Maggie, even if deeply attached to each other, form an eternal and perfect contrast evident in the childlike accidents of their childhood and in their serious actions of maturity. They also seem to represent two distinct family types: Tom, like the Dodsons, is hard-working and practically-minded, showing features of selfishness and self-satisfaction, learning to avoid problems of every kind; Maggie, like the Tullivers, is impulsive and impractical, imaginative and generous, less reliable and less successful, representing the rustic, provincial existence of small farmers and their failure to adapt to the newly created environment.

Like Charlotte Brontë, George Eliot makes her characters act as influences dictate to them, but unlike Jane, Maggie is weak in relation to the milieu and is finally destroyed by common standards and the public opinion. Though the author would have attempted to attack the narrow-mindedness, the family pride and prejudices, the social rules, which are presented, as in Dickens, but unlike Thackeray's satire, with humour and sympathy, she seems not to approve of Maggie's rebellion, didactically showing the dramatic fate of those discontented with their lot. The author herself does not see any other ways of solving her character's problem except by allowing her to be broken by conventions. Eliot suggests, by providing an external solution (the flood on the river), that life is merely a rational problem, hardly allowing for the existence of yet unknown possibilities.

The concern with character and social background, dominant among Victorian realists, takes in *Middlemarch* new perspectives, allowing the involvement of the concept of "normality" which, alongside her omniscient point of view and the consideration of characters as firmly placed in actual social situations, makes her a true realist writer, a remarkable exponent of the Victorian High Realism. George Eliot argues that an individual subject belongs to and is dependent on society, but she also reveals a special insight into human psychology and a keen analysis of the individual: Ladislaw, for example, is never placed in a concrete social situation and he remains a romantic dream-figure, who has failed by Victorian standards. Ladislaw alone, with Dorothea, rebels against the values of the Middlemarch; they both express the idea that one's need to change the world he or she lives in has no place in the deterministic and mechanistic universe of the town. Like in Thackeray, Eliot's static vision of the social background contrasts with her uncommon emotionalism involved in the relationship between Ladislaw and Dorothea. The character of Dorothea Brooke is presented as yearning for a more satisfying life than Middlemarch can give, for she is dissatisfied with the general life of the women of her class, seeking something beyond the narrow selfishness and conformism of her lot and turning towards Puritanism and philanthropy, as with building the cottages for the labourers, to satisfy her unfulfilled aspirations, imagining (disastrously for her) that marrying Casaubon she will accomplish her potential. In earlier chapters of the novel, the examination of Dorothea involves the examination of the Middlemarch's background, and the society gradually becomes the prime matter of concern of the narrative, almost its subject. With the introduction of Lydgate, the basic structure of the novel changes, leading even to a lack of organic unity of the narrative, which is due to the fact that George Eliot actually joined together two novels, originally planned separately.

Middlemarch, intended to be a study of provincial life, is set in a Warwickshire town of the Reform period, and even the title, meaning the "middle of the marches", suggests a typical provincial setting. If the novel is lacking any organic unity, the intention is that Middlemarch itself, as a particular social environment, should be the unifying factor of the narrative, but in fact it is not. Eliot's view of society being static and determinist, it seems that the author is unable to sense the social power of change. Hence is her special concern with the problems of determinism, of personal responsibility, the drama of life in her novel being always a moral debate and an ethical discussion. Hence are her static moral attitudes, her character's individuality being chiefly passive, almost unable to change the outside world, though changed by it. Hence are the unheroic nature of her characters, who do not rebel, and almost no tragic conflict, though there are some moral crises. The character drawing in her novel is very much linked to the theme of compromise, which everyone ultimately accepts, between the life they aspired to and the life which social circumstances allow. To a mediocre reader, Casaubon's life is one to which a human being can only aspire, but Eliot makes the reader perceive the total uselessness of his existence; similarly, Lydgate's financial success and the position of a fashionable society physician is a perfect reward, but Eliot renders the tragic, worthless essence of the inner life of a character who abandons research at his wife's insistence. The characters' actions, their moral crises and decisions are strongly under the prevailing pressure of the Middlemarch way of life, without any vivid suggestions of the all-powerful destiny. "There is no private life which has not been determined by a wider public", claims George Eliot, and this is also shown in the novel by the author's profound analysis of the individual, her special insight into human psychology.

By the time *Middlemarch* was published, George Eliot was at the height of her fame, earning a considerable income from her work, and being widely admired and recognized as the greatest living English novelist. *Middlemarch* is definitely one of the first English novels entirely concerned with intellectual life. Virginia Woolf termed it "one of the few English novels written for grown-up people". Indeed, henceforth the development of English novel will reveal the art of fiction to be not only a product of a sensitive observer but also the means of rendering ideas based upon a conscious rational philosophy, new scientific discoveries and advancement of human thought. But the influence of scientific disciplines upon her work, materialized in the methodical demonstration of certain philosophical and aesthetic theories, in the terminology and concepts borrowed from biology, medicine, mathematics, and so on, as well as her frequent intervention with analyses, explanations and reflections in her work, also alludes to the crisis of the English novel in the second half of the nineteenth century. George Eliot's fiction bears also the influence of the French philosopher Auguste Comte's Positivism, the scientific attitude towards social behaviour, and the cause-and-effect relationship in different areas of human existence (economics, religion, culture) which explains human conduct. Comte saw three stages in the evolution of humanity – theological, metaphysical, positivist – and he believed that Europe was in the Positive or scientific era of development. Eliot insists in her novels that the human being should receive his or her rewards and punishments during his or her life, here and not hereafter, such rewards being not material but consisting in inner well-being.

George Eliot's progressive attitude towards the special issues of social behaviour and determinism prompted her attention to be focused on character and the rendering of characters acting as the influences of the milieu dictate upon them, for they are indeed conditioned by circumstances, education, inherited mores and prejudices. Eliot has broken with the picaresque tradition, still fecund in Victorian fiction (in Dickens, for instance) and has transformed the novel into a study of the individual as a social unit; she is less interested in socially representative types, for she is shifting the emphasis from the factual to the psychological and from plot to character and social background.

2.5 Lewis Carroll

Lewis Carroll (1832 – 1898), by his real name Charles Lutwidge Dodgson, the third in a family of 11 children of considerable literary and artistic interest, was educated at Rugby and Christ Church, Oxford, where he became a lecturer in mathematics in 1855. During his childhood, the Dodgson children produced family magazines which displayed his love of parody, acrostics and other word games and puzzles (he was later to invent many educational board games himself). Carroll was also a keen photographer, with a particular interest in photographing little girls, whose friendship he valued highly. Carroll's most famous literary works include *Alice's Adventures in Wonderland* (1865, originally entitled *Alice's Adventures Under Ground*) and *Through the Looking-Glass and What Alice Found There* (1871), but he is also the author of *Phantasmagoria and other poems* (1869), *The Hunting of the Snark* (1875), and *Sylvie and Bruno* (1889, 1893). He also wrote a number of mathematical treatises, the most valuable of which was his defence of Euclid, *Euclid and His Modern Rivals* (1879).

The theme of the "logical nonsense", or that of psychoanalytic growth/womb-entry, only partly helps us in discussing Carroll's work. However, it seems that Carroll, along with Edward Lear (1812 – 1888), represents the nineteenth-century offspring of the literature of nonsense, whose antecedents are to be found in some earlier instances from the Middle Ages, and which has a long history in Europe to be found in nearly all European languages and literatures. The reader's interest would be in the intentional kind of nonsense, which has become a minor genre in literature during the last 150 years. Carroll himself, both in the stories about Alice and in a number of songs which have become classics, continues the long tradition of the nonsense writers, especially of the brilliant Laurence Sterne. His stories are undoubtedly pieces of genius, containing a form of nonsense in which the logic seems deliberately planned and precise; although his true or positive nonsense writing is never intended to make formal sense, it has a kind of internal logic of its own, often comprising enigmatic variations on the absurd. Also, the success of his works is attributed to the fact that unlike most books for children of the epoch they do not teach anything and have no moral.

Alice's Adventures in Wonderland originated in a boat trip with the young daughters of H. G. Liddell: Alice, Lorina, and Edith, and it was for Alice that he expanded the story into book form. Alice pursues, in her dream, a White Rabbit down a rabbit-hole to a strange world where she meets famous characters such as the Mad Hatter and the March Hare, the Duchess and the Cheshire Cat, the King and the Queen of Hearts, and others. Her adventures in wonderland occur by the workings of a romantic mood intended to bring the memory and imagination which regain childhood. Alice's restoration of infancy happens as a physical retraction, for she gets in "the loveliest garden you ever saw" by shutting herself up as a telescope/microscope/"camera obscura" for Carroll the photographer. The setting and the architecture of the place remind of the Gothic houses – with their dark, small passages and halls – of the English romantic tradition.

The universe rendered in Alice's next dream, where she steps through the looking-glass, is far more complex and more open to interpretation. She enters the chessboard world where all the people are chessmen, and has to move through the game to be crowned queen at the end. The nonsense finally annoys her and forces her awake. Alice can travel through the mirror (which represents a forbidden source of knowledge, the knowledge itself, the perverse alter-ego – as with Dorian Gray's picture – or the access to a superior form of existence. The mirror alters reality by reflecting and reversing it rather than being a mimetic enforcement of actual objects. In the world of the looking-glass everything is the same "only the things go the other way", and, seeing them as mirror images of themselves (in Wilde's novel the picture discloses the inner existence by externalizing it), the author is allowed to render them symbolically. In this respect, one may be surprised how relativistically Carroll handles the concepts of time and space: the Unicorn remarks that Alice does not know "how to manage Looking-Glass cakes", saying that she is supposed to "hand it round first and cut it afterwards"; or the White Queen, refusing to permit it to be today, propounds the rule of "living backwards", which is in the romantic tradition. Wordsworth claimed that human memory works both retrospectively and as prophetic foresight, since the child is the predestining parent of the adult and can remember things before they happen. Carroll's Humpty Dumpty can explain all the poems that were ever invented and many of those that have not been invented yet, and Carroll himself would write letters back to front and play music boxes backwards.

2.6 Oscar Wilde

Oscar Wilde (1854 – 1900) was born in Dublin, the son of Sir William Wilde, a leading oculist and ear surgeon who founded the first eye and ear hospital in Great Britain, and June Francesca Elgee Wilde, a writer. In 1864, he entered the Portora Royal School at Enniskillen; in 1871, the Trinity College, Dublin, and from 1874 to 1879, he attended Magdalen College, Oxford, where he oscillated between the moralism of Ruskin and the aestheticism of Pater, finally proclaiming himself a disciple of the latter and of the cult of "art for art's sake". Wilde also vacillated between Roman Catholicism and Freemasonry and between heterosexuality and homosexuality. In 1882, he scored a great personal success in a lecturing tour of the United States, and in 1883 – 84, he extended his success in a lecturing tour of the United Kingdom. In 1884, Wilde married Constance Lloyd, a woman of means, the daughter of a Dublin barrister, and took a house in Chelsea, an artists' sector of London, where he made friends with James McNeill Whistler and other artists. Later, infatuated with the egocentric young Lord Douglas, Wilde made the friendship public, causing Douglas' father to criticize him publicly. The controversy soon lead to Wilde's arrest for homosexual offenses. He was sentenced to two years of hard labour, making him suffer bankruptcy and humiliation in the press. On release from prison, Wilde went in exile to the continent under the name of Sebastian Melmoth. After being baptized into the Roman Catholic Church, he died in 1900 of cerebral meningitis at the Hotel D'Alsace and was buried at Bagneaux.

Oscar Wilde is one of the leading British playwrights, novelists and short-story writers. While a student, he won in 1878 the Newdigate Prize for his poem *Ravenna*. His first volume of poetry, *Poems*, was published in 1881. He then turned to drama and, in 1882, produced in New York his first play, *Vera*, followed the next year by *The Duchess of Padua*, but both unsuccessful. In 1888, he published a collection of original fairy tales entitled *The Happy Prince and Other Tales*. The following year he published *The Portrait of Mr. W. H.* in *Blackwood's Magazine*, an essay on Shakespeare's sonnets which put forth the theory that many of them were addressed to a man. In 1891 Wilde published several essays and a number of books: *Intentions*, a collection of dialogues containing Wilde's aesthetic philosophy; *Lord Arthur Sanle's Crime, or Other Stories*, a collection of short stories; *A House of Pomegranates*, another collection of stories; *The Picture of Dorian Gray*, his only novel; and produced *The Duchess of Padua*. In 1892, he enjoyed great popular success for the production of *Lady Windermere's Fan* at St. James' Theater. The same year he wrote *Salome* in French, but it was denied production because of an old law forbidding theatrical depiction of Biblical characters. In 1893, he published *Lady Windermere's Fan* and *Salome* in French, and scored another success with *A Woman of No Importance*. The next year he published *Salome* in English, translated and wrote *The Importance of Being Earnest*, often regarded as his dramatic masterpiece. In 1895, Wilde put on this play at St. James' Theater, and *An Ideal Husband* at the Haymarket Theater. In prison he wrote *De Profundis*, a moving description of his spiritual progress through suffering to religious insight, in a form of a letter to Lord Alfred Douglas (published in part in 1905 and in full in 1962). In 1898, Wilde published his best known poem, *The Ballad of Reading Gaol*, and two letters on prison reform.

The aestheticism of *The Picture of Dorian Gray*, the novel which aroused a storm of controversy over its morality, and the author's attachment to the "art for art's sake" doctrine is the first thing that everyone normally discusses with reference to this novel. The term "aestheticism" derives from two Greek words: *aisthēta* (things perceptible by the senses) and *aisthētēs* (one who perceives). Its roots go back to the romantic doctrine and helps defining some of the later aspects of the twentieth-century experimental writings. The German writers of romanticism (Kant, Goethe, Schelling and Schiller) agreed that art must be autonomous, hence the artist should not be beholden to anyone; hence the artist is special, apart from other persons: this idea subsequently lead to the late nineteenth-century development of the image of the artist as a Bohemian and a non-conformist, which is a result of romantic subjectivism and self-culture, and of the cult of sensibility and individual ego. Gautier claimed that art has no utility; Poe created the theory of "the poem *per sè*" and rejected the "heresy of the didactic"; Poe also influenced the symbolism of Baudelaire's *Les Fleurs du Mal* and Mallarme's work. In England, aestheticism has also a close kinship to the reverence for beauty of the Pre-Raphaelites, their tendency to withdraw from the materialism of the Victorian period, and of Tennyson; a part of the movement were also the English Parnassians (Lionel Johnson, Andrew Lang, Ernest Dowson, Edmund Gosse), although their primary concern represented questions of form rather than sharp separation of art and morality. The dominant British figures of aestheticism were Walter Pater and his student Oscar Wilde, who insisted on the separation of art and moral issues, and generally it was the result of the French influence of symbolism and native ideas.

Aestheticism represents the point of view that art is self-sufficient and need serve no other purpose than its own ends; art is an end in itself and is not moral, didactic, political, propagandist, or anything else but itself, and it should not be judged by any non-aesthetic criteria, primarily whether it is or not useful. Art is important not life; art instead of life; life as art; or art as an alternative to life. At its extreme, and its worst, aestheticism turned to mannerism and vapid idealism; at its best, aestheticism was a reaction against the materialism, complacency, hypocrisy and Philistinism of the age, a revitalizing influence searching for beauty and asserting that it has an independent value.

Aestheticism, as an important artistic and literary movement, a mode of sensibility in the second half of the nineteenth century, is closely linked to aesthetics, the study of the beautiful in art, nature, and literature. Aesthetics is also a philosophy, attempting to answer questions such as "What is art?" and "What is beauty and what is its relationship to other human values?"; it has also a psychological dimension:

"how is beauty perceived and recognized?", or "what is the source of aesthetic enjoyment?". The aesthetic study of literature concentrates on the sense of beauty rather than on moral, social, or political considerations, and, when pursued rigorously, it leads to aestheticism and art for art's sake doctrine.

Oscar Wilde was a quintessential aesthete, a disciple of Pater, cultivating an extravagant style of living and defying conventional opinion with his wit. In *De Profundis*, recalling how he read Pater's *The Renaissance* in his first term at Oxford, he calls it "that book which has had such a strange influence over my life". And over his literary activity as well, we may add, for his novel explores the idea of the self-sufficiency of art, and that art has nothing to do with morality, and that it endures while life passes.

Although Wilde has tried to illustrate in his work the self-assumed truth that "aesthetics is higher than ethics", one may not help noticing that the novel does not take a positive view of recognized aestheticism, or fully supports the doctrine – it rather displays its dangers. The novel also displays some of the aspects of the basic pattern of the Bildungsroman as it renders the formation of a Faustian character from an innocent person into an immoral creature. Also, Dorian is presented as progressing, or rather regressing, to art and back to life. There are other two characters that assume a protective role and influence the formation of Dorian, and Wilde regards the three characters as reflections of his own image, explaining to a correspondent: "Basil Hallward is what I think I am: Lord Henry – what the world thinks me: Dorian is what I would like to be – in other ages, perhaps".

Basil introduces him to the realm of art and art as another form of existence. Basil refuses to exhibit his painting because art mirrors the artist's inner existence, art is the image of the artist himself, for the portrait is too revealing for his love for Dorian, as Dorian later fears that it is too revealing of himself, which is in contradiction with Wilde's statement in the book's *Preface* that "to reveal art and conceal the artist is art's aim".

Lord Henry seduces and corrupts Dorian through plagiarizing the ideas and conceptions stated in Pater's *Studies in the History of Renaissance*, ever quoting, or misquoting, without acknowledgment, from this book as a means of expressing judgments on beauty, art, life, the relationship between life and art. Lord Henry, like Pater, proposes a new hedonism attainable through art, stating that "We are punished for our refusals. Every impulse that we strive to strangle broods in the mind, and poisons us. The body sins once, and has done with its sin, for action is a mode of purification. (…) The only way to get rid of a temptation is to yield to it, resist it, and your soul grows sick". Also, when Dorian tells him that he is corrupted by a book, his friend denies it: "As for being poisoned by a book, there is no such thing as that. Art has no influence upon action. It annihilates the desire to act. It is sureptibly sterile. The books that the world calls immoral are books that show the world its own shame. That is all".

Dorian accepts a Faustian pact, with no visible devil, that he will exchange places with his portrait in order to preserve himself as a work of art. Through the presentation of the gradual change of his character, Wilde is able to render the dangers of following the doctrine of aestheticism in real life. Dorian kills Basil and makes his body disappear; another challenging moment of his invulnerable and detached existence is represented by his love and attachment to Sybil Vane, an experiment in the "aesthetic laboratory". As an actress, belonging to the realm of art, Dorian is able to aestheticize her in his imagination: "I have been right to take my love out of poetry and to find my wife in Shakespeare's plays". Like with Gretchen, who poisons herself, their affair ends badly, for she is drawn by love to prefer reality, her fatal weakness in Dorian's eyes being that she values life above art. "All art is but a reflection" of reality, claims Sybil, and Dorian excommunicates her with the cruel words "Without your art you are nothing". She poisons herself in despair, and even her death is rendered aesthetically, firstly by Lord Henry who considers it a performance, "a strange lurid fragment from some Jacobean tragedy", and then by Dorian: "She passed again into the sphere of art". As opposed to Dorian, Sybil gives up the pretence of art in order to live entirely artlessly in this world, only to commit suicide. The great thematic reversal of the novel suggests that Dorian tries to give up the causality of life and to live in the deathless, or perhaps lifeless, world of art, which also means to commit suicide.

2.7 Thomas Hardy

Thomas Hardy (1840 – 1928), son of a stonemason, whose family had known better days, was born at Upper Bockhampton, near Dorchester in Dorset. His father taught him the violin, and in 1849, he began playing it locally. His mother greatly encouraged his early interest in books. In 1848 Hardy began attending Julia Martin's school in Bockhampton, and in 1853, his education became intensive – he studied Latin, French and read widely. At 16, in 1856, Hardy was articled to the local architect John Hicks. Around this time Hardy met and studied with Horace Moule, going through the Greek dramatists under his tutelage. In 1862, Hardy travelled to London to work under Arthur Blomfield. There he pursued a hectic London life, exploring the cultural life of London, visiting museums, attending plays and operas, finding time for extensive reading and writing poetry. In 1865 Hardy published his first article, *How I Built Myself a House*. Hardy returned to Dorset in 1867 to continue architectural works for Hicks. Hardy began considering writing as a profession and wrote his first unpublished novel, *The Poor Man and the Lady*. In 1870, he travelled to St. Juliot, Cornwall, to work on the restoration of the church, where he met Emma Lavinia Gifford, the rector's sister-in-law. In 1874, he gives up architecture for writing, and in September of that year Hardy marries Emma, travels to Paris, and sets up house in London. He moves around and eventually settles in Sturminster Newton. The marriage soon produced intolerable strains, but it also produced, after Emma's death in 1912, some of his most moving poems. He and his wife travelled in Europe and Hardy spent several months of nearly every year in London. In 1914, he married Florence Dugdale. During this time Hardy was already famous, and public honours fell upon him, among them the OM, honorary degrees from Oxford and Cambridge, the gold medal of the Royal Society of Literature, and so on.

Between 1871, the year of his first published novel, *Desperate Remedies*, and the publication of *Jude the Obscure* in 1895, Hardy wrote other 15 novels, as well as many short stories and poems. His novels and short stories, according to his own classification, fall into three groups, namely Novels of Character and Environment:

Under the Greenwood Tree (1872), *Far From the Madding Crowd* (1874), *The Return of the Native* (1878), *The Mayor of Casterbridge* (1886), *The Woodlanders* (1887), *Wessex Tales* (1888), *Tess of the d'Urbervilles* (1891), *Life's Little Ironies* (1894), *Jude the Obscure* (1895); Romances and Fantasies: *A Pair of Blue Eyes* (1873), *The Trumpet-Major* (1880), *Two on a Tower* (1882), *A Group of Noble Dames* (1891), *The Pursuit of the Well-Beloved* (1892, 1897); and Novels of Ingenuity: *Desperate Remedies* (1891), *The Hand of Ethelberta* (1876), *A Laodicean* (1881). In 1913, Hardy published *A Changed Man, The Waiting Supper, and other Tales* as a reprint of a dozen minor novels belonging to the various groups.

After the publication of his last novel, in 1895, Hardy gave up the writing of fiction, which he had always regarded as inferior to poetry, and began to assemble his first volume of verse, *Wessex Poems* (1898). His successive collections of poetry, ending with *Winter Words* in 1928, were received without enthusiasm except by a discerning few, and it was not until long after his death that his poetry began to receive critical acclaim. He published eight volumes of poetry, the other six collections being *Poems of the Past and Present* (1902), *Time's Laughingstocks* (1909), *Satires of Circumstance* (1914), *Moments of Vision* (1917), *Late Lyrics and Earlier* (1922), *Human Shows* (1925). Hardy also published over 40 short stories and an epic drama, *The Dynasts*. Although both his poetry and stories demonstrate a high degree of skill, his reputation in these fields has never approached his reputation as a novelist.

Among Hardy's Novels of Character and Environment, the most celebrated are *Far From the Madding Crowd, The Mayor of Casterbridge* and *Tess of the d'Urbervilles*. Thomas Hardy is almost unique in the general Victorian pattern of fiction-writing, and it is difficult to find any direct alliances to one or another literary trend of the time. It would not be appropriate to do so, though he reveals some aspects of romanticism, realism and even naturalism, some critics say, and he triumphantly takes the English novel into the twentieth century.

The main theme of Hardy's novels is the struggle of man against the indifferent forces that rule the world and inflict on him sufferings and ironies of life and love; in other words, the power of destiny, its stress-mark on the existence of humans. Hardy concentrates firstly on character, and his sharp sense of humour and absurd finds expression in the affectionate presentation of the rustic characters, while exploring the complexity of his characters' inner world and while touching some important psychological issues. Secondly, he is almost romantic in his admiration and observation of the natural world, often with a strong symbolic effect. In the same way, he approaches and reveals attitudes of celebration towards his native Wessex.

Hardy was claimed to possess a bizarre juxtaposition specific to the Pre-Raphaelites, but he is mainly a regional novelist, whose imaginary world of Wessex covers a large area of southern and western England. He reveals in his novels a deep attachment to the rural customs and ways of life, which he knew as a boy, to the close communion and idealized relationship between man and nature, which he praises in, among others, *Far From the Madding Crowd*. Hardy is a poet in many lyrical passages of his fiction, and he writes the formal poetry of his life. If he is often a realist in his poetry, he is a poet in his fiction, and this is much noticeable in this novel, which, unlike his later works, brings up the idea that the tension and violence of human life and nature, though never to be eliminated, can be borne by patient endurance. The title points to the provincial setting of the novel, while the narrative movement, the novel's complex structure on different levels and the huge number of protagonists suggest that there can be strong passions and multiple actions "far from the madding crowd" of big cities and vast human communities.

The main character is Bathsheba Everdene, with a more complex personality than the others, and, unlike the others, she develops and changes as the narrative progresses. She is the central figure who affects the life of every other character in the story. The early part of the novel stresses her high-spirited vanity and provocative capriciousness; her spirit is decided and independent; she is a "new woman" striving for independence and emancipation. One may also notice her love for nature and wilderness, her interest in music and books, her capable adaptation of behaviour towards different people in various circumstances, as well as her physical appearance, admired by many. She rejects Gabriel Oak and the well-to-do farmer Boldwood, preferring the dashing Sergeant Troy, a young cavalry officer, which is her greatest weakness. In her relations with Oak and Troy, she represents the two sides of the currency of life: the wrongs done by women to men and the greater wrongs done by men to women. Sergeant Troy is an atractive personality who introduces powerful sexual symbols in the narrative, masculine virile force, but he eventually turns to be a lady killer, a romantic sentimentalist who ruins his own life and the lives of others, like that of Fanny Robin, whose name suggests the idea of a person-victim. Gabriel Oak, whose name points to both divinity and nature, persists in loving Bathsheba, his passion being the passion of nature itself, proving his moral integrity until his strength provides the prop that she needs, justifying the novel's happy ending.

In his later fiction, Hardy becomes conscious of the social changes and problems of his time, such as agricultural innovation and the power of the new aimed at replacing the old patriarchal relations in rural community, as in *The Mayor of Casterbridge*, for instance, a pessimistic novel expressing his new outlook. The level of tragedy is extended by the author's insights into human psychology and the idea of the imperfection of man dominated by his subconscious passions, the social relations and the mysterious forces that govern human destiny. Michael Henchard, after selling his wife and baby, decides to confront destiny by not drinking for 20 years – this attempt brings nothing but ruin, for, Hardy suggests, human beings are mere puppets bandied about by fate.

Hardy was also aware of the contradiction of contemporary sexual moves, rendered in *Tess of the d'Urbervilles*, a novel which was received with bitter hostility against the author's pessimism and immorality. The subtitle, "A Pure Woman", was important to Hardy's purpose, though it seems to be difficult to prove the adequacy of innocence and purity to the selling of body and the later murdering of a man. Throughout the novel, Tess lives on spiritual and physical levels, the former leading to a moral, spiritual regeneration through suffering and the latter suggesting her physical degradation in selling herself for the sake of her family. Again, the stress-mark of destiny is seen in the past and in the present, in the decay of d'Urberville to Durberfield; the glorious past of the family is compared to the present state of degradation of Tess and her family, and the past is never buried in her case. She experiences a dangerous journey to womanhood and motherhood, and her baby becomes a symbol of her sin – the seduction by Alec. Tess is a strong presence in the novel, all other characters being viewed through her personality: Alec is associated with animalism and the physical dominance over her; Angel Clare exerts a spiritual and emotional dominance, having "the face of the one man on earth who loved her purely". Later, despite having a family and a husband, she is alone, making the reader aware of the fact that she has never known the bright side of life, all her journeys, both spiritual and physical, ending in tragedy and suffering. Her dream-like state is a refuge from reality, which she can never escape. The only happy moment of her life is the time spent with Angel, when, after being maddened by the second wrong that has been done to her by Alec, she kills him to liberate herself and to revenge on her past. After a brief period of concealment with Angel Clare in the New Forest, she is arrested at Stonebridge, tried and hanged. Hardy symbolically renders her death in relation with the ancient rituals of human sacrifice, involving the best representatives of the tribe, who usually were innocent children or young virgins.

2.8 Alfred, Lord Tennyson

Alfred, Lord Tennyson (1809 – 1892), son of a rector, George Tennyson, was born and raised in Somersby, Lincolnshire. In 1827, he entered Trinity College, Cambridge, where he joined the Apostles and became friend with Arthur Henry Hallam, son of an eminent Victorian historian, himself a gifted critic who is said to represent romanticism to Tennyson. He was engaged to marry Tennyson's sister Emily, the muse of his mature work and the most important experience in Tennyson's life. It was under Hallam's influence that Tennyson became a Keatsian poet. When Hallam died suddenly of a stroke in 1833, in Vienna, at the age of 22, it was Tennyson's most terrible experience, and very much of what he wrote afterwards shows the mark of the loss and most of his best poetry is elegiac in nature (*Ulysses, In Memoriam*, for instance, or *Tears Idle Tears*). Tennyson's first volume of poetry was published in 1830 as *Poems, Chiefly Lyrical*, and, though unfavourably reviewed, it contained such outstanding poems as *The Poet, The Lady of Shalott, The Palace of Art*, and others. His second volume, *Poems*, appeared in 1832, including, among others, *The Lotos-Eaters*. His next volume, *Poems*, appeared only in 1842, consisting of a selection from the previous two volumes, and containing also the poems *Ulysses, Morte d'Arthur, The Two Voices*, and others.

The theme of escapism and the concern with major problems of the time represent the dominant aspects of Tennyson's poetic activity. He is largely considered the greatest figure of Victorian poetry, the idle of the age, with larger audience and more veneration than any other English poet. His escapism is rendered in *Ulysses*, for instance, by assuming the position of Ulysses, the ancient hero of Homer's *Odyssey*, and rendering other temporal and spatial realities, capturing the moment of Ulysses' return home, his feelings and ideas raised by his present position of boredom and unsatisfactory state of mind, and the final desire to escape the present moment by continuing the travel on sea, or perhaps the oppressiveness of the despairing grief for Hallam. The poem, written in the autumn of 1833, is a dramatic monologue of Ulysses who is now in the position of an idle king and who has no action to fulfil. The first five lines show Ulysses as a High Romantic Hero, detached and keeping distance from other humans (as Childe Harold, for example), or rather being above them, denying the very essence of human nature, "a savage race, / That hoard, and sleep, and feed, and know not me", and scorning his son's sense of responsibility. As a romantic figure, he appears to lack the capacity to love other people (except his mariners, perhaps); he is a person of outstanding capabilities, experiencing everything in a very concrete way. Ulysses has found delight in the violent actions of the past, which brought him fame ("I am become a name", "honoured of them all", and so on), and identifies with his past experience: "I am a part of all that I have met". Claiming that experience is an arch which you can never reach, Ulysses intends to start moving westward because of his "grey spirit yearning in desire / To follow knowledge like a sinking star", Tennyson exalting his hero's eternally restless aspiration. The glorious past is praised and desired, the present is unbearable, while the future is unimaginable. Ulysses has an experience in the past and projects an improbable, uncertain future, which would perhaps bring death, and "Death closes all". It is a kind of death in action, in active life, different from the spiritual death of other human beings, which Ulysses rejects and is terrified of. For him, it is the action that counts, not the fact that he may finally reach the desired islands, or die washed down by the gulfs. The last lines of the poem make clear the tension of his dramatic monologue, yet with a definite note of optimism, hope and reconciliation, and even a satanic note of rebellion: "To strive, to seek, to find, and not to yield". As Tennyson himself points out, the poem "was written soon after Arthur Hallam's death, and gave my feeling about the need of going forward, and braving the struggle of life perhaps more simply than anything in *In Memoriam*".

The romantic quality of the poem is rendered by the character of Ulysses, his superior condition, rebellion and demonism, his heroic, sustained drive for knowledge, and, perhaps to a lesser degree, by the natural objects reflecting and participating in human moods and feelings (for example, "barren crags" and Ulysses's barren soul, or the "lights begin to twinkle from the rocks" at the moment when he expresses desire to move and seek a newer land).

Tennyson's characterisation of Ulysses as an admirable and resourceful figure relates the Tennyson's persona to the hero of Homer's *Odyssey*, and not to its Dantesque version of the legendary hero, where in Canto XXVI of *The Inferno* in *The Divine Comedy* Dante introduces the "crafty" Ulysses as a "false counsellor", and the poet together with his guide Virgil meet the hero as "double-flame" which he shares with Diomedes, his compatriot from the Trojan War.

The idea of the close relationship between man and nature, the natural objects mirroring the human condition, is to a greater extent explored in *The Lotos-Eaters*, another poem related to Homer's work. The first five stanzas are Spenserian and consist in the description of the land, where "all things always seemed the same" – a land of contraries with a static existence between lightness and darkness, motion of life and deadly pause. Words like "afternoon", "weary dream" and others help create the atmosphere, and especially the memorable "slender stream / Along the cliff to fall and pause and fall did seem", perhaps one of the longest lines in English poetry because of the repetition of the words and the use of long vowels. However, the line is remarkable for its uncommon ability to grasp and define the setting which would eventually become the condition of the mariners themselves. They taste the fruits offered by the mild-eyed melancholy Lotos-eaters (whose pale faces, which "pale against that rosy flame", fit the general atmosphere) and lapse into a sort of existence consisting in a number of contrasts between life and death, deep-sleep and reality, day and night, spiritual activity and physical inactivity – mariners speak but their voices are thin, "as voices from the grave"; unable to move, the Lotos-eaters sat them down "upon the yellow sand" – splendidly rendered in juxtaposition with the natural phenomena of "sunset", "afternoon", "red West".

The mariners' state of is *ataraxie*: a trance, a sweet death, yet alive, a static experience of tranquillity and calmness, an unnatural state for man, where the "music in his ears his beating heart did make" (as in Robert Frost's *Stopping by Woods on a Snowy Evening*, stating that "The only other sound's the sweep / Of easy wind and downy flake"). Ataraxie also a kind of escapism from the real existence, the abundance of life's actions: they lose their identities, refuse to continue the way home, and render the idea of the worthlessness of past glory and action, compared to the ecstasy that can be found in inactivity. The total detachment of the mariners is presented in the "Choric Song", which consists in the descriptions of the land alternating with the mariners' present state, leading to the idea that the poem embodies many feelings of the ideal proposed by aestheticism, namely asserting that "Death is the end of life; ah, why / Should life all labour be?".

The poem denies the whole existence, the brevity of life, and is more or less directly expressive of his grief for his lost fiend. Explicitly inspired by Hallam's death is the elegy *In Memoriam*, completed in 1850, when he was made Poet Laureate. It was first published anonymously in the volume with this title in 1850. The 131 sections or separate poems that compose it were written and rewritten from 1833 to the time of publication. Two of the 131 sections were added in later editions: LIX in 1851, and XXXIX in 1872. The sections can be read as separate poems, but they are unified by themes, ideas, and verse form. The poem is written in memory of Hallam and explicitly mourns his death. Although written without any plan at first, the parts of the poem were finally arranged in a pattern to cover the period of about three years following Hallam's death. Tennyson himself insisted that it is "a poem, not a biography (...). The different moods of sorrow as in a drama are dramatically given, and my conviction that fear, doubts, and suffering will find answer and relief only through Faith in a God of Love. I is not always the author speaking of himself, but the voice of the human race speaking through him".

The poem centres on a number of major spiritual problems of Victorian age, such as the conflict between religion and science, the doubts raised by science regarding the immortality of the soul, the meaning of life, the predestined values and existence of man in the world, and so on. The author speaks here in his own name, disclosing the workings of the soul and expressing a split personality concerned with the major problems of the time. The double vision of the poet-hero consists in counter-pointing his belief in development, progress and established values to the personal negation of the Victorian definiteness and respectability; or how can the poet's soul in pain hope to find consolation and peace in an indifferent world? In this respect, as T. S. Eliot remarks, Tennyson was "the most instinctive rebel against the society in which he was the most perfect conformist".

Many of the narrative poems included in *The Idylls of the King* (1842, 1859 – 1885) reveal the same sense of loss and more or less directly mourn the death of Hallam. The collection contains poems on the Arthurian legends, such as *The Coming of Arthur*, *Lancelot and Elaine*, *The Holy Grail*, *The Passing of Arthur*, which represent the author's effort to deal, in disguise, with major problems of his time. The dominant theme of the poems is the attempt by Arthur to establish standards of morality, of marital faithfulness, useful action for self and society, self-control and attachment to the spiritual norms represented by the Holy Grail. The counter-theme may be suggested by Tennyson's own words: "I intended Arthur to represent the ideal soul of man coming into conflict with the warring elements of the flesh", that is to say, the extermination of the spiritual by the physical, the quest of a self for a universe free from the rise of materialism and sensualist drives, corruption and deprivation of any moral or spiritual values. With the death of Arthur, Tennyson suggests, a magnificent ideal collapses, and one cannot help noticing the author's sense of loss, of nostalgia for times gone by, for an ideal past recreated by the poet's imagination within the framework of an imaginary world in which he could flee from the horrors of daily life, and this is actually the very essence of the literature of escape.

Tennyson was essentially romantic in tastes, conforming in utterance and peculiarly careful about poetic technique, following the tradition of Spenser, Milton, Shelley, Keats by favouring the ornamentation of the text, emphasizing pleasant musicality and sound, elegant and smooth verse, its refinement, grace and pathos, which set him apart from a number of contemporary to him poets, especially from the more experimental and colloquial Robert Browning.

2.9 The Brownings

Robert Browning (1812 – 1889) was born in a well-to-do family in Camberwell, near London. He derived from his parents a deep, though unconventional, religious sense and a love of books, music and painting. His father was a clerk in the Bank of England. His mother was of German-Scottish descent. Browning's strong will determined him to become a poet against his parents' wishes. In 1844, while revisiting Italy, he met Elizabeth Barrett. Browning began corresponding with her in 1845, after he read and became an admirer of her 1844 *Poems*. In 1846, they married and settled in Casa Guidi in Florence where he composed many of his poems. Elizabeth died in 1861, saddening Browning greatly, which drove him back to London where he became a well-known figure in London literary circles. From 1866, after the death of his father, he lived with his sisters, generally spending the "season" in London, and the rest of the year in the country or abroad. He died in Venice on 12 December 1889, and his body was interred in Poet's Corner, Westminster Abbey.

Browning's first published poem was *Pauline*, in 1833, inspired by Shelley's *Alastor* and consisting of a series of musings on poetic sensibility. Also inspired by Shelley were his poems *Paracelsus* (1835) and *Sordello* (1840), but the collection of poetry, entitled *Dramatic Lyrics*, published between 1840 – 42, already revealed his characteristic form and technique of writing – the dramatic monologue. In 1855, Browning published *Men and Women*, considered the masterpiece of his middle period and containing 50 monologues, among which *Andrea del Sarto*, one of the finest. His 1864 collection of *Dramatic Personae* began to revive his reputation and earn him a definite place among the poets of the time. The revival was completed by the triumph of *The Ring and the Book* (1869), by which he achieved the reputation of a major poet, equal to that of Tennyson. The volume brought out Browning's interest in the Italian scene, moral casuistry, and the complexity of the human personality. The publications that followed include, among others, *Balanstion's Adventure* (1871), *Fifine at the Fair*

(1872), *Red Cotton Night-Cap Country* (1873), *Aristophanes' Apology* (1875), *Dramatic Idylls* (1879), *Jocoseria* (1883), and others. His last volume, *Asolando*, was published on the day of his death.

Browning is chiefly praised for his novelty and experiments with dramatic monologue, language and syntax, which make him a forerunner of the twentieth-century literature. The speakers in his monologues are painters of Renaissance, physicians of the Roman Empire, musicians and other artists, or just common persons belonging to different ages, all masks for the poet who displays his energy to explore the problems of good and evil, faith and doubt, the role of art, the role and condition of the artist in the modern world, and others. In the advertisement to *Dramatic Lyrics* of 1842, Browning stated that his poems are "though for the most part Lyric in expression, always Dramatic in principle, and so many utterances of so many imaginary persons, not mine". Tennyson, similarly, would often claim his detachment from the nature of the characters he created. In both of them the characters express the author's opinion, often under the mask of a duplicitous discourse in long dialogues and narratives, and especially in dramatic monologues which Browning termed "introspective drama" and "drama into character". His characters are often failed artists, imperfect poets, unhappy lovers, fanatics, monomaniacs, presented at the moment of psychological crisis and revelatory emotional stress, usually when reality provides new interpretations in moments of involuntary self-revelation, similarly to epiphany. They express a huge amount of ideas under the stress of emotion in a world of imperfection, a world as a moral battleground, a life of trial and probation, of limitations to the soul and spiritual insight provided by the flesh and senses as the necessary conditions for moral testing.

Like Tennyson, and the romantics, in general, Browning is chiefly interested in the individual consciousness, in the individual man, and in the dramatic conflicts which arise from the juxtaposition of the spiritual and the fleshly, the fulfilment and the inevitable failure. He proves to be a subtle psychological explorer, whose apparently unitary human personalities contain a multiplicity of selves. Like in Tennyson, there is a major contradiction in his conception and thought: the belief in God, in the existence and the immortality of the soul versus the delight in the sensuousness of the material world, the acceptance of new scientific discoveries, especially those of the natural sciences regarding the doctrine of evolutionism. Some present-day critics link Browning to the progressive-minded school of post-romantic poetry known as the "Spasmodics", or "The New Poets" (1825 – 55), who attempted both to explore and overcome the contradictions evident in the literary achievements of the romantic movement.

Unlike Tennyson, who views the universe in terms of acceptance, order, wisdom and regularity rising from the workings of a divine rule, Browning inhabits it with strong characters, dramatic conflicts and great passions. His conception of the universe is a dynamic one, full of passion and energy manifest in all aspects of creation. God is the symbol of the original principle of energy, of high tension, unbound passion, and of the presence of vitality as the axis of the universe. In his poetry, the persona attempts to escape the imperfect and incomplete essence of the material universe, permanently aspiring towards God.

Also unlike Tennyson, Browning experimented with language and syntax, applying to his poetry grotesque rhymes, abrupt, violent, and law-breaking diction of a direct, colloquial style, which turns to be modern and difficult. The contraction by ellipsis, the emphasizing epithets, the crowding of determinatives, and many other elements separate his style from the general style of the Victorian age, represented chiefly by Tennyson and Rossetti. Browning's style follows especially the tradition of John Donne, a more colloquial and discordant one, even stenographic, leading to obscurity.

My Last Duchess, for instance, one of Browning's best-known dramatic monologues, enables the reader, speaker, and the poet to keep an appropriate distance from each other, aligned in such a way that the reader must work through the words of the speaker, rendered as a normal, even colloquial speech, towards the meaning implied by the poet himself. From the Duke's one-sided conversation, the reader pieces together the situation, both past and present, and understands what sort of woman the Duchess really was, and what sort of man the Duke is. Ultimately, the reader comprehends the meaning of the poem and what the poet thinks of the speaker he has created. Such a statement as "I give commands", , betrays the Duke's power of dominance over people, or can imply the idea that he may have caused her death, following his reproach to her openness to everybody, including the artist who painted her. The painting represents a substitute for the dead woman, it is an object that he possesses and is not willing to share with anyone else. The Duke keeps the painting covered – the instinct of possession – but her smile annoys him because it expresses some joy of life he is not able to experience. He implicitly warns his future wife that he wants total submission and he expects her to let herself be entirely possessed; he wants his next wife to be an object just like the former wife is now an object (a picture, a portrait). From evidence outside the poem we know that Browning had a special aversion for domestic tyrants, such as his father-in-law; *The Ring and the Book* is the story of a man who, like the Duke, is irritated by his wife's virtues.

My Last Duchess is based on incidents in the life of Alfons II, Duke of Ferrara, in Italy, whose first wife, a young girl, died in 1561 after three years of marriage. Following her death, the Duke negotiated through an agent to marry a niece of the Court of Tyrol, with its capital in Innsbruck. Brother Pomdalf is an imaginary painter, and Claus of Innsbruck is probably an imaginary sculptor, too.

In order to write *Andrea del Sarto*, first published in *Men and Women* (1855), Browning draws upon Giorgio Vasari's *Lives of the Painters* (published in 1550) for the details of Andrea's life. Andrea (1486—1531) was the son of a tailor in Florence, and hence is the name "del Sarto". Having served his apprenticeship and learned his craft, he was engaged to do a series of frescoes for the Church of the Annunciation in Florence, and then to do another series for the Church of the Recollets. It was these paintings that secured his fame and earned him the title "Il Pittore senza Errori", the "faultless painter". During this period he married Lucrezia del Fede, a widow, who served as a model for a number of his pictures. In 1518, Andrea was invited by Francis I of France to come to the court at Fontainebleau. The next year Francis gave him money for the purchase of pictures in Florence for the palace of Fontainebleau, and Andrea left France on this commission. According to Vasari, through Lucrecia's persuasion Andrea used the king's money to build himself a house in Florence, never daring to return to France, and in effect destroying "the eminence he had attained with so much labour", Much of Vasari's story has been doubted by modern scholars; nor are they inclined to share Vasari's (and Browning's) view of the limitations of

Andrea's art. The accuracy of Browning's poem as biography or as art criticism is, however, of doubtful relevance to its success or its meaning.

Inspired by the life of this Italian painter, Browning presents to the reader the tragic fate of both man and artist, unhappy in marriage and a failure in painting. Also, through the speaker's statements uttered in a crucial moment of intense suffering, and through his half-dramatic, half-ironic, sometimes sarcastic voice, Browning discusses the condition of the artist as craftsman and as inspired creator. Andrea speaks half to himself, half to his wife, suggesting the decline of their love, a moment of crisis in their relationship, along with the crisis and failure of his status as an artist. Though indirectly, he blames her for the present situation, her infidelity and sensuality. As an artist, Andrea finds refuge in the universe of his art, and he is a real master in painting. His hand is sure enough to draw without sketches: "No sketches first, no studies", suggesting that he is a complete craftsman, but this is assisted by "This low-pulsed forthright craftsman's hand of mine". According to Browning's conception of art as craft and art as inspiration, this is not enough to create complete, perfect paintings. Andrea's art is almost perfect, his paintings are near heaven, but they lack inspiration. Others, among whom Rafael, are not perfect craftsmen, yet they have access to heaven, a superior form of experience, the source of true inspiration, that is shut to him. This is also not enough, for, Andrea says, even if the other painters "enter and take their place there sure enough", they "come back and cannot tell the world", meaning they lack craftsmanship. A perfect, complete art, Browning implies through his speaker, has to combine craftsmanship and inspiration, the artist has to be true to life and to possess "a truer light of God". Andrea finds imperfection in Rafael's design; he intends to correct it because it is not true to life, but he understands that he cannot change the fame of Rafael. Aware of his limitations as a craftsman, bound to an unfaithful wife, who is perfect as a model but lacking spirituality, Andrea discloses his inner tension, the crisis of his artistic career, the end of his artistic power, a sort of artistic impotence: "And I'm the weak-eyed bat no sun should tempt", which will eventually be defeated in heaven, after death, where he places himself near Leonard, Rafael and Agnolo.

Elizabeth Barrett Browning (1806 – 1861) was born in Durham, the daughter of Edward Moulton-Barrett, who made most of his considerable fortune from Jamaican sugar plantations. She spent her childhood at Hope End, in Herefordshire, where she lived a privileged childhood, riding her pony around the grounds, visiting other families in the neighbourhood, and arranging family theatrical productions with her eleven brothers and sisters. Although frail, she apparently had no health problems until 1821, when Dr. Coker prescribed opium for a nervous disorder. Her mother died when she was 22, and critics mark signs of this loss in *Aurora Leigh*. Elizabeth, an accomplished child, read Shakespeare's plays, parts of Pope's Homeric translations, passages from *Paradise Lost*, and the histories of England, Greece, and Rome before the age of ten. Although largely self-educated at home, she became deeply versed in the classics and in prosodic theory, and later published translations from ancient and Byzantine Greek poetry. In 1832, the Barrett family moved to Sidmouth, and in 1835 to London. In 1838, seriously ill as a result of a broken blood-vessel, Elizabeth was sent to Torquay, where, two years later, her eldest brother Edward drowned, to her lifelong grief. She returned to London in 1841, still an invalid. In 1845, Robert

Browning started correspondence with her which led to their meeting and to an engagement, necessarily secret since her tyrannical father ruled his adult sons and daughters as they were still children and forbade any of them to marry. In September 1846 Browning and Elizabeth were secretly married and left for Italy. Mr. Barrett disinherited her, as he did to each one of his children who got married without his permission, and he never gave his it to anyone. Unlike her brothers and sisters, Elizabeth had inherited some money of her own, so the Brownings were reasonably comfortable in Italy. Casa Guidi in Florence became their base for the rest of Mrs. Browning's life, though they paid long visits to Rome, London, and Paris. In 1849, they had a son, Robert Wiedeman Barrett Browning. Throughout her life in Italy, Elizabeth Browning was actively interested in politics, those of Italy and France, and was a passionate supporter of Italian independence and unity. Her political enthusiasm played an important role in and influenced many of her poems, especially *Casa Guidi Windows*.

Mrs. Browning's *The Battle of Marathon* (1820), *An Essay on Mind, with other poems* (1826), and a translation of *Prometheus Bound* (1833) appeared anonymously, the first two being privately printed at her father's expense. *The Seraphim, and Other Poems* (1838) was her first work to gain critical and public attention. Her next set of *Poems* appeared in 1844 and was highly regarded. At her husband's insistence, the second edition of her *Poems*, which appeared in 1850, included *Sonnets from the Portuguese. Casa Guidi Windows* followed in 1851 and *Poems before Congress* in 1860. In 1857 she saw the publication of the verse-novel *Aurora Leigh*, her *magnum opus*, written in the tradition of Bildungsroman, which today attracts more attention than the rest of her writings.

The place of Elizabeth Barrett Browning's poetry and the critical evaluation of its literary value decreased in the twentieth-century, but during the nineteenth century, no other female poet than Elizabeth Browning was held in higher esteem among cultured readers in both the United States and England. Her poetry had an immense impact on the works of Emily Dickinson who admired her as a woman of achievement. She was recommended as a possible successor to the poet laureateship that was left vacant by Wordsworth's death in 1850, but it went to Tennyson.

Barrett's treatment of social injustice (slave trade in America, the oppression of the Italians by the Austrians, the child labour in the mines and mills of England, and the restrictions placed upon women) is manifest in many of her poems. Two of her poems, *Casa Guidi Windows* and *Poems Before Congress*, dealt directly with the Italian struggle for independence. The first half of *Casa Guidi Windows* was filled with hope that the newly awakened liberal movements were moving toward unification and freedom in the Italian states. The second half of the poem, written after the movement of liberalism had been crushed in Italy, is dominated by her disillusionment. After a decade of truce, Italians once again began to struggle for their freedom, but were forced to agree to an armistice that left Venice under Austrian control. Barrett wrote *Poems Before Congress* as a response to these events, accusing the English government for not providing aid. One of the poems in this collection, *A Curse For a Nation*, attacked slavery and had been previously published in an abolitionist journal in Boston.

Though Barrett's popularity waned after her death, and late-Victorian critics argued that much of her writing would be forgotten, she is widely remembered for *The Cry of the Children, Bertha in the Lane, A Musical Instrument,* and most of all *Sonnets from the Portuguese*. These sonnets are actually love poems which describe the growth and development of her feelings for Robert Browning, at first hesitating to involve him in her sorrowful invalid life, then yielding to a gradual conviction of his love for her, and finally rapturous in late-born happiness. In *When Our Two Souls*, a highly elaborate Petrarchan sonnet, having something of a metaphysical wit and made up of questions and imperative constructions, the two souls of the lovers "stand up erect and strong", suggesting the intensity and purity of their feelings, the sonnet itself being rather an argument for that. The poetess renders the existence of two kinds of love: the ideal, spiritual one, developed in high spheres, and an earthly type of love, closely linked to the motif of carpe diem: "Let us stay / Rather on earth (...) and love in for a day", but they can experience their love as pure spirits on earth as well as in heaven. If the high sphere regards poetry, then their love would be poeticized, and the poetess seems not to agree with that, for she would rather prefer love on earth, human love, without poetry.

A Musical Instrument, another of her best-known lyrics, was published in *Last Poems*, issued posthumously in 1862. The poem reveals the destiny of Pan, half-god, half-man, who invents the flute by which he makes sweet music. In order to produce pleasurable art, Pan has to destroy something from nature, has to deviate from the natural *status quo*: to make the flute he destroys the reed. His laughter after he finishes making the instrument represents the triumph of art, but, being aware of his destructive act, Pan assumes the position of a god, justifying his action: "The only way, since gods began / To make a sweet music, they could succeed". The poetess indirectly rises the question, without providing any answer, about the condition of the artist (poet): is the poet a man, or a beast, or a god, for turning the natural language into the language of poetry implies deviation from common rules, in a way that destroys it only to allow the existence of art? Although the creative act involves destruction, "cost and pain" (the artist as beast), the power of art provides aesthetic pleasure, revives the destroyed material, and re-creates the natural order and universal harmony (the artist as god): "And the lilies revived, and the dragon-fly / Came back to dream on the river".

2.10 Matthew Arnold

Matthew Arnold (1822 – 1888) was born at Laleham on the upper Thames, son of Thomas Arnold, an eminent historian, educator, and a leader of the Broad Church Movement of the Church of England. In 1828 Arnold moved to Rugby School, where his father became famous as an educational reformer, and in 1844 he took second honours at Balliol College, Oxford. The same year he took post as assistant teacher at Rugby School for one year. In 1847, Arnold was appointed to the post of private secretary to Lord Landsdowne, a liberal peer. In 1851, he married Frances Lucy Whightman, the daughter of an eminent judge. To support his family, Arnold took post as Inspector of schools, a position he kept for 35 years. In 1857, he also became Professor of poetry at Oxford, for ten years, and in 1867, after resigning, he gave up his poetic career. Arnold published his first volume of poetry, *The Strayed Reveller, and Other Poems*, anonymously in 1849. In 1852, he published, also anonymously, his second volume of verse *Empedocles on Etna, and Other Poems*, containing, among others,

Tristram and Iseult and some of the "Marguerite" poems, including *To Marguerite*. In 1853, Arnold published another volume of verse, *Poems*, containing his famous Preface. The volume includes extracts from his earlier books, as well as *The Scholar Gipsy*, *Sohrab and Rustum*, *Memorial Verses to Wordsworth*, and others. In 1855, he published *Poems, Second Series*, a volume impregnated with melancholy, nostalgia, and the sense of loss. During his work as a Professor of poetry at Oxford, Arnold published several books of literary criticism, among which *On Translating Homer* (1861), *Essays on Criticism* (1865, including the famous *The Function of Criticism at the Present Time*), *On the Study of Celtic Literature* (1867), and *The Study of Poetry* (1888). After he resigned from Oxford and gave up the poetic career, Arnold's interest began to include religious and social criticism, publishing *Culture and Anarchy* (1868), *Friendship's Garland* (1871), and *Literature and Dogma* (1873). In 1873, he published the essay *Wordsworth* as the preface to *The Poems of Wordsworth*, by which returning to his beginnings in literary criticism. Arnold toured for the first time America in 1883, for which he prepared lectures on *Literature and Science*, *Emerson*, and *Numbers*.

Having read widely ancient and modern European literature, Arnold felt the necessity of the contemporary English literary productions to attain an intellectual and philosophical grasp comparable to what he admired in recent German poetry and French criticism, and especially in ancient philosophy and critical theory. Hence Arnold's "reapplication of classical criteria to literature" in his literary criticism, claims Charles E. Bressler, who continues:

> Quotes and borrowed ideas from Plato, Aristotle, Longinus, and other classical writers pepper his criticism. From Aristotle's *Poetics*, for example, Arnold adapts his idea that the best poetry is of a "higher truth and seriousness" than history – or any other human subject or activity, for that matter. Similar to Plato, Arnold believes that literature reflects the society in which it is written and thereby heralds its values and concerns. Similar to Longinus, Arnold attempts to define a classic and decrees that such a work belongs to the "highest" or "best class". (Bressler 41)

Arnold's creative and critical writing reveals his almost obsession with the second-rate position of the English literature and education, the separation and the cultural gap between the general European, Mediterranean culture and the northern one which English culture belongs to. Hence is the critic's deep conviction of the necessity of their union, his urge to cultivate or "Hellenize" his contemporaries. This aspect is also expressed in some of his poetry, for instance in *To Marguerite* and *Dover Beach*, where the idea is raised on the philosophical level coloured with a wide range of human concerns and natural symbolism. On the subject of translations of classical books, Arnold is acclaimed for his lectures *On Translating Homer* and his essay *On Translating Homer: Last Words* (1861-1862). In these works, he prescriptively draws attention to the fact that every translator of Homer should remember that the ancient writer is noble, rapid, plain, and direct in language and in thought, and that every translator should preserve all these qualities in every new translation of the classic. From 1851 for thirty-five years, Arnold was also one of "Her Majesty's Inspectors of

Schools, struggling inside the grinding inadequacies of the English education system" (Davis 217-218).

The poetic career of Matthew Arnold constitutes an important part and plays a significant role in the general Victorian literary background. It is often claimed that Arnold is less concerned with technique and poetic imagery, laying emphasis on idea and philosophical message in his literary discourse. *To Marguerite*, for instance, renders the apparently common theme of two lovers being separated, their unfulfilled relationship of love, but it takes new perspectives when raised to a more general level: the separation of the lovers becomes the separation of all humans ("We mortal millions live alone"), of the entire universe, as islands are separated by "the watery plain". The poem is an elegy for love, while the image of the sea suggests both the union and the separation of lovers, the poet's desire of togetherness and his awareness of the inevitable solitude of human life. The nightingale's song shared by every soul expresses the communion through the beauty of art, the night and the song creating an illusory image in which love, linked to human isolation, provides a lack of communication. The poem also expresses the poet's note of hostility against God, the lyrical I asking "Who ordered, that their longing's fire / Should be, as soon as kindled, cooled? / Who renders vain their deep desire?", and answering: "A God, a God their severance ruled!" The impossibility for religion to solve the problem of human isolation suggests religious scepticism, enhanced by the scientific developments of the age, for instance, the theory of the world's formation from an initial single continent. Arnold follows John Donne's words that no man is an island, all humans are parts of a continent, pages of a book written by God, and propounds the belief in a future synthesis between northern and Mediterranean civilizations.

The same idea of separation between humans, leading to an almost absurd existence, and between the general European, Mediterranean civilization and the northern, including English, one is also expressed in *Dover Beach*, a poem which dates from his honeymoon. The idea is presented through philosophical speculation and is coloured with deep feelings and fine imagery, the concern with human interests and symbols rendered by natural objects: Dover beach, the nearest point to France, and the French coast separated by the channel, along with many other elements which embrace a great range and depth of significance. Arnold creates a moon-blanched landscape to disclose the melancholic preoccupation with the thought of the inevitable decline of religious faith, finally expressing the predetermined division of and disillusionment with peace that only increase the reality of love and other genuine human values, to which the world is hostile and which are discoverable nowhere else but in human relationships. The opening lines render a series of particular items suggestive of a serene, peaceful, solemn mood which the lyrical I desires for himself: "The sea is calm to-night, / The tide is full, the moon lies fair (...)". Then follows a tender appeal to the poet's companion ("Come to the window, sweet is the night air!"), along with the "grating roar" and other images which admirably define the richness of natural motion and the inner state of the speaker, the sounds made by waves, breaking on shingle, alongside a combination of metrical and stylistically centred devices to make these images vividly present to the reader. After a short reference to Sophocles (perhaps to secure credibility to his own speculation), the poet employs the image of the waves to begin his own commentary in a quite explanatory tone, stressing, like in *To Marguerite*, on the idea of the past, when people were united, and the present isolated state of humans ("The sea of faith / Was once, too, at the full, and round earth's shore"), which brings one, melancholically, to the impossibility of believing that the world is in some degree adjusted to human needs. Only in the last stanza Arnold fully reveals the horror of his analogy (the sea and human condition), the images changing the feeling and constituting a memorable poetic comment on the modern world, an indignation against the opacity of his age. Also, like Tennyson, Arnold was sensible to and rejected the positives and certainties of his age, concealed under an exterior of Victorian responsibility, saying that

> the world, which seems
> To lie before us like a land of dreams,
> So various, so beautiful, so new,
> Hath really neither joy, nor love, nor light,
> Nor certitude, nor peace, nor help for pain,

and, like Tennyson, expressing a sense of social responsibility, which is a basic attitude that obviously differentiates them from the romantic poets. Arnold refused to reprint his poem *Empedocles on Etna*, in which the Greek philosopher throws himself into the volcano, because it set a bad example.

A poetic comment on the modern to him Victorian world is also rendered by Arnold in *The Scholar Gipsy*, a pastoral elegy in which he opposes two types of knowledge, two ways of living, two settings: pastoral and intellectual, countryside and Oxford, past and present. The antitheses used on different levels present the spiritual values of the past and the materialism of his own age; the "gipsy-lore" and the knowledge given by the modern, institutionalized education; the past which allowed individuals personal fulfilment and the present which do not; "one aim, one business, one desire" and the divided aims; life as wondering, not depending on society, and life in a conventional society.

The poem follows the story of a seventeenth-century Oxford student, of "pregnant parts and quick inventive brain", who, "tired of knocking at preferment's door", leaves Oxford in a kind of Byronic rebellion to join a band of Gipsies. Arnold gives the following note from *The Vanity of Dogmatizing* (1661), written by Joseph Glanville:

There was very lately a lad in the University of Oxford, who was by his poverty forced to leave his studies there; and at last to join himself to a company of vagabond gypsies. Among these extravagant people, by the insinuating subtlety of his carriage, he quickly got so much of their love and esteem as that they discovered to him their mystery. After he had been a pretty while exercised in the trade, there chanced to ride by a couple of scholars, who had formerly been of his acquaintance. They quickly spied out their old friend among the gypsies; and he gave them an account of the necessity which drove him to that kind of life, and told them that the people he went with were not such impostors as they were taken for, but that they had a traditional kind of learning among them, and could do wonders by the power of imagination, their fancy binding that of others; that he himself had learned much of their art, and when he had compassed the whole secret, he intended, he said, to leave their company, and give the world an account of what he had learned.

Arnold was inspired by this story, which gave him the opportunity to write a pastoral elegy: the setting is pastoral, the lyrical I invoking the shepherd to accompany him in his quest for the scholar gipsy who represents his reverie, and elegizing the setting. The locality described is in the immediate neighbourhood of Oxford, Arnold himself writing in 1885: "I cannot describe the effect which this landscape always has upon me – the hillside with its valley, and Oxford in the great Thames valley below.' The scholar gipsy becomes practically a legend, expecting a spark from heaven in hope, a full-believer, while other humans, Arnold implies, are only half-believers because they expect without hope. His escape represents "an unattached, gipsy rejection of the consequences of the urban civilization of the nineteenth century" (Sanders 447). Allusions to ancient civilizations may suggest that the scholar gipsy is a modern Tyrian trader, Gipsies are Iberians, while the Greek system of values represents University, modern life, so much rejected by the hero. The poem thus celebrates the student's escape from routine and the poet's own attempt to escape into history unburdened by present uncertainties. This is actually the great poetic appeal expressed in the work, coloured with a tragic account of the confusions in the human existence and differing from the tradition of the pastoral elegy in that at the end there is no hope and joy, and no idea expressed that death is the beginning of life, for "And then thy glad perennial youth would fade, / Fade, and grow old at last, and die like ours".

Matthew Arnold's poetry is a companionable one, especially for rather lonely natures, and the author is a spectator in it. He expresses the half-humorous, half-apologetic stoicism of an academic type of mind in the Victorian age, his conviction being that his poetry possesses intellectual qualities and keen psychological insights.

2.11 Gerald Manley Hopkins

Gerald Manley Hopkins (1844 – 1889) was born in Stratford, Essex, the eldest son of middle-class parents who combined strong High Anglican principles with a deep interest in literature and art in general. In 1863, he entered Balliol College, Oxford, and had Walter Pater as his tutor. There he was deeply affected by the Oxford Movement and turned to Roman Catholicism. Hopkins burned all his completed verse in 1868, after deciding to enter priesthood and considering his poetry writing inappropriate to his vocation, and resumed poetry writing in 1875, before his ordination in 1877. His work as a priest proved not successful, and he spent the rest of his life teaching in Roman Catholic colleges and writing poetry, his remarkable experimental verse, unknown during his life, gaining widespread attention in the twentieth century and influencing numerous poets of our age.

The modern qualities and technical devices of Hopkins's poetry emerge from a number of characteristics of his verse and a number of new techniques of writing poetry which he created and which he explains – in letters and in the preface written for *Bridges* (1883) – in his own terminology. The technical devices of his writings include the so-called "inscape", which is the essential form and meaning of any experience or any object, and each of his poems is more or less an attempt to apprehend an inscape; "instress", the means by which the inscape of the object or experience is perceived, intensified, and communicated. Hopkins's new techniques also include the "running rhythm", which is the standard, conventional syllabic meter of English verse; "counterpointed rhythm", the reversing of metrical feet within the running rhythm; "sprung rhythm", which is actually the Anglo-Saxon principle of versification, where a line is measured by stress, the number of unaccented syllables not being important; as well as the "rising rhythm", "falling rhythm", "rocking rhythm", and "rose-over".

The modernity of Hopkins's verse also emerges from the way in which he uses the English language, especially as a result of his own direct interest in language as a living thing, exploring its resources and potentialities in order to create poetic imagery (critics have noticed that his handling of the language associates him with Shakespeare). Hopkins departs from his contemporary literary idiom, the sheer melody of Tennyson, applying instead the language to a spoken purpose rather than to a literary one; his words and phrases are actions as well as sounds, ideas, and images aimed at rendering the sense of physical motion. His poetry is an attempt to violate as far as possible the contemporary expectation of what poetry should sound like, mingling the surprisingly colloquial with the surprisingly unusual to make a poem "explode". That is why he would always demand his poetry to be read aloud: "read it with the ears, as I always wish to be read, and my verse becomes all right".

Now regarded as a proto-modernist poet, an important discovery of the twentieth century, the most famous devotional poet in English since the seventeenth century, Hopkins's poetry was unknown to the public during his lifetime, and would have bewildered his contemporaries due to its difficult artistic message, impregnated with a metaphysical conceit, or a technique of his own, and the difficulty is essential to the comprehension of the message and its meaning. Hopkins's application of his own technical devices provides a remarkable association of a number of musical effects with the possibility of expressing complexities of feelings, states of mind and movements of consciousness; of the physical, muscular tensions with an inner, spiritual stress, when an apparently trivial event becomes a symbol of universal resonance, which is directly linked to the workings of the soul and the mind (as in *The Leaden Echo and the Golden Echo*, for instance, or *The Wreck of the Deautschland*).

Hopkins's extensive employment and application of assonance, alliteration and internal rime are primarily for dramatic effect, as well as for a musical one. Hence is his one of the most important modern qualities, that of "dramatic lyricism", which, he claimed, combines the power of rhythm and the naturalness of expression. Other features of his writings, as aspects of his modernism, where urgency and excitement are also produced by charged language and unexpected rhythms, include his remarkable "compression and density", to reveal the fullest intensity of feeling; his "multiple meanings and ambiguity", to unify simultaneously the image of several distinct aspects of observation; his "elliptical statement", to move from image to image and to reproduce the workings of the mind in thought or that of the soul in feeling; his "concern with psychological complexities", to dramatically reveal in his work the permanent conflict between the man and artist (artistic individualism), and the Christian priest (love of the world), and, indeed, religious, Christian motifs and themes are frequently present in his work.

Pied Beauty (1877), for instance, an eleven-line poem (sonnet), praises the world's remarkable diversity, the creation of God, as a cause for venerating divinity, where the twofold nature of all "dappled things" is suggestive of Christ's human-divine nature. Similarly, *The Windhover: To Christ our Lord*, which challenges Eliot's *Waste Land* as the most discussed poem in the twentieth century, "the best thing I ever wrote", as Hopkins himself claimed, praises the power of divinity. The kestrel, a type of small falcon, hovering in the wind, provides a dramatic inscape, speaking to the poet's "heart's in hiding" and showing him the beauty and glory of Christ, where the most common natural objects can suddenly reveal their peculiar beauty, some aspects of which symbolize Christ's sufferings and wounds. In point of form, the lyric is a "sprung rhythm" sonnet, though it also displays the influence of the Welsh "cynghanedd", which is an elaborate pattern of alliteration and internal rime, given that the poem was written in Wales, as all his poems from 1875 to 1877.

Creating and cultivating his own philosophy of art, poetry and beauty, Hopkins was one of the most remarkable technical inventors who ever wrote, a major poet, and, of all poets theorizing about their art, he is perhaps the only one who most fully materialized in poetic practice what he theoretically attempted to accomplish.

2.12 The Pre-Raphaelite Poets

The Pre-Raphaelites are remarkable exponents of Victorian poetry, whose contribution to the nineteenth-century English literature was crucial. The most important representatives of the Brotherhood who produced valuable poetic writings are Dante Gabriel Rossetti, William Morris, and Charles Swinburne.

Dante Gabriel Rossetti (1828 – 1882), whose all Christian names were Gabriel Charles Dante, the son of Gabriele Rossetti, an Italian patriot who came to England in 1824, was brought up in an atmosphere of keen cultural and political activity which contributed to his artistic development more than his formal education at King's College School, London. He studied painting with Millais and Hunt, and in 1848, with them and four others, founded the Pre-Raphaelite Brotherhood. In 1850, he met Elizabeth Siddal (Siddall), whose own painting and writing he encouraged, and who modelled for him and many of his circle. In 1854, Rossetti met Ruskin, who did much to establish the reputation of the Pre-Raphaelites, and in 1856 William Morris, whom he greatly influenced. Rossetti and Elizabeth married in 1860; she died in 1862, from an overdose of laudanum, which may have been taken deliberately (she was an invalid and gave birth to a still-born child). Rossetti buried with her the manuscript of a number of his poems (in 1869 he arranged the exhumation of these poems to publish them), and, later that year, he moved to 16 Cheyne walk, Chelsea. In 1868, he showed a new interest in painting and poetry, possibly inspired by the renewed contact with Jane Morris, the wife of William Morris, whom he had previously painted. In 1871, Rossetti and Morris took a joint lease of Kelmscott Manor, where Rossetti continued his intimacy with Jane, with Morris's apparent approval. Rossetti's later years were overshadowed by ill-health, although he continued to paint and write and was recognized by a new generation of artists, the aesthetes, including Pater and Wilde, as a source of inspiration.

For many years, Rossetti was known as painter, though he began to write poetry early. Some of his poems, among which *The Blessed Damozel*, and a prose piece, *Hand and Soul*, were published in *The Germ* (1850). In 1869, he published in *The Fortnightly Review* sixteen sonnets, including the *Willowwood* sequence. In 1870, Rossetti published a volume of *Poems*, containing *Sister Helen*, *Troy Town*, the first part of his sonnet sequence *The House of Life*, and others. It was well received, partly because Rossetti took care that his friends reviewed it. In October 1871 appeared R. Buchanan's attack, *The Fleshly School of Poetry*, in *The Contemporary Review*, which accused Rossetti and his associates of impurity and obscenity (especially the sonnet *Nuptial Sleep* was singled out for particular criticism). Rossetti's reply, *The Stealthy School of Criticism*, appeared in *The Athenaeum* in December 1872, and the controversy finally ended, with the Pre-Raphaelites on the whole victorious. Rossetti published many other poems, his *Poems* and *Ballads and Sonnets* both appeared in 1881. The first was largely rearrangements of earlier works; the second completed *The House of Life* with 47 new sonnets, and also contained other new writings, including *The King's Tragedy* and *The White Ship*, both "historical ballads".

The master-mind of the Pre-Raphaelite Movement, a proponent of English aestheticism, Rossetti was a sophisticated artist, having as models Dante, Coleridge and Keats, being like them a sensualist, and Shelley, given his passionate search for absolute truths, generalizing the concepts of Love, Life, Death. Some of his works show in contrast a Pre-Raphaelite concern with detail, a huge range of undeniable emotional and erotic power. In addition, in some of his works Rossetti rejects nature, especially when the physical (natural) is dissipated into a sort of vague spirituality, for he knew little of nature, his concern with love and beauty coming from his interest in art and poetry. He manages to remove aestheticism from mysticism, but combines the physical with the spiritual, and his poetry often seems artificial.

The Blessed Damozel, one of his most influential poems, expresses Rossetti's alliance to the Pre-Raphaelite interest in medieval sacramental symbolism (three lilies, seven stars, a white rose) and his conception of an ideal, Platonic love, which he was to develop in later works along with the emphasis on sensuality of the human feelings. His concern with detail is revealed by the description of heaven, indeed artificial, out of which a young virgin is leaning and watching – from a great distance and time difference – the world below, which is just an illusion, mourning and praying for union with her lover, so their love would be complete in heaven, the place where lovers meet, "in the shadow of / That living mystic tree" (the tree of life), but where they eventually lose their individuality. The poem generally represents a vision of the Lyrical I, though in the last stanza he seems to comprehend physically both the hope of reunion ("I saw her smile") and the drama of separation ("I heard her tears"). Significantly, these two lines and the two stanzas in brackets point to a movement from physical relation (touch of hair/leaves) and spoken contact (singing/birds) to highly emotional appeal of eternal unity.

The poem was revised for publication in *The Oxford and Cambridge Magazine* in 1856, and again before its appearance in *Poems*, 1870. Thirty years after its first appearance, Rossetti told Hall Caine that he had written *The Blessed Damozel* as a sequel (parody, pastiche, allusion) to Poe's *The Raven* (published in 1845): "I saw that Poe had done the utmost it was possible to do with the grief of the lover on earth, and so determined to reverse the conditions, and give utterance to the yearning of the loved one in heaven", and it also seems that Rossetti follows Poe's famous statement that the "death of a beautiful woman is, unquestionably, the most poetical topic in the world". Rossetti's early study of Dante, especially the *Paradiso*, has influenced the general conception and many of the details of the poem, too.

William Morris (1834 – 1896), the son of a successful businessman, was educated at Marlborough School and Exeter College, Oxford. He was assigned to the architect G. E. Street, and in 1858 worked with Rossetti, Burne-Jones and others on the frescoes in the Oxford Union. In 1859, he married Jane Burden, one of the most painted by the Pre-Raphaelites models. Their home, Red House at Bexley, was considered an important landmark in domestic architecture, adopting late Gothic methods to the nineteenth-century style. The failure to find suitable furniture led to the foundation, by Morris, Rossetti, Burne-Jones, Webb, and others, of the firm of "Morris, Marshall, Faulkner and Co.", which produced furniture, wallpaper, and stained glass. Though the wide public could hardly afford its products, because of the price, the firm's designs brought about a complete revolution in public taste. In 1871, Morris visited Iceland, which stimulated his interest in the heroic themes of Icelandic literature. In 1877, he founded the Society for the Protection of Ancient Buildings in protest against the destruction caused by restoration. From that time on, he turned towards political activity. In 1883, he joined the Social Democratic Federation, the doctrine of which, largely under his leadership, developed into Socialism. On its disruption in 1884, Morris became head of the secessionists, who organized themselves as the Socialist League, and was to lecture and write for the cause with great energy until the end of his life.

Morris was one of the founders of *The Oxford and Cambridge Magazine* (1856), to which he contributed essays, poems and tales. In 1858, he published *The Defence of Guenevere and Other Poems*, which included much of his best poems, all with medieval settings and all marked by a striking mixture of beauty and brutality, and by Ruskin's influence on his view of the relationship between art and work. In 1867, he published *The Life and Death of Jason*, a poem in heroic couplets based on the story of Jason, Medea, and the Argonauts. *The Earthly Paradise*, critically considered his masterpiece, appeared in 1868 – 70. In 1871, he wrote the poem *Love is Enough* (1872). The epic *Sigurd the Valsung* appeared in 1876. His later works, with the exception of *Poems by the Way* (1891) and *Chants for Socialists* (1884 – 5), were mainly in prose. The most important of them were *A Dream of John Ball* (1888) and *News from Nowhere* (1891), both socialist fantasies in a dream setting; as well as a number of historical romances set in the distant past of northern Europe, including *The House of The Wolfings* (1889), *The Roots of the Mountains* (1890), *The Story of the Glittering Plain* (1890), *The Wood Beyond the World* (1894) and *The Sundering Flood* (1898), the latter being completed just before his death. Morris published many other works, including various translations and lectures on art, architecture and politics, the majority of which by the Kelmscott Press, which he founded at Hammersmith in 1890.

The Earthly Paradise established him as one of the most popular poets of the Victorian age. The texts consists of a prologue and 24 long narrative poems held together by a framework, after the fashion of Chaucer's *Canterbury Tales*. But, in contrast to Chaucer, the pattern of the work is almost entirely static, and its narrators undifferentiated. The narratives are supposed to be told on a remote island where some Norwegian wanderers of the fourteenth century, who set sail in search of the fabled Earthly Paradise "across the western sea where none grow old", find the descendants of a band of Greeks who had settled there long before, founding "a nameless city in a distant sea" where the ancient Greek gods are still worshipped. The mariners are hospitably received and there spend their remaining days. The islanders and the strangers meet twice in each month for a whole year, and tell alternate stories from ancient sources – the tales of the elders of the city are on Greek classical subjects (Atalanta, Perseus, and others), those of the wanderers on Norse and medieval subjects (*The Lady of the Land*, for instance, one of the June tales, is a retelling of the shorter story in the fourth chapter of *The Voyage and Travaile of Sir John Mandeville, Knight*, a fourteenth-century century book of travel and romance). Between the tales are interpolated lyrics describing the changing seasons, and the whole work is prefaced by an *Apology* which contains some of Morris's best-known lines, in which he describes himself as "the idle singer of an empty day", "born out of my due time", which allusion to escape the present moment and find refuge in the past, in an imaginary world created by the power of his poetic genius. Morris claims that his poem has no power to change the condition of the mortals, it is not prophetic, though it is eternal, in the line of the art for art's sake doctrine, as everything in poetry is only beauty, and beauty is eternal, possessing the power to change the world by changing its inhabitants. Highly popular in its day, the poem reveals the weaknesses of the Victorian late romanticism and, compared to the freshness of Morris's early writings, is viewed as escapist and archaic.

Charles Algernon Swinburne (1837 – 1909), of an old Northumbrian family, spent much of his childhood in the Isle of Wight. He was educated at Eton and at Balliol College, Oxford, where he was associated with the Pre-Raphaelite movement. His first volume of verse, *The Queen-Mother; Rosamund*, was published in 1860. In 1865, he published *Atalanta in Calydon*, a drama in classical Greek form with choruses which reveal his great metrical skills. Tennyson praised its "wonderful rhythmic invention". *Chastelard*, the first of three dramas on the subject of Mary Queen of Scots, also appeared in 1865. They both attracted much attention and brought him celebrity, though some doubts were raised about their morality. The doubts about the morality of Swinburne's verse were reinforced by the first series of *Poems and Ballads* (1866), which were vehemently criticized by, among others, R. Buchanan and J. Morley. The volume contained a number of notorious poems, among which *The Triumph of Time* stands as the best, which is more personal than other poems and remarkable for its impressive sea imagery which expresses the author's lasting love for the sea, "the great sweet mother". *A Song of Italy* was published in 1867 and *Songs before Sunrise* in 1871, both expressing his support for Mazzini in the struggle for Italian independence, celebrating and encouraging the fighters for political independence in Europe. He then published many more volumes, including *Bothwell* (1874), *Poems and Ballads: Second Series* (1878), *Mary Stuart* (1881), *Poems and Ballads: Third Series* (1889), and others. Swinburne also translated the ballads of Villon and published prose works which

Golban

include two novels, *A Year's Letters* (serialized 1877, republished 1905 as *Love's Cross Currents*) and *Lesbia Brandon* (1952). Swinburne was also an original and important critic, his studies of Chapman, Marlowe, Tourneur, and others were the first remarkable successions to Lamb's in the revival of interest in Elizabethan and Jacobean drama, and those of Blake and the Brontes in many ways laid the foundation of modern appreciation.

As a poet, Swinburne was influenced, in style, rhetoric and versification by Shelley, although on the whole he is compared to Byron due to his rebellious nature, eccentric personality, certain romantic attitudes, and a similar high popularity, making of him much of an "echo" poet, rather than one of exploration and discovery.

In many respects, Swinburne's poetry is unique and highly original; he commanded an impressive variety of verse forms, writing in classical meters, composing burlesques, modern and mock-antique ballads. His poetic production introduces the element of variety and an extraordinary power of suggestion (especially through cadence and imagery), though it caused during his lifetime some sensation because of its exuberance, preoccupation with de Sade, masochism, "femmes fatales" (which he shared with a circle of friends), sensuality, rebellious tone, defiance of established values, lyrical abandon, and especially his outspoken repudiation of Christianity (which was to impress Hardy in *Jude the Obscure*), as in *Hymn to Proserpine*. Proserpine, or Proserpina, was the daughter of Jupiter and Ceres, goddess of harvests. She married Pluto, King of Hell, and as his wife presided over the death of humans. Swinburne's poem is a dramatic monologue of the lyrical I who praises her virtues, disclosing his own existence primarily through senses and, as an atheist and born rebel, expecting the new religion, Christianity (Constantine the Great made Christianity the official faith of the Roman Empire in 313 AD) to be transitory like the old one, along with the expression of a feeling of distrust for the new religious order:

O Gods dethroned and deceased, cast forth, wiped out in a day!
From your wrath is the world released, redeemed from your chains, men say.
New Gods are crowned in the city; their flowers have broken your rods;
They are merciful, clothed with pity, the young compassionate Gods.
But for me their new device is barren, the days are bare;
Things long past over suffice, and men forgotten that were.

The death of the gods is like the death of humans, and death is nothing but sleep, an end, the life on earth ends in death, or sleep, which is an eternal matter of fact ("I shall die as my fathers died, and sleep as they sleep"), the man is a corpse which a "little soul for a little bears up". The lyrical I is aware of the limitations of the human existence, of his own life, he feels unable to engage himself in a struggle for any spiritual accomplishments, or otherwise seems unwilling to struggle. The only value of existence is love, yet not the concept of Christian love of pity and compassion, but rather the love which regards passion, sensation, sensuality and physical pleasure (the opposition is rendered by comparing Mary to Venus). As gods live and die, everything and everybody dies in the end, hence a rejection of life, or yet an escape from it, implied by death as sleep: "So long I endure, no longer; and laugh not again, neither weep. / For there is no god found stronger than death; and death is a sleep".

Closely related to *Hymn to Proserpine* is *The Garden of Proserpine* which has a different stanza, metrical form, line and rhythm, is more balanced and stable, but continues the *Hymn* in its creation of a place of escapism, a transitory state between life and death (the garden), where there is "Only the sleep eternal / In an eternal night". The garden itself suggests life, but its elements, such as white roses, stand clearly as symbols of death. It is difficult to argue whether the poet is inside or outside it, yet one may definitely say that all he desires is a state of complete repose and sleep, in order to escape the transitory moments of existence and life itself, for he is tired "of tears and laughter, / And men that laugh and weep", of "days and hours (…) Desires and dreams and powers". Swinburne, more than other Victorian poets (except Tennyson, perhaps), is obsessed with the idea of the absurdity and worthlessness of the human condition, as with regard to any conventions and established values of all types, searching for a possible escapism in the realm of death, equalled to sleep which is, to follow the affirmation of Lucian Blaga, a superior form of existence.

CONCLUDING REFLECTIONS

In Victorian Age, two theoretical tenets co-exist arguing that, on the one hand, as prompted by social theories and realism, art is a product of society (as for Hippolyte Taine), and, on the other, a moral-humanistic attitude claiming that art affects and improves society (as for Matthew Arnold). Aestheticism and avant-garde art, on the whole, challenge both, declaring that life imitates art, not art imitates life, and that art is useless, including its moral didacticism. Victorian Age consists of a great number of movements and trends co-existing during one period and as such reifying the co-existence of the traditional and innovative element in literature. The former manifests as realism which rejects romanticism and continues a neoclassical emphasis on rules and ethics, and the interest in the actual, immediate reality. The latter – rejecting tradition, rules and prescriptive doctrines, and as a continuation of the romantic rebellious attitude in art – is the real source of literary complexity in the Victorian period.

Innovation in literature and arts growing out of romanticism has a twofold perspective. First, innovation from romanticism and heavily influenced by romantic attitude, thus comprising a great number of romantic characteristics. Second, innovation out of romanticism, which is less influenced by romantic attitude but still continues a number of its features. The first kind of innovation manifests as post- and neo-romantic trends, including most of Victorian poetry as well as some of the fiction of the period, such as the Gothic novel of Emily Brontë and the later colonial prose of Kipling, Stevenson, Doyle, Wells, and Conrad. The second type of innovation manifests as symbolism, aestheticism, impressionism, decadence, expressionism, and other trends which represent the artistic avant-garde of the second half of the nineteenth century. It gives, together with other manifestations of innovation as well as tradition, the literary and artistic diversity in Victorian Age. Symbolism, impressionism, aestheticism, and decadence are regarded as the strongest reactions against the principles of realism and naturalism, and as influencing directly the rise of modernism. A more trenchant opinion, that of Edmund Wilson in *Axel's Castle* (1931), considers symbolism to be a development out of romanticism and that "the literary history of our time is to a great extent that of the development of symbolism and its fusion or conflict with naturalism" (Wilson 25).

This opinion has been very popular, other critics maintaining that symbolism follows "the Romantics in their devotion to the imagination" (Faulkner 11) and contains "within itself a shift from a Romantic to a modernly ironic aesthetic" (Scott 206). Symbolism developed in its turn into a more complex range of experimental and innovative trends and movements (surrealism, Dadaism, cubism, stream of consciousness novel, and so on) which are assembled and assigned together as "modernism". A major impact was provided by the new developments in philosophy and psychology which challenged the traditional values and views, and especially

Man's understanding of himself was changing. Anthropology was probing the primitive roots of religion: James Frazer's *The Golden Bough* appeared in twelve volumes between 1890 and 1915. Philosophers like Nietzsche and Bergson had already emphasised the importance of instinct rather than reason. Psychologists like Freud and Jung were showing the power and significance of the unconscious. (Faulkner 14)

In ideology, politics, and society, the Victorians brought astonishing innovation and change: democracy, feminism, unionization of workers, socialism, Marxism, and other modern movements took form. In fact, this age of Newton's mechanics, Darwin's evolution, Comte's view of society, Marx's view of history, Taine's view of literature, and Freud's view of human psyche appears to be not only the first that experienced modern problems but also the first that attempted modern solutions; in other words, the age can be taken to express the rise of the modern. Modern artists who were trying to free themselves from the massive embrace of their predecessors often saw the Victorian writer chiefly as repressed, over-confident, and thoroughly unsophisticated.

The diversity in thought and in social and natural studies is paralleled by the diversity in artistic and literary movements, trends, and styles. In England, like on the Continent, romantic views of art remain strong and in some respects dominant in the late nineteenth century, as in the Pre-Raphaelite poetry or in the poetry and critical essays of Matthew Arnold.

Actually, the expansion of different philosophies and theories alongside different literary movements and trends helped the diversification of literary criticism, too. After romanticism proclaimed the freedom of artistic expression, by the second half of the nineteenth century there were fewer rules to be followed, hence the more artistic experimentation and the diversity of trends and movements (realism, naturalism, impressionism, aestheticism or the doctrine of "art for art's sake", hedonism, decadence, symbolism), along with a greater variety of critical approaches to literature. Victorian criticism marks the transition from the previous literary criticism – dependent on literary practice and literary movements, as well as subjective, defensive, normative and prescriptive – to the twentieth century independent and scientific approach to literature. The primary cause of the "separation" between criticism and literature is the literary diversity in the Victorian age, and the diversity of literary trends is a result of romanticism breaking the linearity of literary development dominated by classical views, reviving the innovative spirit in art, rejecting tradition and rules, and proclaiming the freedom of artistic expression.

Facing a literary diversity, literary criticism developed its own diversity, its own typology which may or may not correspond to the literary or artistic one. As diverse as they were – realistic criticism, naturalistic criticism, impressionistic criticism, aesthetic criticism, historical criticism, humanistic criticism, and others – dealt with the nature of culture, art and literature, mainly poetry and novel, bringing into discussion such topics as the social function of art and literature, hedonism and its relation to art and literature, morality and immorality in art, imaginative faculty of the artist, the style of the literary work, the theory of the comic genre and the presence of the comic spirit in the novel, and many others.

Also, the subjective component in criticism and the critical dependence on literary practice together with the prescriptive nature of criticism and especially its defensive character are rejected and attempted to be replaced by methodological and scientific analysis. We can see this in the great works of Victorian criticism by the leading critics of the second half of the nineteenth-century Matthew Arnold, Thomas Carlyle, John Stuart Mill, George Meredith, John Ruskin, Walter Pater, Osacr Wilde, and others, many of whom being also important authors of literary works.

The literature of Victorian Age is divided into High Victorian Literature (1830 – 1890) and Late Victorian Literature (1880 – 1901). Literary productions become the most important form of entertainment – particularly fiction and namely novel – in a period of rising commodity and consumerism via library facilities, public lectures, clubs, and drawing-rooms, but of central importance for the production, circulation, and consumption of literature – as well as for the critical commentary on the state of literature – stand British periodicals and the whole of contemporary publishing industry.

By early 1830s, literature begins to be published intensely in periodicals (weekly, fortnightly, monthly, or quarterly) with novels in cheap monthly parts and poetry in illustrated annals. It is also important that the periodicals contain both literary texts and critical essays and reviews; significantly, many writers would be members of editorial boards, acting as authors and editors themselves. Dickens's own journals are *Household Words* (1850 – 1859) and *All the Year Round* (1859 – 1895), and the very influential *Cornhill Magazine* was first published in 1860 under the editorship of Thackeray. Other influential periodicals were *Edinburgh Review* (founded 1802), *Quarterly* (founded 1809), *Westminster* (1824), *Blackwood's Magazine* (1817), and others.

The use of newly developing technology led to cheaper printing of books and periodicals, their faster transportation, larger circulation, and consequently lower prices, which would attract an increased reading audience sparked off by an increase of population assisted by an expansion and improvement of education in an age of likewise increased cultural and political awareness.

The literature of the Victorian Age is a kind of public property, for it is indeed indispensable from the complexity of socio-cultural changes, developments, and movements, their dynamics ranging from the changing status of women in society to the growth of the economic and political strength of the middle-class, alongside extensive transportation and urbanisation, to say nothing about the flourishing in the period of various philosophical doctrines and trends, as well as the rise of new disciplines, such as sociology, psychology, and anthropology. Victorian society saw the "Oxford Movement" of John Henry Newman (1801 – 1890) debating on religion; Chartism as a kind of working-class politics; social thinking starts with Thomas Carlyle and his lectures, essays, and pamphlets. Later, French thought becomes dominant to shape the fiction of writers such as George Eliot, but we ought to remember that it is Carlyle who in early Victorian England displays a passion for German culture reified in promoting Goethe, among others, via translation of *Wilhelm Meister Lehrjahre* in 1824 and the publication of his own *Sartor Resartus* to build up and assert a social philosophy and provide critical commentary on contemporary English issues, such as "dandyism".

More importantly, *Sartor Resartus* is an indispensable part of a remarkable experience of literary reception, namely of the Bildungsroman, from German literature into English one. More precisely, it is considered (as argued by Bakhtin in

"The Bildungsroman and Its Significance in the History of Realism: Toward a Historical Typology of the Novel", 1936-1938), that the Bildungsroman exhibits a long developmental history, and we can trace the origins of its characteristic hero to a number of conventions and traditions, especially to the hero of ancient narratives (Apuleius's *Golden Ass*, Heliodorus's *Ethiopian History*, Longus's *Daphnis and Chloe*) and to the picaresque hero who in his travels meets all sorts and conditions of men, and to the romantic tradition, and finally to Goethe's canonical Bildungsroman *Wilhelm Meisters Lehrjahre*. Carlyle fulfils the cultural reception of Goethe's *Wilhelm Meisters Lehrjahre* in English letters on three levels by translating it, developing critical opinions on Goethe's novel, and writing his own Bildungsroman *Sartor Resartus* which can be considered the first in the line of the English novels of formation.

Victorian England is often compared to Elizabethan England, praised as a second English Renaissance for it great expansion of wealth, culture, and colonial power, where, in point of literary form, the Victorian novel parallels Elizabethan drama in terms of both popularity and literary achievement. Much of Victorian fiction belongs to realism which in Victorian cultural background established itself as a regular and definite trend, rejecting romanticism and the doctrine of art for art's sake. Realism first emerged as a recognizable trend in the nineteenth century France in the 1830s, becoming during the last part of the century a definite trend in European literature, in general. It emerged as an anti-romantic movement which had to concentrate on everyday events, the milieu, the social and political realities, and even the hero had to be an ordinary man. This idea was suggested by Champfleury in *Le realisme* (1857), which became a manifesto of the new doctrine, even though the author himself disapproved of the term, and as others, regarded the movement negatively or rejected it as undesirable. At the moment when Champfleury produced his essays, the movement was already very apparent in the novels of Stendhal and Balzac, and in 1857, Flaubert produced *Madame Bovary*, which was acclaimed as a great work of realism. Later, also due to the developments in philosophical thought, notably by Auguste Comte's *Cours de philosophie positive*, which made possible the appearance of the science of sociology, and the conceptions of Feuerbach, Darwin and Marx, realism and realist elements made the prime scene in the fiction of Dickens, Thackeray, Eliot, and, outside France and England, in the works of Tolstoy, Gogol, Turgenev in Russia, and in America in the novels of William Dean Howells and Mark Twain. In England, the tradition was kept alive in the twentieth century by John Galsworthy, H. G. Wells, Graham Greene, the so-called "new social realism" in the novels of the "angry young men" of the 1950s, and so on.

Realism is a dominant literary trend in the nineteenth century, but it co-existed with a number of other trends and movements representing the alternatives to realism by continuing certain romantic principles and rejecting the realistic once. Among them, aestheticism (Walter Pater, Oscar Wilde, Pre-Raphaelite Brotherhood) and symbolism (influence on Pre-Raphaelite poetry and later Yeats) in literature, impressionism in painting, as well as a rather strong in Britain compared to the rest of Europe post-romantic (Emily Bronte and Victorian poetry on the whole) and neo-romantic (Kipling and later Conrad) style.

Subordinating words to their referents, the nineteenth-century realism is more pragmatic and reader-oriented than other contemporary forms of art, becoming an accessible form of entertainment, which offers a semblance of reality amid continuous change, development and progress, and in whose works the audience would find instructions for living and ethical didacticism. Often, as Moretti declares with reference to *Comedie Humaine*, "the moral tends to precede the fable instead of ensuing it"; in English literature too, characters and situations "are often judged, and at times even the essential features of their fate are revealed, prior to the narrative sequence in which they figure as protagonists" (Moretti 161).

Following Yuri Tynyanov's assumptions on the diachronicity of literary development, realism as a literary system receives its elements from other systems, such as neoclassicism (social concern, city, objectivism, language reflecting reality, and so on), eighteenth-century novel (verisimilitude, picaresque narrative, sentimentalism, comic mode, moral didacticism), and romanticism (individual experience), where the individual and society (actually, their relationship) become central elements in the system. Also, contemporary philosophical, economic, and other systems influenced the rise of realism, in particular social theories, historical analysis, sociology, later anthropology and psychology.

Whatever different in their thematic concern and narrative perspective, Victorian realist novels encompass a number of common characteristics, which can be summarised as (1) the focus on verisimilitude; (2) the social concern or the concern with social background; (3) the concern with individual experience; (4) the relationship between individual and society; (5) governing this relationship is the principle of determinism; (6) reader-oriented art aiming at moral didacticism; (7) sentimental outlook and comic mode borrowed alongside ethical concerns from the eighteenth-century English novel; (8) some romantic elements, particularly Gothic, as in *Jane Eyre*; and (9) on the structural level: omniscient point of view, autodiegetic narrator, linear narrative, traditional narrative organization containing many events and characters that are flat and round, static and dynamic, as well as types (social and moral) more than individualised subjects.

In a nutshell, Victorian novel – not necessarily and exclusively the realist one – aims to reflect the complexity of social concern with its public, political and economic issues, including the concern with the rich and the poor, which would become a major-subject matter of contemporary novels by numerous authors ranging from Carlyle and Dickens to Benjamin Disraeli, and likewise notably in works such as Elizabeth Gaskell's (1810 – 1865) industrial novels *Mary Barton* (1848) and *North and South* (1855).

Fiction, in this respect, establishes a new form to tradition representing the trend we call "realism", whereas poetry, still an exponent of romanticism, tends toward the theme of escapism and withdrawal from reality, and embarks on experimentation and aestheticisation reifying anew the principle of innovation. Victorian novel is itself indebted to romantic tradition by laying emphasis on individual experience, but unlike the escapist and solitary persona of the romantics, the realist fiction places the individual in relationship to the milieu and thematically treats this relationship by conveying the principle of determinism. Victorian novel is also indebted to another novelistic tradition, as we can see the moral and comic alongside sentimental outlook inherited from Richardson, Fielding, and Smollett in the early fiction of Thackeray and especially Dickens.

In the process of their artistic maturation, these and other writers would come to reflect the complexity, diversity, confusion, and clamour of contemporary England, and turn best-sellers covering a large spectrum of readers and exploiting a vast section of popular market. Thackeray, Dickens's great rival, would attract readers with his "novel without a hero", *Vanity Fair*, or Charlotte Bronte with *Jane Eyre* (dedicated to Thackeray) would make a sensation with a strong feminist proclamation of female independence and personal identity, integrating genuine fragments of a feminist manifesto (as in Chapter XII) into the literarisation of a female *bildung*.

But it is Dickens who would become, like Shakespeare, the central consciousness of his age, the quintessential artist of his period, faithfully reflecting a new age of contradiction and discontent of an urban civilization but also an age of development, fertility of ideas, and abundance of discovery and innovation. Dickens's works may seem at times thematically and structurally inconsistent and rambling – or, as John Ruskin finds his novels, except *Hard Times*, as exaggerated in the representation of the contemporary world – but they tend toward totality in order to fulfil the assumed endeavour to cover a wide range of life experiences and social situations in a period which itself is confusing and contradictory. Dickens's presentation of London shows how a restless urban civilization can be transformed into art, and this art prompts the idea that humanity cannot definitely be explained or contained, but art, particularly fiction, constitutes a means of making sense of a disordered world in which childhood and maturity, love and hate, mercy and cruelty, sanity and madness co-exist. Not at all reluctant to display his freedom of artistic expression, imaginative flight of a great author, and the ability to incorporate various aspects of literary traditions and elements of popular culture in his works, Dickens preserves in all his novels a sense of optimism in spite of obstructing social and inter-personal determinism, which marks the existence of his characters, and regardless the consideration that his earlier works, such as *David Copperfield*, are pervaded by sentimentality, melodrama, and a comic, largely humorous, world-view, and his later works, after *Dombey and Son*, are far more gloomier and darker. *David Copperfield*, which relies heavily on binary oppositions (as with congenial versus obstructing parental figures, or a happy mother-bound childhood versus an unhappy one of suffering induced by Murdstone, followed later by two different love relations, two professional experiences, and so on) is thematically connected to Great Expectations as two Bildungsromane tracing the process of formation of two protagonists with the success of David and the failure of Pip, whose *bildung* is failure because of the negative obstructing social and inter-human determinism. In this way, realism provides the literary system of the Bildungsroman with various thematic perspectives, such as the relationship between the individual and society, personal development and social demands, individual autonomy and social integration, and so on.

William Makepeace Thackeray is another Victorian novelist who writes a Bildungsroman and who follows the conventions and thematises the characteristics of realism, fusing moral and psychological insight with verisimilitude and satire to give a complex picture of his contemporary social background. The concern with individual experience and the social background; individual experience and the social background presented in relationship; this relationship is based on the principle of determinism; the reader-oriented concern with moral lessons; the exclusion of the supernatural, fantastic, improbable elements, as well as of idealisation and exaggeration; and the narrative linearity, direct utterance, and omniscient point of view on the narrative level – all these and other features of realism can be seen in his *The History of Pendennis*, a Bildungsroman focused on Laura and especially Pen, tracing the latter's becoming a writer and Member of Parliament. But it is his *Vanity Fair*, a novel without a hero, that is probably the greatest Victorian social satire on hypocrisy, opportunism, greed, idleness, and snobbery rendered through the strong voice of an omniscient narrator chronicling the lives of two female characters embarking on social and matrimonial experiences. Amelia Sedley marries Osborne who dies, becomes obsessed with her son and eventually marries Dobbin. Becky Sharp – an intelligent but immoral social climber – marries Rawdon who leaves her, and she finally probably kills Joseph Sedley for his life insurance and returns to England managing a respectable life. *Vanity Fair* is a novel of manners and a historical novel; however, one may truly argue, that there are protagonists, at least one, Becky, who is highly individualised, and then, one may truly argue again, the novel is without a hero but with a heroine.

Apart from romantic and Gothic narratives challenging the supremacy of realist fiction in Victorian period, as with *Wuthering Heights*, the second half of the nineteenth century saw stronger alternatives to realism, as with *The Picture of Dorian Gray* and *Marius the Epicurean* advancing the principles of aesthetic avant-garde. The new forms of the novelistic genre also include the new types of detective and colonial fiction, which is largely neo-romantic, the naturalistic attempts by Thomas Hardy alongside the psychological ones by Henry James (1843 – 1916). Hardy is called a regional novelist, focusing on rustic ways of life and rural traditions, which face agricultural innovations and changing sexual mores, and being faithful to his concern with characters who struggle in a spirit of existential revolt less with social constraints than the power of destiny. More urban concerned is George Gissing (1857 – 1903), whose masterpiece *New Grub Street* (1891) is a study of London literary life in the late 1880s. And it is also Gissing alongside George Moore (1855 – 1903), famous for *Esther Waters* (1894), and especially Arnold Bennet (1867 – 1931), acclaimed for *Anna of the Five Towers* (1902), who would be later influenced by Zola and naturalism. Like Hardy, Joseph Conrad (1857 – 1924) considers life to be a perpetual struggle against hostile and arbitrary forces, his "far from the madding crowd" being not English countryside but seafaring life, since for him society and city are models of threatened order like a ship at sea.

Robert Louis Stevenson (1850 – 1894) propounded fictional romance as an original mode to realist novel; he even argued that romance could be more superior and truthful than the whole realist fiction of his times. Victorian romance largely comprises adventure stories on colonial thematic substratum, where humans escape from constraints and trivialities of social life into foreign, exotic, largely primitive and archetypal forms of existence (as in the adventure novel *Treasure Island* (1883) or the Gothic horror novella *Strange Case of Dr Jekyll and Mr Hyde* (1886)). Rudyard Kipling (1865 – 1936), convinced of the British Empire's civilising role as a great force for good, writes *The Jungle Book* (1894) to further exploit the popularity of romance as a narrative set in other places (and times) offering imaginative escape from an unpleasant actuality of the present. William Morris envisages a bright future in his utopian romance *News from Nowhere* (1891). Unlike Morris, Herbert George Wells (1866 – 1946), one of the major founders of the dystopian and science-fiction genres, creates memorable scientific/science-fiction romances predicting a pessimistic and apocalyptic future. Unlike Stevenson and Kipling, Wells stays rooted in realist doctrine and, faithful to its social concern and assisted by his ingenious imagination and solid scientific knowledge, he touches on bourgeoisie versus proletariat relationship in *The Time Machine* (1895) and clearly criticises imperialism in *The War of the Worlds* (1898).

Sir Arthur Conan Doyle (1859 – 1930) gathered vast readership with his stories about the adventures Sherlock Holmes, juxtaposing romantic and realist modes. Henry James's break from Victorian realist novel occurs through psychologisation and by placing drama and suffering at the core of human relations, which is enhanced by the themes of alienation and betrayal rendering the psychological insight into character, alongside cultural issues involving the Europeans (and their traditions) versus Americans (and their ideals) dichotomy, as in *The Portrait of a Lady* (1881). This novel is also a Bildungsroman and it is this novelistic subgenre that flourishes in Victorian literature to be found as shaped by most of the main literary trends of the period, ranging from the realist *Great Expectations* and *Jane Eyre* to the post-romantic *Wuthering Heights* and avant-garde *Marius the Epicurean*. The Victorian Bildungsroman is largely a favourite of the realist authors who would find in the pattern of this fictional tradition – consisting of the literary treatment of the process of development and formation of a character in relation to society – the necessary extension and complexity to their realist literary concern with individual experience and the social background, a concern which is framed within a large-scale diachronic model of human existence. Regardless its affiliation with one or another literary trend, the Victorian Bildungsroman keeps its structure centred around the principle of formation signifying emergence or becoming ("stanovlenia", for Bakhtin) of a protagonist whose identity is not ready-made or static but subject to a process of development of personality encompassing various stages such as childhood experience, education, friendship, love, social interaction, professional endeavours, and others culminating in a crucial life event that would prompt epiphany leading to change signifying formation by acquiring and asserting an identity.

The drama of Victorian period owns its significance to the contribution of two Anglo-Irish writers, Oscar Wilde and George Bernard Shaw. The former is the author of poetry, drama, essays, and fiction, and is primarily known for *The Picture of Dorian Gray*, inspired by Joris-Karl Huysmans's *À Rebours* (1884), a novel of French decadence, and disclosing Wilde's status as a disciple of Walter Pater, a quintessential aesthete, a follower of "art for art's sake" doctrine. The latter, via the long expository discourses of his dramatic characters, offers witty and at the same time paradoxical debates on various social and cultural problems, ranging from prostitution to linguistics, and by making his plays a vehicle for his social thinking, Shaw discloses his concerns to be with ideas and psychological implications of action rather than with art.

The critical narrative considers poetry of Victorian Age to be peripheral, marginalised by the dominance of fiction, therefore escapist and pessimistic, but it neither fails over creativity nor lacks popular admiration. Succeeding Wordsworth as Poet Laureate, Alfred Tennyson establishes a poetic tradition on romantic premises with his *In Memoriam* and especially *Idylls of the King*, a long Arthurian cycle expressing disillusionment with the present alongside nostalgic appraisal of earlier, now apparently lost patterns of morality and faith. Tennyson also writes in the genre of dramatic monologue, which is a conscious lyrical innovation of Victorian poets, but it is Robert Browning who perfected and experimented thematically and stylistically with the form. Browning's *Andrea del Sarto* and *My Last Duchess*, alongside Tennyson's *Ulysses*, clearly reveal the main features of the new lyrical subgenre whose closest form is soliloquy, but unlike in soliloquy, in a dramatic monologue the reader cannot assume that the speaker is alone, or the speaker is sincere, betraying his mind rather than articulating it. The main elements of the pattern organise the poetic discourse of *Ulysses* as a chain of utterances disclosing the existential problem of the speaker: (1) "there is a problem" and this is shown by the speaker Ulysses being dissatisfied, unhappy, and bored at home: (2) "what is the problem?", and the answer is his inactivity: "I cannot rest from travel"; (3) "what is the reason of the problem?" – it is that "I am part of all that I have met", suggesting identification with the past experience and meaning that he is still there in his former life now opposed to the present, actual world of his homeland in a type of romantic dualism of existence; and (4) "how to solve it?" – the answer is to embark on a new discovery, experience, a new search for knowledge prompting new expressions of romantic dualism and escapism. This is enhanced by the idea that life is short, death conquers all, and experience and knowledge are infinite and never to be fully achieved, as well as by the idea that his son Telemachus can perfectly replace him as a king. These two ideas are used to justify his desire to leave his home, to embark on a new experience, albeit it could be his last one, but the physical death is more terrifying than the spiritual death. The same pattern of the dramatic monologue is preserved in *My Last Duchess*, for example, but here emerges also a necropolitical meaning in speaker's expressed wish to have his next wife as an object in his possession just like his former wife is now an object, which is a painting, the picture of his "last duchess".

Another Victorian writer heavily relying on romantic heritage in his both critical and poetic work is Matthew Arnold, who is also acclaimed as a cultural prophet. In his *To Marguerite*, for example, the two main metaphors of life as a sea and people as islands in the sea of life allude to a painful personal experience – where the separation of lovers is in itself a metaphor for the separation of the entire humanity – and discloses a broader connotation of cultural discrepancies, particularly of British complex of insularity against the general European culture and traditions, which is also remarkably thematised in *Dover Beach*.

Elizabeth Barrett Browning and Christina Rossetti (1830 – 1894) were highly acclaimed alongside their male fellow-poets. The latter's brother, Dante Gabriel Rossetti with William Morris and Algernon Charles Swinburne are major representatives of the Pre-Raphaelitism as romanticism-bound and aestheticism-related form of autochthonous avant-garde. One of the most representative literary works of the Pre-Raphaelite Brotherhood is Dante Gabriel Rossetti's *The Blessed Damozel*. In its approach to the relationship of art to life and reality, which is a central concern of the avant-garde aesthetics, *The Blessed Damozel* reveals intertextual bonds to Shelley (in *Skylark*) and Coleridge (in *Kubla Khan*) constructing the romantic dualism of corporeality and creative non-reality, but the poem is primarily viewed as parody or pastiche, or at least allusion to Poe's *The Raven*. As counter-positioned to *The Raven*, *The Blessed Damozel* presents the female lover's perspective through her behaviour and speech in Heaven. She is the one who now mourns their separation, whereas the male lyrical I discloses through the fragmented lines in parentheses the movement from physical connection (touch of her hair in non-reality which are falling leaves on his face in reality) and spoken contact (her singing in his vision which is the song of birds in reality) to the high emotional appeal of a promised eternal unity which is rendered by other words in parentheses: "(I saw her smile)" and "(I heard her tears)". The reunion of the lovers is possible only in Heaven after his death, but such transitory connections, albeit short, between the dead girl envisaged in Heaven and her lover living on Earth are possible through art. In the case of Poe's lyrical persona, there is no such possibility for fleeting contacts to occur between lovers given his self-imprisonment in a consciously constructed realm of eternal mourning and suffering. Above all, however, the accurate descriptive endeavour, attention given to the symbolism of colours and numbers, artfulness and the deliberate consideration of ornamented details, and especially its alliance to the tradition of the medieval dream poetry make this poem a remarkable example of the poetic art of the Pre-Raphaelites turning medievalists while pursuing new themes and new means of artistic expression.

The most experimental poet among Victorians, particularly with language and technique, is Gerald Manley Hopkins, a precursor of modernism while remaining bound to metaphysical poetry, namely George Herbert, in thematising God's glory and creative power, as well as to romanticism in his concern with nature.

Another precursor of modernism in English literature – or, for many critics, a true representative of modernist poetry – is William Butler Yeats (1965 – 1939), who in his early work, his Christian faith being overturned by his contemporary scientific rationalism, in the footsteps of William Blake, invents his own mythology based on Irish cultural heritage to escape into this ideal world of imagination. Yeats continues to be a myth-maker in his mature poetry, too, mythologising his native land, friends, and family, but his involvement in Irish politics (having fallen in love with Maud Gonne, a famous and beautiful Irish revolutionary) and culture (having founded the Irish National Theatre Company) affects his style into hardening it to produce a poetic work in which love and politics are placed in a tragic conflict. Yeats writes his best poetry long into the first half of the twentieth century and is often placed in the line of great English modernists.

It will be modernism to continue and expand the experimental efforts of the Victorian avant-garde and produce the greatest creative innovation in English literature so as to put an end to its "complex of insularity" and achieve the modernist synchronization of the English with European literary practice, but this, alongside other aspects of the twentieth-century literary complexity, is to be the concern of the next volume in our series on the historical advancement of English literature.

REFERENCES AND SUGGESTIONS FOR FURTHER READING

References

Abrams, M. H., and Harpham, G. G. *A Glossary of Literary Terms*. Belmont: Wadsworth Publishing Company, 2009.

Auerbach, E. *Mimesis: The Representation of Reality in Western Literature*. New York: Anchor Doubleday, 1957.

Baldick, C. *The Oxford English Literary History, Volume 10. 1910-1940: The Modern Movement*. Oxford: Oxford University Press, 2005.

Barry, P. *Beginning Theory: An Introduction to Literary and Cultural Theory*. Manchester: Manchester University Press, 2009.

Barthes, R. *S/Z*. New York: Hill and Wang, 1974.

Beach, J. W. *The Twentieth Century Novel: Studies in Technique*. New York: Appleton Century Crofts Inc., 1960.

Belsey, C. *Critical Practice*. London: Routledge, 1980.

Bergonzi, B. *Wartime and Aftermath: English Literature and Its Background 1939-60*. Oxford: Oxford University Press, 1993.

Bertens, H. *Literary Theory: The Basics*. London: Routledge, 2005.

Blamires, H. *A History of Literary Criticism*. London: Macmillan, 1991.

Bressler, C. E. *Literary Criticism: An Introduction to Theory and Practice*. Englewood Cliffs: Prentice-Hall Inc., 2007.

Cahoone, L. "Introduction". *From Modernism to Postmodernism: An Anthology*. Ed. L. Cahoone. Oxford: Blackwell Publishing, 2003. 1-13.

Callinicos, A. "Marxism and literary criticism". *The Cambridge History of Literary Criticism, Volume 9: Twentieth Century Historical, Philosophical and Psychological Perspectives*. Eds. C. Knellwolf and C. Norris. Cambridge: Cambridge University Press, 2001. 89-98.

Cartianu, A., and Preda, I. A. *Dicționar al literaturii engleze*. București: Editura Științifică, 1970.

Ceuca, J. *Evoluția formelor dramatice*. Cluj-Napoca: Dacia, 2002.

Churchill, R. C. "Charles Dickens". *The Pelican Guide to English Literature, vol. 6 From Dickens to Hardy*. Ed. Boris Ford. London: Penguin Books Ltd., 1976.

Cioranescu, A. *Principii de literatură comparată*. București: Cartea Românească, 1997.

Ciugureanu, A. *Modernism and the Idea of Modernity*. Constanța: Ex Ponto, 2004.

Claudon, F., and Haddad-Wolting, K. *Compediu de literatură comparată*. București: Cartea Românească, 1997.

Cook, G. *Discourse and Literature: The Interplay of Form and Mind*. Oxford: Oxford University Press, 1995.

Cuddon, J. A. *The Penguin Dictionary of Literary Terms and Literary Theory*. London: Penguin Books Ltd., 1992.

Davis, P. *The Oxford English Literary History, Volume 8. 1830-1880: The Victorians*. Oxford: Oxford University Press, 2002.

Dumoulie, C. "Nietzsche, Disciple of Dionysus". *Companion to Literary Myths, Heroes and Archetypes*. Ed. P. Brunel. London: Routledge, 1992. 872-875.

Durant, W. *The Story of Philosophy*. New York: Washington Squire Press, 1966.

Dutton, R. *An Introduction to Literary Criticism*. London: Longman, 1984.

Emig, R. "Literary criticism and psychoanalytic positions". *The Cambridge History of Literary Criticism, Volume 9: Twentieth Century Historical, Philosophical and Psychological Perspectives.* Eds. C. Knellwolf and C. Norris. Cambridge: Cambridge University Press, 2001. 175-189.

Faulkner, P. *Modernism.* London: Methuen, 1977.

Fokkema, D., and Ibsch, E. *Theories of Literature in the Twentieth Century: Structuralism, Marxism, Aesthetics of Reception, Semiotics.* New York: St Martin's Press, 1995.

Frevert, U., and Haupt, H.-G. *Omul secolului al XIX-lea.* Bucureşti: Polirom, 2002.

Gagnier, R. "The Victorian fin de siècle and decadence". *The Cambridge History of Twentieth Century English Literature.* Eds. L. Marcus and P. Nicholls. Cambridge: Cambridge University Press, 2004. 30-49.

Galea, I. *Victorianism and Literature.* Cluj-Napoca: Dacia Publishing House, 1996.

Gengembre, G. *Marile curente ale criticii literare.* Iaşi: Institutul European, 2000.

Ginzburg, L. *On Psychological Prose.* Ewing: Princeton University Press, 1991.

Golban, T. *The Myth of Electra in Ancient and Modern Drama.* Kutahya: Uc Mart Press, 2007.

Graf, A. *Marii filosofi contemporani.* Iaşi: Institutul European, 2001.

Graves, R. "Legitimate Criticism of Poetry". *The Idea of Literature: The Foundations of English Criticism.* D. M. Urnov. Moscow: Progress Publishers, 1979. 276-281.

Grigorescu, D., and Alexandrescu, S. *Romanul realist în secolul al XIX-lea,* Bucureşti: Editura enciclopedică română, 1971.

Habib, M. A. R. *A History of Literary Criticism: From Plato to the Present.* Oxford: Blackwell Publishing, 2005.

Harland, R. *Literary Theory from Plato to Barthes: An Introductory History.* New York: Palgrave Macmillan, 1999.

Harpham, G. G. "Ethics and literary criticism". *The Cambridge History of Literary Criticism, Volume 9: Twentieth Century Historical, Philosophical and Psychological Perspectives.* Eds. C. Knellwolf and C. Norris. Cambridge: Cambridge University Press, 2001. 371-385.

Hartman, G. "Romanticism and Anti-Self-Consciousness". *Romanticism.* Ed. C. Chase. London: Longman, 1993. 43-54.

Hassan, I. *The Dismemberment of Orpheus: Towards a Postmodern Literature.* Oxford: Oxford University Press, 1971.

Highet, G. *The Classical Tradition: Greek and Roman Influences on Western Literature.* Oxford: Oxford University Press, 1976.

Holman, C. H., and Harmon, W. A. *A Handbook to Literature.* New York: Macmillan, 1992.

Knellwolf, C. "The history of feminist criticism". *The Cambridge History of Literary Criticism, Volume 9: Twentieth Century Historical, Philosophical and Psychological Perspectives.* Eds. C. Knellwolf and C. Norris. Cambridge: Cambridge University Press, 2001. 193-205.

La Bossiere, C. R. "Nietzsche, Friedrich Wilhelm". *Encyclopedia of Contemporary Literary Theory: Approaches, Scholars, Terms.* Ed. I. R. Makaryk. Toronto: University of Toronto Press, 2000. 432-435

Larkin, M. *Man and Society in Nineteenth Century Realism: Determinism and Literature.* Totowa: Rowman and Littlefield, 1977.

Latane, Jr, D. E. "Literary Criticism". *A Companion to Victorian Literature and Culture.* Ed. H. F. Tucker. Oxford: Blackwell Publishers, 1999. 388-404.

Lodge, D. *The Novelist at the Crossroads and Other Essays on Fiction and Criticism.* Ithaca:

Cornell University Press, 1971.

Malancioiu, I. *Vina tragică: tragicii greci, Shakespeare, Dostoievski, Kafka.* Iaşi: Polirom, 2001.

Martin, W. *Recent Theories of Narrative.* Ithaca: Cornell University Press, 1991.

Matz, J. *Literary Impressionism and Modernist Aesthetics.* Port Chester: Cambridge University Press, 2001.

Milner, A. *Literature, Culture and Society.* London: Routledge, 2005.

Mindra, M. *The Phenomenology of the Novel.* Iaşi: Institutul European, 2002.

Moretti, Franco. *The Way of the World: The Bildungsroman in European Culture.* London: Verso, 2000.

Munteanu, R. *Introducere în literatura europeană modern.* Bucureşti: ALLFA, 1996.

Nehamas, A. "Nietzsche, Friedrich". *The Johns Hopkins Guide to Literary Theory and Criticism.* Eds. M. Groden and M. Kreiswirth. Baltimore: The Johns Hopkins University Press, 1994. 545-548

O'Gorman, F. *The Victorian Novel.* Oxford: Blackwell Publishing Ltd., 2002.

Onega, S., and Landa, J. A. G. "Introduction". *Narratology: An Introduction.* Eds. S. Onega and J. A. G. Landa. London: Longman, 1996. 1-41.

Pageaux, D.-H. *Literatura generală şi comparată.* Iaşi: Polirom, 2000.

Parrinder, P. "Science and knowledge at the beinning of the twentieth century versions of the modern Enlightenment". *The Cambridge History of Twentieth Century English Literature.* Eds. L. Marcus and P. Nicholls. Cambridge: Cambridge University Press, 2004. 11-29.

Putz, M. *Essays on American Literature and Ideas.* Iaşi: Institutul European, 1997.

Regan, R. *Poe: A Collection of Critical Studies.* Englewood Cliffs: Prentice-Hall, Inc., 1967.

Sanders, A. *The Short Oxford History of English Literature.* Oxford: Oxford University Press, 1994.

Scott, C. "Symbolism, Decadence and Impressionism". *Modernism 1890-1930.* Eds. M. Bradbury and J. McFarlane. London: Penguin Books, 1991. 206-227.

Selden, R. *A Reader's Guide to Contemporary Literary Theory.* New York: Harvester Wheatsheaf, 1989.

Shires, L. M. "The aesthetics of the Victorian novel: form, subjectivity, ideology". *The Cambridge Companion to the Victorian Novel.* Ed. D. David. Cambridge: Cambridge University Press, 2001. 61-76.

Sirbu, A. *Personajul literar în secolul al XIXlea francez.* Iaşi: Editura Fundaţiei Chemarea, 1997.

Stern, J. P. *On Realism.* London: Routledge, 1973.

Stonebridge, L. "Psychoanalysis and literature". *The Cambridge History of Twentieth Century English Literature.* Eds. L. Marcus and P. Nicholls. Cambridge: Cambridge University Press, 2004. 269-285.

Surdulescu, R. *Critica mitic-arhetipală: De la motivul antropologic la sentimentul numinosului.* Bucureşti: ALLFA, 1997.

Thiher, A. *Fiction Rivals Science: The French Novel from Balzac to Proust.* Columbia: University of Missouri Press, 2001.

Valette, B. *Romanul: Introducere în metodele şi tehnicile moderne de analiză literară.* Bucureşti: Cartea Românească, 1997.

Watt, Ian. *The Victorian Novel, Modern Essays in Criticism.* Oxford: Oxford University Press, 1978.

Waugh, P. *Metafiction: The Theory and Practice of Self-Conscious Fiction.* London: Routledge,

1993.

White, M. *The Age of Analysis: 20ᵗʰ Century Philosophers*. New York: The New American Library, 1955.

Wilson, E. *Axel's Castle: A Study in the Imaginative Literature of 1870-1930*. New York: Charles Scribner's Sons, 1953.

Suggestions for Further Reading

General Literary History and Criticism

Abrams, M. H. (Ed.). *The Norton Anthology of English Literature*. New York: Norton, 1986.

Bakhtin, M. M. *The Dialogic Imagination: Four Essays*. Austin: University of Texas Press, 1981.

Bakhtin, M. M. *Rabelais and His World*. Bloomington: Indiana University Press, 1984.

Bakhtin, M. M. *Problems of Dostoevsky's Poetics*. Minneapolis: University of Minnesota Press, 1984.

Bateson, F. W., and H. T. Meserole. *A Guide to English and American Literature*. London: Longman, 1976.

Belsey, C. *Critical Practice*. London: Routledge, 1980.

Bernard, R. *A Short History of English Literature*. Oxford: Blackwell Publishing, 1995.

Blamires, H. *A Short History of English Literature*. London: Routledge, 1984.

Cartianu, A., and I. A. Preda. *Dictionar al literaturii engleze*. Bucuresti: Editura Stiintifica, 1970.

Conrad, P. *The Everyman History of English Literature*. London: J. M. Dent and Sons Ltd., 1985.

Daiches, D. *English Literature*. Englewood Cliffs: Prentice-Hall Inc., 1964.

Daiches, D. *A Critical History of English Literature*. New York: The Ronald Press Company, 1970.

Daiches, D. *The Penguin Companion to English Literature*. New York: McGraw-Hill, 1971.

Day, M. S. *History of English Literature to Sixteen Sixty*. New York: Doubleday Books, 1963.

Drabble, M. (Ed.). *The Oxford Companion to English Literature*. Oxford: Oxford University Press, 2000.

Eagle, D. *The Concise Oxford Dictionary of English Literature*. Oxford: Oxford University Press, 1987.

Ford, B. (Ed.). *The New Pelican Guide to English Literature*. London: Penguin Books Ltd., 1982.

Fowler, A. Kinds of Literature: An Introduction to the Theory of Genres and Modes. Oxford: Clarendon Press, 1987.

Fowler, A. *A History of English Literature*. Cambridge: Harvard University Press, 1991.

Highet, G. The Classical Tradition: Greek and Roman Influences on Western Literature. Oxford: Oxford University Press, 1976.

Kirkpatrick, D. L. (Ed.). *Reference Guide to English Literature*. London: St James Press, 1991.

Lawrence, K. *The McGraw-Hill Guide to English Literature*. New York: McGraw-Hill, 1985.

Legonis, E., and L. Cazamian. *History of English Literature*. London: J. M. Dent and Sons Ltd., 1971.

Lotman, Y. M. "Lektsii po strukturalinoi poetike". *Y. M. Lotman i tartusko-moskovskaya semioticeskaia shkola*. Moskva: Gnozis, 1994. 10-257.

Magill, F. N. (Ed.). *Cyclopedia of Literary Characters*. New York: Harper and Row, 1963.

Ousby, I. (Ed.). *The Cambridge Guide to English Literature*. Cambridge: Cambridge University Press, 1993.

Parrinder, P. Nation and Novel: The English Novel from its Origins to the Present Day. Oxford: Oxford University Press, 2006.

Ricoeur, Paul. *Eseuri de hermeneutica*. Bucuresti: Humanitas, 1995.

Rogers, P. (Ed.). *The Oxford Illustrated History of English Literature*. Oxford: Oxford University Press, 1990.

Sampson, G. *The Concise Cambridge History of English Literature*. Cambridge: Cambridge University Press, 1970.

Shklovsky, Viktor. *O teorii prozy*. Moskva: Federatia, 1929.

Stapleton, M. *The Cambridge Guide to English Literature*. Cambridge: Cambridge University Press, 1983.

Stephen, M. An Introductory Guide to English Literature. London: Longman, 1984.

Thornley, G. C., and G. Roberts. *An Outline of English Literature*. London: Longman, 1995.

Ward, A. C. Illustrated History of English Literature. London: Longman, 1960.

Ward, A. W., and A. R. Waller. *The Cambridge History of English Literature*. Cambridge: Cambridge University Press, 1953.

Wynne-Davis, M. (Ed.). *The Bloomsbury Guide to English Literature*. London: Bloomsburg Publishing Ltd., 1960.

The Victorian Age

Altick, R. D. *Victorian People and Ideas: A Companion for the Modern Reader of Victorian Literature*, New York: Norton, 1973.

Bayley, J. *An Essay on Hardy*, Cambridge: Cambridge University Press, 1979.

Beach, J. W. *English Literature of the Nineteenth and the Early Twentieth Centuries: 1798 to the First World War*, New York: Collier Books, 1962.

Beer, G. *Darwin's Plots: Evolutionary Narrative in Darwin, George Eliot and Nineteenth-Century Fiction*, Cambridge: Cambridge University Press, 2000.

Bergonzi, B. *Gerald Manley Hopkins*, London: Macmillan, 1977.

Bradbrook, F. W. *Jane Eyre and her Predecessors*, Cambridge: Cambridge University Press, 1967.

Brown, D. *Thomas Hardy*, London: Longman, 1961.

Buckley, J. H. *Season of Youth: The Bildungsroman from Dickens to Golding*, Cambridge: Harvard University Press, 1974.

Buckley, J. H. *The Worlds of Victorian Fiction*, Cambridge: Harvard University Press, 1975.

Butler, L. *Thomas Hardy*, Cambridge: Cambridge University Press, 1980.

Chase, K. *Eros and Psyche: The Representation of Personality in Charlotte Bronte, Charles Dickens and George Eliot*, London: Methuen, 1984.

Collingwood, W. G. *The Life of John Ruskin*, London: Methuen, 1985.

Cook, E. T. *The Life of Ruskin*, New York: Haskell House, 1969.

Craik, W. A. *The Bronte Novels*, London: Methuen, 1968.

Davis, P. *The Oxford English Literary History, Volume 8. 1830-1880: The Victorians*, Oxford: Oxford University Press, 2002.

Donovan, F. R. *Dickens and Youth*, New York: Dodd, Mead and Company, 1968.

Ebbatson, R. *Tennyson*, London: Penguin Books Ltd., 1988.

Elliot, A. P. *Fatalism in the Works of Thomas Hardy*, New York: Russel and Russel, 1966.

Ellmann, R. *Edwardians and Late Victorians*, New York: Columbia University Press, 1960.

Ellman, R. *Oscar Wilde*, New York: Vintage Books, 1988.

Fawkner, H. W. *Animation and Reification in Dickens's Vision of the Life-Denying Society*, Uppsala: University of Uppsala Press, 1972.

Fernando, L. *"New Women" in the Late Victorian Novel*, University Park: The Pennsylvania State University Press, 1977.

Forster, J. *The Life of Charles Dickens*, London: J. M. Dent and Sons Ltd., 1976.

Gaskell, E. C. *The Life of Charlotte Bronte*, Leicester: Charnwood, 1988.

Gerin, W. *Charlotte Bronte: The Evolution of Genius*, Oxford: Clarendon Press, 1967.

Gerin, W. *Emily Bronte: A Biography*, Oxford: Clarendon Press, 1971.

Goodin, G. (ed.) *The English Novel in the Nineteenth Century: Essays on the Literary Meditation of Human Values*, Urbana: University of Illinois Press, 1974.

Haight, G. S. *George Eliot: A Biography*, Oxford: Oxford University Press, 1968.

Hanson, E., Hanson, L. *Marian Evans and George Eliot: A Biography*, Oxford: Oxford University Press, 1952.

Hibbert, C. *The Making of Charles Dickens*, New York: Harper and Row, 1962.

Houghton, W. E. *The Victorian Frame of Mind 1830-1870*, New Haven: Yale University Press, 1957.

Irvine, W., Honan, P. *The Ring, the Book, and the Poet: A Biography of Robert Browning*, New York: McGraw-Hill, 1974.

Jenkin, L. *Charles Dickens' Great Expectations*, New York: Monarch Press, 1964.

Johnson, E. *Charles Dickens: His Tragedy and Triumph*, New York: The Viking Press, 1977.

Joseph, G. *Tennyson and the Text*, Cambridge: Cambridge University Press, 1992.

Kestner, J. *Protest and Reform: The British Social Narrative by Women 1827-1867*, Wisconsin: The University of Wisconsin Press, 1985.

Killham, J. (ed.) *Critical Essays on the Poetry of Tennyson*, London: Routledge and Kegan Paul, 1960.

King, J. *Tragedy in the Victorian Novel: Theory and Practice in the Novels of George Eliot, Thomas Hardy, Henry James*, Cambridge: Cambridge University Press, 1986.

Knoepflmacher, U. C. *Laughter and Despair: Readings in the Novels of Victorian Era*, Los Angeles: University of California Press, 1973.

Knoepflmacher, U. C., Tennyson, G. B. (eds.) *Nature and the Victorian Imagination*, Los Angeles: University of California Press, 1978.

Laski, M. *George Eliot and her World*, London: Thames and Hudson, 1973.

Leavis, F. R., Leavis Q. D. *Dickens the Novelist*, New Brunswick: Rutgers University Press, 1979.

Lindsay, J. *William Morris: His Life and Work*, New York: Tamplinger Publishing Company, 1979.

Mankowitz, W. *Dickens of London*, New York: Macmillan, 1978.

Martin, R. B. *Tennyson: The Unquiet Heart*, Oxford: Oxford University Press, 1980.

McKenzie, G. *The Literary Character of Walter Pater*, Berkeley: University of California Press, 1967.

Moglen, H. *Charlotte Bronte: The Self Conceived*, Wisconsin: The University of Wisconsin Press, 1976.

Neale, C. *George Eliot: Middlemarch*, London: Penguin Books Ltd., 1989.

Newsom, R. *Dickens and the Romantic Side of Familiar Things: Bleak House and the Novel Tradition*, New York: Columbia University Press, 1977.

Norbelie, B. A. *"Oppressive Narrowness": A Study of the Female Community in George Eliot's Early Writings*, Uppsala: University of Uppsala Press, 1992.

Otis, L. (ed.) *Literature and Science in the Nineteenth Century: An Anthology*, Oxford: Oxford University Press, 2002.

Pearson, H. *The Life of Oscar Wilde*, London: Penguin Books Ltd., 1960.

Pearson, H. *Dickens: His Character, Comedy and Career*, London: Methuen, 1949.

Polhemus, R. *Comic Faith: The Great Tradition from Austen to Joyce*, Chicago: The University of Chicago Press, 1980.

Ray, G. N. *Thackeray: The Uses of Adversity 1811-1846*, New York: McGraw-Hill, 1955.

Ray, G. N. *Thackeray: The Age of Wisdom 1847-1863*, New York: McGraw-Hill, 1958.

Smith, G. *The Novel and Society: Defoe to George Eliot*, New Jercey: Barnes and Noble Books, 1984.

Southall, R. *Literature, the Individual and Society: Critical Essays on the Eighteenth and Nineteenth Centuries*, London: Lawrence and Wishart, 1977.

Spanberg, S.-J. *The Ordeal of Richard Feverel and the Traditions of Realism*, Uppsala: University of Uppsala Press, 1974.

Stone, D. D. *The Romantic Impulse in Victorian Fiction*, Cambridge: Harvard University Press, 1980.

Stonyk, M. *Nineteenth Century English Literature*, New York: Schocken Books, 1984.

Sucksmith, H. P. *The Narrative Art of Charles Dickens: The Rhetoric of Sympathy and Irony in his Novels*, Oxford: Clarendon Press, 1970.

Sutherland, J. *Who Betrays Elizabeth Bennet?: Further Puzzles in Classic Fiction*, Oxford: Oxford University Press, 1999.

Thomson, E. P. *William Morris: Romantic to Revolutionary*, New York: Pantheon Books, 1977.

Tillotson, K. *Novels of the Eighteen-Forties*, Oxford: Clarendon Press, 1954.

Tucker, H. F. *Tennyson and the Doom of Romanticism*, Cambridge: Harvard University Press, 1988.

Tucker, H. F. (ed.) *A Companion to Victorian Literature and Culture*, Oxford: Blackwell Publishers, 1999.

Watson, J. R. *The Poetry of Gerard Manley Hopkins*, London: Penguin Books Ltd., 1987.

Watt, I. (ed.) *The Victorian Novel: Modern Essays in Criticism*, Oxford: Oxford University Press, 1978.

Welsh, A. *The City of Dickens*, Cambridge: Harvard University Press, 1986.

Westburg, B. *The Confessional Fictions of Charles Dickens*, Illinois: Northern Illinois University Press, 1977.

Wheatley, J. H. *Patterns in Thackeray's Fiction*, Cambridge: The M.I.T. Press, 1969.

Wilson, A. N. *Eminent Victorians*, London: BBC Books, 1989.

Wright, T. *The Life of Walter Pater*, New York: Haskell House, 1969.

www.ingramcontent.com/pod-product-compliance
Lightning Source LLC
Chambersburg PA
CBHW050346030726
47503CB00008B/2637